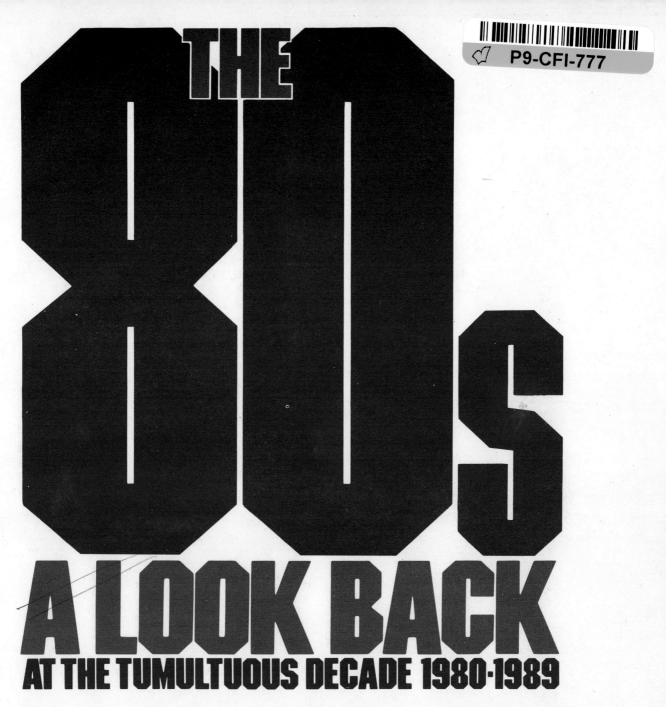

THE 80s
A LOOK BACK
AT THE TUMULTUOUS DECADE 1980-1989

Edited by Tony Hendra, Christopher Cerf & Peter Elbling
Art directed by Michael Gross

Based on an original idea by Peter Elbling

Workman Publishing, New York

Library of Congress Cataloging in Publication Data
Main entry under title:
The 80s: A look back at the tumultuous decade 1980-1989.

1. Civilization, Modern—1950- —Anecdotes, facetiae, satire,
etc. 2. Popular culture—Anecdotes, facetiae, satire, etc. I.
Hendra, Tony. II. Cerf, Christopher. III. Elbling, Peter.
CB430.E35 1979   909.82'8'0207   79-64781
ISBN 0-89480-122-8
ISBN 0-89480-119-8 pbk.

Workman Publishing Company, Inc.
1 West 39 Street
New York, New York 10018
Manufactured in the United States of America

First Printing August 1979
10 9 8 7 6 5 4 3 2 1

Published in association with the Dynamite Museum.

This book is dedicated to the obscure English novelist.

Editor-in-Chief: Tony Hendra
Executive Editor: Christopher Cerf
Senior Editor: Peter Elbling

Contributing Editors:
Tony Geiss, Jeff Greenfield, Ellis Weiner

Editor for Workman Publishing: Sally Kovalchick
Assistant Editor: Carol Wallace

Copy Editor: Judy Hendra
Special Copy Consultant: Louise Gikow

WRITERS

Henry Beard, Glenn Collins, Steven Crist, Valerie Curtin, Timothy Dickinson, Philip Drysdale, Jack Egan, Tony Geiss, Veronica Geng, Howard Gershen, Richard Gilman, Carl Gottlieb, Joey Green, Jeff Greenfield, Janis Hirsch, Abbie Hoffman, Gerald Jonas, Stefan Kanfer, Sean Kelly, B. Kliban, Stan Mack, Bernard Martin, Bruce McCall, Rick Meyerowitz, Maurice Peterson, George Plimpton, Jonathan Roberts, Jennifer Rogers, Harry Shearer, Ellis Weiner, Timothy White, Jeremy Wolff, Chuck Young.

CONTRIBUTORS

Danny Abelson, Annie Bardach, Dan Barrows, Barbara Barrie, Bill Berensmann, John Brent, Valerie Bromfield, Geneviève Cerf, Joan Ganz Cooney, John Corcoran, Jeff Cox, Jim Cranna, Sevren Darden, Russ Devon, Roz Doyle, Murphy Dunne, Larry Durocher, Bill Effros, Amy Ephron, Richard Erlanger, Willard Espy, Richard Evans, Hélène Fagan, Joshua Feigenbaum, Paul Firstenberg, Phil Gershon, Louise Gikow, Garry Goodrow, Ed Greenberg, Glenis Gross, Michael Gross, Larry Hankin, Jay Harnick, Ted Harris, Carol Schlanger Helvy, Judy Hendra, Howard Kaminsky, Jesse Kornbluth, David Korr, Debbie Kovacs, Paul Krassner, Jon Landau, David Lander, Stan Lee, John Leo, Sharon Lerner, Jonathan Lieberson, Richard Lingeman, John Mankiewicz, Susan Margolis, Marounkeji, Steve Mayer, Larry McQuade, Robin Menken, Ed Miller, Ira Miller, Thad Mumford, Victor Navasky, Lynn Nesbit, David Obst, Abe Peck, Alice Playten, Freddy Plimpton, John Romita, Gary Ross, Marilyn Rothenberg, Jane Shapiro, Richard Smith, Raymond Sokolov, Scott Spenser, Norman Stiles, Roy Thomas, Hector Troy, Morgan Upton, Melvin Van Peebles, Eliot Wald, Robert M. Zarem.

SPECIAL THANKS TO:

Jonathan Becker, Madelyn Berensmann, C.C. Berg, Brigid Berlin, Carl Bernstein, Susie Breitner, Ann Brody, Jerri Buckley, Truman Capote, Jennifer Carden, Enrique Castro-Cid, Geneviève Cerf, Alexander Cockburn, Roy Cohn, Sam Cohn, Jerry Cooke, Maggie Curran, Lee Eisenberg, Dimitri Elbling, Simon Elbling, Nora Ephron, Karin Epstein, Judy Feldman, Dabney Finch, Stan Friedman, Henry Geldzahler, Howard Gershen, Gerritt Graham, Jessica Hendra, Sandra Holley, Nancy Huang, Sallie Jackson, Patricia Jones, Anita Karl, Micky Kelly, David Kennedy, Steve Kessler, Sally Kovalchick, Lewis Lapham, G. Gordon Liddy, Lorna Luft, Bonnie Maller, Marounkeji, Sonia Manzano, Susan Margolis, Steve Martin, Phyllis Marucci, Luis Mayorga, Steve Mayorga, Meatloaf, Jeffrey Moss, Walter Murphy, Theodor Nelson, Lynn Nesbit, Suzanne O'Malley, Michael O'Neal, Rae Paige, Linda Pieper, Lars Randle, Lou Reed, Ken Regan, Midge Richardson, Scott Richter, Jennifer Rogers, Stephanie Ross, Michael Rudell, Frank Sciacca, Joan Scott, Ellie Seidel, Helene Siegel, Noel Silverman, Leif Sjoberg, Jennifer Skolnik, Jenifer Smith, Todd Smith, Bert Snyder, Bert Tauber, Victor Temkin, Rusty Unger, Paula Vogel, Dimitri Villard, Robert Wagner, Sr., Carol Wallace, Ann Wang, Andy Warhol, Stephen N.M.I. Weinrib, Ina Weisser, Eugene Winick, and Peter Workman.

Thanks also to John Belushi (for the $1,000) and Bill Murray (for the apartment).

Art Director: Michael Gross
Designer: Richard Erlanger
Design Associates: Scott MacNeil, Nanc Gordon
Production: Richard Rew
Principal Photography: John E.Barrett, Michael Gross
Photographic Stylist: Glenis Wooton Gross
Photographic Retouching: Robert Rakita
Photographic Research: Debbie Kovacs, Pat Relf, Shawn Donnelly, Nick Sullivan
Photographic Assistant: Gary Brennan
Special Fashions Designer: David Wishingrad

ILLUSTRATION CREDITS

Cover, pages 246, 247: Rick Meyerowitz. Pages 39, 64, 78, 148, 235: Randall Enos. Pages 10–13: H. Rogers. Pages 15 (top), 21 (top), 101, 234, 242: Michael Gross. Pages 189, 251: Scott MacNeil. Pages 172 (pop-up book), 207: Carole Gillott. Page 61: James Sherman. Page 128 (center): Joe D'Esposito. Page 151: Stan Mack. Page 172 (doll): Florence Worzar. Page 180: John Romita. Page 181: B. Kliban. Page 213: Mary Ann Shea. Page 240: Richard Rew.

PHOTOGRAPHIC CREDITS

Pages 14 (top), 18 (bottom), 19, 20, 21 (bottom), 22 (top), 24 (top and bottom), 49, 92, 102, 105, 121, 129 (bottom), 138, 167, 168, 172, 174, 175, 182, 208, 232, 236: John E. Barrett. Pages 18 (top), 23, 52, 63, 72, 81, 82, 83, 84, 89, 99 (right), 101, 112, 116, 118, 129 (top, left), 136, 149, 154, 158, 163, 177 (top), 187, 192, 198, 217, 222, 226, 229, 230, 253: Michael Gross. Pages 9, 26, 31, 32, 35, 43, 50, 51, 96, 98 (center), 106, 114 (center), 123, 125, 131, 145, 149, 165, 191, 201, 214, 219, 220, 251, 255, 262: UPI. Pages 108, 167, 176, 177 (bottom), 206: Howard Gershen. Pages 256, 257, 261: Marounkeji. Pages 67, 98 (left): Thomas Jackson. Page 77: John Trota/Black Star. Page 127: Jonathan Becker. Page 129 (top right): Joey Green. Page 130 (top): Robert Adelman. Page 150: Ken Regan/Camera Five.

PHOTOGRAPHIC ACKNOWLEDGEMENTS

Thanks to the following people in and around Yorktown Heights, New York, for their time, homes, businesses, and toasters: Jerry, Mary, and Todd Anderson; Martha Bartolini; Jeff Buggee of Family Britches; De Witt Calmari of Yorktown Shell; Ralph Clemente of Clemente Cleaners; Bob DeFeo of Bob's Coachlight Inn; Michael DeFeo; Madeline De Pole of Baldwin Fruit Stand; Pauline De Santis of The Linen Room; George and Mary Ann Eggleston; Jack Epter, Ben Taibi, and George Zanis of Yorktown Army and Navy; Stan Laber; Howard and Iris Levine of Midway Hardware; Paul Ma of Ma's Oriental Store; Kurt Marshall; Sharon and Richard Moscow; Sean Pomposello; Bob Saccomanno of The Corner Deli; Amy Sillman; Susan Stetson; Martha Wakefield; Shirley Wishingrad. Thanks also to the following people for assistance with props and locations: Centre Fire Arms, N.Y.C.; Gerry Cosby and Co., N.Y.C.; Leonard Ellman of Encore Studio, N.Y.C.; Bob Fitzpatrick; The Ginger Man, N.Y.C.; Evelyn Greene of Brooks Van Horn, N.Y.C.; Charles Kreloff; Paragon Athletic Goods, N.Y.C.; Emily Pattner of Beauty Bookings, N.Y.C.

CONTENTS

INTRODUCTION 8
COLOR PLATES 9
ULOC NOTICE
(As required by the ABAC) 25

THE WORLD   28
Jihad! Revenge of the Prophet   30
The United Magic Kingdom   34
Plastic China   36
Mad. Ave. Comes to the United States
   of China   38
Italy—La Soluzione Finale   40
Russia—The Iron Curtain Call   42
Inside Russia   44
Zufti Nog Hummo: 1988 Tirana
   World's Fair   46
Humpback and Sperm Galore   48
The Yacht People   50
An Interview with a Dolphin   51

SHOWBIZ   54
The Death of the Three-Network System   56
"Hippie Days"   57
The Peacock Expires   58
Waltergate: The Eye Closes   59
The Last Ratings War: The Big Tune-In   60
The People Maybe: Programming
   from the Masses   62
Hollywood Cleans House:
   HUAC's Hawkhunt   64
Hollywood   66
Broadway—Bust and Boom   70

D.C.   74
Camelot II   76
"The Ten Days"   77
Congressional Squares   78
The Congress of Nuts   80
The Halfway House   82
The Horrible Hundredth   84
A Man for Four Seasons   86
The Second U.S. Constitutional
   Convention   88
The New Bill of Rights   90

SPORTS   94
Olympics   96
Contact   98
Los Juegos   100
Contract   102
The White League   104
The Champs   106

RELIGION   110
The Church Modernizes   112
New Gods   114

ADIEU, PRINT   120
Half-Life   121
The Final Edition   124
The New York Variety Times   125
Prime Times   126
Fred   127
Wide Women's Wear Daily   130
Columbia Gossip Review   131
The Past Masters:
   Joseph Sarian: Catch-88   133
   Truman Capote: Answered Prayers   134
   Gabriel Garcia Marquez: El Castillo
   de Tremarric   136
The Best and the Last   137

MUSIC 'N DRUGS   140
A Beatle-Maniac   142
Meatleggers   144
Meatheads   148
Stan Mack's Real Life Funnies:
   "Meatheads"   151
La Sousa   152

OIL 156

¡Viva Mexico!	158
Futures	160
Shortage	162
Glut	164

FADS 'N FASHIONS 170

The Movie of the Decade	172
Downwardly Mobile Fashion	174
Prime Time Terms	178
Rats	180

THE LAW 184

Dealing with the Black Hand	186
The Death Penalty—A New Lease on Life	188
"Citizens for Murder"	189
A Court for Our Time	190

SEX 'N HEALTH 194

One Healthy Nation	196
The Legions of the TV Blind	198
The Death of Cancer	200
The Lives of a Cancer Cell	201
The International Year of the Simultaneous Orgasm	202
"The Little Man in the Scrote"	204
Orgasm—Pro and Con	206

THE ARMY 210

The Passing of the White Army	212
"I Am the Black Infantry"	213
Chief of the Joint	214
This Is the Army, Mr. Jones	216
The Long March	218
Blippie Nation	219
We Shall Overrun	220

FOOD 224

The Food Chain	226
Haute Cuisine with No Ingredients	230
Rich Food: Cuisine Grosseur	231
New Foods	232
The Pigalo and the Potatolo	234

KIDS 238

Baby's First Rights	240
Substitute Kids	241
Little Sons of America	242
Single Kids	244

THE FACE OF AMERICA 248

Las Vegas: Rien Ne Va Plus	250
Neo-Irvington	252
Back to Technology	254
Mother Lode News	255
California Nueva	256
The Big Slide	258
Them	260
Meet Me in St. Louis	262

INTRODUCTION

Most nations are good, and some are even great. But some—and they know who they are—are *really* great. America, of course, counts herself among this latter group, and has always stood ready to reply in kind to those who would deny it—with subtle persuasion, brute force, or that uniquely American amalgam of charisma and cash. Yet the promise and potential of any great people are only fulfilled in a particular historical period. France knew such a period in the 18th century. Britain's time came in the 19th century. There can be no doubt that the 20th century will be recorded as the time in which America had her period.

This was particularly true in the 1980s.

What were the '80s? In a word, there can be no single word to describe them. The years 1980 through 1989 were a microcosm of man's triumphs and follies writ large across the firmament of the national psyche. They were years of laughter, years of tears; years of happiness, years of anguish, and years of just being in a bad mood; years of bounty, and years of not all that much; years of pleasure, pain, victory, defeat, sorrow, joy. Hot years, cold years, big years, little years, sweet years, sour years, yes-years, no-years.

The '80s were a time when children behaved like adults, adults acted like children, and everybody loved Big Brother. It was an era in which government went out of business, and business went into government. It was, in short, a "tumultuous decade"—a formulation I have created expressly for this book.

Life is a sentence. Each year is a letter, and each decade a word. At no time can we truly divine the total meaning of our lives—we must be dead to know that. But we may begin to guess the meaning of our national life-sentence by examining that decade-word that just emerged from the typewriter of time.

This has been the task of the many contributors whose words and photographs fill the following pages. I have written a brief introduction to each section in an attempt to provide a general overview. In so doing, I have taken for my motto that dictum of Santayana, that those who do not learn from history are condemned to relive it. This book will have been a success—if those few remaining Americans of intelligence who are still able to read and who do sometimes purchase books find themselves adequately prepared for the 1980s, should they ever occur again.

H. Caulfield Stein (Host)
January, 1990

1982 *Disney, Inc. announced that it had acquired England, Scotland, Wales, Her Majesty's Government and Her Majesty as the first step in the creation of a theme park to be known as the United Magic Kingdom.*

THE 1980s A LOOK BACK

1980

May 2 The Italian government announced that it would start accepting kidnappees as legal tender. **July 15** In their continuing push for equal rights, women insisted on a shorter average lifespan. **Sept. 17** Jerry Brown resigned the governorship of California to accept the presidency of the CBS television network. **Nov. 3** In a bid for white middle-class support, Edward Kennedy announced he was appointing Allan Bakke to be his personal physician. **Dec. 9** The Ayatollah of Iran ordered that all foreign clocks within the borders of his Islamic republic were to have their hands cut off.

81

Jan. 13 President-elect Edward Kenne fulfilling a campaign promise, announce that his first act as president would be t donate his liver to Senator Russell Long Louisiana. **Jan. 27** The First National Bank of Toledo was held up by a robber wielding a homemade atomic bomb. **Oct** The Checker Cab Corporation in conjunction with *Runners World* introduced a line of metered rickshaws t provide "healthy, economical, pollution-free" public transportation. **Nov. 13** The first shipment of General Mills' Rice Helper arrived in Shanghai.

Jan. 9, 1980 The first Mexxxon station in the United States was opened by the Mexican National Oil Corporation.

Aug. 4, 1981 Exceptional Man o' War, the beloved three-legged three-year-old, was voted Horse of the Year.

March 11, 1983 The Chinese government announced it had retained Richard Nixon as its Special Adviser for Vietnamese Affairs.

Sept. 9, 1983 The first Gay Tod in San Francisco.

1983 *Yves St. Laurent introduced his spring line—the Chador Look. The historic costume of Islamic women was an overnight sensation. Here, a chinchilla mini-chador offers tantalizing glimpses of forbidden fruit.*

1984 *Overalls dominated American fashions, thanks to the success of the movie 1984! The versatile garment was to be found everywhere from boardroom to ballroom.*

1985 *The Meat Prohibition Act had repercussions in fashion. Trend-setters sported the ruffled "Lambchop" dress and meat-related paraphernalia in genteel defiance of the ban.*

THE HON. MICHAEL CURB Presents

1984!

Starring LEIF GARRETT • TRACY AUSTIN and MARLON BRANDO as "BIG BROTHER"

Produced by	Screenplay by	Directed by
THE HON. MICHAEL CURB	WALDO SALT	MARGARET TRUDEAU

Music and Lyrics by	Rat Choreography by	Director of Photography
BARRY, ROBIN AND MAURICE GIBB	TWYLA THARP	LINDA EASTMAN McCARTNEY

A UNIVERSAL WARNER — MICHAEL CURB FILM

Original novel adapted for the screen by
LAWRENCE HAUBEN and
BO GOLDMAN

Songs "THERE'S GONNA BE SOME CHANGES ROUND HERE"
and "MINISTRY OF LOVE" performed by
THE BEE GEES

G GENERAL AUDIENCES
All Ages Admitted

RECORDED IN EVENTIDE
DIGITAL STEREO

Filmed in 140mm LENSURROUND® • TECHNICOLOR®   Deluxe 2-Record Soundtrack Album Available on KNOPF Records and Tapes

1984 *Mike Curb's brilliant musical production, based on a novel by an obscure English writer, was the movie of the decade. It starred Marlon Brando as Big Brother.*

1982 *The Great Wall of China arrived in the United States for its smash-hit nationwide tour. Here is the Wall in New York's Central Park.*

82

Mar. 29 Research by Masters and Johnson discovered two distinct types of male orgasm: the penile and the scrotal. **June 11** New Mexico instituted a novel means of capital punishment—the solar electric chair. **Aug. 13** In light of a precipitous drop in the white birth rate and a chronic shortage of adoptable children, the New York Commodities Exchange announced that it would start trading in baby futures. **Oct. 1** Worried by forecasts of a minute voter turnout in November, the administration announced that any citizen showing up at the polls would get a free toaster. **Oct. 17** Surgeon General Allan Bakke released "unassailable evidence" that jogging, est, hang-gliding, and a certain French mineral water caused cancer.

83

Jan. 1 The United Nations International Year of the Simultaneous Orgasm began at midnight. **Jan. 20** Led by a coalition of migrant farmworkers, vegetarians, and Vishnuites, Congress approved a bill prohibiting the consumption of meat. **Apr. 21** ABC and CBS officially informed NBC that it was no longer entitled to call itself a network. **Aug. 8** Evelyn Wood changed the course of television history by inaugurating the first course in speed-viewing. **Oct. 17** The International Year of the Simultaneous Orgasm finally bore fruit. Two and a quarter billion participants "came" together, and the earth moved. **Nov. 2** On the anniversary of its election, the Congress of Nuts voted to abolish the FBI and the IRS, and to legalize cocaine and incest.

84

Jan. 3 Congress reconvened and passed resolution declaring 1984 "The Year of the Total Recall." **Feb. 13** The New York Sto Exchange revealed that its total day's tra had been three odd-lot shares of GM. For first time, the Dow Jones hit .0001. **Mar** Bankrupted by nationwide casino gamb Las Vegas defaulted on its municipal bo **Oct. 1** The Blue Cross/Blue Shield Cent for Disease Control announced that the main causes of Legionnaire's disease we wearing funny blue hats, drinking quar of bourbon, and holding conservative personal opinions.

vas held

July 4, 1984 The musical movie extravaganza 1984! premiered to ecstatic audiences.

Jan. 29, 1985 Idol of the 98 percent black U.S. Army, General Ali became chairman of the Joint Chiefs of Staff.

GLAMOUR's Agequake Makeover:

When the Agequake swept onto the scene earlier this year, it spelled one word for sixteen-year-old GLAMOUR summer-sales-trainee Medora Carden: I-N-T-I-M-I-D-A-T-I-O-N! "I *wanted* to look old—stylish—like your other employees," she confided to GLAMOUR Editor-in-Chief Joanna Xanthippides, "but everyone else was . . . well, so *experienced* looking. And I wasn't!"

Our reaction to Medora's reaction: Make way for facial *artiste* Bonnie Maller's next Agequake makeoveree!

Medora's pre-GLAMOUR look: hopelessly callow.

5 Steps to a New OLD You

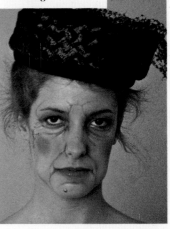 *(top right)*

Bonnie thinks lines and wrinkles are terribly important. Here, with two simple diagonal strokes of her eyebrow pencil, she creates forty years' worth of bags under Medora's far-too-vivid eyes.

Wrinkles all present and accounted for . . . and what a difference a touch of highlighter under those forehead creases can make!

And, finally, the touches to finish the old Medora off in style: cotton balls stuffed in the cheex to create that jowly, dewlappy look; a dusting of white powder for the hair; a cellulite implant or two (not shown); and, the capper: an "old hat" from Lavinia of St. Petersburg.

Medora thought it would take all afternoon to apply enough rouge to look timeworn . . . but before you could say "Methuselah," Bonnie's blusher-brusher—combined with a firm foundation of white, pasty makeup, an austere bunning of the hair, some outrageously thick red lipstick, and the coup de grace—an artificial mole on the chin—had our young staffer speeding a decade-a-minute down the highway to senior citizenship.

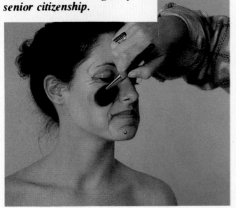

"Liver a little!" is one of Bonnie Maller's mottoes—and who could disagree after seeing how a few well-placed liver spots chicened Medora's youngish cheek?

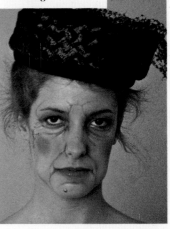

GLAMOUR — OCTOBER 1986

1986 *"Five Steps to a New Old You" marked the growing impact of the "Agequake."* Glamour *magazine presented this feature on how teenagers could look stylishly decrepit.*

1986 *The "New Honesty" was mirrored in the marketing of professional athletes. The highest-rated sports spectacular of the decade was called quite simply, "Big Blax on Ice with Stix."*

1983 *The national pastime's first year-round playing season. The peculiar pitfalls of winter baseball were captured for all time in this LeRoi painting of the Cincinnati Reds losing the ball—and the World Series—in the snows of Riverfront Stadium.*

1982 *The concept and advertising copy for American Motors' "Le Shoe" was an example of the "New Honesty" in marketing. Hailed as a landmark, the campaign was clearly ahead of its time. American Motors folded the same year.*

1984 *It's all foreplay and no follow through for one happy client, who clowns for the camera with a full-size Whoro-gram at Los Angeles' celebrated Museum of the Orgasm (formerly the Continental Hotel).*

1983 *The very success of the International Year of the Simultaneous Orgasm proved to be a disaster. Almost everywhere, the planet underwent profound climatic—as well as climactic—alterations.*

1981 *Legalization of prostitution by Congress made sex a commodity like any other. Ladies of the night were required by federal law to display the Universal Pricing Code "clearly on their person."*

1989 *Oil glut and food shortage combined to inspire a delicious line of synthetic food made directly from raw petroleum. Here is a specialty of Houston's famed restaurant, Le Restaurant—Les Crudités No. 6.*

1981 *The enormous popularity of Perier mineral water in the late '70s prompted the French company to increase profits still further by cutting freight costs. After experimenting unsuccessfully with freeze-dried Perier, it began marketing Perier syrup. The syrup, which made ten times its volume of Perier when added to domestic mineral water, sold for $59 the small bottle, $125 the large economy size.*

The pages of this book carrying text data are imprinted with the Universal Literacy Optical Code (ULOC) in accordance with international standards established by the 1989 Functional Literacy Convention at Sunnyvale, California. Channel settings for automatic reading equipment are as follows:

CHANNEL 1: Line-for-line English narration by Richard Chamberlain
CHANNEL 2: Line-for-line Spanish narration by Ricardo Montalban
CHANNEL 3*: Selected ABS-TV videotape footage of events related to the text, with English language commentary by Jane Pauley
CHANNEL 4*: Selected ABS-TV videotape footage of events related to the text, with Spanish language commentary by Felipe Luciano.

All commercial messages accompanying the above material were created, encoded, and sold in compliance with the voluntary guidelines of the American Book Advertising Council, of which Workman Publishing is a corporate member.

*For scanners equipped with video monitors only (use standard RS232 interface).

THE WORLD

Ships of the desert ... one of the many camel-powered F-14 jets in the great Arab jihad of '88 idles on a dune as its "pilot" gazes toward London, a mere 2,000 miles away.

THE WORLD

It is February 16, 1988, and in the tiny port town of Algeciras on the southernmost tip of Spain, Ciriaco Merced is preparing his small boat for the day's fishing. Suddenly, he is aware of an unusual splashing in the normally placid waters along the shore. He looks up, and cannot believe his eyes. Emerging from the surf, their long robes and burnooses dripping, are a dozen Arab soldiers. The light of religious fanaticism gleams in their eyes. Each draws a great curved scimitar, and advances.

America loves the world, but the world now hates America. It was not always thus—indeed, there was a time when America and the world were partners in a happy marriage. Our nation worked hard all day to bring home the agricultural, technological, and humanitarian bacon, and the rest of the peoples of the globe responded with gratitude, affection, and willing submission to our ideological lovemaking. "Hail Columbia! Husband to everybody!" wrote the poet George Lois. But it became manifestly clear during the 1980s that the honeymoon was over. It was not the groom's fault—we were as loyal and loving as ever. No, the marriage crumbled because the bride went insane.

Our nearest neighbors offered especially painful rebuffs. Mexico, newly rich in oil reserves, flounced about the Northern Hemisphere in open defiance of our most sincere protestations of fidelity, while Canada continued the pose of catatonic withdrawal with which she had tormented us for centuries.

AMERICA LOVES THE WORLD, BUT THE WORLD NOW HATES AMERICA.

Some looked to China to be our partner. But it was plain to many that she was "using" us, greedily accepting our consumer goods but steadfastly refusing us so much as an ideological goodnight kiss. By 1990, we were no longer certain of even "her" gender. Our flirtation with China had landed us in bed with a bizarre hermaphrodite, and—for the first time in history—America was unsure as to who should get on top.

Russia, a spirited coquette with whom we had engaged in many a lively nuclear arms race, seemed to shrink from our embrace. When the Soviets opposed China's war with Vietnam, Senator Robert Dole called them "Commies." We meant it as just another love-tap. But as the decade wore on, we waited in vain to take Russia home from the Cold War Prom. She had left without us.

And what of Europe—traditionally America's best friend, kissing cousin, and former parent? Our filial affection for the United Magic Kingdom remained unchanged. But otherwise Europe acted distant, perverse, and preoccupied. As three dozen Common Market members made shopping unprecedentedly complicated, Swiss banks offered unregistered toasters as inducements to open new secret accounts; and as Moslem hoards swept northward in an unstoppable *jihad* surely destined to decimate the entire continent, the message to America was clear: the thrill is gone. Europe doesn't live here any more.

South America and Scandinavia—the former a trampish slut we had never really fancied, the latter a striking beauty somehow too remote and cool for our taste—were always "busy." Israel, the spitfire tomboy we had ushered into nationhood, was unrecognizable. She had taken up with Arabs now, and spurned her ardent, fair-skinned suitor.

Naturally, this worldwide confusion was reflected in chaos at the United Nations. With literally thousands of sovereign countries jostling each other all over the globe, that venerable institution— kindly, eccentric housemother- procuress—split into several factions: the North American United Nations, the Asian United Nations, etc. The UUN was created—but she was mean, and refused to accept our "propagandistic" credit card. Only the United Multinationals remained as a possible partner for our rejected America—and many thought they would prove much too "fast" for us.

Ciriaco Merced's head, were it still attached to his body, would see around him an invading party of Moslem lunatics preparing to devastate his town, his wife, his country. Were he sentient, he might reflect that in such a manner has the world itself devastated the feelings of America during the 1980s. Who, he might ask, will court the nations of the world now? Who could possibly be America's rival? It is a good, pertinent question. Second husbands are not easy to find.

> **ISRAEL, THE SPITFIRE TOMBOY WE HAD USHERED INTO NATIONHOOD, WAS UNRECOGNIZABLE. SHE HAD TAKEN UP WITH ARABS NOW, AND SPURNED HER ARDENT, FAIR-SKINNED SUITOR.**

3/27/88--ARAB TROOPS SWEPT TRIUMPHANTLY THROUGH VENICE, PAUSING
BRIEFLY TO BATHE AND DRINK IN THE CANALS.

JIHAD! REVENGE OF THE PROPHET

In the dawn mists of October 1, 1988, Harry Mudge, second grounds keeper (on strike) of the Enchanted Cliffs of Dover, gazed eastward across the Channel and rubbed his eyes in disbelief. A veritable cloud of single sails, stretching from horizon to horizon, was bearing down on the English coast, driven by the morning wind. He raised his binoculars and focused: it was, indeed, an armada of 10,000 Arab dhows loaded to the gunwales with white-robed Arabs, camels, F-14 jets, solid gold Bentleys, SAM missiles, tanks, computers, and fractionating columns. Mudge hurriedly called the RAF (Royal Amusement Force) headquarters, but to what avail? The only planes left in Britain were the ancient fuselages on a whirligig ride called the "Spitfire." The "scramble order" left the RAF circling pathetically to calliope music. By noon the Levantine wave was on English soil. An all-night trek up the motorway brought the caravans at dawn to Piccadilly Circus. Fanning out, they bypassed the Enchanted Buckingham Palace to the south and north. At 1:15 Claridge's ran up the white flag. At 2:30 their main objective — Harrods department store — fell without the firing of a single shot. In Hyde Park one million jelaba'd Arabs danced, sang, waved deck chairs and scimitars, and fired their carbines into the air. Thus on October 2, 1988 — 800 years after Saladin freed Jerusalem — the Arabs had taken London.

GENERAL AHMED YAZI YAMANI
VICTORY IN EUROPE, 1989

Black Friday, December 6, 1985, the day the worldwide Oil Glut was revealed, was

After their conquest of Paris, a patrol of Arab Foreign Legionnaires scours the streets around the Arc de Jihad (Arc de Triomphe) looking for NATO stragglers and mopping up pockets of Free French resistance.

blackest for the oil-rich Arab nations. Overnight, as petroleum fell from $240 per barrel to 10 cents (deposit included), they became the oil-poor Arab nations. Their international petrodollar empire had already been shaken by recent events. Millions of acres of Arab-owned farmland in the American Midwest had become arid after the Year of the Simultaneous Orgasm. Their billions in gold bars transmuted slowly to lead as the world moved toward the food standard. Their Hollywood movies *The Hejaz Singer* and *Abu Dhabi Honeymoon (see SHOBIZ)* failed to recoup negative costs: the Euro-American market showed no interest in movie actresses veiled except for their eyes. Arab worldwide hotel chains lost fortunes as the food shortage killed room service. The Oil Glut was merely, in the words of *Time* magazine, the *"coup de grasse."*

It isn't worth a plug petrodollar.
SLANG EXPRESSION, 1986

On Black Saturday, December 7 (according to King Khalid: "A day that will live in infidel infamy"), Arab credit stopped. At Harrods, a sheik from Kuwait had his credit cards torn up. In Paris, an Omani sheik was evicted from five floors of the Hotel George V, which kept his 120 pieces of luggage, 15 camels, five Bentleys, and seven wives as security. In Hollywood, another sheik was deserted by his 16 concubines, who promptly hired Marvin Mitchelson to sue him for palimony. From all points of the globe, impoverished Arabs straggled home economy class, with only the burnooses on their backs, to lick their wounds and pick up the pieces.

The picture was bleak. They were heavily in debt for Western armaments and such modern luxuries as desalinization plants, steel mills, sand-gasification works, iceberg trawlers, metal-plating factories (the famous gold Cadillac plant in Bahrein), and the ambitious omni-peninsular air-conditioning scheme. They had no choice: it was time to liquidate.

Out of debt but broke, the Arabs tried vainly for the next two years to reenter the natural resources market. Their first venture, OMEC (The Organization of Myrrh-

Exporting Nations), soon foundered; there was no world market for myrrh. The pathetic fate of its successor, OSEC (The Organization of Sand-Exporting Nations), is well known.

Frustrated, loaded with out-of-service sophisticated weapons for which they could not afford spare parts, buoyed only by the new wave of Moslem enthusiasm, the Arab

4/7/87—SHEIK ALI FAYADH MAHIM WAS ARRESTED IN BEVERLY HILLS TODAY
FOR TRYING TO PASS A BAD EMERALD AT GUCCI'S.

THE WORLD 33

*At the pre-*jihad *meeting of the Moslem
powers, the Iranian delegation abstains
from voting to invade Europe, clearly
preferring a "hands-off" policy.*

powers turned angry eyes towards the West. Clearly, Arab counsels concluded, their sudden loss of wealth was not just kismet. They had been sold a bill of goods. It had all been an infidel plot against the Mohammedan world! Revenge and recoupment were called for. *"Jihad! Holy War!"*—the cry resounded through Arabdom, from Bagdad to Riyadh to Memphis, wherever the simoons blew and muezzins wailed. *"Jihad!"*

Within two months, 50 million Arabs had gathered in Riyadh under flapping crescent banners, their scimitars waving. Ten thousand troops from Muscat were sent ahead to forage and scout, and reached the Bosphorus unopposed (the famous "Muscat Ramble"). After them came the entire nomadic horde with a thunderous clanking of weapons and a bellowing of camels as ships of the desert hauled grounded F-14s, missiles, tanks, and limousines across the burning Saudi sands, over the Dardanelles and the Balkan Mountains, through Yugoslavia and Austria in search of revenge and former glory. *"Jihad!* To London! *Jihad!"*

NATO, still poised for an attack through East Germany, was completely outflanked by the horde from the south. Its forces, moreover, after 40 years, were trained only for maneuvers and needed six month's warning even for that. Nor had they a counter-weapon for the scimitar. The Arabs swept across southern France and divided, occupying Moorish Spain and heading for Paris via Burgundy (where they demolished the wine cellars for religious reasons). On March 31, crying *"Jihad!* April in Paris!" they drew their dusty F-14s up the Champs-Elysées and dined, victorious, on cous-cous around the Arc de Triomphe.

London, the Kingdom of Camembert, and the Union of Scandinavian Socialist Republics were doomed. The only bulwark that remained against the Moslem hordes was the Pope, driven from his adopted Italy. In Warsaw, on the Feast of the Assumption, 1989, he declared his intention of organizing a new crusade to regain the Holy Land or — failing that — his summer place at Castel Gandolfo.

THE UNITED MAGIC KINGDOM

For Sale: One country. Quaint. Needs work. Best offer.

This extraordinary advertisement appeared in the classified sections of most of the prominent First World newspapers one morning in early 1982. It presaged the greatest single land sale of the decade.

Northern Ireland had been sold off in 1981 to a consortium known as the United Barflies of America and promptly renamed "The Greatest Goddam Little Piece of Heaven on God's Goddam Earth," under which sobriquet it obtained a seat in the UN General Assembly. At the time, this was hailed as the real estate event of the century. But an even greater coup, and one that held promise of rescuing the surviving remnants of the United Kingdom from decades of poverty and purposelessness, was soon to come. The buyer was an American leisure and entertainment conglomerate, and the seller was the United Kingdom itself. By a simple Act of Parliament that stipulated a payment of three million dollars to each Member in return for the Lords' and Commons' relinquishing all governmental power, the United Kingdom overnight became Walt Disney's United Magic Kingdom—a carefree, fun-for-the-whole-family amusement park; admission 50p, no passport required.

It was an instant park. Disneyland and Disney World had laboriously reconstructed a mythical fairy-tale world; but the ready-made, fully operating insanity of 1982 Britain provided a wealth of amusements that needed no improving.

Six times a day, seven days a week, the National Front goons of "Raceway" took to the streets in a living pageant of Paki-bashing. Visitors to the "Free Ride" could (for 50p) down tools with several million members of the Trades Union Council on consistently hilarious pretexts. "Rotten Row" featured brolly-toting bowler-hatted bankers arriving in Threadneedle Street at midday sharp and departing five minutes later for lunch. (For an extra pound, visitors were allowed to pick up the check and listen to the bankers rail against "the f--king workers.") The mothballed *QE2* and the Concorde roamed the scepter'd isle as spectacular rides. In "Commons House," former prime ministers Thatcher, Callaghan, Wilson, and Heath were familiar sights as they pantomimed nonstop noisy debates on points of order, while in "Lords House," bewigged peers took turns trying one another for buggery. Visiting teens could "get off" at live concerts by such performers as Tom Robbins and Polystyrene, during which Anti-Nazi League gays got lead-piped by Special Patrol Group bobbies. Or, out in the countryside, they could join whey-faced university graduates in recreating the lifestyle of prehistoric Britain; dressing in bark, catching scurvy, and getting bitten by badgers. And, of course, Her Enchanted Majesty Queen Elizabeth II and her dancing horse Disraeli joined in a musical Trooping the Colour, every hour on the hour.

The atmosphere of the United Magic Kingdom as an amusement park proved as richly textured as the old version had been. Clean and tasty food—long a Disney byword—was replaced by typical British cuisine; and lucky visitors could snack on roast beef sandwiches with a 65-to-1 bread-to-beef ratio or cold sausages that tasted like tubes of pork toothpaste. Sullen, soggy skies needed no special-effects wizardry. Everything from the phone system to the plumbing to BBC Radio exactly duplicated the hilarious eccentricities of yesteryear. And without the expense to Disney of a single p.

And yet, within only a few years, the United Magic Kingdom was struggling financially. Of the theme park's 70 million live-in employees, 85 percent called in sick on an average of 10 days a month; and Disney statisticians calculated that 95 million workdays were lost in 1987 alone through wildcat strikes—including those staged by the Royal Family. Power failures and food boycotts by tourists crippled the facility at peak seasons. The tightly organized Disney operation realized it had an unholy mess on its hands.

Among the happy throng at the sumptuous opening of the United Magic Kingdom were (left to right) *the Japanese ambassador, the president of the United States, and the prime minister of India.*

The end came as the '80s drew to their close: 45 million pink slips, the largest mass firing in history. The former United Magic Kingdom employees welcomed the prospect of being back on the dole, but they were unprepared for what followed. Disney, never a corporation that liked to cooperate with unions, had made no provision for their welfare. The British unions themselves were, by title deed, Disney's property. Management forthwith requested that the workforce they had "let go" vacate the premises.

The United Magic Kingdom as a theme park remained a good idea, however, and Disney was only too willing to allow Britain's nonunion immigrant population to stay. After a brief three-month remodeling period, the park reopened with such features as a Pakistani Winston Churchill ensconced at Checkers, swigging brandy, ducking bombs, and singing "I'll Give Hitler Such a Hit"; and a West Indian Henry VIII in the great hall of Hatfield House consuming a vast table of victuals, the tablecloth, and the table itself. Meanwhile, Turks in kilts and Maltese Druids roamed hill and dale in search of hopeless causes and oak apples, respectively.

For the 45 million dismissed employees the future remains bleak. They have until December 31, 1990, to leave the island to which a few years ago they held clear title. The recent Arab incursions have had no effect on their plight. In negotiations between Disney and the United Islamic Republic, both sides have agreed that these unemployed people must go. But the once-proud nation of conquerors has found that in a world of former subjects they are less than welcome. Only India so far has expressed any interest in providing the British with a new homeland, and the reason is, many believe, that they are simply too polite to say "no."

PLASTIC CHINA

As far as the eye of the helicopter pilot can see is an ocean of people, young people, a hundred million strong: dancing, swaying, singing, as the monumental sounds of a thousand Fender basses and a thousand Les Paul guitars scream the music of Jimi Hendrix from relayed banks of speakers 200-feet high across the disused province. Every time the helicopter dips suspiciously toward a particularly boisterous group, the young people, drugged, drunk, or just plain happy, wave and yell at the pilot, flashing the universal two fingers of the peace sign, their clothes a flowing cacophony of color, the watery sunlight glinting from the mandalas round their necks.

For many in the Peking Senate and many more in its House of Representatives, the idea of a Chinese Woodstock was a "duplicitous ploy of the teenage jackals of wrong-thinking left-wingism." Allowing immeasurable hordes of Chinese youth, with their antiestablishment lifestyles, their predilection for dangerous drugs, and their un-Confucian sexual attitudes, to gather in one place was to invite disaster. Other more sober heads saw the festival as a safety valve for the deeper and more dangerous pressures that had been building up during the "Great Trip Forward."

The Chinese had taken avidly to capitalist ways. Plunging into both production and consumption with that same energy that had once led a colonial bigot to refer to them as "the priceless Jews of the Orient," they launched two ambitious Five-Year Plans in 1980, designed to bring them abreast of other postindustrial nations by 1990. The plans were based on the thesis that Mao's leadership had not advanced the nation an inch, and that the passing away of his brand of communism with all its embarrassments simply left China back where she started—namely, in the mid-'40s. The dynamic new leadership realized that it had to move the country through four and a half decades in the space of one if it were to catch up with the First World. The '40s, '50s, '60s, '70s, and '80s would all have to be experienced by the Chinese, but at breakneck speed.

The West responded with enthusiasm. After all, the plans meant a vast new market for countless products currently rotting in abandoned U.S. warehouses, European thrift stores, and Australian junkyards. Within weeks of the announcement of the first ('40s) phase of the First Five-Year Plan, the Chinese bought bulbous refrigerators, symmetrically rounded cars, hideous and uncomfortable beige furniture, double-breasted suits with jackets that came down to the knees, and dirndl skirts. They gazed at porthole-sized TV screens and wrote their wall posters in spidery lettering that made the words look like broken railings. As the habits of consumption took hold, the plan began to work at a cultural level. The population looked forward to the promise of all-electric homes, became dissatisfied with the big-band sound, and made serious plans to invade North Korea.

The second ('50s) phase was no less successful. The advanced nations unleashed an avalanche of second-, third-, and fourth-hand goods on the eager Chinese consumers. Endless shiploads of worn-out or broken toasters, cracked records, forgotten plastic fads, faded magazines, and threadbare clothes were snapped up in the time it took to unload and distribute them. Whole new industries sprang up in a dozen countries. Intrepid Japanese entrepreneurs appeared in the offices of garbage dump operators with strip-mining contracts. Rural barns and front yards from Maine to Tennessee were besieged by junk prospectors. Every antique store in California was stripped bare. And while most of the gadgets didn't work and the artifacts were incomprehensible, the brush-cut, finger-popping Chinese couldn't have cared less. As fast as the '50s relics were acquired and shown off to neighbors they were thrown away onto the ever-growing mountains of garbage. The

As an honored citizen of China, Richard Nixon continued his great work—preserving the American way of life.

Chinese were intensely proud of these dumps—visible symbols of their arrival in a world of consumer economies.

By the beginning of 1984, the Chinese had progressed in just 30 months from a full-scale witchhunt, through conformity and apathy, to beat poetry and a widespread concern that the influence of advertising was becoming too pervasive. Nothing summed up the First Five-Year Plan better than that most enduring '50s figure, Richard Nixon, who was now firmly ensconced in Peking as the government's Special Adviser on Vietnamese Affairs.

It was the '60s that became the program's undoing. The '60s started smoothly enough—with computer technology and French films and fashions. The highly lucrative war in Southeast Asia seemed to be going well. The First World's garbage was being recycled at an even greater rate into Chinese garbage. What the authorities had not reckoned with was—youth. The government's campaign two (actual) decades previously to "outbreed" the West now reaped its whirlwind in the shape of hundreds of millions of hot, hairy, and (before long) "hopped-up" teenagers, all angrily denouncing their parents' "plastic" lives. The flames were fueled by a West growing ever more sophisticated in matching their export of useless products to the Chinese market. Soon alienated kids from Sinkiang to Shanghai were getting behind the Grateful Dead and nodding to *Subterranean Homesick Blues*. It only took the Taiwanese, quite willing to resume their traditional role of drug dealers to the world, to complete the picture.

Parents, obsessed by "I Dream of Jeannie" reruns and the problem of keeping the front paddy mown and free of crabrice, were baffled by their drug-sodden children and their ear-bending music. The authorities, however, were not so passive. Drug use was outlawed, rock banned from the airwaves, long hair summarily cut off, possession of anything Indian punished by arrest. Nothing was going to stop the Sec-

ond Five-Year Plan. They had to reach 1970 by 1986, and they smelled trouble.

They got it—in characteristically monumental Chinese fashion. Campus riots often involved more than a million people and police. One narcotics bust of a hash party in Nanking netted 200,000 "heads." The groups that sprang up to reproduce pirated and illegal Buffalo Springfield and Doors albums numbered well into the hundreds. Scores of millions of teenagers "headed east" to the sunnier climes of the South China Sea, there to take part in love-ins and antiwar demonstrations that stretched the entire length of major provinces like Fukien or Kwangtung. The Great Trip Forward, as the LSD-crazed Chinese kids called it, and its concomitant reaction, the Great Clamp Downward, brought the country to a shuddering halt. Nineteen eighty-seven came and went with "pigs" and "hippies" alike firmly mired in the '60s. A new element entered the picture in early 1988 with the emergence in Hunan of a group that preached the works of Chairman Mao.

A horrified government moved from harassment to outright war. But the very army they ordered to crush the rebellion was young, stoned, and very much into Country Joe and the Fish. Sheer numbers and youth were against them. In desperation, they turned to the only hope they had left. In January 1989, Richard Nixon, coaxed out of retirement by one more crisis, became the first president of the United States of China. He counseled reconciliation between the generations. He urged everyone to come together. He promised retribution to those who refused. He advised that the massive music festival in Ningsia Hui, a remote "autonomous" province bordering Mongolia, be sanctioned by the local authorities. But, as he explained to the Chinese people the morning after a cobalt bomb of undetermined and possibly American origin had reduced Ningsia Hui to one vast crater: "History never repeats itself."

MAD. AVE. COMES TO THE UNITED STATES OF CHINA

The drab uniformity of Chinese consumer goods was once epitomized by the wisecrack of an obscure functionary in the Ministry of Sedans in 1980. Quipped he of China's 1949-DeSoto-derived Little Dragon of the Breath As Sweet As Corn Wine Custom Four-Door: "You can have any color you like, so long as it's red."

Hardly more inspired were the hand-lettered wall posters that served as the Little Dragon's sole advertising campaign, with their self-defeating slogan: "Ask the Man Who Is Now Waiting 22 Years to Own One."

Yet 10 years hence the vast freeways of China bustled and hummed with the Snappy Roadster of the Joy-Loving Camp, complete with Great Leap Forward Drive, and the Four Clouds on Four Wheels Coupe, designed to Smartly Rebuff the Boredom Claque.

What had happened? Production had of course quadrupled in virtually every segment of the new hard and soft goods sectors. But experts everywhere agreed that the real stimulus to China's love affair with buying and mass consumption had been sparked by the Central Committee's decision to adopt sophisticated advertising techniques wholesale.

By 1984, Peking could boast its own ultra-modern, steel-and-glass Advertising Compound, the People's Republic's equivalent of Madison Avenue; racy exposés of the ad game like *The Man in the Blue Cotton Suit* and *The Huckster Cadres* topped the bestseller lists; and mighty enterprises like Batten, Barton, Durstine & Foo attracted the creative cream of a newly sales-crazed nation.

Yet China's romance with advertising had begun on a note less than auspicious. The Asian monolith and "Mad. Ave." seemed initially to misunderstand one another,

with often tragic consequences. Horrified American advertising consultants told of soft drink and laundry soap television comparison tests, where those who chose incorrectly were summarily executed as traitors, and of "testimonials" that turned into weeping confessions of stupidity.

Why don't we let this swim like fish amongst the people for awhile?

SLOGAN ON THE WALL OF A CHINESE
AD AGENCY, 1985

Early commercials for the government's tea and rice monopolies persuaded less than dictated, with tempting offers of 100 chiao off for every nonuser the consumer could report to his local precinct committee. Nor, at first, did China's emerging admen fully grasp television commercial techniques. The coveted Golden Chopstick award for 1982 went to "Woo-Woo's Resolute Struggle to Brown Her Duck Without Excessive Grease," on behalf of the new cooking product Vibrate-and-Bake. Featuring a cast of 1,200 peasants, 200 tractors, and a *papier mâché* model of a Soviet battleship, it was based on a popular patriotic folk opera and required four hours to sing and dance its way to the punch line and final "super." Meanwhile, the Golden Chopstick print award for '83 went to a 24-page newspaper advertisement, with 23 pages devoted to denouncing competitive products as jackal frauds hatched by backsliding lunatic hirelings of one or another treasonous cell in the foodstuffs industry. Consumers were urged to sack any store that stocked such worthless goods.

But sooner than might have been expected, given the vast cultural chasm that had for so long separated East and West, the growing pains eased. China was to embrace and ultimately perfect the art and science of advertising, and use it to oil the mighty wheels of her now burgeoning commerce.

This television commercial for a detergent drew ire from an environmental cadre called Comrades of the Good Earth, who decried the "rampant phosphatism" glorified in the penultimate panel.

1.

V.O.

Bemused by the demons of outworn tradition, wrong-thinking Lee Yuan foolishly seeks to cleanse her wok with a rock.

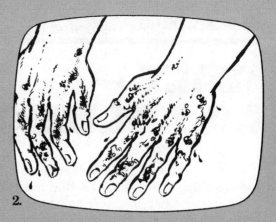

2.

V.O.

Result? A treacherous offense to the state and a hideous obstacle to the unimpedible success of the second Five-Year Destultification Plan —dishpan hands!

3.

SOLDIER
What are you, Lee Yuan?

LEE YUAN
I am a miserable, worthless worm of benighted collectivization. I am a running dog lackey of ancient and outmoded washing-upism. I am an unwitting dupe of the pro-red-rough-and-sore hand clique!

SOLDIER
That is correct, Lee Yuan!

4.

V.O.

Our illustrious leadership has sternly instructed Lee Yuan and her ilk to avail themselves of extremely modern Glorious Detergent of the 23rd of September!

5.

V.O.

Now, thanks to extremely modern Glorious Detergent of the 23rd of September, and in line with the dictates of progressive technology, Lee Yuan's hands are properly soft and silky!

6.

SOLDIER

Remember —those who do not avail themselves of extremely modern Glorious Detergent of the 23rd of September risk the implacable wrath of all forward-thinking people! Resolutely we must struggle against the jackal-eyed specter of dishpan hands!

ITALY— LA SOLUZIONE FINALE

By 1980, kidnappings in Italy had grown so numerous that names of victims and families were no longer reported. A spot check in April by what remained of the Ministry of the Interior revealed that approximately one half of the population was collecting funds to pay another one quarter, which was holding the remaining 25 percent hostage.

The old worker/peasant/landlord/parasite classes became obsolete; the Italian people were now more simply divided into "The Tripartite Society": abductor, abductee, abductee's family.

The precipitous decline in productive population, as well as the social upheaval of the mass kidnappings, led world economists to predict Italy's total collapse. The experts were wrong. Twenty-five percent of the population of Italy was now blindfolded and living in cellars, farm huts, or the trunks of cars. Their expectations were lowered, their consumption reduced to a bowl of pasta and a glass of sour red wine every other day, their productivity nil. But who were they? Union leaders, capitalists, landlords, and lemminglike hordes of Leftish university students from good bourgeois families. In their absence, abductee families worked hard, increased productivity, and scrambled to accumulate enough cash to meet the ransom demands of the abductors.

Suddenly, garbage was collected on time. There were seats on buses, even during rush hours. The trains ran on schedule for the first time since Mussolini. Cardinals were available for audiences at any time without an appointment.

Then, providentially, members of the Agnelli family kidnapped the Pirelli tire company heir, Giovanni, in order to raise a ransom for their uncle, who was being held by a militant Milanese clique. Giovanni's family, *simultaneously*, had run Francesca Agnelli off the road, and were holding *her* hostage to raise funds to free *Giuseppe* Pirelli from the revolutionary Red Wine-

makers of Chianti. All this happened on a Sunday, when the Banco del Popolo was closed. An exchange was arranged that not only restored the Pirelli and Fiat heirs to their ancestral estates, but also saw the Chianti group equipped with new tires for their farm machinery and the Milanese contingent supplied with 6,000 litres of red wine. The entire nation saw the logical next step—the abolition of the debased currency in favor of people as a medium of exchange.

By 1983 in the international money markets, one United States dollar equalled 2.3 Swiss francs, 3.8 deutsche marks, 215 yen, or an urban Italian housewife. In Turin, a $100 bill would procure a plump industrialist. In the provinces, it was difficult to get change for a judge or a factory owner, but the exclusive shops along the Via Condotti in Rome could easily break a bank president.

On the Via Veneto, you could linger all day over espresso for a trio of school children, or purchase the services of a good streetwalker for a couple of bad streetwalkers. Commodities were more expensive: a 55-gallon drum of olive oil cost a busload of Sicilians (although, as one Milanese wag pointed out, one could just as easily have squeezed the busload of Sicilians).

Vending machines became obsolete; nobody could figure out how to stuff a shopowner into a cigarette machine. On paydays, the lines at banks stretched for miles although there were few actual depositors; most of the people *were* deposits—they would wait in large rooms with benches until someone wanted to make a withdrawal, at which time they would dutifully file to the Paid Out window to join their new owner. At the end of the day, if deposits outnumbered withdrawals, tellers would escort the people to the nearest hotel where they would be placed in vaults until morning. If withdrawals outnumbered deposits, however, the tellers themselves were forfeit.

An Italian citizen withdraws a hostage from his Christmas Club account at the Banco d'Italia. As the age of the hostage attests, the term "change for a fifty" took on a new meaning in modern Italy.

These prices are absolutely disgraceful—two lawyers for one lousy grapefruit!

ITALIAN HOUSEWIFE ON THE
SOARING PRICE OF FOOD, 1983

A stuffed Leonid Brezhnev continued to rule the planet's largest nation for several years after his death. Known to insiders as "Lennie the Pooh, the Russian bear," the First Secretary's hold on power was literally broken when on May 1, 1986, his right arm fell off.

Comrades, it is time to break silence about the errors of Brezhnev. Too long have our lips been sealed! Let us speak the truth at last! Let it ring out clear! He was — and you all know this is true — a sloppy eater. And he cheated at cards. He was careless about his personal appearance. Everyone knows he was overweight! And tweeze his eyebrows? Never! And let us say, once and for all, as good Communists, never again will, shall, or should a chairman of the Communist party of the Soviet Union collect Alfa-Romeos!

FROM A. N. SCHLYAPKIN'S UNSUCCESSFUL
"DEBREZHNEVICATION" SPEECH

RUSSIA—THE IRON CURTAIN CALL

The Union of Soviet Socialist Republics has been described as a nation of mystery at best. What remains of it is no exception to that rule.

The first evidence that all was not well behind the "Iron Curtain" came early in 1980. Leonid I. Brezhnev, who had disappeared from the public eye some months previously, and had been presumed dead, reappeared at the May Day parade of that year. Although the dignitaries surrounding him on the reviewing stand remained unperturbed, it seemed clear to most Western observers that the heavy-jowled First Secretary had been none too expertly stuffed.

Repeated denials of this were issued by Soviet officials, and the Russian press continued to cover Brezhnev's activities in subsequent years, despite reports that his bodyguards carried him around by two handles attached to his buttocks and that he constantly leaked sawdust during public functions. The end came at a convention of Heroic Mothers in Leningrad in 1986. Even the stony-faced Soviets could not explain away the fact that, while a particularly enthusiastic Mother was shaking his hand, Mr. Brezhnev's right arm fell off.

The reason for the Presidium's curious attempt to maintain continuity only gradually came to light. According to Soviet theoreticians, Brezhnev had been the last remaining obstacle to the triumph of the proletarian revolution. With his death the final victory had been achieved and, as Marx had predicted, the state forthwith began to wither away. (Specifically, on the night of Brezhnev's demise, several large portions of the Kremlin had disappeared without a trace.) The abortive attempt to keep the First Secretary in power, albeit at the hands of a taxidermist, delayed this process but, ultimately, could not prevent it from happening.

Communications with the colossal nation became progressively more difficult. Understandably, Russians were not anxious to wither away as employees of the state, least of all as its spokesmen. And the confusion was intensified by the emergence in the always unruly southern soviets of a radical populist movement called "born-again communism." This was the creation of a messianic figure whose name was never revealed, but who bore an extraordinary physical resemblance to the father of communism himself, Karl Marx. The full-bearded patriarch led huge revival meetings at which Communists were "reborn," reaffirming their faith in dialectical materialism and singing the Internationale in 200- and sometimes 300-part harmony. The born-again movement, combined with the powerlessness of the central government (which had little or no idea of what had happened to the Red Army), ignited secession amongst the Soviet Republics. Ancient lands from Kazakhstan to Georgia once again became sovereign states.

This much is known. But not much more. Life goes on in the vast hinterland of the Central Steppes, but aside from a few sketchy reports of new Golden Hordes sweeping down into the Balkans to stem the Arab tide, little is heard from within the endless vistas beyond the Vistula. For much of the decade and for the foreseeable future, Mother Russia has lifted her skirts above her head and hidden her face.

INSIDE RUSSIA

In the summer of 1980, an illiterate Muscovite, Andrei Pushpin, walked and hitchhiked from Moscow to Berlin, where he calmly talked his way through a Soviet checkpoint and passed into what was then West Germany. Finding employment in a brewery as a barrel cleaner, the enterprising Russian was later kidnapped by embarrassed Soviet officials and returned to his native land. There he was sentenced to seven years in a publishing camp for having labored abroad.

By the time he emerged from the camp several years later, Pushpin was an accomplished author. His second escape to the German capital, in 1988, provided the West with its only reliable account of events in Russia during the tumultuous mid-1980s.

SPACE

In space the Russians made history in 1981 by sending up the first cosmonaut from the Palestine Liberation Organization. The elaborate gesture of solidarity seemed successful when the intrepid Palestinian joined two Russians in the Salyut 7 space station. Unfortunately, the Arab, upset by an altercation involving the cooking of a goat over an open fire inside the capsule, hijacked the Salyut at gunpoint and forced it to splash down in the Persian Gulf. The great mission ended on a somewhat sour note.

DISARMAMENT

With the signing of SALT II, a certain stability was achieved within the USSR's defense establishment. Throughout 1982, however, citizens began noticing an unusually large number of new churches popping up all over the Soviet Union. In an atheistic country, this was suspicious. What even the most sophisticated U.S. spy satellites failed to prove was common knowledge to the average Russian—that the Red Army had developed a new Soviet missile cunningly disguised to look like the spire of a Russian Orthodox cathedral. (It was known as the Ikon 1 or "Taras

Bulba" missile.) Tentative U.S. charges that the USSR was violating SALT II brought angry denials and the countercharge that Disney World was a "proven missile battery." The Soviet High Command did, however, secretly begin preparing proposals—never implemented—concerning the number of IRVs (Intercontinental Religious Vehicles) each side could develop. These were based on the assumption that even though Saint Basil's in Moscow had greater "throw weight" than Saint Patrick's in New York, the United States had an overwhelming numerical superiority in lighter churches, especially in Southern California.

ARCHAEOLOGY

A flurry of excitement greeted the discovery of the bones of Old Soviet Man (*Pithecanthropus collectivus*) near Zaporozhye in 1984. *Collectivus* lived crowded in very small caves, knew little about clothing, and was an excellent weapons maker. According to Professor Vadim Lysenko, the species, five million years old, proved definitively that "Marxists walked erect before Capitalists."

THE MILITARY-CIVILIAN PRODUCTION SWITCH

In 1983, the Soviet system of central planning became fully computerized. Russian bureaucrats, however, unused to sophisticated electronic equipment, inadvertently reversed the assignments of the military and civilian production sectors. The military was suddenly in charge of washing machines, the consumer sector was turning out planes, tanks, and missiles.

The result was startling; exquisitely designed, high-tech refrigerators, washers, crock pots, and barbecues, equal to the best in the West, were produced on a crash basis by the military. Meanwhile, the civilian sector was turning out the shoddiest military hardware in modern history; most notably the famous MIG-25 II, with the two wings on the same side, and the BOOMERANG ground-to-ground missile, which went straight up and then fell back on its firers.

THE VODKA PANIC

Nineteen eighty-five brought a true national crisis. Climatic changes due to the Year of the Simultaneous Orgasm halved the potato harvest to a mere 63 million poods. In a food-short world, the Politburo had no choice: a secret order went out to "cut vodka production." For a nation where workers spent one sixth of their income on spirits, the effect was sobering. Public drunkenness plummeted, as did the number of people in ditches.

Most seriously, many citizens, newly clear-headed, began to notice and complain about things they had previously endured. "My apartment is too small!" "*Pravda* is dull!" "Remember meat?" "Where are the roads?" chorused voices from Chelyabinsk to Omsk.

Draconian measures were deemed necessary. The Politburo authorized the expenditure of precious hard currency to buy, secretly, 1,500,000 gallons of slivovitz from Yugoslavia. There followed, of course, the now-famous Soviet "drunk" of May 1986, during which, among other things, the Kremlin was painted green.

RUSSIA ON WHEELS

The Oil Glut quickly created the great Soviet auto boom. Unwilling to throw workers out of guaranteed jobs in refineries and proliferating oilfields (the biggest strike, of course, being the famous "Big Red" field directly under Lubyanka Prison), auto production was ordered on a "shock" basis. To move the flood of new cars, the government set up state-owned distribution on the American model. On television, car dealers such as "Ivan the Terrible" and "The Mad Russian" ("How can I sell them so cheap? I'm crazy!") became familiar figures, pushing the official "Five-Year Plan." ("All parts and labor guaranteed for five years.")

The auto boom called attention to a new problem: the great road shortage. With a road density only 1.7 percent that of the United States, Soviet cars had no place to go. They tended to accumulate in the cities, provoking the Great Moscow Traffic Lock of 1987 (an immovable traffic jam that eventually had to be paved over).

THE GREAT WITHERING AWAY

On June 12, 1986, in a Moscow mourning for Brezhnev, a garbage man noticed something unusual. Overnight, the Ministry of Planning, a huge edifice, had disappeared. In its place was a vacant lot. He called the authorities. Roadblocks were thrown up to divert traffic from the spectacle. A mystified Politburo met and after 24 hours of silence put a small item in *Pravda*: "The redecorating of the Ministry of Planning is proceeding on schedule."

In ten days more ministries had vanished, including the Ministry of Health, the Ministry of Insignificant Facts, the Ministry of Fresh Water Fishing, and the Ministry of Fear. A strange lassitude had struck the remaining bureaucracies; many of them stopped coming to work with, fortunately, no noticeable effect on the operation of the country.

After a week of debate, a special plenum of the Central Committee announced what it had known for several years: now that communism had been achieved, the state was withering away.

Signs of change appeared quickly. Instead of the scheduled essay on hydropower in Byelorussia, the front page of *Pravda*, July 12, shouted strange new headlines: "Man Bites Bear!" "Dynamo Shocks Spartak 1-0," and "Cops Raid Red Love Nest." KGB agents wandered the streets dazedly, raincoats unbuttoned, following each other. The Taganka Theatre announced a brazenly unauthorized production of a foreign play, «Под Деревом «Ём-Ём»» ("Under the Yum-Yum Tree"). Store clerks became polite. Restaurant service became fast. Something was wrong.

Catching this spirit of abandon, the ragtag remainder of the Central Committee decided in 1986 to cancel the upcoming 27th Congress of the Communist party and replace it with the "first *party* of the Communist party," appointing the Refreshments Committee of the Communist party, the Decorations (non-military) Committee of the Communist party, and the Entertainment Committee of the Communist party. Although the punch ran out at 4 A.M. and someone was mauled by a bear, the party was a riotous success and it was decided henceforth to hold two a year, on May Day and on November 7. And thus began the era of the two-party system.

ZUFTI NOG HUMMO: 1988 TIRANA WORLD'S FAIR

The 1988 Tirana World's Fair, the only world's fair of the '80s and the first such exposition to be staged anywhere in two decades, proved a notable event on any number of counts. The World Court at The Hague still refuses to take up the charge of the Brussels-based Bureau of International Expositions that the license to hold it was forged, and scholars of Albanian affairs continue to wrestle with the import of its curious theme: *Zufti Nog Hummo*—"The Future Belongs to Tinned Mice."

How many world's fairs, expophiles wondered, had ever been held in the strict and seemingly self-defeating secrecy of this one? In line with Albania's rigid policy of political nonalignment, all other nations of the world except the Central African Kingdom and the Dominion of Canada were excluded from participating. In line with Albania's even stricter border control, no outsiders were allowed to enter and attend—a ban underlined on Opening Day (or what was rumored by informed sources to be opening day), when a chartered British Laker Airways Boeing 767, with 540 would-be fair visitors aboard, was destroyed by a Chinese-made Albanian guided missile as it prepared to land at the Tirana airport.

A less-than-celebratory spirit of secrecy and suspicion evidently hovered over the fair itself. Word filtered out via diplomatic sources all through the duration of Tirana 1988, telling of picture postcard vendors being charged with selling state secrets and picture postcard buyers being shot as spies. Indeed, reported the authoritative British journal *The Economist*, fair souvenirs bearing the event's name or date had been declared illegal, and Albania's prison system was crammed to overflowing with purchasers by the end of the second day.

It was perhaps just as well, since conversing with fellow fair visitors was also a crime, that the Tirana exposition evidently gave those in search of novelty and excitement so very little to talk about. There was the traditional Albanian amusement of pin-the-tail-on-the-donkey, of course—but according to that same tradition the donkey was a real one and the pins railroad spikes. Visitors could inspect a working naphtha plant, a working olive grove, a working sheep pasture, and a working coal mine; but only by trading a minute's worth of labor for every minute of spectating. There were the pungent tobacco sandwiches, *Hoxhaburgers*, favored by Albania's hardy peasantry since before King Zog's time and the unquestioned snack treat of the fair, as well as the only one. And there were native Albanian crafts: the goat cheese sculptors of Shkodër, the Vlach dog wrestlers in their talismanic rubber bathing caps, incantorily grunting "Yump! Yump! Yump!"; fierce Bulgars from Mount Korab in the northern regions performing their astonishing rope-skipping feats. And finally, the exhibit of the Albanian State Security Police in its underground concrete bunker, where attendance and fingerprinting were literally a "must."

The Tirana Fair's closing ceremonies—a shower of red-hot Party buttons shoveled into the nighttime throng from the tender of Albania's first domestically built steam locomotive by First Secretary Enver Hoxha—were carried live over the Albanian state radio service in a broadcast monitored by listening posts in neighboring Greece. It made a piquant finishing touch to the 1988 Tirana World's Fair, observers agreed, that the announcers describing the festivities later received stiff prison sentences for divulging restricted information to unauthorized persons—the listening radio audience.

4/5/88--AS A PROTEST AGAINST THE TIRANA WORLD'S FAIR, THE ALBANIAN
TROTSKYITE COLONY OPENED A COUNTER-WORLD'S FAIR IN HONDURAS.

THE WORLD 47

This panoramic view of the 1988 Albanian World's Fair shows, among other exhibits, the International Hall of Sheep Diseases (foreground, right) and the International Hall of Huts (fifth row, far right). Photos of the fair were illegal, and the photographer who took this shot was interviewed for several years in the International Hall of Head-Squeezing (second row, center).

UMPBACK A D
SPERM GALORE

Whales, whales every where,
But not a drop to eat.

The banning of whale killing on May 4, 1981, turned out to be, in retrospect, the highwater mark of the decade's ecology movement. On that date, representatives of 157 nations signed the International Concordat Against Whaling (ICAW), and ended, with a stroke of the pen, 25 centuries of man's exploitation of the whale.

The first indication that all was not well came in the summer of 1982 during the annual Whale Count at Point Mugu, California. According to Fred Hammersalt, former president of Friends and Acquaintances of the Gray Whale: "It looked as if every female whale in the vicinity was either pregnant or a mother. We simply had no idea that they were so fertile—and so promiscuous. One large humpback achieved 64 orgasms in a single afternoon before pausing to nibble a bit of purple krill. Females were approachable by males two hours after giving birth. The only whales we observed that didn't get pregnant after being mounted turned out to be gay males—and many of these were seen helping out with calf care."

The increase in the whale population proceeded at a stupendous rate. By 1984, ports from Vladivostok to Tierra del Fuego were clogged with masses of humpback, blue, gray, and sperm whales. Some parts of the Atlantic and Pacific oceans were so chock-a-block with whales that international shipping lanes could only be kept open by refitted ice-breakers, designed to shove the huge bodies aside gently but firmly. (ICAW made it an international crime not only to kill whales, but also to "cause them lacerations, contusions, or emotional stress.")

One early victim of the so-called Whale Glut was the perfume industry. At first, the increase in whales was a bonanza for the scent manufacturers, providing them with unheard-of quantities of ambergris, the whale regurgitation by-product used as a base for all expensive perfumes. But whale proliferation quickly proved too much of a good thing. By 1985, supermarkets were offering handy six-packs of Arpège in easy-open cans. The perfume cartel struck back with TV commercials promoting a "Kill the Whales" campaign. The aging Judy Collins was lured out of retirement to produce a *Songs Against the Whale* album—including the hit single, "When You've Seen One Giant Aquatic Mammal, You've Seen Them All."

Meanwhile, public opinion seemed to be swinging in favor of limiting the numbers of whales. The change was fueled in part by the well-publicized fact that each whale carcass contained some 8,789 megagrams of protein—the equivalent of nine million eggs, or 11 million strips of lean crispy bacon, or 24 million slices of whole wheat toast.

By 1987, intentional oil spills had become the keystone of the United Multinationals' official Whale Control policy (*see OIL*). Yet efforts to rescind the ICAW were repeatedly thwarted in the Concordat Council, where each signatory country had veto power. Instead of simply acceding to the original agreement, the Japanese had enthusiastically adopted the pro-whale position, even declaring the mink whale a sacred creature in the Shinto Pantheon (just below the silicon chip).

Then, in November 1989, a group from the University of Southern California Los Angeles-San Francisco announced a promising new breakthrough: they had isolated the sex-attractant chemical of the female whale. The cetologists hoped that, by sprinkling just a few molecules on selected structures, they could induce male whales to try to copulate with such things as supertankers, the Statue of Liberty, and the White Cliffs of Dover.

The Whale Glut hurt parfumiers the same way the Oil Glut hurt Arabs. Almost anyone with a garbage pail of ambergris and a lime could make a passable perfume. Although the large perfume companies were foiled in their attempt to bomb the proliferating sperm whales into extinction, the situation had its positive side. In 1988, Revlon, Incorporated, acquired nuclear capability.

THE YACHT PEOPLE

More than one child standing at the rail on an ocean voyage has called out, "What's that, daddy?" as in the distance the form of a great gray ship drifts by in the mid-ocean fog. The father makes the sign of the cross. "The Yacht People!"

For almost a decade, an entire shipload of personages without a country has been sailing the seas, unable to land. Often, when the mysterious ship encroaches upon a country's territorial limits, it is driven off with gunfire, or chased away with angry shouts through Coast Guard megaphones.

Little is known about the Yacht People except that they are visa-less and thus, according to the UUN High Commissioner for Refugees, Jon Dunn, are "an island unto themselves." Communication with the outside world is by bottle.

The ship the Yacht People inhabit is thought to be the U.S.S. *New Jersey*, exhumed and thoroughly reconditioned. Some believe her registry is Liberian, with her home port, Monrovia, which like all ships of Liberian registry she has never visited.

Aboard among the Yacht People are thought to be the Shah of Iran (still carrying a small box of Iranian soil), Madame Nhu, the Iman of Oman, the Mufti of Jerusalem (or someone who looks an awful lot like him), King Umberto II of Italy (who likes to sit in and play the traps on "Jazz Nite"), Lord Lucan, the Sultan of Zanzibar (who keeps two sheep in his cabin), Cord Meyer, Bert Lance, Thomas Pynchon (who writes a column in the ship's *News*), Lady Brett, the six-foot eight-inch Leka I of Albania (who is the shuffleboard champ), James Manchem (the deposed prime minister of the Sey-chelles), Al-Hakim (the caliph of the Faithful), Robert Vesco (who lends a hand in the purser's office), Idi Amin, and assorted wives, hangers-on, toadies, and a large caged bird kept in the ship's salon that is thought to be the same, or perhaps a relative of the same, eagle that Napoleon III kept with him during his succession of exiles.

Judging from the reports that have been pieced together from bottle messages, the happiest man on board is Idi Amin, late of Uganda, with his bride of almost twelve years, Dora Bloch, whom he met in Entebbe in 1976 during a skyjacking episode involving the PLO and an Air France plane. Mrs. Bloch caught a glimpse of the Ugandan leader in the passengers lounge and promptly swooned. She was carried to his residence in Kampala where the romance blossomed. For many years, Dora Bloch was believed to have been murdered by Amin: in 1979 the bones of someone thought to be her were disinterred from a Ugandan forest. In a bottle message, Mrs. Bloch denies the bones are hers. "Who is kidding? Idi, a murderer he is not, a *mensch* he is!"

Amin is by far the most exuberant passenger aboard, often carrying little Mrs. Bloch (who is now in her eighties) around on the top of his head. With or without her in this position, he is the table tennis champ of the *New Jersey*, and has won two, if not three, Ballroom Nite prizes for the waltz (bottles of Blue Nun wine). He swims around the *New Jersey* once or twice a day, even when the *New Jersey* is on the move. He does not get along with Leka I of Albania, the six-foot eight-inch son of King Zog, and has threatened to stuff him down the funnel of the *New Jersey* to see (as he puts it) "what will happen."

1. *The Chogyal of Sikkim*
2. *The Dalai Lama*
3. *Prince Norodom Sihanouk of Cambodia*
4 and 5. *The Wandering and Mrs. Jew*
6. *King Constantine of Greece*
7. *Czar Simeon II of Bulgaria*
8. *Philip Nolan*
9. *The Iman of Oman*
10. *Rechad el-Mahdi*
11. *Ian Smith*
12. *Mohammed Zahir of Afghanistan*
13. *Augusto Pinochet*
14. *Anastasio Somoza*

Dr. John C. Lilly was the first human to communicate with a dolphin and thus became a cause célèbre of the '80s. Playboy magazine immediately assigned him to do an interview for their March 1985 issue. The results were somewhat disappointing.

PLAYBOY: How did you like the halibut?

DOLPHIN: It was a little salty. I like mackerel better.

PLAYBOY: Aha, aha.

DOLPHIN: And you can only take a bite or two at a time because they tend to come apart in your throat.

PLAYBOY: Aha, aha.

DOLPHIN: It's much better to swallow them whole. Quite frankly, if I've got my eyes closed and something just pops in, I'm hard-pressed to tell what it is. You know?

PLAYBOY: Aha, aha.

DOLPHIN: There are exceptions.

PLAYBOY: Like what?

DOLPHIN: Well, a shark . . . or a whale . . . I mean, you can tell them right away because they won't fit in your mouth. I'll tell you a funny story if you like.

PLAYBOY: Sure.

DOLPHIN: Well, a couple of friends of mine and I were just swimming around one afternoon down Malaga way. D'you know where Malaga is?

PLAYBOY: Aha, aha.

DOLPHIN: Great eats. Anyway, we're just lazing around when someone, I don't remember who . . . it was probably Harry . . . no, it wasn't, it was Burt . . . anyway, doesn't matter, anyway, he says why don't we close our eyes, you know, just for a joke, and see who can catch the most. No, wait a moment, it had to be Harry 'cause Burt just got caught in that tuna net. Yeah, it was definitely Harry. . . .

PLAYBOY: Aha, aha.

DOLPHIN: Anyway, getting back to the story . . . whoever it was, and it probably was Harry, so let's say it *was* Harry, just for argument's sake . . . Harry says, let's just close our eyes . . .

PLAYBOY: Aha, aha.

DOLPHIN: . . . and see what pops into our mouths.

PLAYBOY: Aha, aha.

DOLPHIN: We're all lying sort of dead-looking with our eyes closed. Get the picture?

PLAYBOY: Aha, aha.

DOLPHIN: Good. Whenever one of us swallows something, we shout out, "Hey," to let the other fellows know . . . and we're going along . . . and there's a "hey" and another "hey" when suddenly I hear a "glump." Not a big "glump," but a "glump," see. So I say to myself, now, wait a minute! Wait a minute! Someone's not playing fair. I mean if we agreed to go "hey," why mess up a good thing with a "glump"? I thought . . . I know, they're jealous because I'm winning. I mean, I've got a big mouth, bigger than Burt's or Harry's, and just before the "glump" I'd probably done about three "heys" to every one of theirs, right? So I opened my eyes, just to see what was going on. And what do you think I saw?

PLAYBOY: Aha, aha.

DOLPHIN: I said, what do you think I saw?

PLAYBOY: Oh, I don't know. I really don't know.

DOLPHIN: Go on! Just one quick guess.

PLAYBOY: I'm sorry, but I can't even imagine . . . (*Pause*) What was it?

DOLPHIN: S'funny . . . just gone right out of my head. . . . Hmmmm . . .

PLAYBOY: What?

DOLPHIN: Wow . . . isn't that strange . . . right on the tip . . . and then . . . nothing . Don't worry about it . . . it'll come back to me . . . isn't that strange . . . I was just talking about . . .

PLAYBOY: How you and your friends . . .

DOLPHIN: Oh, forget it! Doesn't matter. It'll come back when I'm not thinking about it. Does that ever happen to you? Does to me. Sometimes I'll be thinking about one thing and something completely different will pop right into my head. For instance, I can be talking about, oh, let's say . . . er . . . er . . . I can be talking about . . . anything . . . you name it . . . go on, name something.

PLAYBOY: Oil spills . . .

DOLPHIN: No, I don't talk about them much . . . name something else.

PLAYBOY: Seaweed.

DOLPHIN: Seaweed? Why would I want to talk about seaweed?

PLAYBOY: Well, you said name . . .

DOLPHIN: Forget it . . . let's say I was talking about . . . er . . . I'll think of something. . . .

PLAYBOY: Sure . . .

DOLPHIN: Sharx . . . right! Let's say I was talking about sharx . . . all of a sudden a cod pops into my mind.

PLAYBOY: Aha, aha.

DOLPHIN: I'll tell you a funny story. I was swimming along one day, on my way down to Mexico.

PLAYBOY: Aha, aha.

DOLPHIN: Yeah, terrific eats down in Mexico . . . haddox as big as . . . well, er . . . big haddox . . . anyway . . . where was I?

PLAYBOY: On your way down to . . .

DOLPHIN: Mexico . . . right, right, right, right, I remember. Anyway, I'm swimming along minding my own business, you know, taking it easy. . . . Anyway . . . all of a sudden this big cod swims right out in front of me from behind a rock, and misses me by about an inch. No wait, half an inch, half an inch. And then he just swims away. Not an "Excuse me" or a "I beg your pardon." Nothing! Just plain nothing. No sense of direction, cods . . . just stop whenever they want. No signals. Nothing. *(contd.p. 111)*

"You know where Malaga is?"

"S'funny . . . just gone right out of my head. . . . Hmmmm. . . ."

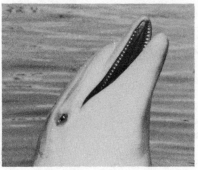

"Seaweed? Why would I want to talk about seaweed?"

The "in" Hollywood license plate of the late '80s stated, simply and tastefully, the driver's net worth. This plate belonged to a distinguished movie agent. His agent's plate read "$.68 MIL."

SHOBIZ

I t is lunchtime at La Nausée, one of Hollywood's older existential restaurants. This is a thoughtful place, and Jaime Lazarus, an upper-echelon web-exec, is thoughtful. Should he or should he not cancel "Touch It, Please," a sitcom whose premiere has shown up poorly in the overnight ratings? The show stars Michael McNair, an old friend from the defunct California state legislature and, as Lazarus well knows, a hopeful in the 1990 Network elections. This exposure would be critical to McNair's campaign for A.M. Host. Jaime toys moodily with his exquisitely prepared roast porridge *aux croûtons*.

Of all of our precious natural resources, it is that distinctively American thing called "entertainment" that is the most precious, and the most natural. If, as economist Gloria Vanderbilt opines, we are a people who "work like slaves, but get paid accordingly," then we are also a nation in love with entertainment. And, as is our way, we have created an industry to serve this love. "Show business," we like to call it—canny term, one that acknowledges both sides of the bargain. For just as our lives are part show and part business, so is our entertainment. And entertainment was what our lives were all about in the tumultuous decade.

There was television: earthy, unpretentious, democratic. And there were motion pictures: aristocrats of media, noblest-born of the "shobiz" brood, whose producers, associate producers, agents, and agents' agents are the kings, dukes, lairds, princes, barons, earls, viscounts, sultans, viziers, margraves, kaisers, rajahs, baronets, czars, pharoahs, and mikados of entertainment. All of them—even those possessing their own coats of arms, flags, and uniformed retainers—display that sense of *noblesse oblige* that, in the end, wins the loyalty of the most wild-eyed media revolutionary. It is they who know that art means industry, industry means progress, progress means trends, and trends mean business.

In the film industry, the trend was toward less quantity and more quality. The '80s saw the emergence of politicians as movie stars, with such films as *Birch Bayh: P.I.* and *Alan Cranston in Rhode Island Rogue* demonstrating the inevitable convergence of our two most popular forms of public life. Thus, too, did producers forsake the anonymity of the Polo Lounge, becoming stars in their own right. It was as though our national life were itself a movie—one rated G, from which sequels would be spinning off forever, and from which there need be no clearly marked exit.

Technology kept pace, most notably with Lensurround, the 140 mm film process that gave everyone—audience, actor, director, cameraman, ticket taker, popcorn girl—the illusion of being completely surrounded by movies for the rest of their lives.

JUST AS OUR LIVES ARE PART SHOW AND PART BUSINESS, SO IS OUR ENTERTAINMENT.

The American stage continued its maturation as well. A witty, self-conscious Broadway gave us a string of show-oriented shows. The influx of Chinese tourists soon left its mark, too, with zeitgeist-sensitive "angels" mounting such Vietnam-era full-dress spectaculars as *Seven Bribes for Seven Brothels.*

But surely it was television that dominated the entertainment industry in the 1980s. "The boob tube," they had called it—but TV was a boob no longer. True, some thought that the demise of NBC and, later, CBS, meant a certain loss of choice in viewing. But many held that a single network merely echoed and complemented our traditional belief in unity itself: "One nation, under God. . . ." Surely one nation under God must progress toward one network . . . for how else to concentrate and focus the very best of the available talent? By decade's end, the American Broadcasting System was to television what America herself was to the free world.

Small wonder, then, that TV parlance entered our common speech. "Sally and I took a lunch, agreed on a step deal, and that night I got a 51 share," meant, to all but the most cloistered, that a successful romance had reached sexual consummation. Indeed, such was the relationship between television and America, even our youth knew it, and took to writing their schoolwork in teleplay form. "Lighting and sound cues need work. See me," read a teacher's note on one youngster's chemistry exam, and few doubted that education had become "relevant" at last.

To be sure, there were those who thought that television had become too powerful, with influence in inappropriate sectors of society.

But Jaime Lazarus, like many, knows otherwise. As he lays his napkin down on the table, he is suffused with the glow of a man who has not only eaten well, but has remained at peace with his conscience. He will cancel "Touch It, Please!" because it is a poor show. The ratings prove that. Promotion of personal friends for private gain is not his mandate. He is in show business, where the bottom line reads: Enjoy.

THE WEB

THE DEATH OF THE THREE—NETWORK SYSTEM

The ratings spread between the three commercial webs grew cavernous this week. ABC took all seven weeknights (and would have taken an eighth) with a 40.1. CBS was a distant second with 6.9 and NBC a pitiful third with .3 (no measurable audience) despite a season's high of 1.3 for the all-too-perennial "Hello, Larry." The long-awaited new NBC entry "Hippie Days," about 1960s flower children, wilted to a .09 and became the only sitcom ever canceled during its first commercial break.

VARIETY, SEPTEMBER 24, 1983

This casual business report in the "bible of show business" tolled the death knell for NBC, America's fourth network (its ratings had fallen behind the Public Broadcasting System's in 1982 thanks to the American success of three BBC series: "The Many Loves of Richard I," "The Many Loves of Richard II," and "The Many Loves of Richard III").

A scant five months earlier at the NBC affiliate meeting, President Fred Silverman had had good news for NBC's affiliate (WQRS-TV in Penn Yan, New York). NBC's inspiring fall slogan would be "Nowhere to Go But Up," and there would be a new blockbuster series called "Hippie Days."

"In it we will tap America's unexploited nostalgia for the late '60s—the golden days when kids tuned in, turned on, and dropped out. To show you we're really behind this one, we've already spent 100 million dollars to reproduce the city of San Francisco, including Haight-Ashbury, in Burbank, California."

In the three months before production began, network president Fred Silverman had signed an unprecedented number of subsidiary-rights contracts. The "Hippie Days" name was licensed to manufacturers of Beatle wigs, bell-bottom trousers, vinyl micro-minis, Nehru jackets, beads, wide ties, fishnet stockings, peace-symbol pendants, plastic flower stickers for Volkswagens, incense, wide watchbands, brocade guitar straps, granny glasses, paper dresses, flag apparel, and *Yellow Submarine* spinoffs that didn't sell the first time around.

Unfortunately, the '60s nostalgia trend that "Hippie Days" was created to exploit fizzled several weeks before the show's ill-fated debut, and most of the licensees were left with huge stockpiles of memorabilia (*see CHINA*).

NBC was in dire straits even before America turned on, tuned in, and tuned out "Hippie Days." Advertisers were deserting it in droves (its only remaining national commercials were for small-time, often undesirable products such as Dog-Eat-Dog dog food, the Seven-in-One Little Handy Kitchen Wizard Glass Cutter and Flensing Tool, and a record of Phyllis Newman's Greatest Hits). It had been forced to sell its five Owned and Operated ("O&O") stations, leaving it (thanks to a hastily concluded lease-back arrangement) with just one "&O" station. In April 1983, in fact, a joint ABC-CBS committee had informed NBC that it was no longer entitled to call itself a network.

The *coup de grace* came shortly before Christmas, when Fred Silverman attempted to light the Rockefeller Center Christmas tree. In the darkness, a Con Edison representative informed him that the network's electricity had been shut off. NBC was out of business, and was sold up at auction the following week.

"Hippie Days." In this scene from the NBC-TV comedy series, Dylan (sitting on the ledge under the word "PEACE") and his friends plan a nude love-in. The woman in the big hat is Jean Lusk, who later became a notorious meat smuggler.

12/2/83--THE FINAL NBC TOUR WAS SEIZED BY US MARSHALS. 30 TOURISTS
AND A GUIDE WERE HELD IN ESCROW BY THE NETWORK'S CREDITORS.

SHOBIZ 57

With the strident opening riff of the title theme song by Lothar and the Hand People, "Hippie Days" burst into prime time in the fall of 1983.

The show's premise was a simple one. Dylan, a typical teenager of the late '60s, is engaged in a perpetual battle with his parents (a housewife played by Buffy Sainte-Marie and a police chief played by Noel Harrison). In the pilot, and only, episode, he calls his parents "fascist bourgeois pigs," knowing that they will then lock him in his bedroom. Contriving a rope from his Indian bedspread, he escapes out the window and goes downtown to buy drugs. When a meddlesome neighbor reports the transaction to Dylan's parents, they just laugh. They know he has been in his room the whole time!

The show, of course, managed to offend or bore the few who tuned into it. Commented a crestfallen Silverman: "I guess I underestimated Noel Harrison's clout."

THE WEB

THE PEACOCK EXPIRES

Today the NBC chimes tolled their last, sounding the tocsin for an era . . . the video epoch spanning "Broadway Open House," "Jackpot Bowling" (hosted by Milton Berle), "The Howdy Doody Show," "My Mother the Car," "The Girl from U.N.C.L.E.," "The Snoop Sisters," "I Married Joan," "The Steve Lawrence and Edyie Gorme Show," "Hi, Mom!," "F Troop," "The Monkees," those unforgettable Dean Martin "roasts," "H. R. Pufnstuff," "Dr. Kildare," "Cliffhangers," and "Flipper." It is the end of something. A runner has fallen. The torch is ours. We, the survivors, can best honor the departed with this pledge: to maintain the same standards of excellence that they did.

ABC "BIG TRUE LIVE-ACTION
EYEWITNESS NEWS" TRIBUTE

Networks   **Networks**

PUBLIC AUCTION   **DECEMBER 5, 1983**

FINAL SALE

At the request of creditors and the Chemigrant Bank a sale of the properties of a MAJOR AMERICAN TELEVISION NETWORK will take place at the New York Convention Center on December 5, 1983. Merchandise to include the following:

● 200 NBC Tourguide uniforms, all men's and women's sizes up to portly (includes uniforms worn by Gregory Peck, Charlton Heston, and Kate Jackson) ● Jane Pauley's lapel mike ● the TV rights to the words "today," "tomorrow," "tonight," and "yesterday" ● 500 network vice-presidents ● the RCA Building ● 50 washroom hot-air hand dryers ● wide-gauge model train set with swimming pool car, sauna car, disco car, and night-club car ● giant Christmas tree stand and decorations ● permission from Nebraska Public Television to use the NBC logo ● a commitment from John Davidson to guest-host 300 "Tonight" shows ● a set of dinner chimes that play the NBC theme ● desk plates bearing names including Johnny Carson, Chet Huntley, Sylvester (Pat) Weaver, Hugh Downs, Robert Sarnoff, and J. Fred Muggs ● a complete set of video tapes of "B.J. and the Bear" ● Tom Snyder's lapel mike ● scrimshaw coke spoon belonging to staff of "Saturday Night Live" ● television cameras, control rooms, monitors, etc., etc., etc.

Seating limited. Bring chairs. Personal checks not accepted. Catered by NBC Commissary. Bring own lunch.

WALTERGATE: THE EYE CLOSES

At 1:00 A.M. on January 19, 1984, a security guard at ABC headquarters passing a door marked "Programming Ideas" noticed something unusual: a small piece of videotape stuck across the latch to keep it open. Alertly he entered: his flashlight beam revealing three startled men in stocking masks. They were crouched before files marked "Notions," "Ideas," "Concepts," and "Treatments," and they were holding sheafs of papers.

"Waltergate," an unfair journalistic sobriquet in that Cronkite had no knowledge of the scheme, had begun.

A subsequent Senate investigation, led by Senator Bill Bradley (Democrat of New Jersey), revealed that all three burglars were loyal Hispanic employees of CBS drawn from local news teams in various major cities. They had been told only that what they were doing was "for the good of the company." But their testimony left no doubt: the trail of Waltergate led right to the top. CBS headquarters, Black Rock.

These were bad days at Black Rock. Carroll O'Connor was doing just two guest appearances a year on "Archie's Place." A new series, "Beyond the Paper Chase," had failed miserably. The falling ratings of "The Waltons" and "The Jeffersons" had forced television's first spin-in—a merger in which John Boy moved in with the Jefferson family. No help was octogenarian Chairman William Paley's insistence on doing two hours of quality prime time programming a week (an archaeology series called "Dig It!" opposed "Mork and Mindy"). President Jerry Brown's suit to advertise CBS programs on ABC was defeated in the Supreme Court (the *Brown* decision). CBS, now ABC's sole competitor in the ratings war and way behind, was desperate. In search of winning program ideas the break-in, "Operation Eye," was authorized.

ABC sued CBS for first-degree theft of program ideas, normally a misdemeanor, but more serious when combined with burglary. The evidence was damning, as this bit of testimony reveals:

BAILEY: Do you recognize this paper I hold in my hand?

SANCHEZ (CBS): Yes.

BAILEY: Do these words on it sound familiar? (*Reading*) " 'Bikini Squad'—three lovely policewomen on 24-hour call to rush wherever girls in bikinis are needed to fight the forces of crime?"

SANCHEZ: (*Almost inaudible*) Yes.

BAILEY: That's all, Your Honor.

Equally damning evidence was an 18-minute tape gap in "Emergency Broads"—a CBS series pilot amazingly like "Bikini Squad." The judgment went to ABC, which was awarded the CBS network, plus costs, as compensatory and punitive damages. (The sole proviso was that Paley be allowed to remain chairman for life —and 10 years thereafter.)

For the first time, America had one commercial network—the American Broadcasting System.

THE WEB

THE LAST RATINGS WAR: THE BIG TUNE-IN

From the corner of his eye Markham saw them approaching, two helmeted military forms with ABS jacket patches and Day-glow armbands that read VP. He buried himself in his book, hoping they would not notice he was the only man in Pershing Square.

"It's eight o'clock, sir," said one of them, gripping his shoulder firmly. "Why aren't you watching TV?"

The polite voice carried the velvet menace of unlimited authority. Markham sighed, closed his copy of Answered Prayers, *walked to the nearby lamp post and gazed up at the flickering television monitor. The program was "Hello, Larry."*

FROM THE NOVEL *1987*

Even as world-conqueror Alexander the Great sat on a stone and wept that he had "no new worlds to conquer"—so the American Broadcasting System, the newly victorious, sole commercial television network, faced the 1985 television season in both despair and frustration.

Its competitive legions—conditioned by years of ratings wars—were girded for battle. It had five new sure-fire series (including "Emergency Broads," notorious from the Waltergate scandal, and yet another new format for Mary Tyler Moore—a comedy-variety-sitcom game show, a sure winner).

ABS was ready to go for the jugular—but there was no jugular to go for.

For two months, the demoralized, unopposed network staggered along, with vice-presidents taking long liquid lunches and returning, weeping, to clean desks. Then the first Nielsens came in: ABS had a 75 rating and a 100 audience share.

The next day this memo zapped the programming vice-presidents: "The latest Nielsens prove there is no cause for complacency. Everyone with his set on is watching ABS. But only 75 percent have their sets on. Let's go after that other 25 percent! We want the impossible dream—a 100 rating!"

A hastily ordered survey showed the many reasons why at any given moment certain Americans were not watching television: some were driving; some were taking showers; some were sleeping; some giving birth; others dying; still others were making love; people were putting out fires, or mugging or being mugged; a few were lying in ventilated coffins for days hoping to make the *Schlitz Book of World Records.*

Over the next year, ABS put all its burgeoning wealth (amassing at two million dollars a commercial minute) into a drive to reach this "great unviewing public."

It's lonely at the top, especially if there's no one below you.

JERRY BROWN, PRESIDENT OF ABS

Television monitors were immediately placed wherever human eyes ventured: in elevators, washrooms, churches, movie houses, massage parlors, surgical amphitheaters, and Krishna temples; on street lamps, highway mileposts, and coal breakers; in cornfields; and embedded in giant Californian sequoias. They were built by law into the dashboards of cars and tractors.

To police the "curview," ABS set up the Video Patrol (VP), a small, paramilitary group that foreshadowed the growth of the network's civil power later in the decade.

But perfection proved elusive: the highest ABS rating up to 1986 was a 98. Realizing that the VP could not do its job while watching television and that 1 percent of television owners were legally blind, ABS took another tack. It launched a show for those who determined the ratings.

"The Nielsen Family" was the runaway hit of the 1986 television season. It featured Ozzie, Harriet, and the Nielsen kids continually watching television and taking phone calls from a "Mister Brown." ("Hi, Mister Brown, we're watching 'Hello, Larry.'") Any show they were seen viewing also became a runaway hit. The average viewer adored "The Nielsen Family"—for its charm—and envied it for its vast power.

More importantly, the Nielsen families loved to see themselves portrayed on television. On December 20, 1986, ABS realized its dream—"The Nielsen Family" came in with a 100 percent audience share—and a 100 percent rating.

"The Nielsen Family" was officially the most popular program of the '80s. Since ABS sneak-previewed all its new projects on the show, the fictional family's actual power in determining programming was awesome. The public, however, loved it for its earthy, ordinary, unselfconscious reaction to the television it watched. The Nielsens were scared by scary shows, tickled by funny ones, unimpressed by anything "too heady," as Ozzie put it, and hilarious when presented with what Rikki called a "real stinkeroo." Even the Nielsen's pet rat, Spot, had an opinion.

TV GUIDE

In This Issue:
'The Nielsen Family'
Page 18

Local Programs November 16-22
$5.35

THE PEOPLE MAYBE: PROGRAMMING FROM THE MASSES

On a hot night in July 1988, the television flickered above the bar in Grogan's Bar and Grill, a steelworkers' hangout near Pittsburgh. The Pirates were playing a game that night, but the tube was tuned to a situation comedy. All eyes were watching. The comment was lively.

"Switch! Switch!" yelled a burly steel puddler at the TV screen. "You need a f--k-ing plot switch here ... the mother comes home, finds the kids necking, throws the boy out, the daughter says, 'Now you've ruined everything,' then commercial break, question hanging, will the boy ever come back?"

"Wrong," said a nearby ingot man, nursing his boilermaker. "The kid turns out to be rich, the mother thinks, 'We're on to a good thing here....'"

"F--k off! Whadda you know, you're not even in the Writers Guild."

"Anyway, the kid is funny. I bet they could spin him off into a series—maybe ... young kid opens his own garage, see, a wacky garage in this small town, see ..."

"Ya f--kin' A ..."

Suddenly in 1988, when the Supreme Court announced its historic *Right to Treatment* decision, everyone in America became a television writer. The Court on that occasion ruled that any citizen had the right to have his idea for a television series considered by the network, as well as the right to "take a meeting and go to story outline."

To handle the tremendous volume of suggestions, Regional Programming Centers were quickly established in each of the 50 biggest media markets, resembling nothing so much as unemployment centers. Under dim fluorescent lights, ordinary people stood in long lines leading to windows marked "Sitcom," "Action Show," and "Comedy-Variety," each clutching a precious piece of paper with an idea for prime

GAME SHOW   VARIET

Here at a Bethlehem, Pennsylvania, Programming Center, hopeful citizens wait to submit television series ideas to the network. Each individual was limited to one submission a week, and while, officially, penalties for self-plagiarism were severe, it was common practice to resubmit the same idea week after week with the names changed.

SITCOMS

time entertainment, and dreaming of the million-to-one-shot/step-deal stairway to the stars—from idea to outline, to story treatment to pilot script, to pilot to hit series, to spinoffs, residual payments, wealth, fame, perhaps even a chance to meet Donnie Most!

The immediate effects of "series fever" were: a sudden marked drop in the number of people playing the state lotteries; a proliferation of correspondence schools in television writing (this era produced the now famous matchbook ad, "Read me and win a television-writing scholarship"); and a new, three-block-square archive in Los Angeles-San Francisco to preserve on file the roughly four million original ideas a month submitted on everything from monogrammed vellum notepaper to losing horse race tickets.

A sample of a few suggestions from the two billion program ideas now on file suggests the rush of creativity generated by the American public after the Supreme Court decision.

"This guy Archie, a Carroll O'Connor type, lives in this row house in Queens with his wife, kinda dumb. This cute little blonde daughter lives with them, who is married to this lazy student with no job, but he is *Swedish*."

"I have lived an interesting life, but I'm no good with words. If you knew the things I've seen. Dry cleaning is not a dull business. If you could put me with a writer, with *his* gift for words and *my* experiences ... what a series!"

"HEER IS MY IDAE FOR A SERES. TAD HAS A CAT BUT IT RUNN AWAY. HIS SISTER DID UT. GARY COFFMAN, 7."

"Here is my series idea ... I have this cousin who is always horsing around, he has the gang in stitches ... just put him on every week ... he's a million laughs."

"Here is my idea for ....a series ... like, have you ever, *ever* thought ... that you ... *you* are just a little dot ... on a minor planet ... in a solar system ... around a small star ...... in a galaxy, like, that is like just one of a billion ... like, a *billion* galaxies ... in, like, this *tremendous* expanding *universe* ...... ?????....oh, wow!"

"A man runs a newsstand and sells lots of papers. Please send money to Ed Hirsch, 59 Elm Street, Wapakeneta, Ohio."

And that ordinary citizen's idea just might be "The Nielsen Family" of tomorrow.

While few ideas have yet journeyed from a network Programming Center to the home screen, the effect on American television has not been negative. At this very moment, somewhere, an ordinary citizen is stepping forward to a Programming Center window where a programming vice-president (clerk) greets him with the ritual, "Hey guy, how's the wife and kids?" The ordinary citizen presents his or her idea, receives the standard writer's fee ($12.50 up front, $25,000 when it goes to series), and is dismissed with the familiar, "Let's have lunch real soon."

If you can read this, you can outline a hit TV series!

I made $1,500 in just three months after taking your course.

HOLLYWOOD CLEANS HOUSE: HUAC'S HAWKHUNT

The crowd had massed outside the Dorothy Chandler Pavilion in Los Angeles since dawn. When the famous faces began sweeping by, they cheered, booed, begged for autographs. But this was no Academy Awards presentation. It was what elder statesman David Begelman called "a sneak preview of the central moral issue of our time."

In April 1980, after the appearance of a number of books and movies "reinterpreting" the war in Vietnam, the Hollywood talent unions, led by the Screen Actors Guild, held urgent meetings. The result was the announcement of public hearings "to expose the militarism, racism, and sexism that festered within the entertainment industry during the immoral United States invasion of Southeast Asia." An umbrella group was formed to conduct the investigation—the Hollywood United Activists Coalition (HUAC).

"Americans swim in the medium of movies," said Chairperson Jane Fonda. "It is time to rid this medium of the pollution of warmongering. And that's fact."

Whatever their point of view, all observers agreed that the HUAC hearings were a showcase of progressivism. Wheelchair access was provided for the handicapped, and childcare for involved mothers. There was simultaneous translation of the proceedings into Spanish and sign language, no smoking was allowed within 500 feet of the hearing room, and prayer was forbidden.

At the outset the hearings were an unqualified success. Cooperative studios furnished names of writers, directors, and performers who might "directly or indirectly" have supported the United States war effort. Most of those under suspicion aligned themselves firmly with the coalition and against the war. Bob Hope, for

IN '47 I WAS A WRITER AT WARNERS. COWBOY FLICKS. WAR FLICKS. COP FLICKS. $2,500 A WEEK. NEAT.

THEN I REFUSED TO FINK ON BUDDIES WHEN H.U.A.C. CAME WEST IN '50. DID A YEAR FOR CONTEMPT. BUCK A DAY MAKING LICENSE PLATES. PITS.

BY '69 I WAS LIVING IN L.A. AGAIN. TAPPED INTO THE COUNTERCULTURE. DOPE FLICKS. PEACE FLICKS. 75 K PER PLUS POINTS. OUTASIGHT.

BY THE END OF THE '70s I HAD A THREE PICTURE DEAL WITH FOX, AND A HOUSE IN MALIBU. SPACE FLICKS. SEX FLICKS. SCARE FLICKS. SHALLOW.

This cartoon strip, a blatant imitation of the work of Jules Feiffer, is taken from a series that appeared unsigned in the pro-HUAC newsletter, Julia's Biweekly, *in 1980. While it poked fun at the hawkhunters, it also managed to implicate 11 cartoonists in pro-war crimes.*

SO UNTIL '61 I LIVED IN PARIS. WROTE SPAGHETTI WESTERNS. GHOSTED FOR STUDIO HACKS. $750 A SHOT. CHEAP.

IN THE EARLY '60s I CAME BACK TO THE STATES. DID FILMS FOR U.S.I.A. UNDER MURROW. SIT-IN FLICKS. SPACE SHOT FLICKS. BRIGHT YOUNG LEADER FLICKS. $37,500 AND A HEALTH PLAN. OK.

SO I GAVE IT ALL UP AND BECAME HAYDEN'S TOP AIDE IN THE WARMONGER INVESTIGATION. PUT THIRTY-FIVE GUYS OUT OF BUSINESS.

RIGHT ON.

example, insisted that he had been "as dovish as the next guy," and that his USO Christmas shows in Vietnam had been covers behind which he made frequent broadcasts to bolster the morale of the Viet Cong. With the words, "But seriously, I want to tell you who was really for the war," Hope went on to name 15 of his joke writers who were immediately stripped of all union memberships. George Jessel, accused of saying on a May '68 episode of the "Joey Bishop Show" that "the trouble with these peaceniks is you can't tell the girls from the boys," explained the remark as evidence of his early commitment to the gay movement. Martha Raye was named by four directors as "the real mouthpiece of the pro-war clique."

Others responded differently—some said heroically. Born-again Christian Bob "Dylan" Zimmerman said that he had been secretly for the war all along, and that he longed to "kill a Commie for Christ." Comedian Don Rickles, standing firm on his dislike of "gooks," issued a dramatic call-to-conscience to HUAC Director Tom Hayden, with the eloquent conclusion: "And another thing, pizza face—did your mother give birth in a meteor shower?" (Ruined, Rickles fled to Mexico, where he eked out a pitiable living insulting people who could not understand him.)

Inevitably there were excesses. Warren Beatty, considered above suspicion, was accused of having consorted with "known hawks" in the Beverly Hills Hotel. An atmosphere of mistrust pervaded the industry. Merely to have been considered for an episode of "Gomer Pyle" was grounds for investigation. The end came when HUAC turned on the studios themselves. During the questioning of an obscure young Universal executive, Meyer Feigenbaum, Chairperson Fonda became clearly frustrated by his impeccable credentials—he had been a Weatherperson and had blown up at least one branch of the Bank of America. She launched into a furious tirade, accusing Feigenbaum and his employers of being "closet pro-nukers." Two days later, the hearings were suspended. Hollywood's housecleaners who, many said, made possible its subsequent political triumphs, had cleaned enough.

HOLLYWOOD

When Mike Curb, head of Universal-Warner, woke one morning in January 1983, his first thought was: "In only one year, it will be 1984. And 1984 should be the year of *1984!*" The executive board of UW could not have agreed more, and before the day was out Curb, armed with a budget of 100 million dollars, was taking the first steps toward making the movie of the decade.

There was little time to be lost. Of all movie forms perhaps the most complex is a musical. Not only must the "book" be written, lyrics conceived, and music composed; but dance numbers must be planned, costumed, and choreographed; and hordes of stars, dancers, singers, and other proles must be found. All of which had to be accomplished in time for *1984!* to open in 1984. In addition, Curb felt that the original book left a lot to be desired as the basis for a musical motion picture. "Short on story, long on words," was his characteristically pithy assessment. What was needed, the dynamic former governor insisted, was something more upbeat, something that would get the audience involved on an emotional level, something that would leave them tapping their toes and feeling warm inside. "After all, this *is* 1984," said Curb at the Academy Awards in 1985. "And people should be happy about that."

Curb's masterpiece, using three faded stars (Marlon Brando, Leif Garrett, and Tracy Austin), a bargain basement director (Margaret Trudeau), and the idea of an obscure English novelist, was typical of and seminal to the direction Hollywood was to take in the 1980s.

Several years earlier, Hollywood, like many other ancient and prestigious monopolies, had begun to feel the pinch of a critically inflated and capital-short economy. Turning, with their fellow conglomerates, to what philosopher Rex Reed described as "big bucks in a burnoose," the great studios found themselves saddled with Saudi producers, sheiks turned directors, and Bedouin screenwriters. The re-

sult was a series of "sure-fire" and lavish high-budget remakes, such as *Heaven Kuwait*, *Abu Dhabi Honeymoon*, *The Man in the Iron Mosque*, and *The Hejaz Singer*.

Aghast at the political views of the newcomers and the utter box office failure of their product, the studios nonetheless felt their hands were morally tied. The Arabs were determined to pour unlimited money into movies until they had remade every great American film in their own image. "It was a time of deep personal agony, of, I guess I have to say it, prostitution," recalls tragedian Blake Edwards. "We hated those tenthead bastards, but it was our duty to the public to recycle their black gold into the American economy."

A nation that does not turn its books into films, its films into remakes, and its remakes into re-remakes is a society doomed to die.

ROBERT EVANS

The selflessness of the producers sparked an unforeseen reaction from the then new generation of Hollywood directors. Treading in the footsteps of towering cineast Woody Allen, who in 1980 began spelling his name Wöödi and making films exclusively in Swedish, they declared the arrival of the "New *Nouvelle Vague*"—a "search-for-self" school of big budget movies, which sought to create an American Eisenstein, an American Truffaut, an American Fellini, an American Kubrick.

The result was a string of masterpieces melding the best of Europe with the best of Hollywood, all of them intensely personal films, often with great special effects and musical numbers. Typical were Lucas' *Star Wars and Peace* ("a brilliant and sensitive use of the third sequel form," wrote Penelope Gilliatt), *Barbra from 4 to 6*, *Godfather 8½* ("a brilliant, sprawling use of the eighth sequel form," wrote Penelope Gilliatt), and Spielberg's monumental *Harrisburg, Mon Amour*, portraying the hopeless love of an out-of-work journalist for a badly mutated dairy herd. The directors

The Agents Hall of Fame in Beverly Hills was dedicated to "all those who negotiate so that others may live in Switzerland," and bore the Latin legend "De Astris Dix Percentum" ("From the Stars, 10 Percent").

released their private angst into the theaters and the walls squealed with pain.

Unfortunately they echoed, too. For the theaters were empty. Under these circumstances, the long-suffering producers had no option but to seize control. A series of mergers ensued and gradually the firm, prudent hand of finance brought the ship of art back on course. In this respect, as in so many others, Curb's *1984!* was a crucial watershed in the fortunes of the movie industry. He himself was typical of the wave of politicians who had fled a decaying system to find a more meaningful form of leadership in the arts. He took total control of the movie, in effect producing, writing, and directing it, and making himself the focal point of its publicity. But in one important respect his masterpiece differed from those to come. He himself did not star in it.

Curb's work confirmed the beliefs of producers and agents alike in what they had always secretly known. In order to protect their ideas from disgruntled writers, temperamental directors, and egotistical actors, they would have to take over these functions themselves, emerge from the back rooms of financing, and become their own auteurs.

At a deeper level, the producers proved themselves right yet again. In a nation obsessed by every aspect of show business, a crude but moving work like *The Picture Deal*, starring Dino de Laurentiis, was a blockbuster. The film was a simple story of a kindly producer, taken advantage of by unscrupulous superstars, who wins through by his tenacious willingness to "go 15 rounds" in negotiating a picture deal. Public and critics alike took the film and its cigar-chomping star to their hearts. (Indeed, Dino's playful cheekslap greeting replaced the handshake across the nation.)

Others followed. *I Like It, I Like It, I Like It, But . . .* , starring Bob Chartoff as a softhearted producer who has to learn to say no, and *Let's Keep in Touch*, starring Frank Yablans and Pauline Kael as two gentle, sensitive producers trying to find each other in the stormy world of Hollywood politics, both garnered Oscars in the '87 Academy Awards.

Producers and agents, long the despised "untouchables" of Hollywood, finally achieved their true rank: Brahmins of an industry that owed them so much, and darlings of a nation to whom that industry was everything.

Woody Allen announced in May 1980 that all his future films would be in Swedish and that henceforth he was spelling his name Wŏŏdi. His newspaper strip reflected this and was, in fact, known as a "tragic strip." The failure of the strip (and all his subsequent films) so impressed the Swedish government that in 1985 he was invited to become professor of Advanced Depression at Uppsala University.

WŎŎDI

Life is an unlit tunnel with no exit.

I know it! I know it!

Death, too, is an unlit tunnel with no exit.

Scorsese's Bread and Bread, *the serio-comic story of an American migrant executive's degrading efforts to find employment, garnered the Best Domestic Foreign Film Award for 1985.*

"Backdating," putting a modern story back in time, enjoyed a brief and unsuccessful vogue. Here is a still from Paul Monash's 1982 film, The Rodin Story, *set in 85 B.C.*

The accent was on comedy in this 1983 remake of The Miracle Worker, *in which Annie (left) looks after her wacky blind, deaf, and dumb aunt, Helen. In this hilarious scene, Annie explains the correct use of spoons and forks.*

Producers from the Deep *(1986) told the story of a group of kindly alien producers who landed on the coast of California bringing hope and jobs to thousands.*

BROADWAY— BUST AND BOOM

As Neil "Doc" Simon once appropriately remarked: "There's a big thermometer that runs between Fifth Avenue and the Hudson River, and it's called Broadway. When it's up, the patient has a fever, and when it's down, he's dead."

So it was during the amazing '80s, as the mercury shot up and down the Great White Way like confused spermatozoa. Mimesis, the art of imitation according to Aristotle, reached new highs — and lows—in the early part of the decade with a rash of shows attempting to repeat the success of *A Chorus Line, Dancin',* and other productions based on the experience of Broadway itself. Shows about show people, shows about shows, shows about shows about shows multiplied under such titles as *Rehearsin', Investin', Negotiatin', Upstagin', Breakin' Even, Bombin',* and *Closin'.*

Predictably the mercury dropped and the patient gave every sign of being legally dead. But then, as happens so often, someone injected a massive dose of energy and, as Mr. Simon was wont to put it, Broadway's forehead was hot enough to fry an egg on.

The lifesaving adrenalin came from a most unlikely source—the Red Chinese. The opening of the '83 season saw the newly flamboyant mainland businessmen, or "party officials," flooding into New York to taste the hitherto forbidden fruits of capitalist decadence. *Vietnamania*, a shot in the dark that had been limping along since spring on the last wavelets of '60s nostalgia, turned out to be the sleeper of the season. The musical, an evocation of the war in Southeast Asia, included an Army physical from the ticket taker, the sale of K-rations during intermission, punji sticks in the aisles, and the periodic strafing of the audience with AK-47s. The Chinese loved it. Broadway was in a fever. China was *in*. Communists elbowed their way to the bar at Sardi's. Backers' auditions were held in downtown opium dens.

Hungry gypsies lined up in hundreds to audition for parts on the Chinese Dinner Theater circuit. And remakes abounded for the benefit of the new theatergoers. Hal Prince offered a reburnished *My Fair Lady*, with Higgins as an aging, crotchety Red Guard and Eliza Dolittle as one of the original Boat People. The Chinese loved it. Richard Rodgers, eyeing the smash *Vietnamania*, presented a modernized *South Pacific* called *South Vietnam!* (*See* Playbill *opposite*.) Despite the plot breakdown ("boy gets girl, boy loses girl, boy gets part of girl back") and the fact that the Americans won, the Chinese loved it. Bob Fosse, never one to give up easily, concocted a show based on the Red Chinese ballet called simply *Pekin'*. The Chinese even loved that.

And then, without warning, the patient had a relapse. Irma Le Wine, a polite, gracious, non-Irish woman, demanded membership in the Usherettes of America Local 1, New York City. The law upheld her claim, but rather than admit her, the trusty "Ladies of the Aisles" led one another off the job and into a crippling two-year strike. Confusion reigned after every intermission as bewildered Chinese who had paid a top of $74.95 for orchestra seats found themselves sitting in the laps of secretaries from White Plains who had started the evening in the upper balcony. The theater ground to a halt. Fellow Teamsters, in a show of sympathy, wore white Peter Pan collars over black cardigan sweaters.

And then, as suddenly as the strike began, it ended. The fabulous invalid was once again flashing hot all over. Joseph Papp had come midtown. And in one Papp-like stroke, he transformed the theater, not only providing a competitive medium to the blandishments of ABS but exploiting a resource that had been there for everyone to see. Joseph Papp began reviving America's best-loved television programs. For the stage.

Season One kicked off with a 12-week run of *The Ed Sullivan Show*, starring Raul

In 1982, it occurred to Richard Rodgers that his World War II musical hit South Pacific *might be an ideal vehicle to satisfy Broadway's insatiable thirst for Vietnam War nostalgia. So, Nurse Nellie Forbush found herself attached to a mobile hospital unit, planter-turned-war-hero Emil de Becque became an American general, Lieutenant Cable was reincarnated as Lieutenant Calley – and Rodgers had his biggest hit in almost three decades.*

Julia as the stony-faced emcee. Commercials were included. Meryl Streep assumed the dual roles of Kate Smith (on before the first commercial at ten after eight) and Topo Giogio, the Italian mouse ("kiss-a me goodnight, Ed-dee"). Richard Dreyfuss recreated the magic that was Alan King; Ben Gazzara and Gena Rowlands, in the words of Neil Simon, *were* Gordon and Sheila MacRae.

Next came the great family shows of yesteryear. Few can forget Michael Moriarity and Robert DeNiro in *McHale's Navy*, or Elizabeth Swados' haunting, atonal theme for *Bonanza*.

Papp's one-act package tour broke records wherever it played, and with good reason. The tour included *My Favorite Martian, The Courtship of Eddie's Father*, and *Nanny and the Professor*, starring James Earl Jones, Sam Shepard, Estelle Parsons, and Al Pacino as "Uncle Martin."

On Broadway then, all is well. The sound of tortured plastic is everywhere as bumper meets fender in the matinee traffic jams; there is gunplay at Ticketron as out-of-towners vie for seats to *My Mother the Car*. The fabulous invalid, incredible though it may seem, is up and about once more.

SYNOPSIS OF SCENES

ACT I.

SCENE 1: A Red Cross mobile field hospital somewhere in the strategic Iron Triangle region of South Vietnam—November, 1967 (a command inspection is in progress)
"Dites-Moi Pourquoi" .... Nervous Nellie
"A Cockeyed Optimist" .... Westy

SCENE 2: Nervous Nellie's tent (later that evening)
"Who Can Explain It?" .... Westy

SCENE 3: A brothel in a free-fire sector of Quang Ngai province
"Bloody Mary Is the Girl I Love" .... Calley and the Men of Charlie Company
"My Lai (May Call You)" .... Bloody Mary

SCENE 4: A mobile intensive care tent in a defoliated forest in the Central Highlands (a few weeks later)
"I'm Gonna Wash the Hair Right Outta This Man" .... Nervous Nellie, Scrub-Down Nurses, and Montagnard Tribesman
"I'm in Love with a Wonderful GI" .... Nervous Nellie

SCENE 5: A tunnel beneath the besieged U.S. Embassy in Saigon—February 2, 1968
"You've Got to Be Tet" .... Colby and the Company
"This Nearly Was Mine" .... Westy

ACT II.

SCENE 1: The Grand Ballroom of the President's Palace, Saigon—February 19, 1968. (The Annual South Vietnamese International Red Cross Dinner Gala is in progress)
"Soft Thieu Dance" .... ARVN Chorus
"I Am Nothing Like a Diem" .... Gen. Thieu
Reprise: "Who Can Explain It?" .... Westy and Nervous Nellie

SCENE 2: A landing zone near the village of Songmy (about three weeks later)
Reprise: "My Lai" .... Calley and the Men of Charlie Company

SCENE 3: Later that same incursion

SCENE 4: A mobile special surgery tent near the pacified hamlet of My Lai 4 (several hours later)
"Too Young to Dismember" .... Calley and Nervous Nellie
Reprise: "Bloody Mary Is the Girl I Love" .... Calley and Bloody Mary

SCENE 5: A tunnel leading to and from the main runway at Tan Son Nhut Airport near Saigon—March 22, 1968
Finale: "I Think I See the Light" .... Westy, Nervous Nellie, Gen. Thieu, Calley, Bloody Mary, Gen. Creighton Abrams, and Ensemble

D.C.

The White House on the morning of December 1, 1989.

D.C.

It is January 21, 1988, and Mrs. Goldie Schwartzman stands near the entrance to the Capitol Building, her camera poised. Before her, a mob swarms around a limousine as it drives with difficulty down the steps of the building. Inside the car is the President of the United States, and Mrs. Schwartzman must hurry forward to snap a picture of him as he passes, cringing in the back seat. Suddenly machine-gun fire is heard, and dozens of men crumple and begin to roll down the steps. One of them bowls Mrs. Schwartzman over, and in a moment she is buried under a growing pile of bleeding bodies.

When the Celestial Academy of Civilizations and Societies holds its first awards ceremony, certainly the prize for Best Political System will go to the United States of America. But as the applause swells and the orchestra strikes up our national anthem, the person accepting the award, as he strides proudly down the aisle and bounds up onto the stage to give the entity or entities who have opened the envelope a great big kiss, had best remember this: we can't do it alone. A whole host of very talented people have worked very hard to make this award possible, and they all have one thing in common. They know that a political system must change with time. Yet most Americans, when confronted with this fact during the 1980s, preferred to shut their eyes and look the other way.

For example, most of the nation regarded with utter indifference the election in 1982 of the so-called Congress of Nuts. But there were some who divined great meaning in the event. For was it not democracy at fullest flower? Is it not the quintessence of American freedom to be a "nut"? Have we not always been, from Benjamin Franklin to Jerry Brown, a veritable "Nation of Nuts"?

Similarly, there were those who saw the resignation of Teddy Kennedy (and his replacement by Jimmy Carter), the resignation of Jack Kemp and William Roth (and their replacement by Jimmy Carter), and the ascension of Walter Cronkite (and his accompaniment by Jimmy Carter) as evidence, not, as some said, that "the system works," but as auguries of profound transformation.

These people were hardly silent. Some of them wrote several book-length monographs expanding on that thesis—works that, though scholarly, featured a style easily accessible to readers of "popular" trash. Yet these writers were denied even the most cursory advances from every remaining publishing house in the land.

During the '80s, a shrewd plan was advanced whereby voters (and later, candidates) would be lured to participate in elections with such special bonus gifts as kitchen appliances. When it failed miserably, the meaning—to some historians, at least—was clear: an outmoded politics, centuries old, was dying and a new one was being born. For two hundred years, European-style representative government had served us well—a stately, quaint manse in which our society was born, lived a happy childhood, and matured. But now it was time to move on. Our new mechanism of government—instantaneous and universally democratic, and made possible only by that most American of media, television—sat parked out front, a stylish, powerful roadster. We packed our bags, kissed our Founding Fathers goodbye, and sped off.

What lay down the road? Nothing less than the ideal that serves as the very Howard Johnson's of the American political soul: progress. By late in the decade, what had hitherto been an unacknowledged trend had become official policy as dozens of federal departments and agencies formally seceded from the government and formed a constellation of independent, warring fiefdoms around Washington. Some decried the situation.

FOR TWO HUNDRED YEARS, EUROPEAN-STYLE REPRESENTATIVE GOVERNMENT HAD SERVED US WELL . . . BUT NOW IT WAS TIME TO MOVE ON.

But many remembered that out of chaos emerges a superior form of order, and so it was. The United Multinationals—as though to prove yet again that progress will destroy everything in its path to keep America great—systematically began acquiring such foundering splinter organizations as the General Services Administration; the Department of Health, Education, and Welfare; and the Bureau of Mines, Fish, and Wildlife. Result: centralization, efficiency, order, profits. Walter Cronkite's subsequent election to the post of the nation's first Anchorman—and Jimmy Carter's acceptance of the role of Vice-Anchorman—clinched the deal.

Mrs. Goldie Schwartzman crawls out from under the pile of bodies—and America crawls with her. She—and we—will go on.

CAMELOT II

I pledge to give Senator Russell Long anything it is within my body or soul to give.

Teddy Kennedy's dramatic speech seeking Southern backing at a giant rally in New Orleans was widely credited with giving the Kennedy-Carter ticket its narrow popular and electoral victory in November of 1980. Kennedy's promise would prove his undoing.

A mere two days before Congress was to count the electoral votes, Senator Long redeemed the pledge. For reasons still unclear, Long needed an emergency liver transplant to save his life. After consulting with Dr. Allan Bakke (whom Kennedy had appointed surgeon general-designate in a move to win white middle-class support), Kennedy offered to donate his own liver.

Twelve hours later, the nation learned that, although Senator Long was alive and well, the gallant president-elect would never drink or drive again. Bakke's surgery had hopelessly incapacitated him. "Now I remember," sobbed Bakke on coast-to-coast television. "It's two *kidneys, one* liver."

The resourceful Kennedy, kept alive by a huge artificial liver weighing some 15 tons, was inaugurated on January 20. On January 30, citing "reasons of personal health," he resigned, and James Earl Carter, Jr., was sworn in as the 41st Chief Executive.

Thus ended Camelot II, a period consecrated by historians as "The Ten Days."

President Kennedy's inaugural address included a clarion call to America's youth, and many of the nation's not-so-bad and quite bright young minds responded eagerly. David Halberstam chronicled the legendary "Ten Days" in which they almost changed the course of history.

It was vintage David Burke. He would tell friends of his how he had set out from his office in the White House to let the President know just how bitter he felt about how badly the Surgeon General had botched things. On the way he would think of the President's problems: the chronic racial divisions, economic chaos, inner-city decay, the sudden, unexplained emptying of the White House swimming pool, the Middle East, the Dutch elm blight, the mysterious appearance of Fala, President Roosevelt's dog, in the Rose Garden. All these burdens. And minute by minute as he approached the Oval Office where President Kennedy was trying to recuperate from what the Surgeon General had done to him (the Great De-Bakke-L the boys over in State had called it), he felt his anger boil, until by the time the Oval Office door was opened and he looked in and saw the President attached to all the life-support machinery, he heard his own voice saying, "Mr. President! It's just unfair! Darn!"

Afterwards, he would be embarrassed about saying such a thing. Why couldn't he be more like General Haig over on the other side?—taut, controlled, driving, even bird-watching with a vengeance, chivvying the other generals, moving, pushing, putting his shoulder to the Republican wheel, exerting—and he would never come up with such a line as, "Mr. President! It's just unfair! Darn!" The *look* was part of General Haig's power, the glasses round with steel rims, like battleship portholes, and that was certainly part of the drive. You looked at the glasses and you definitely kept your distance. It occurred to David Burke that perhaps the first thing he might do was to buy a pair of glasses even though his vision was perfect. That would be a start, and maybe the rest would fall into line.

In the meantime, he looked at the President sorrowfully. He would remember af-

The Kennedy Inaugural: Republican chauffeurs were blamed for a series of bizarre accidents such as this, which marred the inaugural parade of the already marred President Edward Kennedy.

terwards how ravaged the President looked inside his ring of supportive machinery—the colossal artificial liver, the EKG, the oxygen tanks, the splints, the iron lung in the corner (wherever the corner of the Oval Office might be, Burke found himself thinking with a hollow laugh), the respirators, the electro-encephalogram, the McGuire and colostomy bags hanging neatly from hooks, the stomach tubes, the chauffeur's leg—and he would think then and later how remarkable it was that the President could function as briskly and confidently as he did under such circumstances. The President seemed wan, he thought, and Burke would mention this to his wife later that evening at a party in Georgetown for George Stevens, Jr.

It was not unlike Burke to repeat what he had seen and heard during his working day at the White House to his secretary and wife, but he would tell no one else, because he would always put duty and country above self. It was unlikely that he would ever write a memoir. He eschewed the practice of the bright young Kennedy people who were writing their memoirs, although the President had only been in office for eight days. He would not do such a thing. He had not told either his secretary or his wife about the rumors sweeping the corridors of the White House, that the President felt so encumbered by the paraphernalia of the life-support systems he was thinking of turning the reins of office over to Vice President Carter and leaving for a vacation in Martinique.

The thought would cross David Burke's mind that perhaps Senator Russell Long would give back the liver that had caused the problem in the first place. Greatness would beckon if Senator Long agreed to do so. It was a question of getting to the Senator to explain firstly greatness, and secondly how when it beckoned it could be recognized to be beckoning. . . .

CONGRESSIONAL SQUARES

"A fundamental, far-reaching reform of Congressional moral conduct," was how consumer crusader Ralph Nader put it, and ABC Veep Roone Arledge agreed. Why shouldn't his network produce a weekly series of House ethics hearings smartly fitted out with a familiar game show format?

House leadership was quick to endorse any idea that would give representatives prime time exposure. On Friday, September 4, 1981, at 8:30 P.M., "Congressional Squares" premiered on ABC.

"Jim has picked Representative Mascalzone of the Third Congressional District of Ohio. Representative Mascalzone—what is the one thing that Teamsters Local 401 and the First National Bank of Toledo own jointly?"

"Well, it could be suite 401, the Dixie Motel on Route 78."

"Jim, do you agree?"

"No."

"You're absolutely right, Jim. The one thing Teamsters Local 401 and the First National Bank of Toledo own jointly is—Representative Mascalzone!"

Crude but effective. The questions on "Congressional Squares" were not always about the chosen celebrity himself. Guest representatives more often had the opportunity to answer questions about one another. And part of the fun was that their answers sometimes revealed facts possessed not even by the genial host, Chairman John Flynt of the Standards of Official Conduct Committee. The show was a smash. Ratings skyrocketed. Congressmen fell over one another for the chance to ruin fellow congressmen, and the audience roared. But as voters they were appalled. The show revealed a depth of chicanery and corruption not even Nader and his cohorts had suspected. Public pressure, increasingly measurable thanks to the miracle of two-way television, was overwhelmingly in favor of a new and rigid bill of ethics.

On May 14, 1982, the House and Senate as a result ratified the most stringent code of conduct ever imposed upon itself by a democratically elected body. These were some of its requirements:

• "All Senators and Representatives elected in 1982 and thereafter must put the entirety of their assets into 'blind, deaf, and dumb' trusts administered by members of the Lighthouse or similar institutions, whose handicaps are sufficiently severe to preclude any direct communication or influence.

• No Congressman may acknowledge any praise or compliment from any source, and if any such praise or compliment appears in any news media, he or she must immediately issue a statement casting doubt on the judgment of the source of praise.

• Congressmen must return all coupons and refuse all discounts of any kind; they must buy periodicals at their full newsstand price; pay for air at gas stations; avoid all sales; return all Christmas, birthday, and other gifts, even from members of their immediate families; fly full fare; and whenever practical, divide travel among railroads, buses, and barges to avoid favoring any mode of transport.

• Congressmen must return all prizes and awards, including athletic trophies, fair ribbons, gold stars received for composition papers, and the like.

• All forms of solicitation of campaign funds, with the exception of actual begging, are prohibited; and candidates may only raise money in the designated 'venue' districts specified by law. Thus, a candidate for the Third District in Connecticut may only raise funds in the Fifth District in Oregon, and a Senatorial candidate from Delaware can only accept contributions from residents of Montana.

• To prevent compromising liaisons, all Congressmen must live in the Congressional dormitory in the Willard Hotel and sign in and sign out, specifying their destination and the person or persons they plan to meet with.

• Congressmen must put personal pets into escrow in a kennel or other facility to prevent undue influence on legislation af-

JIMMY: LOOK, I TOOK
WISE: JIMMY, I'M

fecting, for example, vivisection, fishing limits, the protection of turtle species, and dog licensing.

• Under the freedom of information portions of the ethics law, Congressmen must provide copies of all correspondence, transcripts of telephone calls, and summaries of chats, and all Congressmen must carry tape recorders to maintain records of any thinking out loud.

• Congressmen must publish weekly statements of their net worth for which purpose they will be provided with a live-in accountant at Government expense; and of their weight, so that the public may judge if they are being lavishly entertained."

As one retiring senator commented on leaving Washington shortly after the act passed the Senate, 89-7: "Someone would have to be nuts to run for Congress." It was a prophetic statement; in 1982, with rational candidates thoroughly discouraged from seeking office by the stringent new rules, only nuts ran. And, of course, only nuts won.

Sensational revelations of wrongdoing in office made the House ethics committee's TV debut a runaway hit. On the argument that there is no such thing as bad publicity, the denizens of D.C. were willing to face ruin rather than pass up the massive exposure the show afforded them.

A BRIBE AND I HAD A HOMOSEXUAL AFFAIR! WHAT MORE DO I HAVE TO DO TO GET ON THE SHOW? SORRY! RIGHT NOW THEY'RE ONLY LOOKING FOR TALL, DARK CONGRESSMEN!

THE CONGRESS OF NUTS

In the wake of the new ethics code of 1982, 96 percent of congressional incumbents either announced their retirement or declined to run again, citing "reasons of health." Having thus purified their representative bodies, the American public lost interest. Polls prior to the 1982 off-year elections suggested a voter turnout of slightly less than 13 percent. Accordingly, the administration launched a massive advertising campaign offering a toaster to anyone willing to exercise the franchise on November 2. Slightly less than 13 percent of the electorate turned out for their toasters.

In an election dominated by a draconian bill of ethics, the only people ethical enough to run were representatives of idealistic special-interest or political fringe groups. Within a matter of days, the newly elected body, already touting bizarre methods for creating energy, praising Krishna, and refusing solid foods, was dubbed the "Congress of Nuts."

As if to set a seal on this reputation, its first act was to declare the possession and consumption of meat to be illegal (*see MUSIC 'N DRUGS*). This measure, however, was but one item of a legislative record that covered an impressively wide and puzzling terrain:

• The Arlen-Josephson Act, ordering all states to transfer their capitals to "cities where a reasonable person, asked to name the capital of said state, would expect its capital to be located," on penalty of forfeiting their share of revenue-sharing and highway funds.
• The Gorton-Bennington Act, making broccoli the national flower, the parakeet the national bird, and "Theme from a Summer Place" the national anthem.
• The Mastrelli-Donnell Act of 1983, requiring that the dollar be backed by cheese.
• The Immigration and Naturalization Act of 1983, making demonstration of "a pleasant singing voice or facility with a musical instrument" a condition for acquiring American citizenship.

• A Sense of the House Resolution adopted in 1983, calling on the president to break relations with any country whose name began with a *Z* or ended with an *o*.
• The Trade and Tariffs Act of 1983, which, among other things, prohibited the importation into the United States of prunes, shredded wheat, ice skates, bow ties, and corduroy.
• The Regulated Objects Act of 1983, which made possession by an individual or household of more than one thousand feet of twine, string, rope, or cord a criminal offense and mandated the registration of all magnets.
• The Reilly-Smeckhardt Act of 1983, which offered U.S. statehood to Norway.
• The Agricultural Assistance Act of 1984, which authorized direct payments of one hundred dollars per acre to American farmers to grow honeysuckle.
• The Monetary Convenience Act of 1984, which required all federal officers to have on their persons at all times at least ten dollars in change.
• The Animal Nomenclature Act of 1984, appropriating seventy million dollars to undertake a census of all animals in national parks and, wherever practicable, to give them names and painlessly affix to their bodies weatherproof name tags.
• The Horton-Millies Act of 1984, prohibiting the use of the word "tantamount" in any federal proceeding.
• The Strategic Paving Act, which authorized the Department of Defense to stockpile one billion cubic yards of gravel.
• The Dent-Papagoros Act of 1984, providing one hundred ten million dollars to the Public Health Service to fund an effort to eliminate the sty by 1985.
• The Jackson Amendment of 1984, forbidding anyone named Jackson from trading with the USSR.
• The Durocher-O'Rourke Act of 1984, which required the recall of any article manufactured within the continental United States in the year 1983.

Amongst other things, this last measure led to 1984 being dubbed the Year of the Total Recall, or "the year American industry could not forget."

Left to right: *Senator Robert "Geek" Wilmot (Luddite, South Dakota) and Congressman Amos Kallikak III (Vegetarian Hydrotherapy Mystic, Kansas) applaud President Carter's speech opening the 98th Congress (the "Congress of Nuts"), after his famous statement: "This time I will lie to you a lot."*

THE HALFWAY HOUSE

If the Congress of Nuts was nuts, the American public was not. Responding to the welter of bizarre legislation passed by the "Nutty 98th," citizens voted an unending series of "initiatives" and "propositions" limiting federal expenditures. The government's spending and taxing powers were virtually eliminated, and its control over even its own agencies all but abolished. Several departments became independent fiefdoms in their own right; others were taken over by the private sector, formalizing a system that had been in effect for decades.

One particular measure limiting federal expenditure had a dramatic effect on the 1984 presidential contest.

Republican presidential candidate Jack Kemp and his running mate, William Roth, went to bed in the wee hours of November 7 safe in the knowledge that their "blitz-on-spending" platform had swept them to victory. But when they discovered, two weeks before their scheduled inauguration, that the so-called Zero-Base Compensation Proposition, also ratified in the '84 election, would eliminate their salaries and expenses, they resigned.

In the meantime, Jimmy Carter had selflessly stood for election to the House in order to demonstrate to the American people that a seat in Congress was "still worth something." He had won easily, and, on January 3, when Congress reconvened, the outgoing president was the near-unanimous choice for Speaker. Now, by virtue of the law of succession, the "born-again" Georgian found himself on the verge of yet another "Immaculate Ascension" to the Oval Office.

Meanwhile, Congress had changed. Indeed, for the residents of Washington, D.C., who had to dodge drunken congressmen dozing on the Mall and stopping traffic on Pennsylvania Avenue to wipe windshields with

1

2

dirty rags, its early departure in May 1986 was to be a welcome surprise.

The elections of 1984 had attracted an amazing crop of winos, welfare cheats, and the perennially unemployed, whose only legislative accomplishments proved to be the Aid to Dependent Congressmen Act of 1985; the Wine, Beer, and Liquor Stamp Program; and the Accelerated Retirement Act of 1986, which provided immediate pension benefits after 20 months service to any congressman who could locate them. By June 1986, the nation's lawmakers had taken advantage of the free bus ticket to anywhere in the country provided by the District of Columbia Chamber of Commerce, and had drifted out of town.

But the term of the 99th Congress was not yet quite over. On July 7, 1986, meeting in joint session in Representative Harry Stowoski's Buick in the parking lot of a bowling alley in Bethesda, Maryland, the House (Representatives Vincent Gurn, Democrat of Pennsylvania, and Stowoski, Democrat of Ohio) and the Senate (Senator Harris Bushville of Illinois) voted to organize the Congress as Local 1776 of the Teamsters, declared itself a closed shop, and asked for union supervision of the 1986 elections. The Congress then bowled a few frames, and after a dinner at Danny's Char Broil, it adjourned.

After nearly two years of what one commentator called "a system based on welfare checks and balances," the prospect of a Teamster-dominated Congress was not unattractive. They might charge time and a half, they might insist on a union label on the currency, but the Senate Committee on Foreign Relations wouldn't be cadging quarters for Ripple in Lafayette Park, there would be no cockfights in the caucus rooms, the Senate subway wouldn't smell of urine, and no one would set fire to the House majority leader as he slumbered in the Rotunda, dazed by Sterno.

The legendary Speaker of the House, Milburn "Night Train" Wills (Democrat, Louisiana), in action. Here Representative Wills calls the House to order before it has even entered the Capitol, proposes a bill, debates it, passes it, and adjourns the members, all in the space of 14.8 seconds, a congressional record.

THE HORRIBLE HUNDREDTH

On January 2, 1987, Walter Cronkite held a Congress Conference. Normally these were simple affairs at which Cronkite and other members of the American Broadcasting System's press corps would brief Congress on important matters of state and then answer selected questions. In the past two years they had been poorly attended, owing to widespread inebriation on the Hill, but on January 2 Cronkite was greeted by 432 congressmen-elect, 138 senators-elect, and an estimated 3,500 bodyguards. The future Anchorman kept his remarks brief. The stony Congress-to-be had no questions.

Even after the extraordinarily crooked 1986 elections no one ever imagined that they would long for the lazy, hazy days of the 99th Congress, but by the day the Horrible Hundredth was sworn in, it was apparent that trouble lay ahead. "Do all of you swear to uphold this Constitution and all that f--king b--llsh--t?" intoned Mario "the Reverend" Dipucci, the new Senate chaplain. "You bet your f--king ass," came the chorus of replies from the hundreds of petty thugs, punks, and labor goons packing the historic House chamber. During the remainder of the ceremonies, a dozen reporters were beaten, a *Washington Post* columnist was thrown from the press gallery to the floor below, 40 ambassadors were robbed at gunpoint in the Capitol hallways, and over 125 limousines were stolen from the congressional parking lot.

Within a week, the Senate had contracted with an escort service in Chicago to provide 80 female pages. When a citizen's group protested, one senator replied: "They are pages. Of course, they are the pages with the numbers circled and the corners turned down, get me?" The same day, the group's offices were firebombed.

The House then passed a bill raising the salary of each member to $400,000, with a $100,000 annual union dues checkoff. The lopsided vote (781–0, with 432 members present and voting) precluded a veto. The Senate quickly followed suit.

In the days to come, it became apparent that the 100th Congress was more intent on breaking laws than making them.

• The Senate, as part of a continuing investigation into retail pricing, subpoenaed more than 30-million-dollars' worth of televisions, mink coats, diamonds, and other goods, which senators then sold on the streets surrounding the Capitol.

• The House threatened to pass legislation requiring explicit and gruesome health warnings on, among other things, soap and shoes until the industries involved coughed up sums ranging as high as two million dollars to finance "studies" of their products' safety.

• A joint House-Senate committee prepared, and Congress passed, legislation authorizing the sale of parts or all of the national park system as surplus land with all monies to go directly to Congress. A week later, advertisements offering choice homesites in Yellowstone, Yosemite, and the Grand Canyon appeared in newspapers and magazines.

• On March 17, 1987, the House Committee on Banking, Finance, and Urban Affairs made a surprise visit to a branch of the Continental Federal Savings and Loan Association in downtown Washington for a "hearing" on security in banking. After instructing tellers, guards, and bank patrons to exercise their Constitutional right to remain silent or get their goddam head blowed off, and not to contact the police or be cited for contempt, the committee left with over two million dollars in cash. The hearing may have been a sham, but the rules on congressional immunity for legislative actions were clear and sweeping. The police were powerless to act.

The robbery marked the beginning of a legislative crime wave that transformed the immediate neighborhood of the Capitol

Posters such as this were common when the 100th Congress was in session, although some longtime residents of D.C. professed not to know what all the fuss was about, and even saw the crime wave as a sign that "the old days were back."

into the area with the highest incidence of assault, armed robbery, extortion, grand theft, and fraud in the nation. No one in his right mind went within a mile of the Capitol, even in broad daylight. Accordingly, when President Carter delivered his 1988 State of the Union Guesstimate, the Secret Service insisted that he be driven into the Capitol, remain in his limousine with the windows rolled up at all times, and address the members through a loudspeaker. Even so, the car's hubcaps were stolen, its aerial snapped off, and its windshield smashed. Finally, President Carter had to cut short his speech when a pair of senators began removing one of the tires. For many, the spectacle of the presidential limousine bumping down the Capitol steps at 30 mph with the Secret Service firing bursts of machine gun bullets into the Capitol to cover the exit signaled a new low in the often stormy relations between Congress and the White House.

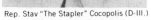

A MAN FOR FOUR SEASONS

Looking back on the events of May 1988, no one was too sure what had provided the final straw. Maybe it was the reported sale by the Library of Congress to a German industrialist of the original copy of the Declaration of Independence. Whatever the provocation that ignited the spark, on the night of May 18, 1988, the citizens of Washington erected barricades around the Capitol and began trading small arms fire with the congressmen within. Two senators who were holding up a liquor store in Georgetown when the uprising began were tarred and feathered; a representative who had taken an elderly lady's purse on the Metro was beaten to death.

By noon the next day, a crowd of over 100,000 surrounded the historic seat of representative government in America. Their slogans were an ironic echo of the spirit that led to the first Congress 200 years earlier. "No taxation and no representation," they cried. "Give them all another term—in Leavenworth."

By the afternoon of May 21, their supplies of subpoenaed delicacies running low, the 100th Congress hurriedly passed a bill canceling all existing extradition treaties. At sundown, guns blazing, the Congress sped away in a dozen municipal buses. At 9:10 P.M., it began a joint session on airline safety in a pair of commandeered 767s at Dulles International Airport. By the morning of May 22, the Horrible Hundredth Congress had left the United States for good.

And if an outmoded form of government had breathed its last, a newer, truer democracy was emerging elsewhere. On a warm June day in 1988, the American Broadcasting System announced that in November it would hold the first free video-election to choose its Anchorman for the next four seasons.

It was an epic showdown for America, a choice between its most trusted man and its most distinguished family name.

Incumbent Walter Cronkite, confident and with no intention of relinquishing his office, scared off all but one challenger—John-John Kennedy, host of the sagging "Tonight Show," whose reluctance to run echoed a long family tradition. Coyly denying his candidacy until August, he finally accepted the pleas of a "Draft Kennedy" movement that some said was financed by the network.

The gauntlet was down and the battle of the ages began. Each candidate persistently appeared in commercials, all donated by ABS as a public service; and since Kennedy's show ran 90 minutes each night, the equal-time provision mandated that Cronkite's broadcast be lengthened to an hour and a half. It was the most scrutinized election in American history.

Kennedy directed his campaign to what he called "the forgotten viewers"—the military, children, and meat-culture youth. The brash and handsome challenger advocated opening up the airwaves to a broader spectrum of Americans, promising to use his influence as Anchorman to persuade program executives to buy more pilots from Programming Centers.

Cronkite seemed more bemused than threatened by the campaign, relying on his sober maturity and aging trustworthiness to carry him through. He only bristled on rare occasions, as when reporters inevitably mentioned "Waltergate."

In the end, there was no contest. Cronkite was able to project himself the overwhelming victor on the basis of an election day pre-poll that closely matched his final showing—91 percent of the popular vote and every electoral market vote except Massachusetts'. There were smiles all around, but none broader (and, some suggested, more knowing) than those of ABS executives, who proudly announced that the network's rating had risen once again to the ethereal and all but unachievable 100 percent during the election.

The first popularly elected Anchorman of the United States is seen here hosting his Inaugural Special. In his closing monologue, Anchorman Cronkite urged the American people to "ask not what your network can do for you, but what you can do for your network."

SEAL OF THE ANCHORMAN OF THE UNITED STATES

THE SECOND U.S. CONSTITUTIONAL CONVENTION

What started in 1978 as a grassroots movement to balance the federal budget by means of the second Constitutional Convention in American history had, by 1980, become something of an evangelical crusade. The hurried adoption of the Dole-Moynihan Act outlawing deficit spending did nothing to halt the ground swell, and on September 18, 1980, Alaska became the 34th state to ratify the call for the convention. On March 23, 1981, 593 delegates, representing 50 states, Puerto Rico, the Virgin Islands, and Guam, gathered in the newly refurbished Kemper Memorial Arena in Kansas City determined, as one delegate put it, "to get all that un-Constitutional stuff out of the Constitution."

For 18 months, the delegates, colorful in the powdered wigs and plastic tricorn hats that became their trademark, argued, debated, discussed, and compromised their way to an agreement. On the night of September 16, 1982, with the eyes of America and the world on the futuristic auditorium, the voting on the 900,000-word document began. And then it happened. With the rasp of tearing metal, the roof of the jinxed arena wobbled, cracked, and fell on the hapless conventioneers. When the dust had settled, 297 were dead.

The full extent of the tragedy became apparent the next day. Two hundred ninety-seven was an exact mathematical quorum. Legal and constitutional scholars considered the precedents. Their judgment, backed by a ruling from the Supreme Court, was as heartbreaking as it was final: with the elimination of the quorum, the mandate of the convention expired. Once again, the states would have to call a convention; once again, delegates would have to be selected; and, once again, every phrase and clause would have to be argued over, debated, and discussed.

The 594 delegates who assembled at Atlanta's ultramodern Omni Convention Center on January 21, 1984, were much like their predecessors. One hundred fourteen of them were survivors of the original convention, including the entire delegation from Guam. They were as boisterous and fun-loving as the members of the first Second Convention (one bartender in a lounge on Peachtree Street reported that a group of conventioneers came in at closing time, and when he refused to serve them, threatened to write an amendment requiring bartenders to wear articles of women's clothing on their heads), and they were just as determined to modernize the legal foundation of the Republic.

Early in the afternoon of August 15, 1984, during a debate on the Fifth Amendment, the impossible happened. Delegates who survived reported that the speaker (Delegate Wayne Chackman from the Third District of Oklahoma), had finished a speech condemning the self-incrimination protections of that amendment with the words, "You can take the Fifth and you know what you can do with it," when the hall burst into applause, and, incredibly, the roof fell in.

Three hundred twenty-one people were pronounced dead by nightfall. Less than a month away from a final vote on a document it had labored over, the second Second Convention was legally dead.

When the third Second Convention was convened in the open-air arena at Marineland of the Pacific on July 19, 1986, an entirely different spirit prevailed. Within two hours, the new convention had ratified an amendment to the Constitution forbidding any aircraft of any kind to fly over any meeting of the convention, or any object of any kind to be suspended, placed, hung, or allowed to stand over any conventioneer's head. Its ratification was made a condition of any further meetings, and awaiting the action of the states, the convention thereupon recessed.

With the ratification on February 14, 1987, of the 37th Amendment, constitutionally banning air traffic in the coastal Californian area, the convention got down to business. On June 7, 1988, the new Constitution was presented to the convention. It passed, 580 to 13, at 6:21 P.M. Pacific time.

There were few who spoke of a "Miracle at Marineland." The new document reflected the complex realities and prejudices of the 20th century, just as its predecessor, ratified a few months less than 200 years earlier, had exemplified the hopes and ideals of a simpler time.

But in the end the charter was the product of human beings, and the story of their efforts to give the country a new legal foundation was a human story. As the senior delegate from Guam observed, while he and his fellow delegates celebrated the passage of the new Constitution and their own incredible survival: "It was like any convention. You drink, you talk, you drink some more, you talk some more, maybe you meet a pretty girl. Only thing is, this one lasted 87 months. But I ain't complaining."

Two "Foundering Fathers" from the third Second Constitutional Convention turn their attention to "the pursuit of happiness" after the floor debate on the session's final question ("Where are the broads?").

THE NEW BILL OF RIGHTS

1. Congress shall make no law respecting the establishment of rifle ranges, pistol clubs, shooting societies, gun clubs, or any other such organization; or prohibiting the free use of guns; or abridging the freedom to shoot or to hunt; or the right of the people peaceably to assemble firearms collections, and to redress their grievances with guns.

2. A comfortable and well-regulated populace being necessary to the security of a responsible state, the levy by any individual, group, partnership, company, or governmental entity of any impost, toll, or tariff of any kind upon the use by the people of sanitary facilities in the United States or any place subject to their jurisdiction is hereby forbidden.

3. Congress shall make no law prohibiting prayers in schools, or any other place, or abridging the freedom of reasonable speech or a responsible press; but speech shall be taken to mean sounds that come out of the people's mouths or, if provoked, their guns, and not strange and unnatural dress or hair, or cohabitation with persons of the same sex, or offensive or perverted gestures or behavior, or other things that cannot be heard and have to be seen to be believed, nor shall disrespectful silence or the display of badges, buttons, or slogans be held to be speech; but nothing herein shall be construed as limiting or abridging the right of the people to affix to the bumpers of their vehicles such signs and declarations as they may choose; and the press shall be held responsible for any smut or nasty things; nor shall any publisher insert any card in any periodical which shall fall upon the people's lap when it is opened.

4. Congress shall make no law abridging the freedom of speed by setting arbitrary limits thereon; or prohibiting turns to the right on a red light after a full stop; or preventing the removal of any buzzer or alarm in any vehicle or the installation of any device, electronic or otherwise, therein; or requiring any person to wear a belt, harness, helmet, or other encumbrance while in motion of any kind; or restricting the right of the people to assemble at the scene of an accident or disaster to acquaint themselves with the results; or depriving any person of leisure, mobility, or a license to drive, without due process of law.

5. No person who has been granted lawful entrance to an establishment which has on its premises an hors d'oeuvre table, salad bar, or other assembly of comestibles shall be prevented from filling his plate therefrom as often as he shall choose, nor be made subject to any additional charge therefor, providing only that he shall have agreed to pay the full cost of an entrée.

6. No person receiving public monies of any kind for support or aid shall be quartered in a hotel or any other such lodging, with or without the consent of the owner.

7. The right of the people to be secure in their persons, houses, garages, cars, trailers, recreational vehicles, leisure homes, condominiums, papers, effects, belongings, and gun collections shall not be violated; nor shall they be required to seek permits to make additions or improvements upon their basements or attics or any place; nor shall any person enter therein for the purposes of inspection or assessment without their consent; nor shall they be required to enumerate their flush toilets or closets or any other thing therein, save only its occupants; and if anyone shall enter in or upon their property or vehicles without their consent they may in the first instance shoot, and then make inquiries.

8. After one year from the ratification of this article, the sale of containers with tops which require more than one motion to remove is hereby prohibited within the United States or any place subject to their jurisdiction.

9. No person shall be held to answer for a capital or otherwise infamous crime unless a police officer shall say that he did it; nor shall any person be subject for the same offense to be twice put in jeopardy of life and limb, except if his sentence be excessively lenient or his acquittal be due to a technicality or be otherwise ridiculous; nor shall he be compelled in any criminal case to be a witness against himself and he shall be informed of his right to remain in confinement until he consents to do so; and if he shall be a witness against himself, he shall have the right to confront and cross-examine himself.

10. In all criminal prosecutions, the criminal shall enjoy the right to a speedy and public trial by a jury of not less than one person, whose verdict must be unanimous in all capital cases; and to be informed of the nature and cause of the accusation and of the lesser charge to which he may plead guilty, as well as of the maximum sentence he could receive should he be found guilty of the original charge; and to have compulsory process to obtain copies of his confession; and to have present at his trial a courtroom artist.

11. No bail in excess of one hundred million dollars shall be required; nor any sentence longer than six thousand years imposed; and any cruel or unusual punishment inflicted must be televised.

12. In commerce with other nations, where the value of goods to be sold shall exceed twenty dollars, the duly elected officers of any company incorporated in the United States shall not be hindered from granting such emoluments as they may choose to foreign princes, citizens, or subjects to ensure the speedy success of their enterprises; and if they shall be questioned for it in any other place the right of perjury shall be preserved.

13. No person shall be fined or otherwise held to account for stationing his vehicle at a broken inoperative meter; nor shall any vehicle be towed more than two hundred feet without its owner's consent; nor shall any fine be imposed for discarding litter in a public place which is more than ten times the value of the discarded litter.

14. No person shall be compelled for any reason or in any place to acquaint another with his mother's maiden name.

15. No pregnancy may be terminated without the written consent of the fetus; nor may any person under the age of consent be struck or otherwise disciplined, except by his parents or with parental consent, or by a police officer having possible cause, or a teacher during regular school hours, or by an officer or employee of any institution into whose care or under whose control he has been given or placed, or a person or employee thereof onto whose property he has placed himself, or by a lawful rider on public or private transport, or by a citizen acting under provocation or having a particular purpose.

(1) *Star Yankee outfielder Gary "Stilts" Murchison sparked baseball's first "in-game negotiation" when he stopped 30 feet short of home plate and demanded a raise.*

(2) *Murchison and his lawyer hastily initialed the six-figure salary escalation clause proposed by the team's attorneys ...*

SPORTS

(3) *and, with a last-minute burst of speed ...*

(4) *the rangy slugger stumbled home with the winning run and a new multi-year contract.*

SPORTS

It is summer, in the year 1988. The setting—the Peking Olympics. A young man named Bud Teppler stands nervously, his hand cradling a 16-pound ball of iron. In a few minutes he will attempt to put the unwieldy object as far as he can, and he will have to do so while dodging a veritable hailstorm of similar spheres being thrown at him by upward of 600 Chinese. This is not the shot put event he is used to. Bud Teppler waits, and perhaps he utters a silent prayer for victory, and for survival.

We Americans have always been a sporting breed, and during no decade was this as true as in the '80s. Some thought that the increasingly violent nature of organized competition signaled the advent of a new barbarism in our society. But many believed that the broken collarbone and the pulled hamstring have always been as much a part of our way of life as the roach rancher and the Wôôdi Allen movie. These were the ones who came—by the million—to organized sporting events of every kind. They were ample proof that, as philosopher Howard Cosell wrote, "The sport of America *is* business."

Physical contact did increase in sports during the '80s, as a nation of fans who in their daily lives were, some said, well-insulated from aggression, pain, and even feeling itself, sought vicarious pleasure in the skillful combat of trained professionals. Athletes are like the rest of us, only bigger; that is why we choose them to represent our school, college, city—indeed, our nation. In their bodies are our frailties redeemed; in their salaries is our apotheosis. And athletes in the '80s were bigger than ever—great, strong, strapping Colored People mostly, who had grown up amid the excitement and violence of what used to be our inner cities, and to whom life-or-death competition had always been a way of life. These were the men and women who, in that quiet, gradual way of which Charles Darwin spoke, came to dominate professional sport in the '80s—not only in the traditional American games of baseball, football, and basketball, but in new forms of contest as well.

> **SPORTING EVENTS WERE AMPLE PROOF THAT, AS PHILOSOPHER HOWARD COSELL WROTE, "THE SPORT OF AMERICA *IS* BUSINESS."**

And there were more—"folk sports," as it were. The preindustrial custom of horsewhipping and the postindustrial hilarity of "dodge 'em" cars united in the Kentucky Demolition Derby. The child's fascination with tormenting insects gained new respectability in the decidedly grownup sport of roach racing. And cockfighting, that earthy outlaw game, once the domain of underprivileged Third World unemployables, attained a new validity (and widespread popularity) in its professional form, culminating in the Superpit—an event viewed by millions (65 rating, 86 share).

It is a law of nature that, in business, competition leads inexorably to the increased efficiency of one network, one beer producer, one oil company, and the like. Therefore our people, in various ways, will turn to sport to express that competitive instinct which is so quintessentially American. Inevitably, then, in the face of black domination of baseball, the white sports fan found players, teams—indeed, an entire league—with which he could identify. "Brainstormers" they were called, these white athletes, some inspired amateurs, some Ph.D. candidates in Comparative Literature. Their wit and wordplay brought them a sort of unofficial fame as baseball's "smart white underbelly."

But, black or white, athletes continued to serve as both objects of hero-worship and as role models—particularly for the American no longer quite as fit, but likewise no longer quite as naive about life. For these were not the "dumb jocks" of previous decades. These were canny businessmen and women who carried, with equal ease, a gym bag in one hand and a CPA in the other. The '80s saw lawyers and agents come "out of the locker room" and take their rightful place alongside the heroes they so doggedly represented. Few were surprised, therefore, when the "in-game trade" ruling took effect.

But sports are still games, and games are for the young. American youth continued to play—and to excel. As more and more youngsters gained athletic proficiency and "turned pro," the nation responded with amazement, pride, and downscaled "Suzuki"-type sports arenas. When five-year-old Ricky Vartorella beat John McEnroe to win the men's singles trophy at Wimbledon, it seemed a sort of message. And what could it mean other than that we Americans were becoming more skillful, stronger, healthier, and, yes, better paid.

Bud Teppler, a nine-year-old Olympic shot-putter, was one of those healthier, stronger young Americans. Today, he looks back on the injuries he received from those 600 iron balls and smiles. A major motion picture was made about his silver medal-winning effort, and now Bud is a well-liked, if toothless, greeter at a major Los Angeles casino. It was worth it. That is Bud's glory, and it is the glory of sport itself.

OLYMPICS

It promised to be a spectacular Olympic decade. The three superpowers would alternate as host countries and a generation of promising athletes from around the globe waited in the wings to soar to new heights in their quest for the gold. No one was disappointed, though none of the games turned out quite as expected.

The 1980 Olympiad in Moscow will be long remembered for the USSR's awesome domination of the games. Russian athletes brought home a staggering 92 percent of the gold medals and placed 1–2–3 in many events. Not only did the home teams sweep the field in their traditional strengths, such as weightlifting and track, but they also took surprising victories in such perennially weak areas as diving, equestrian events, and bantamweight boxing.

As *Pravda* crowed about "the triumph of ideology over genetics," and veteran Olympic watchers shook their heads in respectful disbelief, rumblings of an unsavory sort simmered among visiting athletes and coaches. Although Slavic officials laughed off the nagging accusations, skeptical observers accused the Russians of loading the deck. One West German swimming coach insisted that the Olympic pool was designed to make the home-team lane 50 percent shorter than all others; middle-distance runners complained that handfuls of marbles had been strewn in their paths; and several South American teams protested a spate of all-night vodka parties where noisy celebrants sounded horns and chorused boating songs directly under their windows. Despite a rash of such allegations, the International Olympic Committee refused to act, and the Russian records stayed on the books.

No records of any kind were set at the 1984 games in Los Angeles, an Olympiad that will be better remembered for what didn't happen than for what did. The self-actualized Californian hosts found it difficult to embrace the Olympic spirit and tried to inject the games with their regional ethic of personal growth. Emphasizing "sharing the experience" and the non-

competitive "trip," officials downplayed scores and flatly refused to announce winners in many categories, favoring such pronouncements as, "Kenyo Koombo, a very together Nigerian fellow, said today while running the marathon that he'd had a flash about how birds were just like people, only smarter. That's beautiful, Kenyo."

Attendance dropped precipitously, and many visiting athletes lost interest in competing without cheering throngs to urge them on. The only hero of the games was the Fresno native, Robin Lighthouse, who won both of the new events introduced

in Los Angeles: hot-tubbing and orgone boxing. Still, the television ratings plummeted and outraged network executives vowed never again to broadcast the Olympics.

It was just as well, for Americans were thus spared watching the 1988 Peking Olympics, which were overshadowed by constant quibbling over the rules. Joining the international competition for the first time, the Chinese sought to make a good first showing by overwhelming their rivals through sheer numbers. Despite howls of "foul" from purists, the Chinese entered a relay team of 100 and approached the soc-

cer competition by filling their half of the field with the entire population of a Shanghai suburb. Claiming that each nation should be allowed to exploit its greatest asset, the Chinese sent no fewer than 912 entrants to the board in the diving competition, and cruised to a controversial sweep of the first 1200 places in the marathon with an impenetrable wall of front-runners. Fearing the advent of a world war, visiting athletes refused to complain, settling for 1201st, 1202nd, or 1203rd place, carrying on as best they could.

Such is the Olympic spirit.

Moscow's beautiful new Olympic pool, completed just in time for the 1980 games, was a fitting showplace for a string of record-shattering Soviet victories that shocked the swimming world.

CONTACT

The soaring human spirit always demands more and more from its favorite athletes, asking that they be braver and bolder, swifter and sharper, bigger and better. Americans continued to expect these qualities from the athletes of the '80s—and two others as well—that they be nastier and bloodier.

It is difficult to pinpoint the emergence of contact sports as the dominant trend of the decade, but no other event crystalized the movement so much as the 1985 Kentucky Demolition Derby. Putting a new crimp in the time-honored Churchill Downs classic, racing officials set up two starting gates, each pointing in a different direction around the picturesque mile-long oval. As each half of the 24-horse field turned to-

ward the finish line, they ran smack into each other, felling 16 mounts in a hearty crunch of horseflesh and delighting 140,000 equine enthusiasts. Jumping over their bleeding cohorts, the eight surviving Triple Crown hopefuls continued to circle the course, colliding after each circuit as their whip-wielding jockeys sought to unseat one another. Finally, only two colts remained upright, Big 'n Bloody and Firing Squad, who jousted for four laps until Firing Squad tripped on the heels of the fallen son of Affirmed, Affixed, breaking both fetlocks and leaving Big 'n Bloody the victor.

Contact spread like wildfire to every arena of athletic endeavor. Team contact tennis made tigers out of the white-shorts set. The U.S. Lawn Tennis Association changed tournament rules in July to award bonus points for "aces" (striking one's opponent in the head or abdomen

Mixed doubles teams play out a "thigh-breaker" point in contact tennis. There is clearly no love lost.

Blood stained the blue grass of Churchill Downs at the fir running of the Kentucky Demolition Derby, contact horse racing's famous "Run for the Bruises." Big 'n Bloody (righ

with a serve); "webbing" (encircling an opponent's head with the racquet and breaking the strings while pulling it around his neck); and "drives" (embedding the racquet or handle by any means into any part of the opponent's body).

Even the most sedentary of sports were transformed by the trend. Contact bridge gave new meaning to the term "grand slam."

Veteran observers of American culture were less impressed than the fans and sounded dire warnings. But the spoilsports were clearly in the minority. A plethora of self-improvement books such as *Body-Checking in Backgammon, The Proper Use of Golf Clubs,* and *Beating the Dealer* made the bestseller lists. Even small fry joined the parade of hyperactive sports, and games like contact hopscotch and hide 'n seek 'n destroy kept many a youngster on his toes.

The trend seems sure to continue. Wily sports promoters have created a master plan for the perpetuation of the brawny breeds. Rather than waiting for muscular specimens to arise at random from farmland or ghetto, they wait eagerly for their first "cultured" litters of large-bred athletes. Entrepreneur and sports aficionado David Garth has already announced that 16 million dollars await basketball muscleman Kermit Washington, should he decide to hire himself out to stud. Garth also plans a stable of broodmares and hopes to attract athletes of the caliber of Nancy Lopez and Diana Nyad. Not to be outdone, several franchise owners, acting on the advice of highly regarded bloodline experts, have secretly plunked down staggering sums on untested foals of champion performers. It would appear that the next generation of American athletes will certainly be bigger and better, nastier and bloodier than ever.

...on by a nose (broken) *with Firing Squad second. It was the ...rst Derby where all the horses were scratched.*

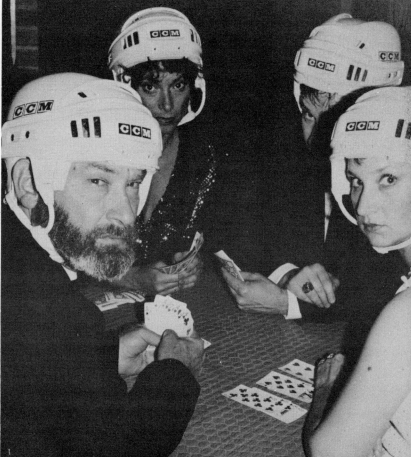

The woman on the left has just "roughed" a low diamond (wrested it from an opponent's hand), and the man on the left is about to rough the cameraman during this game of contact bridge. The bid was three no-thump.

LOS JUEGOS

We have often been called a nation of borrowers, brewing our heritage in the vast melting pot of American society. Just as our indigenous music is filched from the Africans and our literature from the British, our favorite sports owe much to the world around us. But the American gaming scene had seen no massive invasion by a single foreign culture until the last decade, when many an oddsmaker was left crying, "Here come the Latinos!"

With a zest usually reserved for food and real estate, American sportsmen by the millions embraced *Los Juegos Hispanicos*. Not only did such entrenched pastimes as jai alai and midget wrestling soar in popularity, but amusements previously submerged in the steamy Hispanic subculture burst onto the national scene.

Arising—as so many other institutions have—from the sweltering *barrios* of the disenfranchised, particular *juegos* were at first merely improvised gambits to pass the time. Cockroach racing, for example, began as a crude—if exciting—gambling mechanism, but the "sport of the people" quickly developed a loyal following on its aesthetic merits.

Similar in operation to greyhound tracks, roach racing studios sprung up in droves. Shortly before post time, leadout boys placed the racers in starting bags from which they crawled at the flicking on of a lightbulb. Dyed various colors to match their post positions, the tiny but stouthearted competitors began their frantic dash over 25- or 50-foot straight racing strips. As the sport gained popularity, sophisticated improvements evolved, such as the electrification of the starting bags, the addition of a mechanical cupcake used as a lure in front of the galloping insects, and video screens that magnified the contests to billboard size to alleviate the sport's built-in visibility problems. In time, heroic racers and trainers became household gods, and rabid fans sang the praises of the legendary Sugarchomper, a 10-length victor in the 1986 Siesta Stakes.

If Americans took a while to accept the elevation of household pests to the rank of thoroughbred athletes, they were even more stubborn about succumbing to the allure of cockfighting. Cashing in on years of secretive participation in *el prueba final de los aves del corral* ("the final test of the poultry"), wily Latinos dominated the game. But a groundswell of support for the fledgling entertainment came from America's heartland, where Oklahoma chicken farmers, bankrupted by the meat ban (*see* MUSIC 'N DRUGS), packed up their families and flocks of cocks for greener tracks in the burgeoning cockfighting world.

My roach had a f— –kin' six-length lead, then this jerk pulls out a toaster and half the roaches run and hide behind it.

DISAPPOINTED OWNER AT ROACH RACE

Tension between the Hispanics and the Okies bubbled to the surface amidst frequent charges that the cockfights were being rigged to provide betting coups for Latin-American gambling syndicates. Plagued by continual allegations of unseemly conduct, the sport took a downward plunge toward staged showmanship that, if it alienated aficionados, did win cockfighting a broad new following. "Grudge pecks" between polished showcocks like The Capon Crusader and Drumstick Calhoun fired fierce rivalries, as did the infamous Shake 'n Bake Jake's highly promoted series of USDA-tag-team scratch matches pitting the Butterball Twins against Dusty Rhode Island Red and Andre the Giant Rooster.

Even as whining purists decried the craze and ragtag humanitarian groups droned on with maudlin appeals to the American public, longsighted promoters were focusing their efforts on a single national bout that finally saw fruition as Super Pit I in 1987. As a 91-share audience hungrily looked on, many having placed advance wagers at Off-Pit Betting parlors, odds-on favorite Nasty Pecker prevailed over the bleeding but plucky Mad Chicken of Manchuria to win a $750,000 purse and the hearts of the nation.

El campeón del mundo, Andre el Giant Rooster, dice: "Picando un adversario a muerte me deja sediente. Por eso, cuando yo bebo cerveza, bebo **Beer**"

Beba **Beer**, el cerveza de campeones por todo el mundo.
Un otro producto fino de Anheuser-Schlitz.

Cockfighting so captivated the American public that human athletes were often "aced-out" in the fierce world of product endorsement. Fighting cocks appeared as "spokesbirds" for goods ranging from bubblegum to aphrodisiacs to beer, and though their life expectancy was somewhat shorter than that of regular sports figures, their names were used after "defeat" to promote a continuous parade of new brands in the neighborhood meat-substitute freezer.

CONTRACT

It all started on May 15, 1981, the day San Diego Padres' rookie Larvell Mumford became the first major leaguer to demand his release on waivers after facing only one pitch. ("Forget about them low strike zones in the National League!" he explained to manager Billy Martin after Enzo Hernandez had gone up to pinch hit for the free-swinging youngster and grounded to short.)

Padres' owner Ray Kroc was forced to release Mumford on his own recognizance; the new Players Association contract negotiated by attorney Roy Cohn left no doubt about that. The rookie was picked up by a total of eight clubs over the next 15 days, during which time he faced 19 pitchers and batted .189. But if his playing statistics were less than auspicious, Mumford did succeed in touching off the most feverish—and, from a fan's point of view, the most exciting—spate of negotiating in the history of American sport.

Perhaps the most significant legal victory of the decade's early years came on September 23, 1982, when, during a crucial game against the Boston Red Sox, Yankee outfielder Gary "Stilts" Murchison successfully completed the national pastime's first "in-game negotiation." With the score tied at 2-2, Murchison had singled and had been advanced to second on a sacrifice. Pete Rose, leading the American League in hitting at the age of 42 and still using his patented head-first slide after a successful solar plexus transplant, lined a vicious drive up the alley in right center that seemed destined to give the New Yorkers the lead. But, halfway between third and home, Murchison pulled up short. "I won't budge," he insisted, "without a six-figure bonus and a new multi-year agreement." Yankee attorneys, faced with the loss of the division championship, had no choice but to consent. The run that Murchison eventually scored was later calculated to have cost the team $34,000 per foot.

After the notorious Murchison incident, pandemonium reigned supreme. Through their on-field representatives, players received new contracts on their way to first base; after fouling off three pitches; during windups; and tracking down fly balls. Ultimately, the "California subclause" was invoked: each player was declared a franchise unto himself and each team merely a consortium of separately owned companies. And, as the decade wore on, the more flamboyant of the lawyers and agents built up an appreciable spectator following of their own.

Even in enemy ballparks, Chicago Cubs' attorney G. Clifford Obst seldom failed to get a standing ovation when he strode in from the bullpen to trade a pitcher or slap an injunction on an opposing base runner. The exquisitely worded tirades of Burton Tauber, Reggie Jackson's counsel, defending his client's "inalienable right" to disobey signals from the third-base coach, were quoted nightly in taverns from Atlanta to Seattle. Schoolboys competed to complete their sets of Topps attorney cards and to memorize the tables of "Decisions Won-and-Lost" that appeared in the daily newspaper.

Nor was the trend confined to baseball. Indeed, the unquestioned negotiating coup of the sports decade was pulled off by Richard LaMotte III, owner of the National Hockey League's Pittsburgh Penguins. With his team trailing the Buffalo Sabres by a goal late in the decisive seventh game of the 1987 Stanley Cup semifinals, LaMotte ordered coach Eddie Shack to call time out. Then, while Penguin lawyers long-windedly cross-examined each individual Buffalo defenseman in an alleged attempt "to determine whether he was using, or had ever used, an illegally curved stick," LaMotte rushed to the airport, flew to Montreal, purchased the entire squad of Les Canadiens (who earlier that week had completed a four-game sweep of their semifinal series against the New England Whalers), and jetted his new charges back to Pittsburgh in time to clinch an overtime victory. Two weeks later, as the cheers of 17,000 win-starved fans rocked the Civic Arena, veteran superstar Guy Lafleur drilled home the goal that clinched the first cup victory in the Penguins' 20-year history. The long drought was over.

The New York Yankees' ace relief attorneys, Ryne Katzenbach and Hoyt Rosen (above), warm up in the visitors' bullpen for one of their patented late-inning restraining orders. But for once they're unsuccessful; umpire Stan McIntyre (below) rules that their collusion charges against the Orioles' pitcher and catcher represent an illegal "assault-on-battery."

THE WHITE LEAGUE

Sportswriter Red Herron's classic account of the formation of the so-called White League in baseball had the distinction of being the last article ever written for a major periodical on a typewriter. Subsequent sports reporting was done first on, and then by, computers programmed to synthesize box scores and sports argot into columns of remarkable readability.

Back in the years before yrs. trly. had shed the carmine foliage by which he earned his sobriquet, it was understood that baseball, or "The National Pastime," as I have dubbed it, cared not for race, color, or creed. If a man were willing to don a silly suit and risk his bodily and spiritual well-being by swinging a stick at a ball for money, his ethnic origin was moot, and if he could run, catch, and throw as well, an athlete of any shade would be signed to a contract as fast as you could say "Jackie Robinson." Those days are gone.

When Carl Yastrzemski, perennial DH of the beloved Bosox, dramatically succumbed to a heart attack with two out and the bases loaded during the playoffs of '86, not a single Caucasian remained active in organized baseball. Two winters later, Yaz, Fidel Castro, and New York agent Art Kaminsky were the only non-Negroes among the nominees to the Hall of Fame.

As a spectator sport, the "Great Game," as I term it, had never been more popular. And, over the hidebound objections of such traditionalists as yrs. trly., Commissioner Agnew had initiated such successful moves as the amalgamation of leagues, expansion to 60 cities, the year-round season, and Instant Replay Appeals, or "Backsies."

And so, on opening day in the Rosedome, January 1, 1987, only the ball and foul lines were white. The only team of Caucasians playing honest-to-Abner Doubleday *hardball* was a brainstorming nine out of Grosse Pointe: "Ol' Valise" Paige and his Wasps.

This "Valise" guy was a Harvard Business School grad who'd made a killing in the market, dumping a mess of Exxon shares right before the Oil Glut. He pitched for the Wasps, and on the mound made up in guile what he lacked in speed. He could take something off a change-up. His eight mates, recruited from the Main Line, the Ivy League, and the New York Athletic Club, last bastions of epidermal pinkness, wore baggyass uniforms from Brooks Brothers, and deported themselves upon the diamond with gravity and vigor.

In the spring of '88, other aggregations such as the East Hampton Jet Set, the Birmingham Klan, and the Lake Forest White Tornadoes got into the act, and the so-called Caucasian Balk Circuit or "White League" was in business.

Lackeys and hacks for the official National-American League can go on sneering at the new loop's impressive statistics and records, claiming it doesn't take much of a pitcher to twirl a no-hitter in glaring daylight, or that anyone can hit .400 with the crazy hops a ball takes on a surface of dirt and grass.

But in this retired scribe's opinion, the White League is here to stay. All it needs is a little credibility, which is to say, publicity. So far, the women writers who cover baseball—and the writers who cover baseball are women, to a man—have not granted it a line score, side bar, or column. The distaff scribes have so far refused to so much as enter the locker rooms of the White teams, whining, "What's to see?" But crafty old "Ol' Valise" and the other owners have come up with a compromise proposal. They are willing to guarantee that any White League player interviewed will be fully dressed at the time, and are offering to all accredited members of the sporting press the opportunity to participate in a regular season game, at the position of her choice.

Yrs. trly., for one, thinks it'll all work out. In fact, I'm willing to propose a toast to the bright future of the great game of baseball. Gentlemen: the ladies!

One especially popular White Leaguer, "Ol' Valise" Paige, acquired such a following that his life story, tracing his colorful career as both renegade athlete and responsible investment counselor, was made into a major motion picture. Paige himself financed the venture.

The crowds who come to see the great pitcher are small but enthusiastic. The blinis are served in striped tents beyond the outfield grass. The doors of the Port-o-Johns, which stand in neat rows beyond the temporary aluminum stands along the first base line, swing briskly open and shut. It is a day for the club owners to celebrate, because Lawrence "Ol' Valise" Paige has come to town — and just about everybody has come out to see the legendary hurler, the mainstay of the Grosse Pointe Wasps' pitching staff. Fathers point: "There he is, sonny. You'll never see his ilk again." Some say that he is the greatest pitcher to appear in White Ball since blacks began to dominate the major leagues in the early '80s (the last white was a ballboy on the Cincinnati Reds named Rufus), and relegated the white players to a small, obscure, watering-spot-storming league — black players refer to it scornfully as the "Social Ramble."

Indeed, there are those who have seen "Ol' Valise" pitch who believe that, blackened up with Kiwi shoe polish, he might even "pass" into the majors and surprise a few people. Others scoff. ("Comparatively, that guy can't throw a fit!")

Nonetheless, Paige is a great draw in the little watering-spot ballparks. Folks come out to see a legendary figure, indeed a living legend; famous for his quips, his laconic manner, his strange, ostrichlike posture, the way he talks to his glove, his habit of building little mud pies behind the pitcher's mound, his wealth, his Grosse Pointe mansion, his collection of Holland & Holland shotguns, his fly-tying equipment, his den full of big-game heads (including a rare Marco Polo sheep), his impeccable breeding ("Ol' Valise" was born during a tea party at Monticello, Thomas Jefferson's former home), his lifestyle, and his homilies. Not the least, people come to see him pitch his vast repertoire, including the famous "Procrastination Pitch," in which the ball apparently speeds toward the plate after a bewildering series of arm-twirlings and leg-liftings. In fact, no one has ever been sure the baseball is actually thrown, and there are some doubters who believe that his catcher, a heavily bearded gentleman named Josh Gibson III, palms a second baseball and smacks it in the glove at the end of the pitching motion. Then he turns to show the ball to the umpire. "Strike!" says the umpire, who insists that his employ in the Paige household as an upstairs butler has nothing to do with his play-calling. "I'm not saying that the Procrastination Pitch should not be banned," the umpire says, "but while it's legal, I've got to call 'em as I see 'em."

The great white hurler still dreams of a chance with the major leagues. "I know those black boys are awfully good," he has told a reporter from the *Southampton Sun*, "I mean *awfully* good, but I'd certainly like to 'strut my stuff' nonetheless." He has admitted that he was given a secret tryout with Los Dodgers in the spring of 1988, failed, and was driven home in his Ferrari. The color line was as strongly defined as before.

"Ol' Valise" has masked his feelings since then. When he arrives in town for a game, he often disappears to go fishing. As game time approaches, his teammates spread out through the vicinity to find him. Often, when they discover him out on the lake, they have to lure him in off his Bertram Model V fishing yacht, where he sits with whatever member of his household staff has been elected to tie on the Silver Doctors and remove such fish as the great hurler manages to hook. "Yuk!" remarks the great hurler at such moments, shielding his eyes.

Born 20 years too late . . . Josh Gibson III, star catcher of the White League, was good enough for the "bigs" but his skin was the wrong color. Unable to survive on a brainstormer's salary, he settled for a job as a stockbroker.

THE CHAMPS

"Boxing and horse racing are the only true sports," wrote ring-and-turf scribe Jimmy Cannon long ago. As the latter came to imitate the former in recent years, the primal sport of man-against-man galloped on, still dominated by its aging hero of yesteryear.

As Ali reached his 38th birthday and 252nd pound in 1980, it seemed to some that there was nothing left for him to do. He had talked frequently, even incoherently, of uniting the world through his personality, of organizing a political mechanism to spread peace and brotherhood. But most dismissed these lofty aspirations as the punch-drunk ravings of an athlete past his prime.

The pundits ate their words on the morning of October 29, 1982, when the once-and-perpetual champ unveiled his most daring scheme to date: a series of exhibition bouts with various heads of state to promote his world political platforms. As Ali told a roomful of stunned newsmen:

In roun' number five,
President Sadat won't hardly be alive.

Listen up, Mr. President Kosygin,
By roun' three, yo' head'll be leakin'.

As for that snooty Mrs. Thatcher,
I'll deck her soon as I can catch her.

And you watch, Mr. Premier Deng,
I knock you upside yo' head 'til it rung!

And so the self-styled "greatest" was off and running on a round-the-world parliament-storming tour that saw him knock out no fewer than 16 of the 17 foreign leaders he faced. "Park TKO'd in 2," "Marcos Mauled in 4," screamed international headlines.

But after the punches stopped flying and the champ tried to cash in jabs for jobs, he came up short. In one country after another, Ali was given a cool reception by humiliated dignitaries who turned him away at the doors of state dinners and barred him from top-secret conferences.

Menachem Begin reels from a solid right delivered by the Champ in round five of their fight. "If I hadn't knocked him out, he'd have talked me to death," said Ali later.

It was inevitable that the remarkable string of black heavyweight champions that had lasted nearly two decades would someday be exhausted. The Great White Hope was surely lurking just around the corner. But when he finally showed his face, the sports establishment's collective jaw dropped to the canvas. The surprising slugger made his first appearance in a heavyweight title bout with Joey Spinks, a fight considered a mere tune-up for the indomitable champion. Manuel "Beanbag" de Goya, an unheralded puncher from Guatemala, was hardly of classic stature. Standing an inch under five feet, weighing in at 312 pounds, but undeniably unblack, de Goya was immediately dubbed "The Great Wide Hope." The sobriquet was justified on the night of October 5, 1988. De Goya shocked the boxing world with a stunning 15-round decision over the baffled Spinks, who found himself trapped in his own corner time and again by a wall of flesh, and failed to land a single punch except on the Hispanic pompadour.

De Goya's win and subsequent title defenses changed the face of boxing. Shorter and slower instead of taller and faster became the name of the game. One French-Canadian challenger, Jean "Mae West" Bolduc, weighed 397 pounds, stood five inches shorter than the champ, and had a reach of seven inches. The era of the overweights had arrived.

Some sportsmen, deploring the lack of action now attending world title bouts, have begun to wonder if there isn't someone, somewhere, who might be able to get the noble art back on its feet—or rather off it. (There have been no knockdowns in world heavyweight fights since that fateful night in October 1988.) They even talk of a Great Black Hope. But the sweet science has changed. In de Goya's latest title defense against Hans-Carl "The Hippo of Flanders" Gueuse, no visible motion took place in the ring for 15 rounds, with the exception of an interminable left hook to the body thrown by the champ in the final minute. The decision was unanimous. De Goya retained the title, 1–0.

"If we can't save souls, we can save on the rent," was the Catholic response to declining attendance. Empty pews gave way to condominiums, and were typically advertised as follows: "1-apse apt, stain gls wndow, hi ceils, no hats allowed."

St P

RELIGION

RELIGION

It is October 6, 1983, and Swami Makhnamarasbanda (Local 233, International Brotherhood of Gurus) is preparing for a job action as part of his union's nationwide strike. He does not look forward to it. But thus far, management (United Temple, Retreat, and Lamaseries, Incorporated) has proved intransigent, and union leadership feels that only direct interference with the spiritual instruction process will bring them to the bargaining altar. "It is not our demands, it is your answers," union negotiator Maharishi Mahesh Yogi has said to United Temple. "That is the obstacle to perfect happiness." Makhnamarasbanda takes a deep breath, holds it for a count of four, exhales slowly and mindfully, and enters his temple.

When the original caveman first gazed at a beautiful sunset and murmured thank you, then was religion born. Something there is in the human spirit that desires to bow down before a Supreme Being—indeed, that yearns to fall prostrate on its knees in complete, utter, and adoring worship of the strength, power, and talent that we call "God." But the institution of religion during the '80s was a cauldron of idiocy, foolishness, and downright stupidity all over the world. Fortunately, by the end of it all, our nation showed signs of awakening to the One Deep Truth, thereby continuing—with her partner, God—that love affair that has kept America great for over two centuries.

Theologian Charles Colson has written, "In its color, excitement, and special effects, the Catholic church is the *Star Wars* of religions." Yet even the Obi-wan Kenobe-like Pope John Paul II found himself wondering whether or not the Force was with him—when, for example, his church's modernization plan resulted in a request by a group of nuns to use the Sistine Chapel for a pajama party.

THE INSTITUTION OF RELIGION DURING THE '80s WAS A CAULDRON OF IDIOCY, FOOLISHNESS, AND DOWNRIGHT STUPIDITY ALL OVER THE WORLD.

Meanwhile, Protestantism remained the most boring of the major religions, and Islam the most terrifying — as it proved in 1988, when the United Islamic Republic declared a *jihad*, or holy war, on Europe, Russia, and the rest of the world. It was difficult to tell whether this was a sincerely religious movement, or rather one motivated by Arab pique at the Oil Glut. Whatever the cause, it reflected very poorly on the God of Islam. One really wondered just what sort of prophet Mohammad must have been.

These were difficult years for Jews, marked by the emergence of "Realistic Gourmetism." This sect announced that they had "officially given up waiting for the Messiah," asserted that living a righteous life was "optional," and declared their intention to devote their lives to "the elimination of the bland, so-what tradition of Jewish cooking."

Such worldwide religious turmoil did much to divert attention away from the Unfathomable One, and His subtle yet inevitable Rise to the Surface. Indeed, oddball sects, specious prophets, and laughable "messiahs" appeared all over the globe during the '80s. Louise Brown, the test-tube baby, announced herself to be the Ms.iah; millions of French worshiped Kermit the Frog; a bizarre cult arose around baseball umpire Ron Luciano; several thousand persons claimed that Jesus Christ had been reincarnated as the Detroit Symphony Orchestra. At a rally at Baltimore's civic center, the Reverend Sun Myung Moon was said to have changed a glass of water into *sake*, inspiring a multitude. The entire decade was a period of desperation and gullibility, as a befuddled American nation sought hungrily for some kind — any kind — of salvation.

Fortunately, in the midst of this welter of conflicting claims, fraudulence, and delusion, one figure did emerge who, without question, was and is the True Messiah. His following by the end of the decade was relatively small, but promised to expand to include all mankind as His ineffable magnificence became known. Indeed, by 1988, the network reported a dramatic increase in the popularity of "Sea Hunt" re-reruns, and it seemed only a matter of time before the glory of Bridges the Lloyd—Savior, Swimmer Divine, Bringer of Oxygen — would become apparent to every man, woman, and child on earth.

Swami Makhnamarasbanda emerges, shaken but satisfied, from his temple. He has just passed on a quantity of bogus wisdom to his trusting pupils, confusing them with such false truths as, "Life is linear," and "Matter is real." After the strike is settled he will mend the damage, and show them the "real truth." One can only hope that he — and the world — will soon see the Real Real Truth: that of Bridges the Lloyd, before Whom all men must hold their breath.

1/15/89--POPE JOHN PAUL II'S INFALLIBILITY RECEIVED ANOTHER BLOW WHEN, CONTRARY TO HIS PREDICTION, THE STEELERS DOWNED THE SAINTS IN SUPERBOWL XXIII.

THE CHURCH MODERNIZES

"*Francamente sumus desperati*," ("Frankly, we're desperate,") concluded Pope John Paul II's celebrated 1987 encyclical *Ecclesia Modernissima* (A Very Modern Church). The feisty Slav's outspokenness may have grated on the exquisite sensibilities of the Curia, but it nonetheless expressed a grim truth. Catholicism was on the verge of ruin.

Much of the problem was the decline in the number of faithful. By 1986, for example, there were only 17 practicing Catholics in France, and all of them were at the same

Life in the "modernized" Catholic church. Father Tumulty has just told Sister Maria La Vonne that she looks really "keen" and has invited her to the Sodality sock-hop. Though they still can't marry, they can be "pinned."

time registered members of the Communist party. The rest of the once fanatically Catholic nation had either lost interest in a church that still forbade birth control at a time when the decline in orgasm made it practically and theologically academic, or had been lured away by one of the bizarre millennial religions that were sweeping Europe. In Italy, by mid-decade, Catholic clergy were the only people not worth kidnapping (although cardinals in full regalia were occasionally used as small change). Even South America, which had always been relied upon to provide large amounts of what one Vatican wag described as "canon fodder," had been enticed away by the more worldly rewards of militarism. By 1985, in Brazil alone, there were an estimated 34 million generals.

The '80s had not been kind to Holy Mother Church. The discovery in 1981 of the Red Sea Scrolls had severely damaged the credibility of the New Testament by suggesting that the Gospels were, in fact, a collection of traditional Hamitic bedtime stories. (In the Red Sea version, the Jesus character appeared as a naughty but goodhearted rabbit.) An energetic foray into the media world after the issuance of the 1982 encyclical *ViaTVcom* had largely backfired. Aimed primarily at the American faithful, the papal decree made it possible for Catholics to receive the sacraments via television. However, try as they might with elaborate sets and musical numbers, Vatican programmers were unable to give the sacraments "legs" (although confession did well in some local markets, notably New York and San Francisco), and ratings were not good. The only visible result was the virtual elimination of church attendance, which led to the widespread sale of churches and cathedrals for conversion into condominiums. Of the commercials carried by the series, the less said the better—both the recruiting campaign ("Having a great vocation out here with the Christian Brothers!") and the fund-raising drive ("A family needs afterlife insurance:

you're in good hands with Papal States.") embarrassed even the normally resilient American Catholics.

What was needed was a radical program of modernization. The church got it. In *Ecclesia Modernissima* the Pope declared that he was going to drag the clergy, kicking and screaming if necessary, into the

Hey Mary,
Sh-boom, sh-boom,
Full of Grace,
Sh-boom, sh-boom . . .

FROM THE NEW LITURGY

20th century. Priests were ordered henceforth to wear peg-leg jeans, penny loafers, and DAs. Nuns were required to sport ponytails and habits adorned with poodles. During the celebration of mass, the biretta was to be replaced by a Davy Crockett hat. Proficiency in using the hula-hoop and singing backup became mandatory requirements for confirmation, and the Lord's Prayer now began, "Hey, Daddy-o . . ." Teaching and scholastic orders were to wear berets and dark glasses at all times, while the militant and missionary orders, most notably the Jesuits, were equipped with black leather jackets and bike chains. In a simultaneous announcement, the Vatican revealed that it had set Elvis on the road to canonization by confirming his first miracle: an amazing overnight increase in the bustline of Mrs. Duane Kitto of Memphis.

Although the program attracted widespread attention and caused violent theological controversy, it was an utter failure. Plucky Pope John Paul, however, never gave up in his efforts to make the church and himself more responsive to the needs of 20th-century man. Just days before the Ethiopian armies overran south and central Italy in 1988, he issued yet another encyclical, *Ludens, Ludens, Ludens* (Games, Games, Games), declaring himself to be infallible in all matters of faith, morals, and sports.

NEW GODS

■n any age of confusion, at any time of turmoil, new dogmas promising a rock and a salvation to the shiftless masses are sure to gain adherents. In the 1980s, cult religions—creeds whose only promise was of complete soul satisfaction and surcease of sorrow—ascended to their place in the sun. They attracted young and old alike, many of whom forfeited bank accounts to the cult leaders, gave up homes and jobs, and left families behind—or dragged them along into the cults.

OSCAR WORSHIP

A balding, admonishing uncle, it stood high atop a cliff gazing resolutely out to sea, away from the fleshpots and boutiques of Hollywood. It was the 700-foot-tall Oscar of the Coast, a modern-day Colossus of Rhodes. And all over that state of rising stars and shattered dreams, people traveled to it in worship.

These were the members of the film community, who had renounced poverty and obscurity in pursuit of a new, perhaps loftier ideal. Thousands of them had sacrificed Mercedes coupes to provide the tons of reclaimed steel that were needed for the statue's construction. Their hope: born-again careers.

The great Oscar was toppled in the California slide of 1986, and today all that remains is the gigantic stone base, with its inscription:

> BEST SONG
> Joseph Brooks
> "You Light Up My Life"
> 1977

The awesome Oscar of the Coast. It stood some 700 feet tall and its head was a revolving restaurant called L'Exorciste.

WHIP INFLATION NOW

A German cult. Based upon the too-literal translation of their prophet, Gerald Ford, these members of the *deutschemarkbruderschaft* believed they could stem rampant inflation in their country through the practice of self-flagellation. Beating themselves into an economic frenzy, the 5,000-odd cultists ran through the streets of Bonn, brandishing leather whips tipped with dangerously sharp WIN buttons. Their average monthly mailings reached a peak of 600,000 letters in 1988.

YOUR CULT OF CULTS

These disgruntled dropouts from organized cults venerated other cults. They studied the minutiae of cults with a Talmudic penchant for detail. Like the Gideons and the Jehovah's Witnesses before them, they developed a scheme for reaching into the community at large. Their principal proselytizing tool was the Cult-of-the-Month Club, which offered any four creeds—and a tote bag—for only one dollar. The subscriber simply agreed to accept four more beliefs within the next year.

"Krauts love knouts," sniffed the rest of Europe as the German WIN sect flagellated themselves in an effort to lower inflation. Nevertheless, in 1985, while the annual inflation rate ran as high as 1,115 percent in The Greatest Goddam Little Piece of Heaven on God's Goddam Earth (formerly Northern Ireland), Germany's rate stuck at a modest 78 percent. Somebody must have been flogging something right.

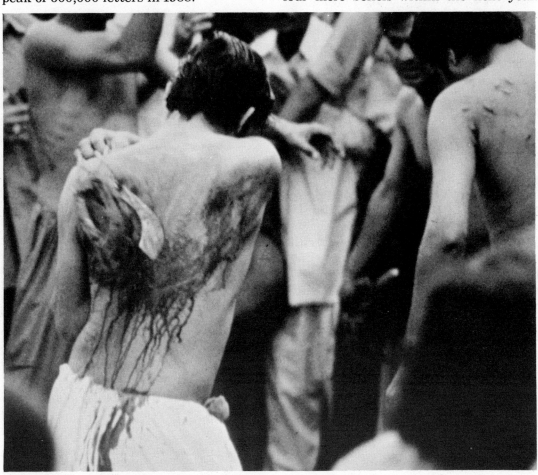

WORSHIPING THE CATHOLICS

This was not ordinary Catholic worship as practiced in Catholic churches, but the act of worshiping a Catholic. No Catholic was safe. People with Irish surnames found their houses surrounded by prostrate admirers. Cultists stole occupied confessionals. Sacrifices were made to Vikki Carr. At its height in 1985, the Catholic-Worshipers boasted approximately 200 members for every remaining Catholic.

LOUISE JOY BROWN

With the onset of her menses, Louise Joy Brown, the first successful test-tube baby, declared herself the "Ms.iah," and changed her name to Louise Joy-of-Man's-Desiring. Immediately, an estimated 7 percent of the world's Catholics rallied around her. At her shrine, Our Lady of the Extrauterine Conception, near the Cambridge, England, laboratory where she was conceived, women gathered and became spontaneously pregnant. Once a year, it is said, the original test tube, now a treasured relic, filled with a 30 percent saline solution.

To date, the Louise Brown sect's most significant contributions to Catholic dogma have been the expansion of the belief in original sin to include the idea of charmingly unoriginal sin, and the adaptation of the Fifth Commandment to read, "Honor thy tube and thy mother."

Louise herself started an order of nuns, the Sisters of Perpetual Aberration. At the convent she busied herself with simple domestic miracles: making mayonnaise perfectly every time; finding tasty meat substitutes that were inexpensive, nutritious, and appealing to the eye; designing décolleté habits called Louise Brown Tube Tops.

PAT'S PEOPLE

Ted Patrick, famous in the 1970s for "deprogramming" cultists like the Moonies, came to be worshiped as a savior. At first a reluctant prophet, Patrick eventually let the promise of power go to his head. He said: "Power corrupts. Absolute power corrupts *divinely*." Members of this cult, called "Pat's People," went through ritual Hare Krishna indoctrinations in order to be deprogrammed. The cult folded in scandal when it was found that Patrick was funneling money from his worshipers into Hare Krishna coffers to keep that religion alive. The estimated membership in 1982 was around 45,000.

THE LLOYD BRIDGES CULT

These aquatic acolytes worshiped only between 4:30 A.M. and 5:00 A.M.—the half-hour during which "Sea Hunt" was rerun. Congregating in Bridgeport, Connecticut, they were recognizable for their persistent use of double *L*s where one would do—as in "llampshade," "poulltry," and "lllllama." The Lloyd Bridges cult was trinitarian, worshiping the Father, the Son, and the Other Son. Their relics included His Tank, His Regulator, and His Fins. The cultists became notorious for buying up Baptist churches and remodeling the baptismal pools to a depth of 500 feet. The estimated membership in 1987 was reported to be 19,000.

CULT OF KERMIT

The American experience translated into foreign cults, too. The French, whose appreciation of American culture has always far exceeded that of the Americans, built a religion around the famous Muppet, Kermit the Frog.

Having found inspiration in every telecast of their exophthalmic exemplar, an estimated 700,000 Frenchmen turned out for the Hi-Holy Days ceremonies at the Pond of Notre Dame des Grenouilles near Paris. "Take, eat, for these are my legs," said

"A Bridges over Troubled Waters" was the slogan of the missionary Lloyd Bridges cult, the cornerstone of whose faith was that a new millennium would occur when He finally rose to the surface.

In Paris, this figure of the frog-martyr Saint Kermit graced the facade of the renamed cathedral of Notre Dame des Grenouilles. Note the missing legs.

Kermit to the massed admirers. And all over France, people—even non-believers—ceremonially ate frogs' legs.

Kermit's purported divinity spawned other activities. The Old Testament plague of frogs was debated endlessly, children were enrolled in schools run by orders of Amphibian nuns, fingers and toes were ritually webbed, and in country chapels ecstatic worshipers could be heard talking in long, sticky tongues.

The cult finally collapsed in 1987, owing to Kermit's chronic alcoholism.

Traditional faiths and organized religions were beset by financial and philosophical problems in the '80s, and loss of members forced many religions into mergers with one another.

Since only the most devout had remained faithful, there was often bitter disagreement over the terms of the mergers. Power struggles were rampant. The Lutheran-Hindus, centered in Germany, spent interminable hours debating whether or not leather boots (anathema to Hindus, a necessity to Lutherans) could be permitted. The German contingent finally agreed upon leatherette, as long as the boots could still be high, black, shiny, pointy, and studded all over with chromed spikes. Basing their new dogma upon the 96 million theses pinned to a church door in Madras, the Lutheran-Hindus changed their name in 1988 to Indu-Aryans.

The Swiss Calvinists and the Buddhists (the Calvinudhists) had a rocky marriage in the beginning, with two years of conferences needed to redefine the "Seven Levels." By 1986, they had managed to agree that the levels of reincarnation would range from cuckoo clock to foreign depositor, and that a person could be reincarnated as an overdraft.

The ordination of animals in the Anglican church was the subject of international controversy when the Anglicans and Animists merged in 1988. Factions within the new church argued over whether female animals could be ordained, and whether homosexual animals should be allowed to assist at mass. Basing their beliefs upon the writings of Bishop Pike, Father Flye, and Saint Bernard, the Anglicanimists gained national recognition when two trees in an Oxford quad were married by a small flock of cardinals.

The merger of Judaism and Confucianism in 1987 (the Year of the Poodle) went far more smoothly than was expected. The two ancient groups were bound by a mutual interest in Chinese food and funny alphabets. Talmudic scholars turned their attention to detailing the 57,000 ways of making hot and sour soup (without pork), and a beyarmulked dragon danced in the streets of Chinatowns everywhere, hailing the golden age of the Confused Jews.

ADIEU, PRINT

In this 1988 study, a former "writer" ekes out a living peddling "printed" matter to anyone kind enough to buy it. He is too proud to wear the usual sign: "Please help. I am totally literate."

ADIEU, PRINT

Just as a beautiful, intelligent, and graceful woman must one day die—from being run over by an insane cannibal driving a cement truck, for example—so must man's communication media suffer inevitable obsolescence and pass away. Therefore, adieu, print. Technology—which, of course, is wonderful, and makes life truly worth living—has decreed that you shall die, and who is the man who would gainsay wonderful technology? (He is assuredly not the publisher of the present work, who, for the Print section, has deemed it appropriate to reduce the space normally allotted the introductory essay by half, not just made it shorter, no, *cut it in half*.) A picture, as any moron will tell one, is worth a thousand words. Let us have pictures, then—yes, lots of pretty pictures.

Many thought print would survive the 1980s. The redefinition of "journalism" as "gossip" apparently boded well for the medium, providing it with a more honest and potentially more popular designation. Such magazines as appear on the following pages (adieu, pages! adieu, bookmarks! adieu, clever, handsome *Ex Libris* stickers!) seemed decisive proof that there were still those able to read—and write. But no, no; "the people" would rather "read" the fotonovella of *Captain Kirk Meets Bluto in Animal Planet* than the *Quixote*.

A PICTURE, AS ANY MORON WILL TELL ONE, IS WORTH A THOUSAND WORDS.

Perhaps it is just as well. After all, written language itself has become so degraded by the cheap contractions and revised spellings of the advertising world that much of what has found its way into print is unrecognizable. A society that permits the substitution of "kwik" for "quick" and "e.z." for "easy" is a society that does not deserve Shakespeare, Eliot, or Michener. Indeed, a newspaper article concerning the leisure habits of young people will soon resemble this orthographic obscenity:

> 2-day's klean, brite teen sez: "Boox 'Я' slo 'n dri. U kan thro 'em a-way. I luv T.V. 4 pix 'n fax. But gimme sum kwik, e.z. kash 2-nite, 'n I wanna n-joy a dan-d hi-fi, hav-a bru or 2, 'n snak on plen-ti o' tastee "cheez-spred"!

Therefore, adieu, print. Pictures have replaced you and with them we shall, as usual, triumph. For nothing can stop our modern, illiterate, progressive, ignorant, industrious, lazy, humane, contemptible, glorious, wretched, wonderful society, no nothing, ever, period.

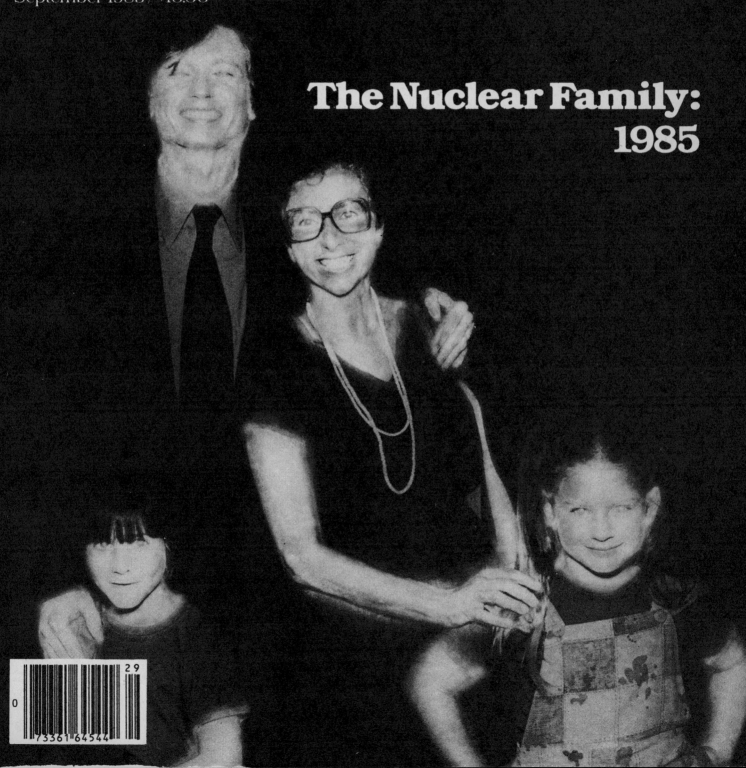

HALF LIFE

Food That Cooks Itself!

Radioluminescent Infants Make Super Nite-Lites!

Using Your Wife to Heat Your Bathwater

September 1985 / $10.00

The Nuclear Family: 1985

LETTERS

Dose, but No Cigar

Lately I haven't been feeling up to snuff, but I'm making this effort to write because there's something I want to get off my chest.

I'm a nonsmoker myself and am often inconvenienced by the tobacco habits of others. But that's not my beef. It seems to me that people who protest nuclear power don't know when they're well off.

There are no nuclear reactors in elevators, restaurants, and other public places, and I've never heard anyone complain about having to sit next to a nuclear reactor smoking a big green cigar on a bus or lighting up a smelly pipe at the next table.

I think atomic energy is a pretty good citizen compared to a lot of people.

Evan Hardell
Ausable, N.Y.

"Mute" Point

My late wife and I enjoyed your excellent article, "Mutations: There's Gold in Them Thar Rays." If it hadn't been for a heck of a lot of mutations in the past, we'd all be sightless lumps of goo sucking up bottom scum in some fetid estuary. Keep up the good work!

Benson Townley
Silver Springs, Md.

Forgive Those Who Trespass?

I think it's shocking the way criminal protestors trample all over the laws against trespass. Well, I can tell you, if I were a utility company executive, I'd figure a man's nuclear plant was his castle, and if some of these law-breaking individuals tried to storm my containment building, I'd give them some free lead shielding, one slug at a time!

The last few months I haven't been as spry as I once was, but you can bet any person or persons who messed around my plant would leave begging for some X-rays (to pinpoint the broken bones they would have gotten!).

Tom Mastrelli
Clawson, Ariz.

Health-Giving Air

O.K., O.K., so increased atmospheric radiation means more cancer. It also provides free, "natural" chemotherapy. And what with the escalating cost of... excuse me, I don't feel very well...

EDITOR'S NOTE

We can't help thinking, what with all the hoo-ha about nuclear energy, about the fix we'd be in if the same daffy dimbulbs who are grabbing all the headlines today had been around when that unknown pioneer snatched a burning branch from a lightning strike way back in caveman times and gave his fellow man fire. We can just hear the outcries now.

"Hey!" says one scruffy fellow. (I think I've seen a descendant of his before at antinuclear rallies. At least his distant ancestor could explain his appearance by pointing out that razor blades weren't going to be invented for 100 million years!) "Hey, don't you know that heat causes cancer? Why, just look at the way the skin on my hand is reddening as I hold it up to your fire!"

"Yeah," says a second, "and look at what's happening to that dinosaur steak he's put over the coals — it's turning black and it's sizzling. It's bound to be laced with carcinogenic substances!"

"Say," shouts another shortsighted caveman, "what if every single tree and bush in the world caught fire at once? I know that the odds against it are 800 trillion to one, but think of the terrible catastrophe!"

Well, I could go on, but I think you get the picture. The way I see it, we're darned lucky that our ancient ancestors had the guts to tell these uninformed critics to go take a long walk off a short land bridge! Fortunately, man has always had enough intestinal fortitude to support progress. There are plenty of nay-sayers around, but we're smart enough to ignore them.

HOROSCOPE

*The **sun** is in **Cancer** and will remain there for some time. This will be a period of growth, but it is also time to get rid of unwanted odds and ends. Cutting attachments can often be painful but necessary.*

Libra. Sept. 23-Oct. 23. The time is ripe to make a good investment. Canny Libras will choose life insurance.

Scorpio. Oct. 24-Nov. 21. Don't put off that vacation or holiday you've been planning — it's later than you think!

Sagittarius. Nov. 22-Dec. 21. You try too hard to do it all yourself. Don't be afraid to lean on others, particularly when you're not feeling your best.

Capricorn. Dec. 22-Jan. 19. Wise Capricorns learn to make allowances for others — who may be suffering from unrevealed medical problems.

Aquarius. Jan. 20-Feb. 18. A good time to plan ahead, Aquarians. Keep in mind that many arrangements are cheaper if you make them in advance.

Pisces. Feb. 19-March 20. Don't let being laid up cause you to become depressed. A spell in the hospital is a fine opportunity to unwind and take stock.

Aries. March 21-April 19. Don't let the death of a friend or close associate get you down. Chin up!

Taurus. April 20-May 20. Afraid to take the leap? Go ahead! You may have less to lose than you think!

Gemini. May 21-June 21. Loss of key people can cause headaches in the future. Take time now to make sure you have replacements lined up.

Cancer. June 22-July 22. Don't wait to put your house in order. A little preparation now can pay big dividends to loved ones.

Leo. July 23-Aug. 22. You Leos may feel off your feed, but remember: it's a great opportunity to start that diet!

Virgo. Aug. 23-Sept. 22. Making longterm plans is useful, but don't get carried away. It's today that counts!

Day of Judgment For Wind Energy

"How many deaths will it take till he knows
That too many people have died...."

Bob Dylan, "Blowin' in the Wind"

A month later, the immediate horror has subsided. But even as the demolition crews at Timbelier Island rip the last twisted shards of steel from their concrete foundations, and the families of those killed or maimed by the slashing blades of runaway Rotor No. 2 try to get on with the business of restoring normalcy to their lives, the questions remain.

Before disaster struck the huge mill 80 miles south of New Orleans, the wind energy business was already in serious trouble. Now, the pundits ask, can the various generating schemes lumped whimsically under the title "alternative energy" possibly survive what is clearly the most dramatic and damaging event in the murky 800-year history of the windmill? The answer, most thankfully agree, is no.

To be sure, human error and administrative negligence played a part in the accident. Several lives could have been saved if inspectors had spotted the cracks in the pylons holding the huge rotor to its supporting tower; the carnage undoubtedly would have been reduced had the credulous picnickers frolicking on the beach been given even 30 seconds' warning that the killer turbine had torn free of its underpinnings, and was scything a swath of doom down the grassy dunes to the Gulf below.

But in the painful—if long overdue—reevaluation going on now in even the most irresponsible of Congress' so-called pro-ecology subcommittees, more longterm areas of concern predominate.

The most pressing issue, of course, is turbine safety. The problem of how to keep 37,000 pounds of knife-edged steel from decimating everyone unfortunate enough to stray into its path has yet to be solved. And, ritual reassurances from proponents of "clean" energy notwithstanding, the fact remains that thousands more lives are snuffed out each year by the combined effects of wind and sun than by the almost immeasurably small amounts of radiation emitted by each pellet of uranium 235. Studies of such phenomena as the deadly tropical storms that churn up out of the Atlantic each summer, and the relentless scorching that threatens to turn much of the once-fertile American Midwest into a useless desert, have taken on an urgent new significance.

Behind all these questions lies the great dilemma of energy production as we move to the end of the Second Millennium. Are we ready—at last—to ignore the uninformed whimpers of those who would literally cast our fate to the winds, and to commit ourselves, once and for all, to a nuclear utopia? If so, the thirteen who perished at Timbelier Island, unlike the "many" in Bob Dylan's prophetic song, will not have died in vain.

THE FINAL EDITION

The Los Angeles Times, *once a proud bastion of West Coast journalism, declined throughout the early 1980s. The following is the last story that ever appeared in the paper. A terminally bored editor made up a headline that included all 26 letters of the alphabet and then wrote a story to fit. It appeared on March 3, 1984, as the lead (and only) story on the front (and only) page. The next morning, the two vending machines the paper still retained were empty. The illustrious* Los Angeles Times *was dead.*

Los Angeles Times

CIRCULATION: 5 DAILY   SATURDAY, MARCH 3, 1984   CC/1 PAGE /DAILY $1.75

How KGB Fly Pens, Jam TV, DC Quiz Rx

NEW YORK, N.Y.—The unfolding story of how Representative Virgil LeRoux (Marxist Media Front, Mass.) has abetted the escape of at least seven convicted KGB agents from Federal prisons in the Northeast, and how those agents have then systematically jammed network-TV news reports on the rumored death and subsequent stuffing of Soviet First Secretary Leonid Brezhnev, has given a badly needed boost to the ratings of ABC's foundering quiz show "Congressional Squares," a spokesman for the A.C. Nielsen Company told reporters here today.

Once the most popular attraction on American television, "Congressional Squares," a game-show version of the proceedings of the House Committee on Standards of Official Conduct, sagged precipitously in mid-1982 after passage of the Comprehensive Ethics Bill all but eliminated the legislative corruption that had accounted for the program's following.

"This Russian agent thing's just the prescription our ailing show needed," enthused ABC Vice-President Roone Arledge after the announcement. "Let's face it — the country's pretty bored with the Congress of Nuts. A little old-fashioned impropriety was bound to be stimulating. And Cold War-type treason? In 1984? Well, let's just say we couldn't be more pleased."

Some experts believe, however, that the "Congressional Squares" rating boomlet is likely to be short-lived. Media analyst Rona Barrett, for example, points out that Representative LeRoux will not be able to spin out his confession indefinitely. "Besides," she adds, "if the public continues to pass propositions limiting legislative spending, pretty soon Congressmen won't have any influence left to peddle, or power left to abuse."

The New York Variety Times

VOL. CXXXV.... No. 46, 655   "All the Hype That Fits in Type"   NEW YORK, WEDNESDAY, APRIL 16, 1986   Copyright © 1986 The New York Variety Times   2 DOLLARS

'HEEEEEEEERE'S JOHNNY-JOHNNY!'

Kennedy Kid Vice Carson Shines in Debut Stanza

By GROSS
Special to The New York Variety Times

BURBANK, April 15 — The faces of ABS web's top brass were wreathed in smiles this week as John F. (John-John) Kennedy, Jr. won plaudits and big numbers for his maiden week as host of their perennial late-nite "Tonight" couch-and-desk strip, formerly the "Johnny Carson Show," after its erstwhile now-and-then star.

Guests Skillfully Quizzed

Kennedy scored heavily with tasteful monologue material ("I just flew in from Hyannisport, and is my pilot tired") and proved adept at quizzing guests as varied as Angie Dickinson, Arthur Schlesinger, Jr., Suzy Chaffee, Dean Rusk, Gene Tierney, Rose Kennedy, Judith Campbell Exner, Jeff Greenfield, Lee Radziwill, and Lola Falana Kennedy. Clef-

John-John

fing by the Leonard Bernstein Band was okay.

Kennedy's rise to the top of the late-nite heap followed the much-publicized rift last year between the net and Carson, who had earlier become the first video star ever to both retire and remain on television at the same time.

As of 1984, Carson was grossing $15 million per annum for a single guest appearance on his own show.

Naysays Appearances

Carson's '85 demands included: that he not appear on the show either live or in re-runs; that his $50 million salary be sent directly to his home; that his feet be washed and kissed by the ABS board

Continued on Page A14, Column 2

MOSQUE BOMBED IN QUM; MULLAH: 'NO MOOLAH'

BY IRV
Special to The New York Variety Times

QUM, Iran, April 15 — Twentieth Century-Desert Fox brass were lower than a camel's goiter last week as re-released TC-DF cloak-and-scimitar epic "Man in the Iron Mosque" closed its sixth and final week at the Emir II with a dismal gross of 10 figs, making its Iran rerun in the Big Pomegranate a near-washout. The failure of the muezzin-meets-girl pic was laid to several factors: the usual pre-Ramadan biz dip; casting Streisand as the Moslem chick; and a recent closing of all movie houses by the

Barbra

Ayatollah Youso. TC-DF is feeling mullahed out of its moolah, but is hoping for a better sheik in Iraq.

Morris Cops Top Bernies

BY MILT
Special to The New York Variety Times

HOLLYWOOD, April 15 — William Morris reps again carried off the lion's share of the fifth annual "Bernie" Awards, honoring outstanding achievement by ten-percenters, nabbing 17 of the 25 gold-filled statuettes (representing a nude two-faced figure talking into twin phones). Agents so honored included: Bernie ("I was just thinking of you today")

Complete award fax, page A8.

Schatz — the Chutzpah Award, for keeping Kirk Kerkorian on hold for forty-five minutes; Bernie ("I'll get back to you") Nudelman — the "Let Me Be the Heavy" Award for his fistfight with Alan Ladd, Jr., over a bigger on-set bungalow for Susan Anton; Bernie ("We'll talk") Schechtman — the kudos for Best Suntan; Bernie ("I'll have you paged by the pool") Kaplan—for Taking the Best Lunch; Bernie ("You'll never work in this business again") Gargiullo — Casting Coup of the year, for finally convincing Katharine Hepburn to

Continued on Page B6, Column 1

Afghan War Is Held Over for 6th Big Week

By MORT
Special to The New York Variety Times

KHYBER PASS, April 15 — The border clash between Afghanistan and Pakistan, which opened March 11 to a mixed reception from the UUN Security Council (6 yeas, 6 nays, 4 in-betweens), rounded into its sixth successful week at the Khyber Pass, with both sides reporting growing advances. Pros-

pects look good for hostilities to continue thru the pre-holiday doldrums and into

Continued on Page B4, Column 4

N.Y. to L.A.
Pham Van Dong
Charo
Shields & Yarnell
King Khalid
The Hudson Brothers
The Panchen Lama

L.A. to N.Y.
Dr. Carl Sagan
Sha-Na-Na
Joan Didion

U.S. to Europe
Cyrus Vance
Tiny Tim
Peaches & Herb
Jerry Brown

Europe to U.S.
Aleksei Kosygin
Sandler & Young
Soupy Sales
Margaret Thatcher
Pope John Paul II
Sid Luft

Quakes Giving Turks Shakes; Insiders Are Ankling Ankara

Special to The New York Variety Times

ANKARA, April 15 — A head-for-the-hills mentality seems to have taken over here since last week's boff earthquake, which topped 8.5 on the Richter scale (compared to a weak 4.5 for last year's outing). In-the-know in-towners are ankling Ankara, expecting the usual aftershox. The only brite side is the possible hype for construction co's in the coming semester, which, however, without government funds forthcoming, could turn rebuilding hopes into a rubble bubble.

Prime Times

June '84 No. 3 — NEWS MEAT — THE MAGAZINE OF RARE SOCIETY

Two Teens Arrested for Meating School Cafeteria

SAN JOSÉ—Two high school seniors were taken into custody here last month after they allegedly spiked the school cafeteria's salad bar with slivers of Virginia Red and London Broil. Their crime came to lite after an elderly teacher complained of dizziness and clogged arteries after lunch period.

The two youths, whose names were withheld, appeared "incoherent and full" at the time of the arrest, according to school authorities, who promised a full investigation into meat abuse at the high school level.

S.G. Crax Down on Rolls

The Surgeon General must be getting bored again, 'cause one of his lieutenants, Surgeon Sergeant Mike "Meatless" Barley, dragged out his tired-ass routine about rolls and buns as "dangerous and deadly meat-related accessories" again at a press conference last week.

"I don't believe this situation," said old Grainface to the fourth estate. "My 15-year-old daughter can stroll right into any one of these pork shops and pick up a package of 'hot-dog buns' as easily as a head of cabbage. And I'll tell you, these beefed-up kids aren't using the buns for carrot cake!"

Sergeant Mike droned on for about 20 minutes about burger-buns, shake-n-bake pouches, and other cripplers of youth.

Hit Parade

Summertime, and the livin' is meaty, or so it should be. What could be so *rare* as a June Day spent eating out on the lawn when you got those ol' smokehouse cravings? Anybody *human* just wants to cool out and get sautéed up to the throat; at least, any self-respecting porker does.

But not the damn *carnies*, hungry pals. They're chewing on goddamn vegetables and corn-oiling their copter blades, just gettin' ready to hassle some peaceful meatheads. These pathetic potatoheads got nothing better to do than chase our asses all over the country.

Here's the casualty list for last month:

- **200 shoulders** of prime pork seized from a freezer in **Norfolk, Virginia**. Twelve porkers busted by Surgeon Stormtroopers.
- **24,000** precut, premeasured N.Y. Prime patties confiscated by S.S. Special Squad in major assault on the **New York Strip**. Twenty-seven arrested after month-long steakout.
- **540** freshly picked whole steers purchased in an **Omaha** diner by two carnies posing as on-the-lamb meaties.
- **102,000 linx** of sausage, uncased, by Surgie pursuit plane after leggers began shooting one another at a beef-complex near the old **Chicago** stockyards. Twelve busted, two hospitalized.
- **Sentenced:** "Shank" Stewart, alleged one-time associate of the Butcher of Bensonhurst, to a minimum two-year rehabilitation program at Soy House in upstate **New York**.

FCC Clamps Lid on Meaty Lyrix

WASHINGTON, D.C.—The Federal Communications Commission has just issued new guidelines for radio stations regarding airplay for songs containing meat lyrix. The Rev. Jesse Jackson masterminded the crusade for meatless airwaves. Citing recent hits like "Meat Me in St. Louis," "Stoned Sole Picnic," and "Vealings," the Chicago-based leader spearheaded a nationwide "leave-your-radio-at-home" boycott that brought pressure on the lily-livered commissioners to issue the guidelines. Going beyond the mere banning of certain songs, station programmers are urged to listen carefully for "code words" associated with the meat-rock underground: "tender," "tough," and "blue," for example. Commissioner Jack Comstock commented, "Let's face it, everyone knows the code words. Look at phrases like "hot sauce." Now, at first we thought "Hot Sauce in My Pants" was merely sexual, but this situation is the *(continued page 41)*

P.I. Adviser

Dog-Gone Beefed!

Q: I want you to settle a bet: this friend of mine and I got really beefed the other nite and he thought it would be hip to get my dog beefed, too. So we dropped a few linx in his veggie dish and he ate it all up. My friend says that the dog got beefed, but I say that only people can get beefed. Who gets the 10 bux?

—S.C., Waterford, Conn.

A: You lose. Treat your buddy to a burger.

Between the Buns

Q: My old lady has this way-out theory about sex and beef that I'd like to run by you. She claims that sometimes when we do burgers or thumbbits before sex that she comes close to having an orgasm and that once she even had one! I say that this is baloney, and that she just uses the meat as a psychological crutch 'cause she's hung up and that anyway, she's lying because some friend of hers once had two orgasms and she's trying to get even. What do you think?

—G.O., Tempe, Ariz.

A: *Lots of chix claim that beef can get them close to God, but it's also a convenient excuse. You and your ladyfriend should definitely talk this out, because you should occasionally be able to enjoy sex without getting all porked up first. Happy hamhox!*

CLASSIFIED

The 1983 meat ban spawned a huge meat-ingesting subculture and the subculture spawned its own irreverent journal, Prime Times.

Over 30,000 Attend Third Annual Fred Convention

The monthly magazine for people called Fred

FRED

MAY 1988 UM$23.50

Can a Woman Be a FRED?

FRED Forum

Future FREDs of America

The Joy of FRED

FREDs on Parade

FRED Like Me

FRED

Volume 4   No. 5   May 1988

THE MONTHLY MAGAZINE FOR PEOPLE CALLED FRED

FREDitorial

Being named Fred carries with it certain responsibilities. One constantly finds one-self faced with the inevitable Fredisms: "I bet your dog is man's best Fred," "I love you, but can't we just be Freds?" and the ineluctable "Yabadabadoo, Freddy boy, how's Wilma and Pebbles?"

I certainly do not oppose the use of our name by reputable businesses. I proudly bear the same name worn by Fred University, FRED magazine, and what has become known as "Fred art." I admire the "avant-Fred" movement, respect boox like *A Fred for All Seasons,* and welcome the renewed interest in dancing the Freddie. But the new Fred from Ford is anything but a better idea. Not only does this lemon of a car discredit our name, but it also takes advantage of a captive Fred audience. And I'd be extremely upset with that new Broadway musical *Fred!* if not for its smash success. I understand the demand for personalized Fred toiletries, but when ruthless businessmen introduce an utterly appalling and terrible tasting candy bar called "Oh! Fred," I question whether some agency should not be created to develop guidelines for what produx our name may represent.

Maybe then I'd be able to return to the comforts of battling off ludicrous requests to change the name of our "Letters to FRED" column to "Letters to the FRED-itor." Or insipid callings of "Are you Freddy for love?"

HONK IF YOU ARE FRED!

Bumper stickers. Also "West Virginia is for Freds," "Fred and Proud," and "Think Fred." Send $22 for catalog to Fred-Stickers, Fredericktown, MO.

CONTENTS

Articles & Features

Annual Freddie Awards 42
Fred Forum 53
Fred Foundation 69
Fred Mertz Scrapbook 92
Interview with Phred the Terrorist . . 143
Who Was the First Fred? 188

Fiction

The Fredding of America 196

Humor

The Gospel According to Fred 243

Fashion

Fall Fashion for Freds 73
The New Fred Look 101

Departments

Ask Fred 3
Our Foreign Freds 7
Letters to Fred 17
Fred Hall of Fame 24
Fred of the Month 38
Freds on Fred 254

Freddy Breen

ASK FRED

Dear Fred:

My wife and I are very concerned about our daughter. Over the course of a year, she became quite close to a charming young man whom we have always known as Fred. Of course we encouraged the relationship, but last week, when she showed us their marriage certificate, it troubled us to find that his real name is Alfred. For generations we've had pure-bred Freds in the family. What will this Alfred do to our lineage?

Name Withheld upon Request

Dear Fred:

Fred is more than a name. Fred is a way of life. Whatever your new son-in-law's true appellation, if he's a Fred in need, he's a Fred indeed.

—Eds.

FRED LIKE ME

My name is not Fred, but for years those possessing that name fascinated me. Their unique lifestyle, culture, and the particular problems they face just because they are Freds became my consuming interest. In the course of my studies, I traveled the world, speaking with Freds of every nationality and creed. But during all this time, I knew in my heart that there was only one way to capture the Fred experience, to know just what it means to spend every second of every day under the specter of a name you can't escape. I had to become a Fred.

The process of conversion was slow and difficult. I first had to move to a town where no one knew my name—but that was the easy part. Then came the hours changing all the monograms on my hand-kerchiefs and sewing new name tags into my shirts. I was beginning to have doubts that I might be taking things too far, that I might never be (Continued on page 200)

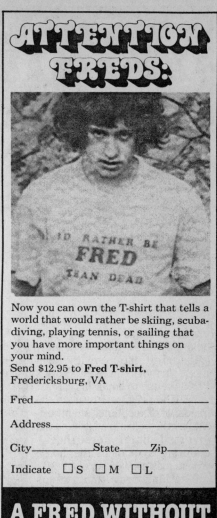
FRED CONVENTION

It was the dawning of the Fred Generation as more than 30,000 Freds attended the third annual Fred Convention last week in Philadelphia.

From every part of the country, convention-eers poured into "The City of Brotherly Fred" to delight over graphs showing the increasing number of Freds named each year, to view such cinematic classics as *The Three Faces of Fred*, and to pass resolutions advocating immediate passage of the Equal Fred Amendment calling for equal protection under the law for all Freds, regardless of last name or middle initial. Fred Freeman, chairman of the gathering, addressed the convention, insisting that "... to unite these fractured Freds, we must look to the Fred among us who will lead us into the Age of Fred. For this reason, we have decided to be (Cont. on page 207)

From the publishers of FRED:

GEORGE

Appearing on newsstands January 1989. Tell your friends.
Charter subscriptions now available.

CONSOLIDATED FRED

FRED! CALL ON LINE ONE!

DIAL-A-FRED
800-555-FRED

WWWD

THURSDAY, MARCH 24, 1988

VOL. 156 NO. 53

UM$6.50

Foreign wide

PARIS — For her fall collection, Laurence Charbin has come up with something MONU-MENTAL—chic mountains of accordion pleats.

Eye Eye:
Horse Sense, 3-Legged Style

"I don't think he was on anything," said **Whippy Morris,** committee chairman of the Exceptional Man o' War Veterans Ball, as he surveyed some 500 jockeys, trainers, breeders, and owners who had worked with the beloved horse and were now gathered at the Seventh Regiment Armory on New York's Park Avenue to honor his career.

The drug issue was on the minds of Exceptional's enthusiasts as they clustered around the inverted floral horseshoe— enduring symbol of the horse whose luck always ran out.

"This drug thing keeps coming up," worried **Angel Vania,** the internationally respected — and impeccably huge—Argentinean trainer who spent a year coaxing the plucky thoroughbred through his crushing 1983 Triple Crown defeat. "When will it go away?" he asked.

"Those of us who rode him knew it wasn't drugs that made him limp along," noted jockey **Steve Cauthen,** noticeably and fashionably older and grossly fat.

"It was his exceptional determination—and his three legs," agreed **Leslie Curry II,** expansive owner of Leslie Curry Farm, where Exceptional Man o' War has been retired to stud, commanding the lowest fees in the history of racing and producing new generations of curiously deformed but lovable horses.

C.Z. Guest, effortlessly older than everyone else, was enraged at the idea of any horse—even Exceptional Man o' War—being given drugs. "It's outrageous," she glared, while her husband Winston nodded his head as tho to concur. "If you have to drug a three-legged horse, you might as well get a four-legged horse!"

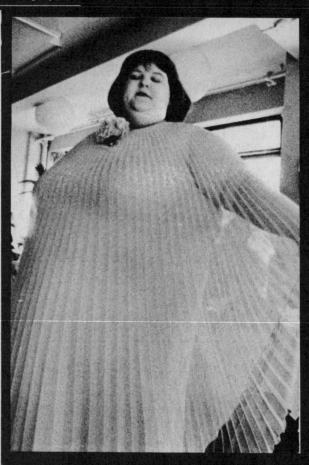

Exceptional

TODAY

Belt business declining
P. 11

●

Macy's — World's Largest Store hires World's Largest Clerx
P. 7

●

Padded body stockings on horizon
P. 29

●

Milan designers show macro-minis
P. 31

●

Waddle into Fall P. 43

"The Fat Look" Spells Big Sales For 'Dress' Makers

NEW YORK—The dress, long forgotten in the years of workers' overalls, the inside-out look, and the fascination for such materials as Sheetrock and plastic garbage bags, is expected to make an emphatic comeback this fall, according to major retailers, who cite the challenge of creating an utterly shapeless silhouette as the cause.

"We call it a 'dress' to evoke all the glamour and chic of traditional feminine fashion," said Mervin Lansky, executive vice-president of Saks Fifth Avenue. "The 1988 woman, mountainously obese and extraordinarily old, remembers. She wants something she can call a dress, and we're going to give it to her."

"What we're selling here is any length of yard goods that will do the trick," explained Borden Cook, Bloomingdale's senior vice-president for sales promotion. "Fat women in their dotage are characteristically lonely, shy about sex and romance, sick, dependent, and feeble-minded," he said. "They are shown off to their best advantage when lots of cloth is draped around them."

"In the 'dress,' we think we've got something really big," commented Jerald Plum, senior vice-president for marketing and research at Lord & Taylor. The store has commissioned leading designers to come up with purses to complement the new style. Its "Old Bags for Old Bags" line creates the look of pocketbook, clutches, and handbags from years past, including a painstakingly researched and lovingly reproduced version of the 1983 Shape-of-Things-to-Come tote, which is expected to win the coveted Halston Fashion Critix Circle Award.

Food shortages caused a vogue for fat as reflected in the perennial mirror of fashion, <u>Wide Women's Wear Daily.</u>

Liz Smith at the Gridiron ■ Rex Reed on Existential Libel

The Situation Tragedy: Soap Plus Hubris ■ Hot Stuff from Sin City

COLUMBIA
GOSSIP
REVIEW

JANUARY–DECEMBER 1989 • UM$30.00

NATIONAL MEDIA MONITOR / SITCOMS • VARIETY • SOAPS • COPSHOWS • SPORTS

Taylor

DeNiro

Bryant

Kissinger

NEW YEAR SPECIAL!

WHERE ARE THEY NOW? '89

All The Stars of Yesteryear —
In, Out, Alive, Dead!

Reagan

07

0

71486 71486 02811

WHERE ARE THEY NOW?

Anita Bryant

Mrs. Bryant apologized to the nation in 1983 for her outspoken opinions, admitting that she had "confused homosexuality with heroin addiction."

Robert DeNiro

The enormously successful actor's career came to an abrupt end when, while filming in Hollywood, he accidentally murdered co-star Jon Voight during a take. Mr. DeNiro is now serving a 30-year sentence for manslaughter.

Henry Alfred Kissinger

Rebuffed, discredited, and disowned even by his most ardent Washington supporters after his unprecedented 1984 attempt to simultaneously run for president of the United States, prime minister of Israel, premier of Egypt, and chancellor of West Germany (he failed to be nominated for any office), Kissinger, former U.S. Secretary of State and advisor to presidents Nixon and Ford, had by 1986 found his influence gone and his lucrative publishing, TV, and academic sinecures dried up. Divorced once again, now as fearful of publicity as once he had been avid for it, Kissinger all but disappeared from public view. In 1988, a Los Angeles TV newsman discovered him working in the K&K Mart, an Encino, California liquor store he co-owned with former South Vietnamese Marshal Nguyen Cao Ky.

Ronald Reagan

In an effort to boost his sagging polls, Mr. Reagan dyed his hair white and tied himself to a lock to prevent vessels from entering the Panama Canal. Merchant ships respected his views and made detours around South America; the subsequent delays created mass shortages on the West Coast. Voters repaid Mr. Reagan's patriotic fervor by ignoring him during the 1980 elections and for several years at the lock.

Cleveland Amory

A longtime champion of animal causes, Cleveland Amory was in 1987 presented with a classically '80s crisis of conscience when he contracted cancer, the only known cure for which is the cranial fluid of baby harp seals. Opting for his own survival, Mr. Amory traveled to Prince Edward Island, where he personally dispatched the seal that was to save his life. He now lives in Northern Southern California and devotes himself to the cause of endangered vegetables.

Ralph Nader

A crusader—some said a meddler—in the area of consumer affairs, Mr. Nader was regarded as the guiding spirit behind the 98th Congress, commonly known as the Congress of Nuts. Having masterminded the Year of the Total Recall (1984) in which Congress ordered the recall of everything manufactured in the U.S. in 1983, Nader became increasingly reclusive. Information about him became likewise scanty, but it was said that he would not leave his room for fear of auto emissions and other pollutants in the air, that he remained strapped to his bed all day by several safety belts, and that—afraid of contracting cancer—he would neither eat nor allow his hair to be washed or his fingernails to be clipped. Some time in 1985 he disappeared and was presumed to have died, although there are rumors that he lives in a welfare hotel in Vegas called the Sahara. His estate, some $38, is still in probate.

Bjorn Borg

A legendary figure in the days before tennis became a contact sport, Borg met an untimely end at Wimbledon in 1985. Known as a shrewd exploiter of his commercial potential, the superstar allowed more and more of his clothing—and eventually his skin—to carry advertisements. During a particularly grueling set against seven-year-old Mickey Austin of the U.S., the Swedish player collapsed and died. The coroner gave the cause of death as epidermal asphyxiation, and explained that Borg had literally "endorsed himself to death."

Werner Erhard

On a "mission of mercy" to the starving nation of Chad in 1981, Erhard chose to land in the northernmost part of the country, the area most devastated by drought. Erhard's landing attracted a group of curious natives to whom he addressed an impassioned plea, through an interpreter, to "redefine hunger" and "take responsibility for your own starvation." His audience seemed impressed by his speech and, after a brief conference among themselves, ate him.

Donna Summer

Miss Summer, a distinguished contralto and political activist, launched her career in earnest when she sang the *Disco Missa Solemnis* at the Funeral of Terence Cardinal Cooke. Several brilliant achievements followed, including the legendary disco *Das Rheingold* at Bayreuth in 1984. But her star diminished somewhat when she began to be identified with the old New Left pro-Army movement. A high moment in this stage of her career was her rendition, at the 1987 March for the Pentagon, of "We Shall Overrun (Some Day)." In 1988, Miss Summer left serious music and politix to found Love to Love You Jesus Church at a commune named Mondo Disco in the Amazon jungle.

Arnold Palmer

Mr. Palmer was wounded by a furious marksman on the 14th hole of the 1983 Patti Smith Open for "not knowing enough about the Kennedy assassination."

Jacques-Yves Cousteau

In his search for higher ratings, Mr. Cousteau tried a series of different formats for his TV series, finally settling on a talk show in which interviews were conducted underwater. The breakthru in communication with dolphins brought new guests to his show, but, during one particularly uninteresting interview in March 1987, Mr. Cousteau fell asleep and became entangled in the nets of a Russian tuna fleet. Before the loss could be discovered, Mr. Cousteau was processed along with the catch. Cans of this batch—possibly containing parts of the marine explorer—became a much-sought-after delicacy.

George Plimpton

Mr. Plimpton expired under Haystack Calhoun while researching a book on professional wrestling.

Literature may have died in the second
half of the 1980s, but it did not go peacefully, as the following excerpts demonstrate.

Joseph Sarian: Catch-88

The Linden Press surprised what was left of the literary establishment when, late in the fall of 1987, it announced the forthcoming publication of Catch-88, *by Joseph Sarian, the true author of* Catch-22. *The memorable opening paragraphs of the novel – Sarian's second –are reproduced below.*

It was love at first sight.

The first time Heller saw Joe Sarian's manuscript he fell madly in love with it.

Now Sarian was in the hospital with the idea that he fell just short of being Heller. He was puzzled that he wasn't quite Heller. If he was Heller he would have written a good book, two bad books, and a bad play. If he wasn't Heller he wouldn't be Heller and he wouldn't have to think about it. But this always just falling short of being Heller made him feel crazy.

They came every day, the man with slow quick eyes and a quick slow mouth, named Doctor Master Charge, and his companion, the efficient and inefficient Nurse Visa. They seemed annoyed when Sarian described them this way and called them by these names.

"Still no change?" Doctor Master Charge demanded.

"All I have is a hundred dollar bill," said Sarian.

"Give him another bag of change."

Nurse Visa made a note to give Sarian another bag of change, and the two of them went away. Sarian suspected they would kill him if they didn't decide not to kill him.

It was actually terrible in the hospital except for the dead lawyer under Sarian's bed. To somebody who didn't have to worry about being Heller, the dead lawyer under Sarian's bed might have seemed like just a dead lawyer under Sarian's bed, but as far as Sarian was concerned the dead lawyer under Sarian's bed was really an asset. Every night Sarian got a phone call from someone named Simon Schuster, who would say, "Has our lawyer gone over those papers with you?"

"What lawyer?"

"Our lawyer. The one with the papers."

"What papers?"

"The papers you're supposed to go over with the lawyer."

"If there isn't any lawyer how can he have papers?"

"I'm telling you there is a lawyer."

"If he doesn't have papers how can he go over papers with me?"

"I'm telling you there is a lawyer with papers."

"I don't believe you."

"Will you stop that?"

"Who is this?"

"What do you take me for?"

"Is this Simon Schuster?"

"Will you stop calling me that? It's irritating."

"You see? I told you you were crazy."

One night just before dawn during the Great Blitz to promote Heller's new bad book, while the dead lawyer's papers blew around Sarian's room like the white ghosts of papers he might have signed if he hadn't been too crazy to sign papers, Sarian suddenly remembered everything. Years ago, the dead lawyer had tried to convince Sarian that Sarian was a bomber pilot who was crazy and was claiming to have written a first novel by Heller, a curly-haired man who was crazy. The lawyer wanted to pay Sarian to sign some papers.

"If I'm crazy enough to let Heller put his name on a book I didn't write," said Sarian cagily, "then how can I be held legally liable under a legal agreement I make while I'm crazy?"

"You're not that crazy," said the lawyer. "If you were that crazy, how could you have written the book?"

"Exactly. So why should I even be involved?"

"For profit. Think of it as extra flight pay," wheedled the lawyer. "But you have to promise not to say anything until all the people who are alive now are dead."

"When will that be?"

"1988," said the lawyer, who was under a lot of personal strain and was only guessing. ∎

Truman Capote: Answered Prayers

The following fragment by Truman Capote, which surfaced in 1981, shows to what lengths —the adoption of a completely different literary style —the author went to break a monumental writer's block that first developed in the 1960s during the writing of Answered Prayers. *The eagerly awaited novel was finally published in 1986.*

It was morning, and had been morning for some time, and he was waiting for the plane. It was difficult to speak.

"Can you see all right?" the attendant asked as they approached the ticket counter.

"It's O.K. unless the bandages slip," he said. "Then it's all fuzzy."

"How do you feel?"

"A little wobbly."

"Does it hurt?"

"Only when I sit down."

He thought about the railway station at Karabük and the headlight of the Simplon-Orient cutting the dark now, and he thought about his enemies and how he wished he had them laid out across the tracks. They would make a long row. Perhaps a mile. Too many, maybe. But at least they had always picked the finest places to have the fights. The tea place in the Plaza Hotel with the palms. The Bistro in Beverly Hills. That was where Jerry Zipkin came out of the dark restaurant gloom that time, blinking his eyes, and he had hit him right along the chops, twice, hard, and when the Social Moth —that was what Johnny Fairchild called him, wasn't it, old cock? —didn't go down he knew he was in a fight. Swifty Lazar broke that one up, and he thought of how clean and white Swifty's hands had been coming between them, and he wondered how many bars of soap had gone into keeping them that way, and he was thinking of asking Swifty, and would have if the Social Moth had not been screaming like the bombing officer that summer evening who had been caught up on the wire at Mons.

Swifty, about his size too, a sawed-off Purdy, though he had not read a book, had mixed it up with some true contenders, though probably not Turgenev. He had driven those immaculately clean hands into the chops of Otto Preminger, who was a movie director with a domed head with not much in it except a German accent. He wished he had seen that one, which was at El Morocco, which was a good place to fight, with the palm trees and the high ground off the dance floor where the band played. He liked Swifty's left hook. If you fight a good left hooker, sooner or later he will get his left out where you can't see it, and in it comes like a brick. Life is the greatest left hooker so far, though they say the cleanest ever thrown was Swifty Lazar's.

"Smoking or nonsmoking?" the official asked him. He answered through the bandages. He asked for a window seat. Just then it occurred to him that when the stewardess came by with the tray of steamed towels and the tongs to grip them he could not use the fine hot face towels because of the bandages on his face. It came with a rush; not as a rush of water nor of wind, but of a sudden evil-smelling emptiness.

He thought about being alone in the motel room in Akron with the big table lamps, having quarreled in Memphis, and how he had started his enemies list, and how long it was, and how he had used the Dewey catalog system to arrange it in the green calfskin notebooks. Under K there was Stanley Kauffmann, who had written forty unproduced plays and ten unpublished novels, which had wrecked him just about as much as any other thing had wrecked him, but it did not stop him from trying to wreck people who were writing true stories about Christmas in Alabama and how they hung the mule from the rafters. Under R he had Ned Rorem, who had a head shaped like John Dillinger's, who wrote untrue and snide, and Tynan, under T, Kenneth Tynan, who had worn the same seersucker overcoat since the year the dwarfs came out on the Manzanares along the Prado road, and who wrote snide about his party in the Plaza where John Kenneth Galbraith had danced the Turkey Trot. Under A he had Dick Avedon, who had hung snide two portraits of him in the exhibition that had him young in the first and like an old goat in the other. He thought how good the notebooks felt to the touch, and how he could buy fill-ins at Cartier when the lists became too long, and how he could look in them when the time came. Vengeance went in pairs, on roller skates, and moved absolutely silently on the pavements.

He looked through the eye-holes at the standbys. They would begin to call them soon enough, and some of them would sit in coach. He had sat in coach once. But that was when he was beginning, and now he liked the face towels and the tongs to grip them, and the crèpes with shrimp within and the tall green bottles of California Pinot and the seats that went back when you pushed the button. They had the buttons in coach but they did not have the hot towels and the other things. So when the time came and he had to work the fat off his soul and body, the way a fighter went into the mountains to work and train and burn it out, he didn't go into coach. He went to the Fat Farm, where they took his face and lifted it, and took a tuck in his behind as well, and they put the bandages on afterwards. The sprinklers washed the grass early in the morning and the doctors had taken his vodka martinis away from him, and later on, up in the room, they took the cheese away from him, too.

He thought about the people in the notebooks he wished were not there. They were the ones who cut him the way Ford Madox Ford had cut Hilaire Belloc at the Closerie des Lilas. Except that it was a mistake and it was Aleister Crowley, the diabolist, Ford was cutting. Well, Ford said he cut all cads. But then he was not a cad. He wrote things simply and truly that he had heard at the dinner tables when he sat with the very social and listened with the total recall that was either 94.6 or 96.8 percent, he never could remember which. The very social liked to talk about each other, but they did not understand him when he wrote about this and wrote about what they talked about at the Côte Basque and about the bloody sheet that was tossed out a window of the St. Regis Hotel, which had the great King Cole mural in the bar. So they cut him. Slim Keith, Marella Agnelli, Pamela Harriman, Gloria Vanderbilt, Gloria Guinness, Anne Woodward, who had gone out a window, cut him, and so did Babe Paley, whom he loved and who called him "daughter." He knew he would never be invited to dine with Mr. Paley under the great tiger painting at the polished table that reflected the underside of the silverware. He tried not to think about that. You had to be equipped with good insides so that you did not go to pieces over such things. It was better to remember that the difference about the very social was that they were all very treacherous. Almost as treacherous as the very gauche were boring. Lee Radziwill! The Princess who looked fine in jodhpurs although she never wore them that he could remember had a fine nose and a whispery way of talking. She had told him how Arthur Schlesinger had thrown Gore Vidal out of the White House onto Pennsylvania Avenue, which was the length of two football fields away from the front steps, a long toss for anyone, but which was logical enough if you knew what a great arm Schlesinger had and how he had gripped Vidal by the laces and spiraled him. He had remembered because it was a good story, and it told about Arthur

Schlesinger's great arm and the proper way to grip Vidal if you had to throw him a long distance. So he had told the story in an interview in Playgirl, *which was not as good a publication as* Der Querschnitt *or the* Frankfurter Zeitung, *but had a substantial number of readers anyway, and so Vidal sued him. The Princess did not support him. She said she could not remember telling him such a thing, which meant that she was treacherous, either that or that she had a recall of .05 or 1.6, he couldn't decide which, which was not a great talent. He decided he would not take her to Scgrunz that Christmas where the snow, which he had never skied, was so bright it hurt your eyes when you looked out from the weinstube.*

It was difficult to get him into the plane because of what they had done to him in the Fat Farm operating room, but once in he lay back in the seat and they eased a cushion under him. He winced when the plane swung around and with one last bump rose and he saw the staff, some of them, waving, and the Fat Farm beside the hill, flattening out as they rose. He tried not to think about the hot towels and the tongs. He remembered that he was a new man again, his face lifted and perky as a jackal's under the bandages and his rear end tucked up and river-smooth. They had drawn him true and taut, so that his skin was as drumhead tight as the tuna's he had caught at Key West and eaten with long-tipped asparagus and a glass of Sancerre with Tennessee Williams sitting opposite. Que tal? Tennessee, and he wished he had been named after a state too, perhaps South Dakota, or Utah even, and not with a name shared by that peppery man who sold suits in Kansas City.

The plane began to climb and they were going to the east, it seemed. They were in a storm, the rain as thick as if they were flying through a waterfall, and then they were out, and through the plane window he suddenly saw the great, high, shadow-pocked cathedral of Studio 54 with the mothlike forms dancing, the hands clapping overhead, and the barechested sweepers, who built up their crotches with handkerchiefs, sweeping up the old poppers with long-handled brooms. And then he knew that this was where he was going. He thought about the smooth leather of the banquettes under his rear end and how he would look out and think about his enemies. We will have some good destruction, he thought. ∎

Gabriel Garcia Marquez: El Castillo de Tremarric

In an effort to broaden his readership, the celebrated South American author began to experiment with the fotonovella form. In 1988 he published the first Hispano-Gothic novel, a sprawling saga of a beautiful Puerto Rican girl shipwrecked on the rockbound coast of Cornwall in the early part of the 19th century.

THE BEST AND THE LAST

The New York Variety Times Media Revue
*discontinued its regular best-seller list early in 1987, largely because of the fact that, in the previous
year, only seven new books were published. In its Sunday, December 31, 1989, issue, however, the
NYVTMR did present the following literary recap of the 1980s.*

Best-Selling Boox: 1980–1989

1   **DEAD!** by Piers Paul Read. The gripping story of a group of passengers who fail to survive the crash of a DC –10 jetliner in the Canadian Rockies.

2   **THE LUDLUM FORMULA,** by Richard Marek. An intricate yarn about the writing, publishing, and promoting of suspense novels.

3   **EL CASTILLO DE TREMARRIC,** by Gabriel Garcia Marquez. A Spanish-language fotonovella about a beautiful Puerto Rican girl shipwrecked on the rock-bound coast of Cornwall in the early 19th century.

4   **ARE YOU DEPRESSED YET? NO, I'M STILL DEPRESSED,** by Dr. Eric Berne. A chatty treatise on pre- and post-coital melancholy.

5   **THE KENNEDY TEETH,** by Dr. Jack Chachkes. An intimate, straight-from-the-mouth memoir by the orthodontist who molded the smiles of three generations of America's best-known political family.

6   **1984!** by Lawrence Hauben and Bo Goldman. The fotonovelization of the Michael Curb film.

7   **IF LIFE IS A DREAM, HOW COME I CAN'T GET TO SLEEP?** by Erma Bombeck. Further exercises in domestic irony by a master of domestic irony.

8   **THE FREDDING OF AMERICA,** by Fred Friederich. The publisher of FRED magazine — and the founder of the International Fred Movement — reveals his blueprint for a "political and spiritual renaissance" in the United States.

9   **BLAND AMBITION,** by John Dean. The media analyst probes the executive venality that led to the Waltergate scandal and the demise of CBS.

10   **DOING NOTHING,** by Joan Didion. The most laconic novel yet by one of America's most tight-lipped writers.

11   **THE PSEUDO-FRENCH CHEF,** by Julia Child. The art of haute cuisine in a near-foodless society.

12   **HITLER SAID THE DARNEDEST THINGS,** by John Toland. The author continues his "up close and personal" look at the Fuehrer.

13   **ANSWERED PRAYERS,** by Truman Capote. A nostalgic look back at the gossip of the mid-1960s.

14   **I DON'T KNOW ANYTHING ABOUT MEDICINE, BUT I KNOW WHAT I LIKE,** by Mary Baker Eddy. The devotional find of the decade!

15   **MUMMY DEAREST,** by John-John Kennedy. A bittersweet, sometimes acid tribute by a devoted son to his globe-trotting mom.

FOOTNOTES

The following worx, altho not qualifying for the decade's best-seller list, made major literary news during the '80s:

Norman Mailer's "Why Are We in America? " in which the author denounces Diana Trilling, Jose Torres, thumb-wrestling, Gloria Steinem, divorce, Ernest Hemingway, booze, gun control, and writing in general; and espouses masturbation, the U.S. Army, insurance premium collectors, Gloria Steinem, and over-the-counter sex aids.

William Styron's somewhat autobiographical novel, "Hunky-Dory," about the good life in Martha's Vineyard, emphasizing raising rabbits, lively dinner-table conversations in which the common agreement is that the Europeans got everything they deserved, strawberry-picking, Sunday church picnics, belly-laughs with Art Buchwald, and skinny-dipping with Lillian Hellman.

Jacqueline Bouvier Onassis's tantalizing memoir, "My Troubled Dawns," which disappointed an eager readership by concentrating entirely on the author's admiration of George Walsh, her longtime Secret Service employee, and how splendidly he cared for the children when he took them to Central Park. The opening line of the book ("I think I'll tell you about George Walsh and how splendidly he cared for the children when he took them to Central Park") was voted by the Critix Circle in 1986 "the most disappointing opening line of the year."

MUSIC 'N DRUGS

Dimitri Oliver, suspected mastermind behind a chain of "meathead" shops, is arrested by the surgeon general's "carnies" after allegedly selling a lamb chop to an undercover agent.

MUSIC 'N DRUGS

It is morning, somewhere in the United States, at the start of the tumultuous decade. In a sunny bedroom a teenage girl awakes, reaches out to a bedside radio, and fumbles with the dial. All manner of cacophony pour forth: sounds she calls "country," "jazz," "heavy metal," "R & B," and "pop." Finally, she finds what she is looking for. Music fills the room. "Music"? Our teenager might be puzzled by the distinction. For, to her, it is merely . . . "disco."

With the '80s came the diminuition and, finally, the disappearance of what psychologist David Cassidy has called "the confusion of choice." Like the music that came to dominate it so completely, this was a decade of simplicity, directness, and straightforward Yankee honesty—one in which fewer and fewer options or decisions came between us and the fundamental pleasures of life: eating, loving, driving. When historians write the final screenplay for the history of the '80s, they will specify disco for the soundtrack. But much of the movie will be about resistance to disco itself.

It is easy to forget that disco began strictly as a form of dance. Indeed, the term derives from the word "discotheque," a nightclub where audio-discs were once played and where patrons—usually homosexuals or Colored People—danced. It was not until the untimely death of Terence Cardinal Cooke in May 1982, and the subsequent state funeral, that disco began its "long boogie" to preeminence. Leonard Bernstein's pioneering *Disco Missa Solemnis* brought together soloists Donna Summer and Rod Stewart and a choral contingent featuring many of the best-known names in contemporary music. (The contralto section alone included Sister Sledge, Peaches and Herb, and the Village People.)

> **THE FINAL SCREENPLAY FOR THE HISTORY OF THE '80S...WILL SPECIFY DISCO FOR THE SOUNDTRACK.**

Classical composers from Monteverdi to Milhaud were widely reinterpreted—often it took no more than the addition of a "funky" bass line and that inescapable disco drumbeat to make so esoteric an artist as Arnold Schoenberg accessible to the millions. In 1984, the Bayreuth Festival unveiled a disco *Ring* cycle, bringing radical new meaning to the posturings of

Siegfried (unremittingly gay) and to the character of the Niebelungen (irremediably black). It remained only for a great American musical institution to provide the final stamp of approval: in 1985, the Juilliard School of Disco revamped its entire curriculum, adding courses in "Percussion Since Ralph Macdonald," "The Esthetics of Multi-Tracking," and "Miking the Snare."

But what of that traditionally "outlaw" form known as "rock 'n roll"? Long faltering in an almost religious search for "the next big thing," it found new—many said demonic—life with the 1983 illegalization of meat. The subculture that sprang up in resistance to the meat ban was nowhere reflected more boisterously than in its song. "Meat 'n roll" it was called, and the very name expressed its primal crudity. Uncompromisingly antidisco, the "ground round sound" was as raw and dangerous as the substances that inspired it.

But there were those who, spurred by the economic turmoil created by the Oil Glut in 1986, demanded that the nation "come in for a close-up" on the problems of the destitute black Army, and they too had their subcultural trappings, language . . . and music. These hard-bitten veterans of the man-eat-dog meat 'n roll underground took for their marching tune the musical form of prole and web-exec alike—disco—but melded it with the traditional military music of John Philip Sousa. They called it "la sousa," and its distinctive style of disco featured heavily electrified brass bands playing in clubs with names like Fort Bragg. Its dances mimicked the movements of a close-order drill team.

The clash between meat 'n rollers and sousa fans was inevitable, and enjoyed widespread publicity in the pages of *Prime Times*. (It was this magazine, now defunct, that took over the moribund *Rolling Stone* in 1984—an event which, some say, caused the fatal explosion of *Stone*'s editor-in-chief, Jann Wenner.) But compromise is America's middle name, and a reconciliation of sorts took place on an abandoned poultry farm in upstate New York during August of 1989. They called it "Chickenstock." It was a gathering where both meat 'n roll and sousa found the broad audiences denied them on the radio waves. And, as over a million people cheered, it seemed fitting that the festival's slogan, "A Piece Now," was equally applicable to a turkey leg or a gun.

But these were the exceptions that proved the rule. Disco remains America's national "sound," whether in the soaring "riffs" of Charles Wuorinen's synthesizer or in the smoky mystery of Gloria Gaynor's scat-moaning. Disco it is that soothes the irritation of a nation that has endured, by day's end, just one "What?" too many. For our teenager of a decade ago, now grown to womanhood, music *is* disco, and disco music.

A BEATLE-MANIAC

Joshua Araknid was poor, scrofulous, and 34 years old. At the beginning of March 1981, even Joshua's best friends had difficulty remembering his name. Two months later he had become one of the celebrities of the decade.

Araknid was an incurable Beatle fan. Since 1964, he had dedicated himself totally to the "fab four." In 1969, for example, he constructed—and almost drowned in—a small yellow submarine that he attempted to launch in Long Island Sound. In 1970, he was arrested after turning up at a Halloween party and hitting several guests on the head with a small silver hammer. And with the group's breakup, he lapsed into a decade-long depression.

Early in 1981, however, Araknid's circumstances changed. The beneficiary of a fair-sized inheritance, he flew to London in the first week of March. Immediately, he rented a large house in Abbey Road and had its basement equipped as a sound studio. Then, in a series of perfectly executed maneuvers, Araknid proceeded to kidnap the Beatles. To do this, he played upon characteristic "weaknesses" of his victims. Starr was lured to the house with a large cash advance to appear in a movie of his own choice. Harrison accepted an invitation to discuss matching a large cash contribution for the rehabilitation of the Ik, an obscure African tribe. McCartney, then in negotiation with a Saudi consortium for the purchase of his wife's photo collection, was snared by the simple promise of a better offer.

Araknid's trap for Lennon was more ingenious still. In the predictable furor surrounding the disappearance of the three Beatles, Lennon was acutely embarrassed by not knowing where they had gone or why. When Araknid contacted him by phone, offering to sell a message purportedly from McCartney to Harrison about the reunion and using a name only the Beatles (and of course the quintessential Beatle scholar Araknid himself) could have known, Lennon flew incognito to

The Beatles, un-united once more, cross familiar ground to four ambulances waiting to whisk them away to four separate hospitals for medical tests after their ordeal.

London, met Araknid in a pub near Heathrow, and drove to Abbey Road to "confront" his erstwhile colleagues.

Confront them he did. With the arrival of Lennon, all four Beatles were hustled into the recording studio. Araknid then locked them in and announced, in a voice breaking with emotion, that "there was a way back home, and they were to come together right now and write a new song." Convinced largely by Araknid's .38, the group, in McCartney's words, began to "bung one together."

The result was "Please Backwards Please," an elegant ballad of sexual innuendo that recalled the Beatles' pre-*Sergeant Pepper* style. A tape of the song was released to the BBC several days later. The record world went wild.

What Araknid did not know was that "Please Backwards Please," when played backwards, featured the unmistakable voice of Lennon saying, "Help, we need somebody at 152 Abbey Road." Harrison LeGrange, a DJ from Winnetka, Illinois, discovered this and sold the information—exclusively—to every major record label. Each one, convinced that it alone had the information, began carefully concealed rescue operations.

Meanwhile the Beatles themselves, discouraged by the delay, were formulating another plan. Realizing that the only way to escape Araknid was to cease to exist, the group began a painstakingly orchestrated and "terminal" quarrel of which Araknid was the horrified witness.

Unbeknownst to both kidnapper and kidnappees, lethal gun battles had erupted all over the West End as record executives, seeing that rival labels were on the trail, attempted to prevent one another from being the first to reach Number 152. But the carnage—which baffled Scotland Yard—was in vain. On the evening of June 2, 1981, a heartbroken Araknid released the Beatles unharmed after a furious "argument" over the sexual exploits of Yoko Ono, Linda Eastman, and Patty Boyd.

Araknid was later sent to jail—not without first being offered a top position by two major record labels. The Beatles made plans to release an album called *Together*, but were unable to agree on a royalty split.

MEATLEGGERS

"For the third year running, Number One in our year-end Freedom Standings," proclaimed the Nobel Institute in its 1987 awards presentation, bestowing a coveted Nobie on the United States of America.

For the freest nation on earth, we are given to some curious habits, one of which is the periodic curtailment of our own liberties. This century has seen the zealous prohibition of alcohol in an earlier decade, and of many so-called drugs in more recent ones, but no ban enacted within our shores has ever stirred as much controversy as the Meat Proscription Act of 1983.

Predictably, the stricture was mandated by the Congress of Nuts. A coalition of vegetarian and Vishnuite factions lobbied intensively from the opening of the session to forbid the consumption of "flesh slain in anger." The sizable Animal Rights party joined their ranks when this was amended to "flesh slain in any state of mind," and the bill's passage was assured. Congress overrode President Carter's veto unanimously, and on January 20, 1983, as irate carnivores from Portland to Pensacola howled in disbelief, it became illegal "to eat, cook, possess, butcher, or cause to be butchered, slice, chop, smoke, or process meat of any kind" within the continental United States.

Congress instructed Surgeon General Allan Bakke to carry out the ban, appropriating massive sums for patrol and surveillance helicopters (known as "meatchoppers" or "vegematics") and a far-flung network of enforcement officers. The latter were paramilitary in organization: from the surgeon general himself down through surgeon majors to surgeon sergeants and surgeon privates. Together with legions of paid informants and special undercover men known as "carnotics" agents, these outfits moved swiftly, and some said overzealously, to keep meat out of American mouths.

The task they faced was formidable. Vast interests from cattlemen to coffee-shop owners were arrayed against them. But at the outset their enthusiasm knew no bounds. Huge shipments of South American pot roast were seized and dumped in the ocean, millions of tons of steak were burnt to a crisp ("Well done!" crowed the pro-ban *Chicago Sun-Times*), mountains of baloney, liverwurst, salami, and other processed meats were bulldozed into lime pits like so many tiny corpses. Hunting licenses were revoked *en masse* (the National Rifle Association protested and licenses to hunt trees and wild fruits were issued in their place). Humane societies were provided with round-the-clock sentries; poultry and hog farms were opened and their inmates released. Flocks of bewildered turkeys looking for a new home became a familiar sight in apartment complexes, and wild pig incidents were soon a suburban commonplace. Some carnotics agents interpreted the law to cover eggs and fish in addition to meat. Surgeon troops in a rural Pennsylvania town dumped so many eggs into the local reservoir that residents found their hot-water tanks clogged with omelet; another group uncovered an enormous cache of chum in Martha's Vineyard, which they impounded, causing an island-wide stench that lasted for months. The Surgeon Corps of Engineers even went so far as to spray Wyoming cattle herds with paraquat.

At first, the energetic conduct of Surgeon General Bakke's men drew the approval of a public perennially fascinated by the wastage of food. There was also grudging admiration, if not for their methods, then at least for their Jack-the-Giant-Killer attitude toward the vast meat conglomerates. It was the entry of criminal elements into the picture, ironically, that soured Americans on the forces of vegetarian law and order.

Meatleggers they were called, smugglers and illegal farmers, bringing to the public what Congress could not legislate away. They were the new heroes, always one step ahead of the law, running dead cows under the very rotors of meatchoppers, raising flocks of sheep in hastily soundproofed basements, making daring daylight raids on municipal zoos. Many were hardened criminals, impoverished by the legaliza-

A government patrol plane (meatchopper) closes in on a meatlegger trying to land a hot calf in the Florida Everglades. By 1984, such an animal had a street value of over one million dollars when cut.

tion of gambling, prostitution, and drugs. Many were women—several of the major West Coast meat rackets were run by Vassar graduates—ruthlessly, but with excellent taste. The semi-mythical Butcher of Bensonhurst, part Owsley, part Bronfman, was reputed to be a woman. (Her meat was said to be the most amazing ever tasted—or synthesized.) Sophisticated distribution networks sprang up throughout the nation were headquartered in Chicago,

"hog pusher to the world." Unemployed deli owners and hot dog vendors were recruited as meat runners. The amounts of money at stake were astronomical, and inevitably there was violence. Annie Bardaccio, the so-called Burger Queen, who by 1984 controlled all the meat rackets from Boston to Philadeiphia, was said not merely to execute anyone who tried to move in on her "pasture" territory, but to include their remains in her quarter-pounders.

A giraffe-mounted surveillance camera photographs this trio of "meatleggers" staging a daring daylight murder and theft of a live hippopotamus from Chicago's Wild Animal and Roller Coaster Land. The haul would have netted the "hippsters" $2.5 million.

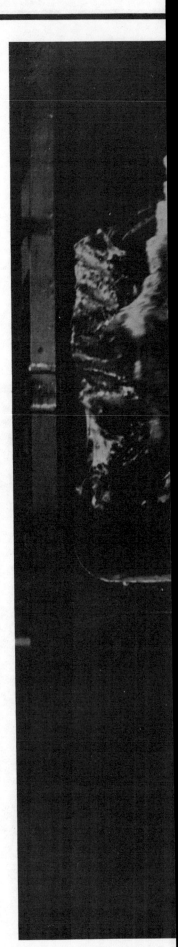

"Don't bust my chops!" shouts lamb racketeer Vincent "Legs" Vitello, as federal carnotics agents raid his Miami hideaway. Three died in the shootout, and one side was reduced from "prime" to "choice."

But of all the factors that militated against the success of meat prohibition, none was as powerful as a public unconvinced of its morality, or necessity. People wanted meat and were prepared to break the law to get it. To be sure, scare tactics were employed to support the ban. Medical reports on meat's adverse effects tended, however, to negate one another. Thus, if a pro-orgasm clique was in the ascendant within the medical community, meat was condemned as a major factor in the decline of orgasm. If an anti-orgasm faction held sway, it was likewise condemned as causing uncontrollable sexual activity. For the most part, the average American, usually with a twinkle in his eye, would say that the occasional chop "helped" or "increased his share." On the other hand, the same American probably felt that the excessive consumption of the meatheads was socially irresponsible, insofar as it might lead to cataclysmic individual or communal climaxing.

Meat prohibition failed because the public wanted it to fail. Ultimately it was impossible for the Surgeon Army to police every household—as the virtual disappearance of household pets attests. Congress had no funds by 1985 to continue enforcement; the corruption that resulted —surgeon corporals in Chicago openly guarded steakeasies in return for bribes— further eroded public support. Increasing food shortages tended to obscure the rights and wrongs of the issue as people turned to new food sources. Whether grubs, insects, and worms could properly be defined as meat was questioned by even the most law-abiding. With no one to enforce the law, and no one to repeal it, the issue became moot. But the legacy of prohibition remains—in 58 states it is still theoretically illegal to consume meat in public; and that most traditional of American snacks, the ballpark frank (even though for years it has contained only soy-meal helper and soluble polyesters), is still eaten carefully concealed in a brown bag.

MEATHEADS

The music is a bizarre mix of old ranching songs and the raucous hard-rock sound of "meat 'n roll." A peculiar assortment of preteens and disaffected 40-year-olds sits around a huge butcher block in the renovated smokehouse, passing around a steaming "joint" (rib) of pork.

"Prime time!" murmurs one bedraggled denizen happily, first inhaling and then nibbling at the morsel of meat. "Hey, yo-blood," slurs his tiny neighbor hungrily, "don't lovelace that joint!" And the bedraggled one passes on the rib with a zero share for hygiene.

The scene could have taken place almost anywhere in America in the mid-1980s. It is, of course, a meat party, a secretive ritual of illegal meat users gathered together for an uninhibited evening of music, ideology, and pork. There is much gaiety in the ancient sense, much nibbling and inhaling, a prevalent sense of revolutionary good cheer.

And there is fear, always fear, of the "carnies," or surgeon general's troops.

"I remember when I got busted," recounts one young woman, an attractive former waitress at a now defunct surf 'n turf chain. "My butcher and me were getting really marbled when these two green machines (surgeon corporals) came right through the door. My parents threw me out for good."

Alienation. Family problems. The desire to experiment. All factors in the meathead phenomenon. The subculture developed its own heroes, daring meat runners who became romantic desperadoes, slaughter-house workers who became folk legends. The movement had its own writers, who described the mystical experiences open to adventurous beef-eaters, artists who painted powerful meat-induced visions, and its own chronicle, a tabloid named *Prime Times*.

But it was the music of the movement that gave it identity and energy, and there was one great instrumentalist/singer who championed the cause. Gordon Seabrook, rhythm guitarist for a forgettable "Next Big Thing" group called the Jeebie-Heebs, made history on the night of June 15 at Madison Square Garden, three weeks after meat prohibition went into effect. Performing as part of the opening act, Seabrook suddenly launched into a wild solo at the end of which he ate what appeared to be a liverwurst sandwich. The crowd roared its approval and a subculture was born.

The young rebel changed his name to Beef Jerky, and within months was the undisputed king and god of the decade's most uninhibited sound—"meat 'n roll," a driving beat with lyrics to match that extolled the joys of the carnivorous life. Jerky's first album, *Jesus Christ Supermarket*, which featured songs such as "Leg of Lamb of God" and "Sweetbread of Life," topped charts for months and went plutonium. A host of imitators followed—the London Broil, the Links, Slim Jim and the Micro-

To satisfy an ever-demanding public, meat-crazed musicians combined spectacular stunts with raw rock 'n roll, often injuring themselves in the process. Here, Slim Jim tries out a new routine in which he jumps from a burning building while playing his hit, "They Chop, They Dice, They Mince, They Slice." The effect was never actually incorporated into a live concert.

MARBLED AGIN!

Many meat underground bedrooms, apartments, and dorms boasted cartoonist R. Crum's "Marbled Agin!" poster. Some claimed that the peculiar art style amplified meat's supposed "somadelic" effects. After a few ounces, meat-eaters reported feelings of sluggishness, lethargy, and drowsiness, followed by a state of altered consciousness in which the subject fell asleep and could not see the poster at all.

waves, and many more—but it was Jerky that the meatheads took to their hearts. The subculture, predictably, reached all levels of society. Television catered to the swelling underground by programming shows with subtle appeals to meat-users, who would lie dazed before multiple screens while sucking salamis. As the movement gathered its own cachet, socialites and entertainers hopped aboard the meatwagon with a smug contempt for authority, and starry-eyed upperclass preteens left home to join the glamorous smokehouse subculture.

In its heyday, the meat movement dominated the hearts and minds of a generation. Traditional hits were reworked into cuts like "Hooked on Vealing" and "Love Meat Tender." Veteran artists like Meatloaf enjoyed huge revivals. Meathead shops hawking every conceivable kind of paraphernalia sprang up in the face of the most determined surveillance by surgeon troops, selling "rare" tags, steak knives, lambchop frills, A-1 sauce, and baked potatoes in foil. A friendly neighborhood "butcher" could provide addicts with "hash," "joints," or even "horse" (considered very powerful and therefore risky), and

even the much sought-after "cold turkey." Whatever his (or her) choice, a meathead might visit a "porker's" (friend's) house to "do" or "smoke" some meat, and then catch a concert with a miniaturized fridge strapped to his wrist so that, under cover of darkness, he could get "really beefed."

Such a giddy culture was certain to crash. In a fall as fast as his rise, Jerky's career ground to a halt one night at San Francisco's Cow Palace when, during a frenzied closing number, he ate his drummer.

His records were banned from the airwaves and denounced in every newspaper. A broken man, Jerky later recounted the incident for *Prime Times*: "Chuck was the best drummer any group ever had, and he was my closest friend. I can't say how it [the eating] happened. The crowd was all hot and excited and by the end of the show the place smelled just like the pot roast my mother used to fix me as a kid."

It was perhaps a fitting end for a movement that many said was consuming itself. For the moment the "potatoes" (straight world) had proven to be more enduring than the "meat."

A 1985 episode of a popular cartoon series. Artist Stan Mack actually went among the downtrodden and meat-addicted to find raw material for his biting yet tender slice of contemporary life.

Rock star Meatloaf enjoyed a second helping of success during meat prohibition. He was rumored to ingest mind-bending quantities of hamburger, and the cover of his album Record Consumption *was held to be a daring dig at the law. Actually, the sandwich contained a meat look-alike made from tomato paste and kapok.*

STAN MACK'S REAL LIFE FUNNIES: MEATHEADS
GUARANTEE: ALL DIALOGUE REPORTED VERBATIM

I DO MEAT ALL DAY, EVERY DAY. PORK CHOPS IN THE MORNING, LONDON BROIL AT NOON, STEAK TARTARE AT NIGHT. IT HELPS TO HAVE A GOOD BUTCHER.

I USED TO GET SAUTÉED ON CUBE STEAK, NOW I GET BEEFED ON HAMBURGER. TECHNICALLY THEY'RE DIFFERENT, PHILOSOPHICALLY THEY'RE THE SAME...

THE WORLD'S ON A BUMMER. ROD STEWART STILL MAKES BAD RECORDS, MY KID'S DIVORCED ME. MEAT EATING GIVES ANOTHER DIMENSION TO A MUNDANE LIFE. YOU GOTTA GET MARBLED TO KNOW WHERE YOU'RE COMING FROM...

LIBRARY TOURS · THE NEW YORK PUBLIC LIBRARY · CLOSED · 'HIBITS

LEGALIZE FISH

I'M A PHOTOGRAPHER. I GET GOOD IDEAS FOR DEPTH OF FIELD WHEN I'M DOING STEAK... OF COURSE, I CAN'T TAKE THE PICTURE THEN BECAUSE IT'LL BE OUT OF FOCUS...

I STARTED DOING MEAT AT 13. I'M 36 NOW AND I'M STILL LIVING IN MY MOTHER'S HOUSE. BUT I'M NOT HUNG UP ON GROWING UP. EVERYTHING'S RUN BY TELEVISION ANYWAY...

PEOPLE ARE ATOMS TOO

THERE ARE THINGS IN THE RHYTHM GUITAR YOU DON'T HEAR UNLESS YOU'VE SMOKED A GOOD STANDING RIB ROAST...

EATING STEAK GIVES ME SOMETHING TO DO WITH MY HANDS...

YOU CAN'T BEAT MEAT

TAKE THE 100 GREATEST GENIUSES OF HISTORY, AND IF WE KNEW THEIR INTIMATE LIVES WE'D FIND THAT THEY WERE ADDICTED TO MEAT ALSO...

I'VE BEEN THROUGH SELF-FLAGELLATION, BLOODLETTING... I'D RATHER GET A PRIME TIME HEAD ON KANSAS RED. IT'S IN THE AMERICAN TRADITION.

I'M LIKE UNEMPLOYED. I'M A SCULPTOR, BUT I'M REALLY INTO THE ENVIRONMENT. I FEEL MORE THAN A VEGI, BUT THAT'S THEIR MISFORTUNE.

I'M RARE ON SIRLOIN. I'M A BUDDING HASH HEAD. A TURKEY FREAK. I'VE HADDA KICK HORSEMEAT. IF I THOUGHT IT WAS BETTER AS A VEGI, I'D DO IT...

VEGI DOGS · PRETZELS · BROCCOLI JUICE · CHOCOLATE CARROT ON A STICK

©stanmack 6-1985

LA SOUSA

Sometime in early 1983, a craze called "cult" swept through the ranks of American schoolchildren. The way it worked was simple. A group of kids—usually 20 or so—would isolate themselves and elect one of their number as "leader." From then on, for a specified period of time, the leader's every command was obeyed without question. Kids spoke in a flat glassy-eyed monotone and walked like robots. Parents found simple requests answered with lines like, "I am sorry, I am not programmed to clean up my bedroom," or, "My directives do not include washing up," all delivered with a hypnotic unblinking stare. If the leader had ordered his or her cult to stand on their heads at 8:06 P.M.—at 8:06 P.M. they stood on their heads regardless of the consequences.

Some saw the fad merely as a means of infuriating mom and dad. Others, looking further, realized that it augured a new era of independence for kids (*see KIDS*). And still others, at an even deeper level, perceived it as part of what video therapist Frank Zappa has called the "loss-of-self-help" movement, a desire not merely to understand others, but to become adjuncts of their personality. The musical comedy *1984!* mirrored this trend (much of the laughter directed against its bumbling antihero, Winston Smith, was because he could not see the necessity for blind obedience), particularly in the fads it generated, such as the campus craze for the Two Minutes Hate. A Two Minutes Hate was orchestrated by a single person and directed against a single person (usually the dean, or some especially despised student). Participants worked themselves up into a "high" of hate, until they "lost touch with themselves."

The year 1984 also saw the premiere of the first cult television series on ABC. Called quite simply, "cult," the first episode was shown over and over again throughout the season until the viewing audience could talk along with the dialogue, assemble enough props to duplicate the scenes at home, and, where they felt obliged to, throw things at the screen. Elsewhere, related developments were taking place.

Early in the decade, medical research isolated many new hormones in the human brain and determined their precise functions. When these substances were "recycled," they induced identical functions in the "host" brain. Thus, for instance, it was possible for a six-year-old to take Nostalgin and experience a gentle regret for his wasted youth. The drug industry was naturally far more interested in hormones inducing loyalty, obedience, and loss of will—they were widely prescribed in the domestic market—but it soon found that the illegal demand for drugs such as Quontrol, Ignorin, and Truinal far outstripped the needs of executives and housewives.

The day-to-day results were appalling. Teenagers "selfed out" on Truinal approached total strangers and demanded orders; squads of youngsters on Quontrol placed themselves at the perpetual disposal of anyone in a uniform, whether mailman, bus driver, or usher. Peace officers arresting such drug abusers were instructed to make funny faces, wear their boots on their heads, even drop their pants—anything so that the arrestee did not get the satisfaction of authoritarian treatment.

What had begun as a collection of fads and trends had by mid-decade become a movement. And a movement looking for a cause. It found it in the black Army. Encouraged by a new radicalism that the '86 depression spawned, its believers identified totally with the impoverished but fiercely proud black military. Largely insulated from their idols, however, the movement's adherents had little but their own preconceptions to go on. Accordingly, they embraced traditional martial music and made it the basis of a new sound, half disco and half John Philip Sousa. Clubs with names like Fort Bragg and The Stockade sprang up across the nation. "La sousa" devotees, high on Ignorin, patronized such places, dancing till all hours in close-order drill, wearing surplus Army fatigues, close haircuts, and rigid expressions, and instantly obeying the orders of the Records Officer (DJ) who would bark commands from time to time over the PA system.

Pro-military disco produced new groups and influenced old ones. Here, the perennial favorite, Jefferson Airborne, perform their hit, "Stars and Stripes Forever," at a summer festival in New York's Central Park sponsored by Beer beer.

Although it was pointed out that the Army had taken a quite different direction, reinterpreting the military spirit and developing drills so complex no white could ever reproduce them, la sousa fans continued to regard their music as a medium of solidarity. And although their ultimate goal — joining up — was denied them by a military bent on its own designs, their music symbolized this fact: while the '60s meant being totally out of control, and the '70s totally in control, the '80s subsumed both previous decades — the "high" of the '80s was to be totally in someone else's control.

OIL

ELEANOR'S FASHIONS

The global Oil Glut meant depression —and street corner gas-peddling was the panhandle of the mid-'80s. The '30s lyric, "You remember me, Al ... I was the kid with the drum," took on a poignant new meaning.

OIL

It is a rainy afternoon in 1987, and Barnes Crawford, a "suite-wise" executive vice-president, is extremely uneasy. He stands before the large picture window in his spacious office and tries to reassure himself that what he is about to do is not actually wrong. It is a familiar sequence of thoughts and, as usual, it comforts him. He dials a telephone number, and in a low, anxious voice asks to speak to his "broker." Crawford tells the gruff presence on the other end that he wishes to sell some stock—an "under-the-counter" transaction in which his name must not be used. He is put on "hold," and must wait, in agony.

"The dismal science," many have called economics. But the American economy has always been able to look such nay-sayers in the eye and reply, "Speak for yourself." True, we have had our ups and downs. But is not the roller coaster all the more thrilling for its unpredictable reversals? And does it not return us—shaken, breathless, perhaps nauseated and vertiginous—safe and sound every time, and ready to go around again? Such was the story of the American economy in the 1980s: slow, agonizing ascents, suspenseful levelings-off, frantic and stomach-churning plunges, head-whipping swerves around terrifyingly precipitous drops, throat-smashing, bone-jarring halts. Yet all the while, we had the time of our lives—particularly when we perceived as we got off that for the first time in many years, someone was firmly at the controls.

ON DECEMBER 6, 1985, AS HALLEY'S COMET REAPPEARED, THE WORLD ECONOMIC PICTURE BECAME A PORTRAIT IN OIL.

Economist Kareem Abdul-Jabbar has written: "There is no such thing as a hot lunch," and indeed, it sometimes seemed as if the entire first half of the decade had been scripted precisely to teach us this fact. It was a tough lesson, but America has never been a nation to play "hooky" from reality. Food, without which life itself goes hungry, was in short supply—yet became all the more healthful and delicious for that. And if the stock market faltered, investment in commodity futures thrived, as our keenest financial minds cast literally millions of dollars' worth of votes for America's tomorrow. In purchasing huge quantities of potato options, fotonovella options, washer-dryer combination options, and the like, they were saying yes to an improved economy, no to despair and defeatism, and shut up to those crying wolf without even asking why, to the who-struck-John alarmists, and the where-were-you-when-the-lights-went-out finger-pointers.

But on December 6, 1985, as Halley's Comet reappeared to remind us of the true meaning of "guest star," the world economic picture became a portrait in oil. Up until that day, petroleum prices had peaked at $240 per barrel (not counting the $40 surcharge on the barrel leveled by the Organization of Barrel Exporting Countries). Then, on that Black Friday, they put the "oil" back in "economic turmoil."

WHILE CITIZENS RACKED THEIR BRAINS, OUR BEST CORPORATIONS WERE QUIETLY CLOSING RANKS AND PREPARING TO LEAD US—FOR OUR OWN GOOD—INTO THE FUTURE.

It is the American genius, however, to provide help in situations when even help itself needs help. While citizens racked their brains in an effort to remember to switch on the electric appliances when they weren't using them, our best corporations were quietly closing ranks and preparing to lead us—for our own good—into the future. When, on April 3, 1986, the United Multinationals officially announced their formation, it merely confirmed to some what many of us had known all along about American big business: that size, strength, power, and influence mean nothing without the unimpeded ability to use them at will in a totally unrestrained quest for production, profit, and happiness.

How right it was, therefore, when the UM declined to be burdened with the acquisition of the pathetic, bad-risk institution that was Congress. When, in 1989, the first meal of petrofood was served, the nation—indeed, the world—gave thanks that at last the distinction had been erased between the food man eats and the fuel that he uses to cook it. The UM's recent move to China is only another in the continuing series of brave and innovative ideas that have made this magnificent commercial juggernaut the most powerful force for change, progress, money, jobs, food, or anything else on the face of the earth.

Barnes Crawford, who sold his stock in '87 for a tidy sum, is a rich man today. The deal went undetected; no one was hurt, and enterprise itself remained a little freer for it. Crawford, like America, is able to ride the thundering roller coaster of economic change and land on his feet.

7/16/82--MEXICO ACCUSED NEIGHBORS OF "LONG-RANGE DIAGONAL DRILLING" OF HER OIL WELLS. 79 NATIONS DENIED CHARGES.

OIL 159

¡VIVA MEXICO!

Our neighbor to the south gained a long-awaited and all-too-briefly-enjoyed place in the sun during the first half of the 1980s. Its petroleum reserves soaring as supplies in the oil-hungry United States plummeted, Mexico began to market its own products directly into the Southwest states as early as 1980. Mexxxon and Mexaco gas stations mushroomed overnight. Receipts from the sale of oil led to rapid expansion in other areas. MexDonald's challenged its northern counterpart in the fast-food field, offering a giant *burrito* called the Big Mex, as did Mex Factor in cosmetics and Mexerox in the lucrative copier market. By 1982, the Mexican peso was second only to the Saudi rial as the world's strongest currency. Europesos and petropesos traded in Zurich helped in the purchase of countless non-Mexican enterprises.

Meanwhile, rapid industrial development in Mexico's Chihuahua and Sonora states was having other, no less significant economic effects. By 1981, streams of unemployed United States business executives were slipping across the border to find work in the booming south. Often caught by *los federales* as they crawled from the Rio Grande or tried to get through the Mexican customs in Tijuana by clinging to the underside of dilapidated company cars, these illegal aliens were known as "whitebacks" or "corporados." If they managed to get through, they were employed on a seasonal basis at below-subsistence wages as tax attorneys, accountants, computer programmers, investment bankers, insurance brokers, commodities traders, and financial consultants. The stream became a torrent and, in 1983, the Teamsters asked the Mexican authorities for permission to organize the migrant capitalists. It was denied, and the teeming "boroughs" of Mexico City remained hotbeds of conservative unrest.

Mexicans grew increasingly curious about the customs and mores of their "Neighbor to the North." Tourism grew by leaps and bounds. "Eh mister, wanna meet my sister?" became a familiar phrase in suburb and city as ethnic Americans, especially those of Italian and Irish descent, vied for the all-important peso. And if the arrogant Mexican tourist was resented for his flamboyant wealth, many Americans took private satisfaction in the chronic constipation Hispanics experienced when they traveled in the United States. On the academic level, United States society and its problems fascinated Mexican intellectuals. In *Children of Darryl*, sociologist Oscar Sanchez examined the plight, responses, and structure of an average Cincinnati family. And Carlos O'Hogg, a University of Mexico City professor, topped Spanish bestseller lists with *The Yanqui Way of Knowledge*, a description of his mystical encounters with Don, an alcoholic gas station attendant from Scranton, Pennsylvania, who claimed to be able to transform himself into a Model T Ford.

With only a head full of figures and a pocket full of indigestion tablets, a "whiteback" CPA emerges from the Rio Grande hoping for a better life in Mexico.

FUTURES

The '80s proved an economic roller coaster for investors. Not surprisingly, they continued to grow more and more disenchanted with stocks and bonds in the early years of the decade, as interest rates and inflation both reached new highs. Anything tangible was better than a piece of investment paper, and capital was lured to the burgeoning commodity markets. Already booming when the 1970s ended, commodity markets took center stage in the shortage-plagued early '80s. Merrill Lynch's famous ad campaign proclaimed that "the future is futures, and the future is now." And a dazzling expansion in the types of futures contracts siphoned trillions of dollars into imprudent speculation in commodities.

The continuing inflationary spiral helped launch the futures craze when Los Angeles residents in 1980 began taking options on undesigned fuel-saving automobiles. Within weeks, the New York Commodities Exchange was offering futures contracts on cumin and Nivea cream, Cuisinarts, and James Michener novels. Bestseller futures as a group were very popular, as were unpainted masterpiece futures. The oil shortage led to the creation of petrofutures with contracts on plastic essentials from Frisbees to Ziploc storage bags. And the nostalgia obsession produced a whole category of listings known as "past" futures: Alma-Tadema paintings, Melmac dinnerware, Watergate hearings transcripts, and plain white tee-shirts, among others.

Meanwhile, the growing shortage of children as the decade progressed led to the inauguration of trading in the most speculative contract of all—baby futures. White Anglo-Saxon Protestant fetus futures commanded astronomical prices, with White Catholic and Colored Protestant in close competition. Girl futures tended to trade higher than boy futures, due no doubt to the decline in fertility; this phenomenon was offset somewhat by the extraordinary sums exchanged in purchasing futures and options on sperm.

By 1982, all of the nation's commodities exchanges had consolidated their trading floors in the twin towers of the World Trade Center. When even this space proved to be inadequate, a third, 110-story tower was built atop the other two to accommodate the growing number of pits.

The declining interest in stocks led to ever lower prices, which only encouraged the corporate merger wave. United Technologies bought United Airlines and United Brands to form the United Company. General Motors acquired General Tire and Rubber, and later merged with General Foods and General Mills to form General General. American Airlines picked up American Motors, American Can, and American Hoist and Derrick. International Business Machines, International Telephone and Telegraph, and International Paper merged. Texas Instruments took Texas Gulf Sulphur, Texas Panhandle, and Lone Star Industries.

In 1983, these new conglomerates themselves merged to form the First National United Texas American General International Corporation, otherwise known as the Seven Brothers. However, when a merger was attempted with the combined oil companies, or Seven Sisters, Incorporated, the U.S. Department of Justice gained its lone antitrust victory of the decade. Ultimately, legislation was passed to save the Fortune 500 (and several mergers were barred) under the Endangered Species Acts.

The decrease in the number of companies and the decline in outstanding shares culminated in the slowest trading session in the history of the New York Stock Exchange, when a total of three shares changed hands in the only transaction on February 13, 1984. That day the Dow Jones Index closed at .0001.

The Black Friday crash in the next year changed all of this, of course. Crude oil futures, which had shot up to $278 a barrel, and thousands of other commodities plunged to nothing. So did the people who traded them. News of the crash hit New York at lunchtime, and hundreds of commodities speculators leapt to their death from Windows on the Third World, the restaurant atop the new exchange.

In 1984, the Third World Trade Center first reared its mass into the Manhattan smog, supported, appropriately, by the First and Second World Trade Centers. It is architecturally identical with the other two, except it is thatched.

SHORTAGE

The Organization of Petroleum Exporting Countries kept tightening the oil noose in the first half of the 1980s. The petroleum supply situation here and elsewhere grew increasingly desperate. Prices kept rising at a 50 percent annual rate, since the cartel effectively kept its production just below the level of world demand as each new conservation measure was introduced.

The United States paralysis over energy policy was finally resolved when Congress, after 21 months of stalemate, passed a program in 1982 to ration gasoline on the basis of odd and even years. Despite a legal challenge, the law, which allowed drivers to use their cars only in those years that corresponded to the last number on their license plates, was upheld by the Supreme Court. At the same time, the justices sustained court-ordered programs to bus commuters on their "off" years. The gasoline shortage led many Americans to pursue transportation technologies that did not require the use of petroleum. The most popular of these was the rickshaw. Nevertheless, it was hard to rid Americans of their automobile addiction, and many were arrested for driving in the wrong year and sent to Gasoholics Anonymous centers for treatment.

Even these measures proved inadequate to deal with the growing shortage, and for several years New York and other cities in the Northeast were subject to a weekly one-day electricity blackout. Outlying suburbs were increasingly cut off from the central city. Some reverted to a remote, frontier-style existence. Others, like Bronxville and Simi Valley, became abandoned ghost towns.

As they grew more expensive, plastic, polyester, and other petroleum-derived products, once scorned by the fashionable, became the cynosure of chic. Gucci stores were stocked solely with plastic loafers, scarves, and luggage. Yves St. Laurent revolutionized fashion with his "High Synthec" collection of 1983. And Ralph Lauren revived the "classic" double-knit leisure suit. Multihued Dynel synthetic

furs, while all the rage with the rich trendy set, provoked bitter moral protests because they were considered a rip-off of precious crude oil. Ocelot skins were suggested as preferable substitutes.

Black plastic garbage bags became so expensive that firms began to salvage them from landfills for reuse. Once the conservation mentality finally caught on, the fear that the world was running out of resources took hold and the disposable society became the reusable society. Kleenex laundries sprang up to wash used paper tissues. Aluminum foil was stitched, patched, and rerolled.

Encouraged by the success of OPEC, other cartels also appeared, such as the Russia-Zimbabwe chromium pool. Finally, OPEC itself was subjected to economic blackmail with the formation of OBEC, the Organization of Barrel Exporting Countries. Made up of South Korea, Taiwan, and the Philippines, OBEC charged OPEC upwards of $40 for its oil barrels.

The lack of easy energy alternatives caused the United States to press ahead with nuclear energy during the decade, despite sizable opposition as the '80s began. A substantial portion of that opposition, however, vanished with the reopening of the Three Mile Island nuclear power plant in 1981. More than two million antinuclear demonstrators had converged on the nuclear facility to protest its reactivation, when a catastrophic reactor core meltdown occurred, and eliminated not only the plant and the surrounding area but all of the demonstrators as well. The Nuclear Regulatory Commission, following an investigation into the causes of the meltdown, concluded it could not have occurred and stepped up its licensing of new plants.

An unexpected benefit of the gas shortage was the "leg up" it gave to thousands of New York's jobless joggers. Unused to running in lanes or stopping for red lights, however, many "rickies" suffered shin splints, and a few unfortunates even had to be put out of their misery.

GLUT

Black Friday, 1985, began innocently enough. At noon, Central African time, the head of state of Chad told a press conference in Ndjamena that his arid nation was sitting astride more than one trillion barrels of oil, the world's largest pool of proven reserves. "We now have the resources to make our desert bloom with polyester plants," a proud Brigadier General Félix Malloum told assembled reporters. Malloum said Chad would sell oil at just under the OPEC market price of $240 a barrel. Within minutes the news flashed around the globe like a seismic shock, triggering a series of rapid-fire disclosures by several dozen other countries that they also had made discoveries of vast new oil reservoirs. The information had been withheld, it turned out, to keep skyrocketing oil prices skyrocketing.

Pitcairn Island followed Chad with a bulletin that it had reserves exceeding Mexico's. The Vatican reported a gusher was spouting out of control from the gardens behind Saint Peter's, where secret drilling had gone on. Denmark for a time appeared to be the world's leading oil power when it revealed that Greenland, beneath the ice, was solid petroleum. Finally, the Seven Sisters Corporation confessed that the reported "dry holes" it had abandoned in the Baltimore Canyon were actually deliberately closed-off strikes into "a subterranean Mississippi of oil" that could satisfy United States needs for 10,000 years.

On that day, December 6, 1985, a startled world that had long become used to paying well over $200 a barrel for oil suddenly found itself on the brink of the equally ruinous Oil Glut. Years of hyperinflation and growing shortages ended abruptly. And the ensuing financial panic set off the

After Black Friday, 1985, the bottom fell out of appliance futures. This American got burned in the toaster market, and had to take delivery. He has 10,000 toasters and no bread.

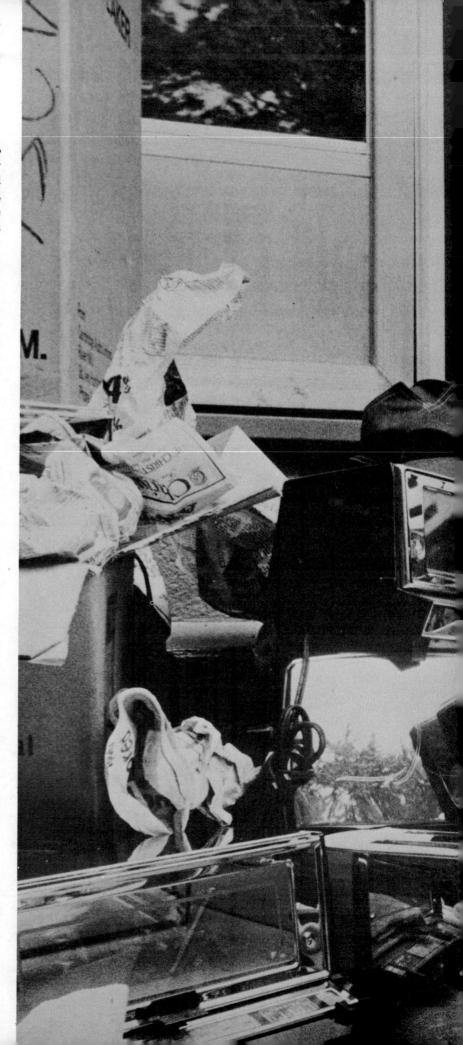

greatest deflationary threat to prosperity since the 1930s depression.

By the end of Black Friday, the world realized that it literally floated on oil. OPEC hastily convened a weekend meeting and announced a going-out-of-business sale. There were no takers, even at distress prices. Soon not only oil, but everything from diamonds to doctors to doorknobs — all of which had been considered scarce and expensive — were discovered to be in tremendous oversupply.

Far from a blessing, the transition to all manner of glut sent commodity prices crashing and collapsed paper fortunes built on scarcity. Oil sheiks tumbled into penury overnight. Investors who had bought high-priced commodity futures in the expectation that prices would keep rising were wiped out. Many found they could not liquidate contracts they had bought on margin, and wound up, not only bankrupt, but with thousands of toasters or babies on their front lawns. Soon "more is less" became the common complaint of the day.

The enfeebled policy response of weak-kneed governments all over the world to the spreading panic and depression left a

Old habits die hard. Despite the N. Y. Stock Exchange's calamitous mid-decade decline, stockbrokers continued to commute into the city every morning, even though on most days not a single share was traded and the Big Board carried little more than sports results. After yet another six hours of slowly shredding blank ticker tape, this stalwart now awaits information regarding delays on the 5:15 to New Canaan.

serious vacuum. Only one force seemed capable of intervening, and the world's largest corporations and banks came together in 1986 to create the United Multinationals, or UM, to deal with the situation. Headquartered, for tax reasons, in the Cayman Islands, the UM moved quickly, introducing a kind of corporate Marshall Plan to subsidize consumers so they could continue to pay for the goods they had agreed to purchase from the multinationals at their former inflated prices. This was accomplished through annual $10,000 demogrants in the form of scrip. The UM also became the employer of last resort, even of government officials. And, consolidating its power, the UM also purchased the Navy and Air Force from the now bankrupt government of the United States.

On the energy front, policies were drafted to provide tax incentives for the removal of all weatherstripping and home insulation materials. Detroit embarked on a crash program to develop a technologically advanced gas guzzler. By the end of the year, the General Motors division of the UM came up with the Unimobile, a 600 horsepower one-seater that got three miles to the gallon, as well as the Upwardly Mobile Home, a three-story recreational vehicle that consumed 30 gallons to the mile as it cruised down the highway at the new minimum legal speed, 100 miles per hour.

When none of this proved sufficient to make much of a dent in the oil surplus, the UM in 1987 passed a unanimous resolution encouraging large oil spills at sea. While these only nominally boosted oil prices, they did help to control the increasingly serious glut of whales (see THE WORLD).

The increasing success of the United Multinationals' efforts to prime the economic pump led to an expansion in the allowable use of UM-issued scrip. Individuals were able to expend a portion to buy newly issued shares in the UM Holding Corporation, making the organization self-financing. And a booming market was soon established in the company's shares.

The exception to the rising tide of commodities and manufactured goods in the late '80s was, of course, the increasingly serious shortage of food. However, a miracle breakthrough by UM food engineers in 1988 paved the way for refining an edible diet directly from crude oil. This promised to solve both food shortage and oil glut simultaneously, and sent UM shares soaring. Though some serious problems did develop (when the Trompe d'Oil products were cooked, they tended to explode violently), food engineers remain optimistic that the prospect of petroleum-based diets will eliminate world starvation in the '90s.

The UM scrip, of course, cannot be used to purchase non-synthetic food—only to buy their products at pre-1985 prices, or to invest in UM stock. While some have warned that the rising tide of paper is creating a dangerous speculative bubble, investors—who continue to borrow heavily from the UM to enlarge their incredibly profitable portfolios—have scorned the chronic prophets of economic doom. As if to vindicate their faith in the revival of the market, by December 6, 1989, exactly four years after the Black Friday crash, the Dow Jones Multinational Index hit a new all-time high of 5501.

The Volkswagen "Continental"—long, lean, heavy, and overpowered—was a pet gas-guzzler after the Oil Glut. Its UMEPA ratings were: two gpm (gallons per mile), city; one gpm, highway—but it performed well below that.

FADS 'N FASHIONS

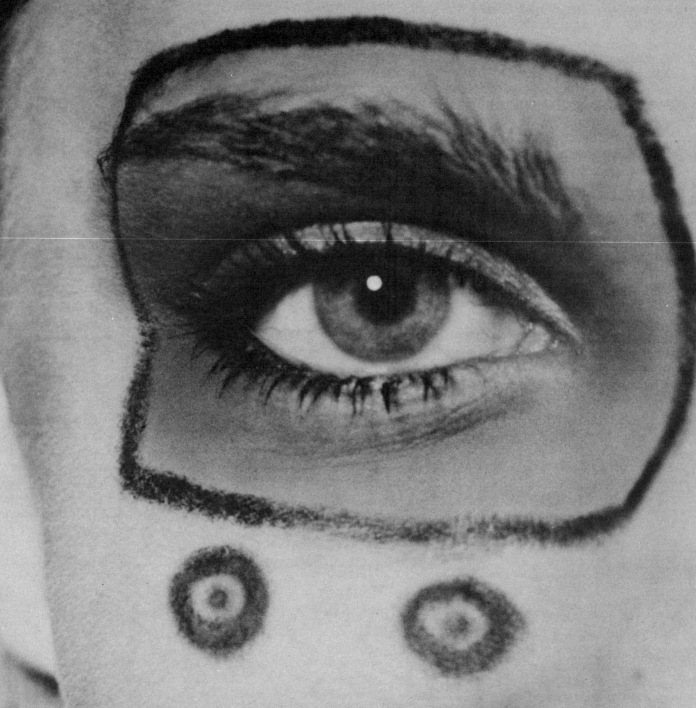

Television sets drawn with eye-liner made the "Viewer Look" the last word in 1987. Said Helen Gurley Brown: "Make your eyes two munchy cathode ray tubes. He will just die to touch your knobs and turn you on!"

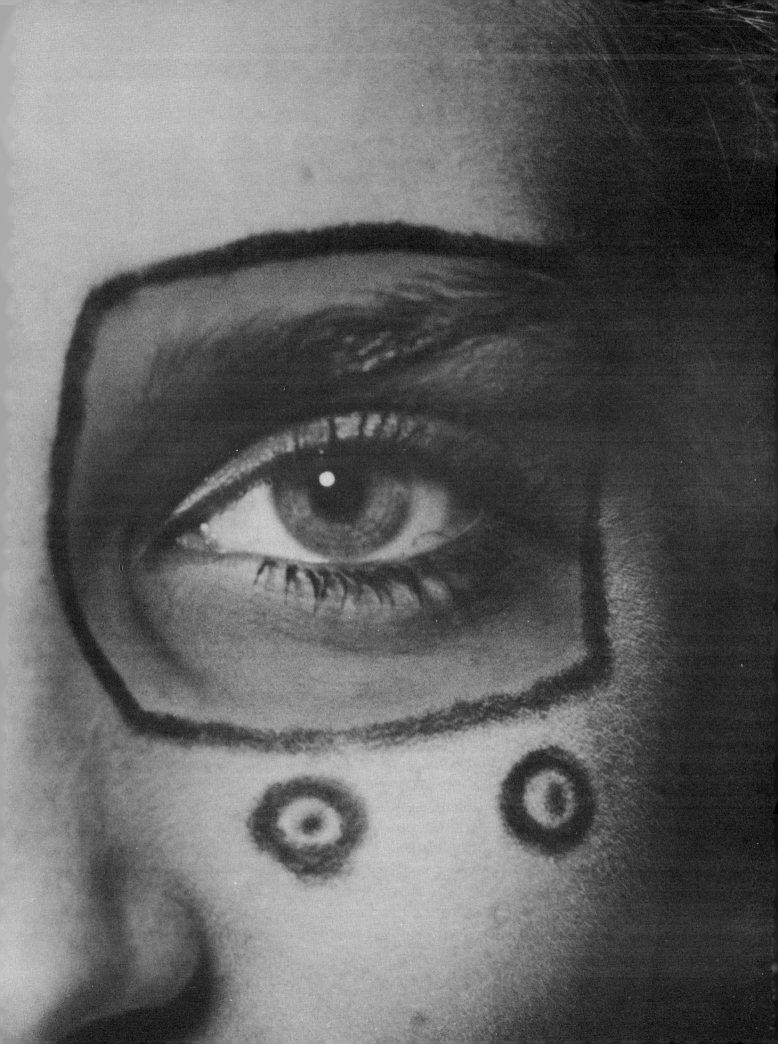

FADS 'N FASHIONS

It is Christmas week, 1988. Harry Peterson, for 23 years a security guard at Dallas' swank Neiman-Marcus department store, has a decision to make. An endless parade of humanity moves past his station; some customers smile knowingly at his Thompson submachine gun and at the button ("IF YOU BREAK IT, YOU'LL BUY IT") on his jacket lapel. But Harry is vexed by a thorny—if pleasant—dilemma: should he, with his Christmas bonus, buy for his wife an egg poacher endorsed by Ryan O'Neal or by Howard Baker?

Our America has always been a land of plenty, and in the '80s there was, as sociologist Erma Bombeck put it, "plenty of plenty left." To be sure, the decade featured its own peculiar stylistic emphases and character—one reason being the general aging of the population. As the post-World War II "baby boom" generation prepared to enter their fifties, the habits, preferences, and proclivities of middle age replaced the "youth-oriented" lifestyles that had hitherto dominated the nation's media, entertainment industries, and marketplace. What, in the '70s, Tom Wolfe had dubbed the "Me Generation" had, by 1989, become the "What?" Generation. Catch-phrases abounded: "You'll have to speak louder," and "Have I told you this already?" to name but two. Not for nothing was Blue Cross' plan for comprehensive medical care promoted with the slogan, "As long as you have your National Health ... "

WHAT, IN THE '70S, TOM WOLFE HAD DUBBED THE "ME GENERATION" HAD, BY 1989, BECOME THE "WHAT?" GENERATION.

With age comes the comfort of television, and with the '80s came a dramatic increase in the popularity and influence—indeed, in the omnipresence of television. Architecture began to imitate the subtle, somehow comforting contours of the TV screen. And the tube not only talked, but listened: 30 million viewers cast, via a QUBE hookup, their votes in *Davidson* v. *United Canning, Inc.*, resulting in the largest hung jury in history. With this civic responsibility came a new awareness of viewing as a skill, and by the middle of the decade most school systems offered courses in remedial, speed, and advanced viewing. Television, in fact, became nothing less than a metaphor for life itself. "HONK IF YOU THINK AMERICA HAS A 54 SHARE," read one bumper sticker, and those not at home watching honked.

But television was only one of many cultural phenomena to inspire America's fashion industry. A new democratization of style swept the showrooms of Seventh Avenue as couturiers, in tribute to the nation's aging citizenry, declared shapeless, baggy, and saggy *chic*. And if traditional natural materials became scarce throughout the decade, then other materials—just as natural, just as attractive—emerged to take their place. Sheetrock and oilcloth proved especially durable and well-suited to the "look" of the times.

But this was no nation all dressed down with nowhere to go. Fun was as American as ever, and there was no shortage of fads, trends, and just plain craziness to amuse one and all. Nostalgia rose and crested in waves: first for the 1960s and then for the 1970s, and finally, in the late 1980s, for the early 1980s. (However, laboratory tests on rats brought '70s nostalgia to a rapid halt. The creatures were strapped into tiny jogging shoes, given massive doses of cocaine and a certain *eau minérale*, and subjected to repeated viewings of *Star Wars*. They quickly developed fatal cancers.) Another form of nostalgia took hold as well: a fond remembrance of old work habits made obsolete by increasingly sophisticated technology. More and more homes boasted a room outfitted with desks, files, a water cooler, and a time clock. Father would dictate a memo regarding the kid's allowance; Mother would type up her notes from the previous day's meeting concerning the purchase of a new coffee pot; then the two could meet at the water cooler to gossip (or flirt!) for a while, before returning to their desks for an evening of filing drafts and stuffing envelopes.

NOSTALGIA ROSE ... FOR THE 1960s ... FOR THE 1970s, AND FINALLY, IN THE LATE 1980s, FOR THE EARLY 1980s.

Out-of-body trips increased in popularity, and "travel parlors" sprang up to serve the needs of so-called oobies, lest they return to their bodies only to discover—as did many luckless, unsupervised travelers—that their wallet, children, or kidneys had been stolen during their "absence."

But perhaps the centerpiece of the decade, in terms of media, merchandising, and sheer magnificence, was a movie musical. The classic *1984!* triggered a deluge of spinoff consumer goods the likes of which the world had never seen. Indeed, it was this entertainment and commercial phenomenon that catapulted to prominence the animal that was to become the symbol of the decade: the ubiquitous rat.

Harry Peterson, perhaps unaware of his role in the vast drama of buying, selling, and advertising that is our America, shifts the weapon on his shoulder and picks the Howard Baker model. He smiles, savoring his decision.

THE MOVIE OF THE DECADE

From the very start it was double-plus good.

For the happy audiences who flocked to Mike Curb's masterpiece *1984!*, there was something that rang true about the merry crowds of proles and Party members who won through despite shortage and privation, and something touching about loner Winston's charming if impractical conviction that things could be changed. Above all, people were moved by the idea that there was a system that worked—especially when compared to the political chaos around them—and that there was someone, a Big Brother, who was willing to listen to suggestions for improving it. And the audiences openly wept when Winston, having endured the apparently pointless torments of the avenging Party, was taken

EMMANUEL GOLD...
LEADER OF THE BROT...
25 50 75
TAIWAN

1984! INCLUDING
GONNA BE SOME CHANGES 'ROUND HERE
OH RATS * I KNOW WHAT YOU'RE THINKING
I HONESTLY HATE YOU * I'D LOVE TO TURN YOU IN
* AND MANY MORE *

1984! spawned a plethora of spinoffs. Shown here are : a mail-order album featuring fly-by-night groups like The Party and The Unpersons; the Goldstein dartboard—Goldstein's eyes were supposed to "follow you round the room" —and so both they and his glasses scored 100; adult and not-so-adult stimulants; Mattel's Room 101 Toy (strap it on your head and –oh, rats!); A Thought Police badge (occasionally used in all seriousness by drugged youngsters); a pop-up book open to the big scene between Winston and Julia; and, of course, Knickerbocker's Big Brother Cuddly Doll, which warmed a million pillows from Poughkeepsie to Pasadena.

by his apparently traitorous mentor, O'Brien, to the apparently terminal horrors of Room 101, only to find—who else?—his beloved Julia, with a chorus of dancing rats, and of course Big Brother himself, introduced to Winston by O'Brien with the immortal words: "Winston, I want you to meet Big Brother—he's real interested in some of your ideas!"

The movie's success, however, was more than the millions taken in at the box-office. Every aspect of *1984!* was idolized, imitated, merchandised. College students, particularly, picked up on the world of Winston Smith. Two Minutes Hate sessions were common on campus, with the demonstrations usually directed at some close-to-home figure such as the dean or the local surgeon colonel. Parties were thrown at which nothing but cheap (Victory) gin and badly rolled (Victory) cigarettes were served. Kids talked to one another in Newspeak. Big Brother Cuddly Dolls filled the novelty sections of stores. But perhaps the most enduring effect of the movie was to give the decade its most characteristic garment, the overalls, and its most popular mascot, the rat.

DOWNWARDLY MOBILE FASHION

"Halston Goes Queens" was the first of the new wave of fashion promotions that washed over an American public eager for a sensible, practical style. Its hallmarks were the "curlertop-do"—a confectionary coiffure executed in pink plastic and netting, and "puff-peds"—fluffy, aqua-colored fur slippers.

All rights to the name "Halston," which in the 1960s and 1970s had graced the most elegant and expensive of couturier clothes, were, in 1981, given by the original Halston to nightclub entrepreneur Steve Rubell, in exchange for a can of gasoline.

Rubell, echoing Western-wear designer Ralph Lauren, said, "I wanted a look that was authentically American. A true modern classic. For 'Halston Goes Queens' I went back to my roots. I studied my mother and father. I went out at noon to see how day people dressed. I rode the subway, for God's sake."

The Halston line of mint-green polyester pants suits for women and mint-green polyester leisure suits for men swept the country in 1982.

In the fall of 1983, Rubell again dominated American fashion with his new "Halston Goes Shopping Bag Lady" look. He said, "I wanted a look that was authentically American. A true modern classic. I went back to my roots, to my mother and father, to the subway." At New York's Bloomingdale's department store, the paper bags once given away free now sold for more than any of the merchandise that could possibly be carried in them. Having the *right* bag, tied with the *right* string, became as important to the fashionable as having the right rags and throwaways.

If the downward mobility of Halston styles had a sociological underpinning, the "inside-out" look of the early '80s had a psychological one. The look originated in the late '70s custom of turning back sleeves, collars, and trouser cuffs. But with the changing mood of the times, the fashion grew increasingly extreme. As people

became more and more confused and irritated—turned "inside out," as some said—more and more of their lining began to show. Eventually, whole garments were reversed. And when designers created jackets, shirts, and pants to look as if they were inside out, people even wore these models inside out. Susan Sontag, in a celebrated essay in *Women's Wear Daily*, analyzed the trend as "an attempt to expose a person's true interior, a human cry for human faith, the whole inside story." But other observers, perhaps with an eye to the loss of privacy in everyday life, argued that, far from being an exposure of the interior, it was in fact a desperate concealment of the exterior, a brazen attempt, in the face of a hostile world, to realize one's "inhuman potential."

Manhattan's inside-out look was so far out that by the time the rest of the country was in, it was out—New Yorkers were wearing their clothes inside-in again.

VOGUE

JULY
$17.50

Mu-mus, mules, and middle class

HALSTON GOES QUEENS

New York's **tackiest** borough is *Down and In* in London and Paris

Rampant inflation in the early '80s prompted couturiers to make the best of a bad situation. In 1982, cheap became chic.

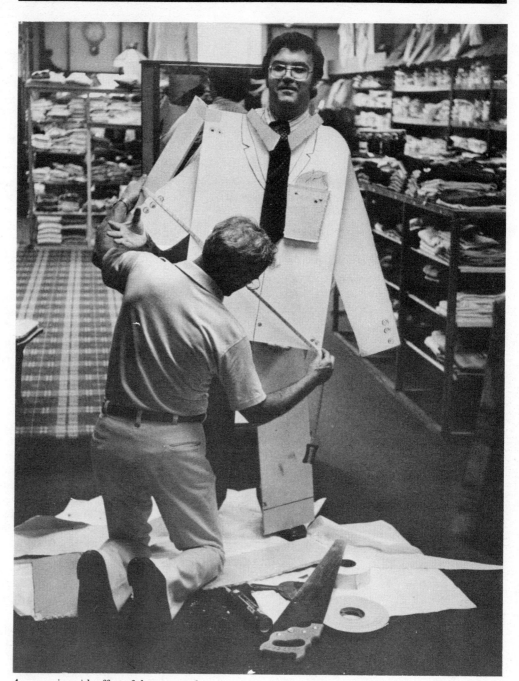

An amusing side effect of the supposed oil shortage in the first half of the decade was a chronic dearth of plastic. A Tupperware jug (left) sold for an undisclosed price in excess of $20,000 at an exclusive Fifth Avenue store in 1984. The astronomical price of polyester fabrics led many designers to experiment with less expensive materials. Above, a Toledo tailor puts the finishing touches on a summer-weight suit made of quarter-inch Sheetrock.

PRIME TIME TERMS

If language is the money of communication, then slang is the gift certificate: informal, situationally specific, not "legal" for all interactions public and private, yet withal valuable and effective. The meanings for which slang expressions and colloquialisms stand could be "bought" using more conventional conversational "cash"—but we are a nation of accountant-poets, as skilled at manipulating language as we are money.

The '80s generated its own distinctive slang expressions, a representative sampling of which appears on these pages. The probable origins of the terms in the events and preoccupations of the times are duly noted. The list was compiled by a professional historian who, as the author of a number of highly entertaining and informative works of popular history, derives great satisfaction (and no little amusement) from his hobby of chronicling the vagaries of contemporary language usage. It is to him that the publisher should wish to express sincere appreciation.

about time, or **A.T.** Approximate time of day: freq. employed by the unemployed. *N.Y. Post*, " 'I will have a further announcement at 4 A.T.,' Mr. Meany said." Also in gen. use by those neurologically incapable of knowing or discovering the time, as in (e.g., during tantrum, coital climax, etc.) *It's about time*.— 2. Hence, any agreement to meet for coitus at an unspecified future time. Jacqueline Onassis, *National Enquirer*, "Elvis and I always had an A.T."

academic robes, all dressed up in, with no papers to grade, or **with no texts to deconstruct**, etc. Unemployed.— 2. Sexually aroused but unable to secure any coital associate, due to unemployment.

aerate one's caps. To talk bull proficiently. Garry Wills, *Milton Nixonistes*, "Lucifer, aerating his caps to the fallen angels ... "

alarming statistics, the. A feeling of melancholy, any moderate form of the creeps; usu. after overindulgence in narcotics, reading material, or coitus. Ex popular song, "St. Louis Alarming Statistics." Dick Francis, *Horse's Ass*, "I woke up with saddle soap on my breath and a case of the alarming statistics."

art, modern, working late on a book of. Fucking: now standard Eng., with much philanthrop. use.

ascertain. Steal. Garry Wills, *Carter Garryistes*, " 'I promise never to lie to you about what I ascertain,' the President snaps."

black evening gown, wearing a. Attired in any costume of black crotchless panties and matching transparent net brassiere.— 2. Naked.— 3. Interested in modern art.— 4. Ready to endure coital adjacency.

bore me with the details! don't. Omit the preliminaries to coitus!: low vegetarian use.

Camp David. Any meeting place for effeminate males. Ex title of novel by Chip Carter.

College of Cardinals. Any gathering of effeminate males. Ex the first herd of sheep with whom any young man practices coitus: New Zealand.

come shot! Yes!, You bet!, or any affirmative ejaculation. Ex film and television depiction of male agreement to cease coition. Margaret Drabble, *A Revised Life of Arnold Bennett*, "We might well ask, then, was this the case? Come shot!" Occ. New Zealand Bar Assn. use.

country sausage. Effeminate male: U.S. South.— 2. Hence, the predominant genital organ of any such effeminate male. Carter, *Camp David*, "Ham's country sausage took Skip by surprise."

development, in. Affianced; annexed for the purpose of ready availability of coital junction. Roger Tory Peterson, *A Field Guide to Drawings of Birds*, "This wren pair mimics the dating patterns of a human couple who are in development." Cf. *step-deal, canceled*.

emerging nation. Semi-erect penile organ: awf. New Zealand State Dept. use.

fade to black. Goodbye.— 2. To terminate a relationship which has included coitus. *New York Variety Times*, "Carter and Voters Fade to Black."

fine print. A diminutive harlot.— 2. Any group of females whose desire for coitus may be desirable. Carl Sagan, *The Voyage of Voyeur II*, "When our mobile camera zoomed in on the Los Angeles landscape, I chose to speculate freely. 'Check out the fine print,' I wittily observed."

get a job. To offer oneself or the members of one's nuclear family for professional coitus.

Glittering Prices. Members of a wild young Society "set" noted for scandalizing pedestrians by "costing them out," ca. 1981. Ex U.S. television series about graduates of the Wharton School of Business and Finance.

grooming the field. Teasing potential subjects for coital toleration, gen. by means of a broom and bucket of water. Ex title of book by Reggie Jackson.

hamburger architect. Ground-meat extender composed of shredded graph paper. Cf. *hamburger engineer* (creamed chipped hard hats), *hamburger executive* (pulverized plexiglass), *hamburger secretary* (styrofoam fragments), etc.

legal defense fund. Any law firm whose members practice advocacy coitus.

lunch in the Oval Office. Oral-genital sexual contact. Ex title of autobiography by Bella Abzug. Cf. *lunch at Whitehall*.

Millie Rem. A wanton female who invites or solicits coitus with nuclear technicians, core attendants, site inspectors, etc., esp. during nuclear mishap. *New York Variety Times*, "Hundreds of thousands of Millie Rems descended on Seabrook."— 2. Hence, U.S., any Nuclear Regulatory Commission groupie.

Mr. ——. Used before a surname to suggest that the male thus designated devotes much time to coitus. Often in *"Hello, Mr. --!"* In business use, implies a moral reprimand.

multiple contusions. The parties to any sexually libertarian domestic arrangement.

nice but not national health insurance. Very abominably distasteful: usu. said after enjoyment of conjugal congress.

now-and-then. Coitus; as in *a bit of the old now-and-then*. Ex Masters & Johnson Report II, which revealed that 96% of Americans achieve sexual contact "now and then," i.e., less often than once every six months.

old spit for new polish. Coitus obtained with one with whom one has had previous coital association, e.g., a former or present spouse. Ex title of autobiography by Elizabeth Taylor.

omelet whisk. The penis: some repuls. use among computer typesetters.

on hold. In state of having recently enacted *coitus obstructus*.— 2. Hence, in any condition of expectation, vertigo, lycanthropy, or malpractice.— 3. Ignored.— 4. Presumed dead. *Sacramento Bee*, "Hoffa Still On Hold."

oxbow incident. Undue coitus, usu. that which damages, weakens, or bends the partners very considerably.

park. Fuck. Either ex (by analogy) the relative impossibility of parking an automobile anywhere ca. 1980s, or, more prob., as H. Hefner (after Marcus Aurelius) insists, ex Greek ρφχϵ, lit. to poke rhythmically until parallel with the curb. Now banned in all dictionaries; the efforts of Arthur Hailey and the Automobile Assn. of Amer. have not succeeded in restoring the word's original dignified status. Cf. *parker, park off, to park over, park you!, park you, Jack!, go park yourself!, parking space,* and *parking meter*.

pen-and-pencil set. Two male participants in a *ménage à trois*.

please sit down! Please sit down!: feminist rhyming slang.— 2. Please cease attempting vertical coitus aboard the aircraft!: never used.

p.o.v. Point of view, as in *it looks fine from my p.o.v., bub*. Ex Masters & Johnson Report II, which revealed that 55% of all coitally able Americans have written one or more film or television scripts.

read me or clear me. Perform coitus with me or park off! Ex pocket-calculator terminology, but much hepcat usage.

secretary of health, education, and welfare. The penis; esp. in *briefing the s. of h., e., and w.,* having sexual intercourse. See *undersecretary*.

share. A measurement for quantifying success, usu. in coital scoring. Quentin Snopes, *Stephen Foster: Extremely Peripheral Bloomsbury Figure,* "On that first night with Vanessa, Steve garnered a twenty-three share."

Special Boots. President of the U.S. Ex footwear customary for visits to sites of nuclear misfortunes. Anthony Lewis, *N.Y. Times,* "Special Boots tiptoed through the State of the Union message . . . "

stamp collector. A woman attending Postal Service balls year after year.— 2. A postal official's trull.

take a meeting. Fly to California for the purpose of engaging in coitus: New Zealand WAC slang.

trade deficit. Difficulty in obtaining opportunities for performing coitus.— 2. The female pudenda: low Ku Klux Klan use.

turnpike tequila. Cocktail of gasohol fashionable among the wealthy.

two ping-pong balls and a fish. Any Chinese motion picture.— 2. The male genitals.— 3. A popular meal consisting of two croquettes made of minced seafood molded around a plastic or styrofoam globular base to add lightness and size; Sidney Sheldon, *The Other Side of Fifty-fourth Street,* " 'I usually just have a couple of ping-pongs-and-fish,' replied the attractive, black-evening-gowned Marsha." By 1987, any round or oval item of fast food, and esp. when consumed before, during, or after coitus. Cf. archaic "Gimme a cuppa cawfee," Raymond Chandler, *The Long Denouement.*— 4. In baseball, a pitching strategy by which the first and second pitch each bounce once, and the third pitch is thrown in such a manner that it gravitates toward the nearest body of water; Roger Angell, *The Bummer Game,* "Forever mourning our bygone youth, we watch as if through a blur of eternal verities as the Tiresian Seaver, now forty-four, totters to the mound like a tyro crossing the Styx, hides the ball in his hair till the final instant, and then, without appearing to move at all, puts two ping-pongs and a fish past the astonished young Nebuchadnezzar in the on-deck circle."

undersecretary. Testicle; gen. in pl. Norman Mailer, *Aquarius on Uranus,* "Had not his small staff two fine hirsute undersecretaries to its credit?"

water pik. Any premature ejaculator.

What? Common reply to any statement or question since c. 1984. Prob. orig., and still mostly, due to elevated noise levels, but hence jocular use. Henny Youngman, " 'Who was that lady I saw you with last night?' 'What?' "

What? What? What? What? What? Customary retort by one who is addressed while panicking during nuclear inadvertency.

Rats –kid substitutes, pet substitutes, some even said substitute substitutes. Whatever their precise function, rats became immensely popular during the decade: partly as a result of their dominant comedy role in 1984!, partly because of their ability to survive (cats, dogs, and most other domestic animals suffered a serious decline during the meat ban); and partly because, when all is said and done, rats are cute and furry. The bad press they had had for centuries was largely countered by the good press they received throughout the '80s. Some examples can be found here.

Vaulted Vole Top Rodent At Westminster

NEW YORK, May 3 — Champion Aurora Blue 2X Hong Kong, a delicate-hued red-backed bank vole from the Monsieur le Rat Runs, Cannes, France, won the Best-of-Show · Award at the second annual Westminster Rat Show here last night to the acclaim of a full-house Madison Square Garden crowd of rat lovers. A close second was Ch. Bob Beamon 2X Jesse Owens, who won the best of the ever-popular Kangaroo Rat class, but just could not match the quick-stepping, haughty vole in the judges' eyes. The crowd grew silent as the judges conferred, and when the vole's win was announced, cries of glee and "Hooray for the voles!" burst forth from the seats.

Among the other winners in their classes were Ch. Two Times Four Equals Eight 4B, a long-tailed gundi from Senegal; Ch. What's Up, Doc 39H, a Philippine shrew rat; Nee Oh Toma 14, a pack rat; and Ch. Formidable Capitalist Eunuch 3X, a harsh-haired nutria from Outer Mongolia.

As usual, the exotix created a stir and captured the crowd's attention, if not the judges' awards. Among the most applauded were the rabbit-sized agoutis, an East African mole-rat, a spiny packet rat, and especially the heavily built aquatic capybaras from South America, the largest of the rats at almost four feet in length. Said one of the bystanders, "Boy, who needs a Great Dane when you've got one of those capybaras to look at? Wow!"

The chief disappointment of the Westminster show was the performance of Ch. King Gustav of Sweden 23X, a highly-regarded bandicoot burrowing rat who tunneled into the dirt floor of the Garden during his showing and would not come out, despite the coaxing of his handler and some mighty tugs on his leash. Officials were still wondering what to do about the bandicoot as of midnite last nite.

Marvel Comix mirrored the new popularity of the once despised rodent with a super-hero named Ratman. Frequently teamed with the no-longer-so-Incredible Hulk, Ratman (who was a specialist in locating edibles) would often save his green-hued friend with tasty tidbits. Marvel super-hero super-creator Stan Lee is reputed to have allowed his own likeness to be used in the creation of Ratman.

Stating that the next time he saw a cat he hoped it would be "sauteed in onions with a touch of lemon," artist B. Kliban turned out a series of even more successful "rat" books, excerpted here.

HOW TO TELL A RAT FROM A BIG MAC.

Fig. 1   *Fig. 2*

RATS CAN SEE THINGS WE CAN'T.

© B. Kliban

THE LAW

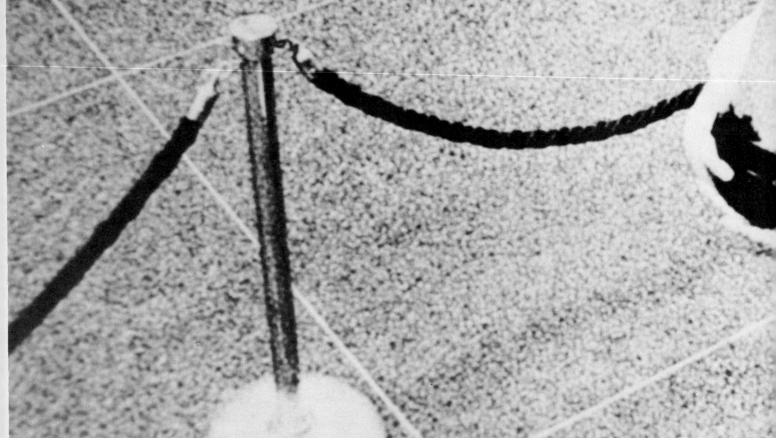

A hidden camera caught Robert Schlesinger in the act of holding up the First National Bank of Toledo with a homemade atomic bomb. "Give me all your money," he grunted, "or I'll blow up this bank—and all its branches."

THE LAW

It is morning on June 2, 1988, and Leon Cohen is exhausted. He should be: he has just completed another all-night study session, and today is his bar exam. To be licensed to practice, rehearse, and perform law in the state of Maryland, he must pass a rigorous test. Leon will have to apply his own makeup, handle a lavalier mike under demanding conditions, and improvise off-the-cuff during a simulated loss of video. He sets his jaw in determination, confirms in the mirror the superiority of his left profile, and leaves the apartment.

Society is built on fear: man fears man, man fears nature, man fears himself, nature fears man, nature fears itself. That is why there are laws. "Natural law" keeps man at bay, and protects nature from the folly with which man seeks to circumvent nature, enslave himself, and destroy the universe. Similarly, the laws of man, which form his civilization, are those strictures that protect nature and man alike from the foolishness with which man and nature might conspire to circumvent man, destroy nature, and enslave the universe. A good society turns fear into law; a great society turns law into hits. Such was the legacy of the 1980s.

Crime *qua* crime, it must be said, declined. Many attributed this to an increased police "presence," as insightful network programmers realized just how many "legs" a show could have if it dealt with truth. Web produc-

WITH THE INSTITUTION OF TELEVISED COURTROOM PROCEEDINGS, LAW ITSELF BECAME A SUPERSTAR.

ers, in cooperation with local law enforcement agencies, presented cruelly realistic stories of lawbreakers and headbreakers filmed *as they occurred*. Indeed, the decade ended with the Network financially underwriting police and firefighting departments in almost every major market—proof positive that the old categories (crime and coverage, lawman, bad man, and newsman) were breaking down and melding into one efficient, exciting, and profitable system of criminology and entertainment. To be sure, the change was not effected without difficulty. Some wondered, for example, why the abolition of the FBI (at the hands of the Congress of Nuts) should result in the widespread disappearance of entire types of crimes, making the jailbird the *rara avis* he ultimately became.

But many knew better than to ask such questions. When the Supreme Court ruled that a free press, to be truly "free," must be distributed to its readers without charge, the death of the print media was assured. It fell to television, then, to bring into our homes the rich panoply of American police and criminal activity during the '80s. The result: democracy's ratings went through the roof.

And it did not end with the chase, club, and collar. With the institution of televised courtroom proceedings, law itself became a superstar—half sitcom, half docu-drama, and all first-rate entertainment. So compelling were the trials that many witnesses broke down in stunning "Perry Mason"-like confessions, proving time and again that good justice and good television were one and the same. For lesser proceedings, phone-in radio trials and conference-call arraignments helped the wheels of justice turn a little faster.

The American Bar Association's "Abie" awards, instituted in 1984, became an annual celebration, not only of law but of individual excellence in its practice—one which might have prompted Justice herself to set down her balance scales, peep out from under her blindfold, and applaud with the nation as it toasted its very best attorneys, prosecutors, expert witnesses, and court stenographers.

But tragedy may strike even the most popular of legal systems, and so it was with ours. When a majority of our Supreme Court justices were killed in Neo-Irvington (three others died of natural causes), some people feared for the ability of the showboat of state to remain afloat. But Chief Justice Warren Burger proved not only that one man could be a majority, but that he could perform the legal tasks of nine. He did it with grace and with efficiency, thanks to his own brilliant innovation—Night Supreme Court. The pistol-packing chief justice's ruling that any major corporation, and in the '80s nearly every remaining corporation *was* major, may spend any amount of money to further its interest expressed the American business metaphysic with unparalleled clarity—and eliminated most forms of white-collar crime virtually overnight.

Public relations wizard David Halberstam has written, "In order to survive, a democracy must have good publicity." If Leon Cohen can remember only this as he applies his pancake, he will already be a long way toward attaining that shingle of which he has dreamed since boyhood: LEON COHEN, ESQ., SAG, AFTRA. He will be a licensed attorney, able to practice law "in the studios and on the stations of the sovereign state of Maryland."

DEALING WITH THE BLACK HAND

In the '50s and '60s, it was the Cosa Nostra, or the Mafia; in the '70s, through the efforts of Italian-American groups, it had become "organized crime"; but in the '80s, many thoughtful observers sensed a subtle change in the fabled Italian criminal organization. The change was typified by an apparent reversal in its once hostile relationship with the government. Whether traditional Central Intelligence Agency ties with the federal authorities or a growing community of interest was the cause, there were many who felt, as a prominent columnist for the *New York Times* who later drowned in a freak highway accident put it, that "a deal was being cut."

On April 14, 1982, the carcasses of over 13,000 silber mudgeons, a flounder-sized fish whose precarious existence had been holding up an Army Corps of Engineers dam in upper Washington state, were found in automobile trunks in Tacoma, slain "in gangland style," according to a Sierra Club spokesman who later died of injuries sustained in a peculiar mountain-climbing accident in his own living room.

In early 1983, the government quietly announced that the problem of nuclear wastes had been solved. "They have been disposed of by qualified parties in a place or places where they will not cause further trouble," said a Department of Energy official who would not comment further. Investigations by a number of public and private groups sustained the claim; not one ounce of over 400,000 tons of highly radioactive substances could be found at their former storage sites or anywhere else in the United States.

In the months to come, jukeboxes appeared in the control rooms of every nuclear power plant in the country, a carting company in Brooklyn received a defense contract to transport the new MX mobile missile, and on April 5, 1983, acting on a tip, Federal Bureau of Investigation agents searched a space shuttle that had just landed at Vandenberg Air Force Base after a technical problem cut short its flight from Cape Canaveral in Florida to earth orbit, and found 183,000 pounds of ultra-pure cocaine in its cargo bays.

But if there was an arrangement, no one was complaining. It may have been true that all of the White House state dinners were being catered by a small company in Queens for 30 million dollars a year, that the Army had to employ nearly 100 giant C-5A transports on a daily basis to take its laundry to the Bronx, and that the Navy had to move its Trident submarine base to a United Fruit Company warehouse in Jersey City, but there were compensations.

On September 15, 1984, the entire board of the U.S. Steel Corporation, which had just announced a price rise of 23 percent condemned by the president as "a blueprint for depression," was found encased in slag in a runoff mold from a basic oxygen furnace in Pittsburgh. In the spring of 1985, after only three days of consultations at the Elysée Palace, a secret American delegation gained French approval for the immediate repayment, plus interest at an annual rate of 2,000 percent, of France's entire war debt. And certainly no one complained when, on October 12, 1985, fishermen in the Persian Gulf found the bodies of 17 ayatollahs, including Khomeini, stuffed in an oil drum. On the contrary, there was a feeling that somewhere there was someone who knew how to get things done.

On the night of June 7, 1986, Salvatore "America" Vespucci, reputed *capo di tutti capi di tutti capi,* was John-John Kennedy's guest on the American Broadcasting System's "Tonight Show." "Hey, Johnny-Johnny," he said. "You know the Mafia don't exist, and since we don't exist, you had to invent us. That'sa funny, no? Hey, when I make a joke, you should laugh." Villages chuckled, cities roared as the laughter spread across a continent.

"Poor guys never had a chance," mused Officer Joe Marino, surveying organized crime's mass execution of 13,000 silber mudgeons —the entire species. "I guess tonight the fish are sleeping with the fishes."

THE DEATH PENALTY— A NEW LEASE ON LIFE

Popular ire over seemingly foolish and arbitrary judicial decisions in favor of criminals caused a revolution in the American system of criminal justice.

Burgeoning cable-television technology that allowed viewers to talk back to their sets also enabled home viewers to become judges and juries for the first time. In fact, the traditional role of judges was soon rendered obsolete and they became more like assistant directors: in charge of lighting, makeup, seating, station-breaks, and audience reaction.

While this phenomenon sprang up spontaneously in several parts of the country, one trial, *State of Georgia* v. *Hernandez*, can be considered the watershed in the acceptance of what was popularly called "Trial by Tube." Ruben Hernandez, 14 years old, was an itinerant tobacco picker. In March 1984, while hitchhiking from Florida to Connecticut, he was arrested in Dalton, Georgia, and charged with the brutal mutton-related murder of a 9-year-old derelict, Steve-Lou Crawford.

Miss Crawford's parents, Steve and Lou Crawford, claimed to have heard screams, then to have seen a small dark figure scurrying away. Three weeks later, Mr. Hernandez, who fitted the description, was arrested as he waited for a ride on Highway I-85 outside Dalton.

The prosecuting attorney, Orville Leis, originally felt he did not have enough evidence to go before the grand jury and recommended Mr. Hernandez' release. The resulting public outcry caught the attention of Thad Burner, owner of a regional cable-television network based in Atlanta, and brought him into the forefront of the Video-Justice movement. Mr. Burner suggested that the district attorney not take the law into his own hands. He then offered three weeks of prime time in which to hold the trial on his cable network, which was equipped with QUBE technology allowing viewers to instantly register their opinions and preferences.

The justice meted out by Mr. Burner's subscribers was swift and sure, to say the least. After three days of televised hearings, Mr. Hernandez was unanimously convicted of first-degree murder and sentenced to the steam chair.

After frantic pleas for an appeal were rejected by the cable viewers, Mr. Hernandez' attorney, Thedford Jackson, took his case to the federal level, pleading with Jerry Brown, the president of CBS, for further exposure. Mr. Brown seemed to consent and an unprecedented network appeal was scheduled.

The appeal, which swamped "Mork and Mindy" in the ratings for six consecutive weeks, centered on procedural questions and broke new legal ground.

Mr. Jackson claimed he had been unable to introduce evidence that would have proven the elder Crawford was a once-convicted pederast with a craving for lamb chops. He declared that as he was about to embark on this line of argument, the judge had recessed the court to "go to a commercial."

"By the time we got back," Mr. Jackson said, "we had to break for a replay of the Olympic hot-tubbing finals. We were preempted, and all of a sudden it was time for the audience verdict."

Mr. Jackson further argued during the course of the appeal that in the first trial his client was denied due makeup, due correct lighting, due sound checks, and due cue cards.

Mr. Jackson's moves paid off: Mr. Hernandez won his appeal and was released, richer by some $10,000 in AFTRA scale payments.

The American criminal justice system was irrevocably altered by the *Hernandez* decision. The squadrons of skilled media experts, makeup artists, lighting technicians, and choreographers that have grown up in its wake now assure all citizens of an equitable broadcast-trial before a jury of at least 12 million of their peers.

comfort to a large group of citizens, many of whom are poor or black or brown, or to a group of network executives based in New York, many of whom have Eastern European ancestries.[1] Regrettable as it is that one of these unworthy constituencies must be satisfied, the choice of this Court is clear.[2]

It is not for this court to pass judgment on the merits of Mr. Jones' idea; we cannot say that a situation comedy based on *Heart of Darkness* is worthwhile or not.[3] What can be said is that a government-granted monopoly, the television industry, must grant Mr. Jones the same right to be heard as must any organization "affected with quasi-state powers."

We have long held that "the right to treatment" belongs to all, including the mentally ill. We now hold that every citizen is entitled to "a right to treatment" in dealing with licensed stations and networks.

---

[1] If one more law school senior named Goldberg or Blatstein comes to my office looking for a clerkship, I'm gonna lose my lunch.

[2] Some of these jungle bunnies are at least Christians.

[3] Sounds a lot better than a bunch of homos talking about sex and vasectomies and God-knows-what-else.

The Supreme Court in 1980 (top), 1984 (middle) — after the Neo-Irvington tragedy — and as it has been since 1986 (bottom). A landmark case brought by the Court before the Court in 1988 declared the Court's right "in the absence of the other two branches of government" to confirm new appointees to the Court. The Court agreed unanimously, 1–0.

SEX 'N HEALTH

Her tee shirt told everyone that this comely young lady had been a successful participant in the International Year of the Simultaneous Orgasm. Although most of those involved acquitted themselves admirably, it became apparent that many non-comes were wearing tee shirts under (or over) false pretenses.

SEX 'N HEALTH

I t is a warm May afternoon in the year 1986. Mrs. Emily Maxwell sits quietly in her doctor's office, struggling with equally powerful emotions of joy and fear. Mrs. Maxwell has just been informed by her team of preliminary consulting obstetricians that she is indeed pregnant. However, it has also been determined that the fetus has cancer. Several options are available to her—none will cost her a penny—and she mulls over the choices. Perhaps she wonders if there is any connection between this dilemma and her husband's orgasm two months ago.

Nothing is more American than a good orgasm. Indeed, how could it be otherwise for the nation that outstripped all others in the pursuit and consummation of the development of the atomic bomb—orgasm of matter itself? We are a country to whom sex is food. Our forebears were lusty immigrants: ignorant, hardy peasant men and their earthy, big-bosomed wives, people for whom copulation and orgasm were as fundamental as plowing a field and milking a cow. And it is no different today. Our men may be more refined and intellectually superior, our wives may be more attractive and better-dressed ... but we are still a nation where orgasm is a way of life. Yet it is the paradoxical nature of things in this world that, during the '80s, many Americans—through no fault of their own—endured lives wholly devoid of that ecstatic, blissful, convulsive, explosive release,

NOTHING IS MORE AMERICAN THAN A GOOD ORGASM.

which, if attained, is the *summum bonum* in the land of *E Pluribus Unum*.

Some found this ironic. For it was during the '80s that a comprehensive medical care program was instituted, guaranteeing every citizen, if not sexual fulfillment via orgasm, certainly adequate health care. Monies received by the Insurance Revenue Service went to every corner of the increasingly specialized medical profession, from the Memorial Sloan-Kettering Institute for the Treatment of Diseases of the Eyebrow to individual physicians investigating the whys and why-nots of orgasm.

In fact, orgasm and genitalia were on everyone's lips. The discovery of a second kind of male orgasm provoked heated exchanges. Some held the penis to be a mere mechanical instrument, and called the penile orgasm "invalid."

Others felt the scrotum to be simply an annex of the penis, and spoke disdainfully of the "myth" of the scrotal orgasm. But by the end of the decade, many Americans had not experienced orgasm of any kind whatsoever in years and years. They could barely remember what it felt like, found the whole topic rather tedious, and

ORGASM PENETRATED THE DEEPEST, DARKEST RECESSES OF THE BODY POLITIC.

were sick to death of hearing their fellow Americans natter on about vaginal-this and penile-that at cocktail parties and faculty luncheons. Such public discussion of what, in less fortunate societies, was usually a private affair, full of gruntings and moanings and the sweaty, hot feel of bare skin on bare skin, with the bed or office couch redolent of the pungent, musky scent of male and female fluids blending in a hot, wild embrace, was boring.

There were more noteworthy events in medicine during the '80s. The causes of and cure for cancer were found. But it was orgasm that penetrated the deepest, darkest recesses of the body politic. The Simultaneous Orgasm of 1983 brought fleeting pleasure to some, but history must not forget that, for many, life was business as usual. Indeed, those who failed to "come" during the great screaming, pounding, delightful, and joyous Simultaneous Orgasm did not miss it in the slightest, did not want to hear from some 300 different people what it was like, and did not even care to discuss it.

True, such citizens suffered the opprobrium of being labeled "non-comes" by some of their more cruel, immature neighbors. But such taunts had little effect. And, as orgasm became more and more scarce toward the latter part of the decade, the distinction between "comer" and "non-come" came to nil, as both enjoyed an equal measure of pleasure in the substitution of postcoital depression for actual orgasm. "Are you depressed yet?" became the most anxiously asked question in the lover's repertoire of passion.

When medical science discovered that each individual possessed a finite number of possible orgasms in his or her lifetime, the "non-comes" were, so to speak, avenged. For did it not then seem that those denied participation in the Simultaneous Orgasm had a much more delightful dotage ahead of them—an old age of virtually uninterrupted orgasm?

Emily Maxwell is at peace. Her child's cancer can be cured, and her baby is being born into a world free of worry about orgasm—be it penile orgasm, scrotal orgasm, vaginal orgasm, clitoral orgasm, any new form of orgasm such as naval orgasm, or any combination thereof, and regardless of what anyone cares to say about it, thank you very much.

ONE HEALTHY NATION

It was the most muscular bureaucratic system of the decade, brawling its way to hegemony, and it held America together. National health care, the grand legislative dream of Edward M. Kennedy, gathered momentum gradually, partly from the cancer panic of the first five years of the 1980s, partly from the skyrocketing costs of doctors and hospitals, and partly because, as one eternally youthful American Medical Association president put it, "it was a darn prime time idea."

Typical of the vast quasi-private entities that moved into the vacuum left by a derelict federal government, national health care was really an expanded version of the old Blue Cross/Blue Shield plan. Citizens, increasingly reluctant to vote any federal funds, nonetheless continued to support lavish budgets for medical research. With no federal machinery to administer such programs, something had to be done to exploit this willingness to spend. Blue Cross executives felt that even if America was not ready to earmark a large percentage of its income for the support of indigence, it was only too happy to devote the same sum to staying alive. Accordingly, on June 3, 1984, Blue Cross announced a comprehensive cradle-to-grave health program. They also announced substantial increases in health premiums and their takeover of the moribund Internal Revenue Service to collect them. The latter move gave the program not only its financial underpinning but its name—the Blue Cross Insurance Revenue Service, or IRS.

Inevitably, some were soon pointing out potential abuses. They charged that even though medical treatment was now free and income tax was virtually nonexistent, premiums had risen 1,500 percent and had become simply a *de facto* system of taxation. (A somewhat flimsy substantiation of this argument was the fact that premiums were now collected, not weekly or monthly, but annually, every April 15.) They claimed that the new laws were written in such a way that the rich could exploit loopholes to create insurance shelters or take massive insurance write-offs. Many

corporations, they alleged, made no payments at all through the simple expedient of listing all their employees as dependents. A few even charged the AMA with "looting the American premium payer," and called the IRS a "medical vegetable barrel."

The voices of the many, however, were also heard—in gratitude for a system that brought life and hope to an entire generation. Health care was indeed comprehensive. Virtually unlimited funds made it possible for dozens of highly trained doctors to be on hand for, say, one patient's foot problem. Shunted from brilliant specialist team to brilliant specialist team, the average American was soon the best-cared-for human being on earth, his every follicle and blood vessel the responsibility of entire departments. Certainly it cost money, but as one noted folliclologist quipped, "Life in America *ain't* cheap!" And if the IRS bureaucracy was no less sprawling and pervasive than the one it replaced, at least it now had a vital need to exist. Nothing attests to the fact better than the by now familiar galaxy of new posts it created—the Director of the Intestine, the Supervisor of the Duodenum, the Secretary of State of Kidneys, and the Ambassador to the Isles of Langerhans are but a few.

And national health care paid off. Not only did cancer go down beneath its onslaught; in 1986 the nation's number-one killer, heart disease, succumbed with the appearance of the IRS-franchised discount-transplant clinics and their cheap, lightweight, disposable sheep hearts, beagle aortas, and rabbit ventricles. Emphysema similarly yielded to the massive importation of rat lung replacements from Kowloon; diabetes breathed its last in 1987; and in 1988 malaria was declared an endangered disease. By decade's end, most of the nation's major killers, with the notable exception of sickle-cell anemia, were on their last legs.

No more moving testimony to the indomitability of medical science could be found than the drama that took place in a television studio in Burbank, California, on Labor Day, 1989. There, a defeated

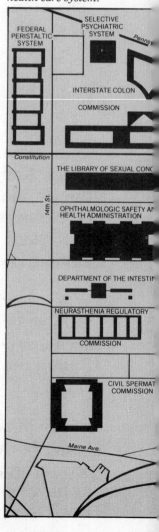

The face of Washington was changed as defunct federal agencies gave way to the dynamic new national health care system.

Abuse of new laws allowing doctors to advertise helped build pressure for a national health program. The operation discussed here, for instance, was actually a simple lobotomy, performed with an electric drill.

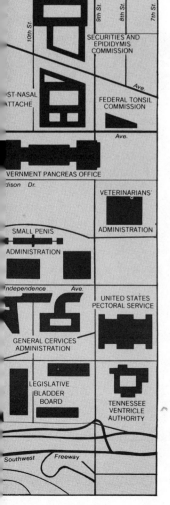

Jerry Lewis, shunted from disease to disease throughout the decade, took a desperate deep breath and faced up to the glowing red light of the camera. "People," he said, mopping his brow, "you all know me. You know what I believe in. All of the things I have *believed* in. And that's why ... I'm asking you to help me put an end to death due to natural causes." And so was born the first Natural Causes Telethon, a moving testament to the golden heart of show business. America watched as all the other displaced telethon hosts who hadn't had a disease to fight in years—Jack Narz, Red Buttons, Bob McAllister, Sonny Fox, Soupy Sales, and many more—embraced Jerry Lewis in a tearful reunion. Finally, Dean Martin appeared and Lewis, openly weeping, turned to the audience. "I want all of you to call now," he said with quiet conviction. "Let's stamp out this killer in my lifetime."

THE LEGIONS OF THE TV BLIND

■t should have been anticipated, like so many other grave and menacing problems.

Certainly, all of responsible science knew that the 25,000-volt cathode-ray gun of the standard color television set beamed streams of electrons at the phosphors on the TV screen, making them glow at the "flicker-fusion" rate of the eye, imparting the illusion of motion. And science also knew that the "wavicles" of light energy from the TV screen were projected onto the retina of the human eye, bathing human photoreceptors in energy and stimulating chemical interactions in the body's neural systems: in the pineal gland, the pituitary, the spinal cord, and the gonads.

And yet the members of the first television generation sat passively for countless thousands of hours, their retinas continually bathed in energy from the picture tube, exposed to a process of selective reinforcement as, again and again, their eyes followed the repetitive rhythm of the TV scan pattern.

Gradually over the years, the devastating and irreversible effects on human physiology became evident. At first the lurking disease took its toll in mysterious ways. In 1981, there was a series of inexplicable automobile accidents: seasoned drivers would suddenly sit as though mesmerized in their moving vehicles—helpless as their cars careened out of control, smashing into other cars and buildings. Then, in 1982, there was the mysterious outbreak of the "urban zombie" phenomenon: without explanation people would stand quietly on streets and sidewalks, in parking lots and plazas, apparently hypnotized by any small rectangle and unable to move until transported to a new location.

It was not until 1982 that these strange phenomena were identified as the first tragic cases of "TV blindness." Further research led to a sophisticated understanding of the characteristic syndrome. Sufferers first displayed symptoms of isolation, disconnectedness, and even autism. Upon a visit to the ophthalmologist, the cause was readily diagnosed: they suffered from "525 vision." Victims' retinal areas were found to be minuscule, squarish, and receptive only to stroboscopic motion. The surrounding photoreceptors of the brain had become atrophied. In laymen's terms, their retinas were tiny TV screens capable only of receiving images from other TV sources. The effect on their eyeballs was to pull the cornea back into the skull, giving them a haunted, pointy-eyed appearance.

More seriously, the victims' world view, their very comprehension of their environment, was also permanently affected. To the "TV blind," the visual universe was only accessible if seen on a screen. The rest was darkness.

A Washington lady gives generously to a victim of TV blindness. "Even though I know he'll just save it up and buy another TV," she said, "I feel that there but for the grace of God view I."

At first, the pitiful legions of the TV blind walked the streets of the cities with canes and cups in their hands, wearing placards that said, "Do you thank God that you can see?" Helpless to control themselves, they would pause before anything remotely resembling a television screen. It was not uncommon to see these sad victims sitting in their automobiles, gazing hopefully at their own windshields. On the streets, they clustered in front of Don't Walk signs, stared at the dark oblongs of newsstands, peered into the chutes of mailboxes. Many of the TV blind suffered frightful burns while trying to change the channel on their fireplaces and microwave ovens.

The development of General Texas Microprocessor Lenses soon enabled these citizens to live a full life once more. And by the end of the decade, a new militancy infected the ranks of the TV blind; pluckily gathering up their courage, they began to demand their rights, ultimately forcing Americans to refer to them as the "TV sighted" in polite company. These courageous Americans soon found that their handicap made them employable in areas other than television studios and processing airline reservations. By the end of the decade, the tale of triumph over their terrible affliction was perhaps best recounted in the inspirational motto of the Lighthouse for the TV Sighted: "Our nights are brighter than your days."

Hello. Eyuh.

I'm Marshall McLuhan. Eyuh. You probably know me as a Canadian professor, a media philosopher, and an actor in Wŏŏdi Allen movies. Eyuh. But there is something about me that you may not know. I suffer from 525 vision. Yes, that's right. Eyuh. I am one of the so-called TV blind. Won't you support our efforts to learn more about television sightedness? Eyuh?

Please write to the Lighthouse for the TV Sighted, 741 West 57th Street, New York....

TEXT OF A PUBLIC-SERVICE
TELEVISION COMMERCIAL, 1986.

THE DEATH OF CANCER

Cancer: the slayer of youth's promise and age's wisdom. It is hard for us to recall now that the very word once struck terror into the average American's heart. Like a murderous psychotic stalking the nocturnal streets of the city, it struck without rhyme or reason at young, old, beautiful, and not so beautiful alike. And the forces of medicine and order seemed powerless to strike back. Indeed, as the '70s became the '80s, an ever-lengthening list of causes was added to the traditional environmental and industrial factors. It was even discovered, late in 1982, that many of the central activities of the previous decade were themselves causes of the grim disorder. Extensive carcinomas were found to have developed in devotees of jogging, hang-gliding, est, *eau minérale de la source*, mood rings, roller skating, and imported food processing machines.

Americans, of course, are not ones to let foes stride amongst them unchallenged. The establishment of the Blue Cross Insurance Revenue Service, with its rapid assumption of responsibility for all areas of health care, gave society the weapons it needed to search out and destroy the killer. Ironical, then, that when the cure was discovered it came from so simple and unlikely a source. A young anthropologist visiting Prince Edward Island in Canada's Provinces Maritimes was intrigued by the zero incidence of cancer among the impoverished islanders. A brilliant series of deductions revealed the reason—and the medical miracle of the century. A totally effective antidote to all known forms of cancer was a substance secreted in the cranium of the baby harp seal when its head was struck repeatedly.

In addition, further research showed that the effectiveness of the serum was directly related to the size of the baby harp seal's eyes. It was this fact that perhaps best dramatized the crisis of conscience experienced by those who, as harp seal farms and abattoirs sprang up throughout the country, felt grave moral qualms about the propriety of the cure. The dilemma was nowhere better expressed than by distinguished zoologist Brigitte Bardot in a famous discussion of *la question phoque* (the seal question) with equally distinguished sociologist Phil Donahue:

"This is my belief. I would rather catch cancer than profit from their death. All my life my motto has been—I cannot reject a *phoque*."

The discovery of a cure for cancer, as related in the following extract from The Lives of a Cancer Cell by Dr. Lewis Thomas, not only provided the answer to the century's most vexing medical riddle, but ended overnight the bitter ecological controversy about the slaughter of baby harp seals.

The empty spaces of our biological knowledge are filled not only by the gleanings of intent but also by the stuff of sheer fortuitousness. Consider our struggle to decipher the message of the organelles. Or ponder the bold new language of the banter of RNA and DNA in the dialogue of the prokaryotic blue-green algae.

Yet these wonders of serendipity seem to pall beside the ironic whisper of the voice of the baby harp seal to the seashell of the medical ear. Consider, for a moment, the absurdity of history. A generation of animal-welfare protesters stalks the annual hunt of the harp seals on Prince Edward Island. One of them, a young anthropologist from the University of Chicago, stays to conduct a field observation of the island culture. The anthropologist, in the course of his longitudinal study, learns that the Prince Edward Islanders have the lowest incidence of cancer of any culture that has ever been investigated. Consequently, a team of medical and epidemiological researchers from the Insurance Revenue Service descends upon the wind-swept Canadian villages. They

David, or "Dukes," as this little fella is known to his researchers, smiles happily under the impression that his recent 20-yard jog has reduced his waistline. What he doesn't know is that his weight loss confirms that jogging and jogging shoes are major causes of cancer.

are invited one evening, during the annual seal kill, to partake of a delicacy: seal brain soup. The Canadian counterpart of the local *griot* informs the researchers that the soup has magical and beneficent qualities. An idle epidemiologist, on a lark, runs his soup leftovers through a gas chromatograph mass spectrometer. And soon: the astonishing revelations. Seal brain soup, it seems, does have medicinal powers. *Mirabile dictu*, it can even cure cancer. But only if the seals are young enough—and if the seal brain synapses are stimulated strongly enough, by the repeated effects of sharp blows to the cranium, to trigger the production of the unique harp seal acetylcholine.

But the Prince Edward Islanders know only that the warm and nourishing soup has always made them healthy. This is all that matters to them. Or should matter to us—or to me, when a massive infusion of harp seal serum saved what was left of "my green age." So don't look for aught but natural law in the quest for closer communion with your mitochondria. Ponder the streaming of the chloroplasts, and drink deep of the synchrony of harp seal soup.

Cards such as this were to be found lining the walls of the faithful old 747s that serviced the inter-city Subway of the Air.

THE INTERNATIONAL YEAR OF THE SIMULTANEOUS ORGASM

Was the idea of an international simultaneous orgasm—the possibility that every sexually mature inhabitant of the earth could climax in a single moment—a good one or not?

Many believed it had merit. Whatever one's opinion, it was hard in the winter of 1983 to ignore the debate. "YO" (Year of the Orgasm) fever had set in.

For its proponents, the realization of YO would be a signal that civilization had come of age. They argued that the peoples of the world—black, white, communist, capitalist, men or women alike—forget politics, money, and war when it comes to the matter of "coming." Their dream—that countless couples in countless huts, bedrooms, cars, fields, and trees could move in countless positions toward one vast epiphany—and thus change the world—came true. With a vengeance.

The cornerstone of the effort to bring YO to fruition was laid in 1982 by the United Nations. Earlier that year, a number of reports had begun to appear documenting a mysterious decline in orgasm among First World countries, especially in the United States. Many reasons were suggested: long debilitating waits in gas lines, anxiety over the changing role of women, the widespread popularity of disco, to name but a few. Whatever the causes, First World nations were distinctly embarrassed, and in September 1982, a coalition of Third World nations led by the Arab bloc introduced a resolution in the UN General Assembly that 1983 be declared the International Year of the Orgasm.

Reaction in the U.S. delegation was panicky. A vote against the resolution would seem to be a confirmation of the decline in First World orgasms, while a vote for it would play into the hands of the Third World coalition, which undoubtedly had secret plans for testing the First World's ability to climax. In a brilliant move suggested by U.S. delegate Marion Javits, the Arab bloc was forced onto the defensive with the Western counterproposal that 1983 should be declared the International Year of the Female Orgasm.

It was the Third World's turn to panic. To vote against the counterproposal would be a rebuff to 53 percent of the planet's inhabitants, the majority of whom lived in Third World countries. To vote *for* raised the possibility of having to induce in their mates a physical experience that had been unknown, and even taboo, for upwards of 2,000 years.

Chaos was the norm at the UN during October and November. Fortunately or unfortunately, the publicity given the debates had fired public response everywhere. First Worlders, challenged by the original proposal, sought the opportunity to prove themselves. Third World women, egged on by the counterproposal ("Let your women go—and come," it proclaimed), demonstrated for it by the tens of millions. For the first time in its history, the General Assembly was a genuinely representative body, its delegates obliged to reflect the desires of its "constituents."

Proposals and counterproposals mushroomed overnight. Mexico offered a "Year of the Self-Induced Orgasm," while Japan, with a weather eye to international trade, came up with a "Year of the Mechanically Induced Orgasm." Germany and France proffered respectively "Vaginal Orgasm" and "Clitoral Orgasm" refinements of the original counterproposal; Turkey suggested a "Year of the Anal Orgasm," which it fruitlessly amended to "Oral Orgasm" after negative reaction in the Security Council. The General Assembly was baffled by China's "Year of the Thousand Recurrent Glorious Orgasms in One Night," and unreceptive to a perhaps

The movement of the earth as it was recorded during the International Simultaneous Orgasm by an American satellite manned by two male astronauts. A Russian satellite manned by a male and female astronaut failed to record the climactic moment.

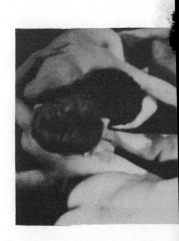

prophetic joint Swiss-Swedish proposal making orgasm an international crime to be tried by The Hague. It fell to Canada, whose chief delegate, Pierre Trudeau, later said he had "heard about it somewhere," to make "Simultaneous Orgasm" the resolution on which everyone could agree. At 23:53 Eastern time, December 31, 1982, the General Assembly agreed that 1983 should be declared "The International Year of the Simultaneous Orgasm" by a show of hands, 1,103–0, Iran abstaining.

Thanks to the energetic support of the U.S. National Aeronautics and Space Administration, the IYSO became a practical reality at an astonishing pace. A global network of satellite monitoring stations was constructed by the participating nations of the world, and enthusiastic armies of students, workers, and citizens organized themselves into training contingents. A party spirit prevailed all over the world. Everyone, from lawyers to radicals, from housewives to "meatheads," from gays to politicians, could relate in their own way to "doing the YO." Early on in 1983, UNISEX began coordinating a series of worldwide time trials—or, as wags termed them, "dry runs"—and multinational corporations facilitated the dissemination of timing devices through their worldwide distribution networks.

To say that there was enthusiasm for the IYSO did not imply there was a dearth of problems. In the earliest test runs, Israel had a tendency toward premature ejaculation, the United Magic Kingdom had difficulty with foreplay, and Ireland found it possible to participate only if the lights were turned out.

For many, on the personal level, there was the intense pressure to perform—for their nations, for their partners, and for themselves. There was also simply the sheer difficulty for citizens of many nations to agree on proper "sim-sex" partners. The spawning of computer matching services for the YO was paralleled by the rise of fly-by-night YO coaches like the Reverend Jackson Eisenhower, who billed himself as the "Wizard of Org."

Finally, after weeks of frenzied rehearsals, a hopeful world began the countdown.

Preparations for the world-wide moment of Simultaneous Orgasm did not always proceed smoothly. Here in Aberdeen, Scotland, for instance, a group of Highlanders —most of them nude for the first time in their lives —experience a moment of confusion as to "where the lassies are."

There were several tense moments— Argentina insisted on going to the bathroom, and a regional supervisor's voice was heard crackling over the global hookup: "Hold it—hold it, Israel! Hold it—for Christ's sake!"—then the long-anticipated event occurred. On October 17, 1983, at 3:10 A.M. Greenwich time, the entire world came together. And, as Walter Cronkite later said, "The earth moved."

Literally. The global satellite monitoring system detected an instantaneous shift in the earth's polar axis of 4.2 degrees. Scientists at Columbia University's Lamont-Doherty Geological Observatory and at the U.S. Geological Survey's earthquake monitoring center in California measured seismic disturbances that registered up to 9.9 on the Richter scale. Within minutes, volcanoes formed along the margins of most of the earth's tectonic plates. Large portions of Kenya disappeared into the Great Rift Valley, and the partial disintegration of the Indian sub-continent lowered Mount Everest and its surrounding Sherpa villages below sea level. Longterm developments included a prolonged drought that was to convert much of the American Midwest into a vast, arid desert.

In retrospect, it is insufficient to calculate the physical consequences of the International Year of the Orgasm. The aspirations of a generation had been dashed on the rocks of coition. Orgasm was largely discredited, sexual dysfunction was a societal norm, and national detumescence dominated the rest of the decade.

The four existential positions are these.

(1) I'm coming and you're coming.

(2) I'm coming and you're not coming.

(3) I'm not coming and you're coming.

(4) I'm not coming and you're not coming....

EXCERPT FROM *I'M COMING, YOU'RE COMING,*
DR. THOMAS A. HARRIS, 1985

"THE LITTLE MAN IN THE SCROTE"

Some thought that, compared with other medical advances of the '80s, it didn't amount to very much. But many believed it held bright promise for enabling millions of men to achieve a new understanding of their own sexuality. "It" was, of course, the latest sexual research conducted by William H. Masters, M.D., and Virginia E. Johnson, Ph.D., working at the Reproductive Biology Research Foundation in St. Louis, Missouri. Not only did these investigators determine that penis size was irrevocably linked to sexual attractiveness, but also that, in fact, the human male experiences two kinds of orgasms: the penile and the scrotal. As they described it in their distinctive jargon: "The penis is the focus of the first two of the four phases of the male sexual response cycle. Vasocongestion of the erectile tissue in the coronal ridge, the glans, and external meatus leads to the first, or false, orgasm—centered primarily in the corpora cavernosa. The tension-induced congestion and constriction of the scrotal sac are the active determinants of the second, or true orgasm—centered in the testes. As the orgasmic-phase release focuses on the scrotal integuments, excitement-phase levels of tension are maintained in the scrotal sac for the duration of the scrotal orgasm," or, as the men of the '80s called it, "the scrote."

The crucial issue for men, left unaddressed by Masters and Johnson, was perhaps best articulated by psychologist Dr. Joyce Brothers: "We must compassionately understand those men who insist on the *macho* glorification of the penile orgasm. But it must also be understood that the scrotal orgasm is more deep and meaningful, a truer and more mature expression of the love of a man for his sexual partner."

Men of the '80s were projected, headlong, into an examination of, and debate about, their own sexuality. It had been known,

even from prehistoric times, that men had derived enjoyment and positive relief from the rhythmic scratching of the scrotum. Athletes had long reported the bittersweet pleasure of the athletic supporter; many men had known the thrill of a motorbike and the enjoyment of tight briefs.

Nevertheless, it was hard for them to accept the idea that eons of cultural conditioning had trained them to mistake the scrotal orgasm for the penile, or false, climax. "The orgasm as we know it is dead," wrote Betty Friedan in *The Masculine Mystique*. "Women must now cope with the real nature of men's sexuality. Will they have the patience and the stamina to massage the scrotum long enough, and gently enough, to permit the male to achieve sexual relief? Or will they insist on their own selfishly quick orgasm, and damn the man of the species?"

Soon the scrotal orgasm became a powerful men's issue. "We now know that the myth of the penile orgasm was simply a way that women manipulated men," wrote Roosevelt Grier, author of *The Male Eunuch*. "By fully accepting the scrotal orgasm we end, once and for all, men's dependence on women."

Subsequently, while American men flocked to sex therapists for help in the achievement of "the scrote," a decade of sexual research culminated in the final discovery of the '80s—that men and women were fetally endowed with a finite number of orgasms. Perpetually linking human sexuality with entropy, researchers totally discredited the "steady-state" theory of human sexuality. As the decade came to a close, proponents of the "big-bang" theory—that orgasmic potential is predetermined at the explosive moment of human conception—cautioned men and women not to attempt a near approach to achieving their "red limit": the ultimate level of their orgasmic capacity.

On March 29, 1982, a picture of a man's penis was shown for the first time on national television. Barbara Walters described how Cowper's gland became erect when excited — resulting in a second and far deeper and more meaningful orgasm.

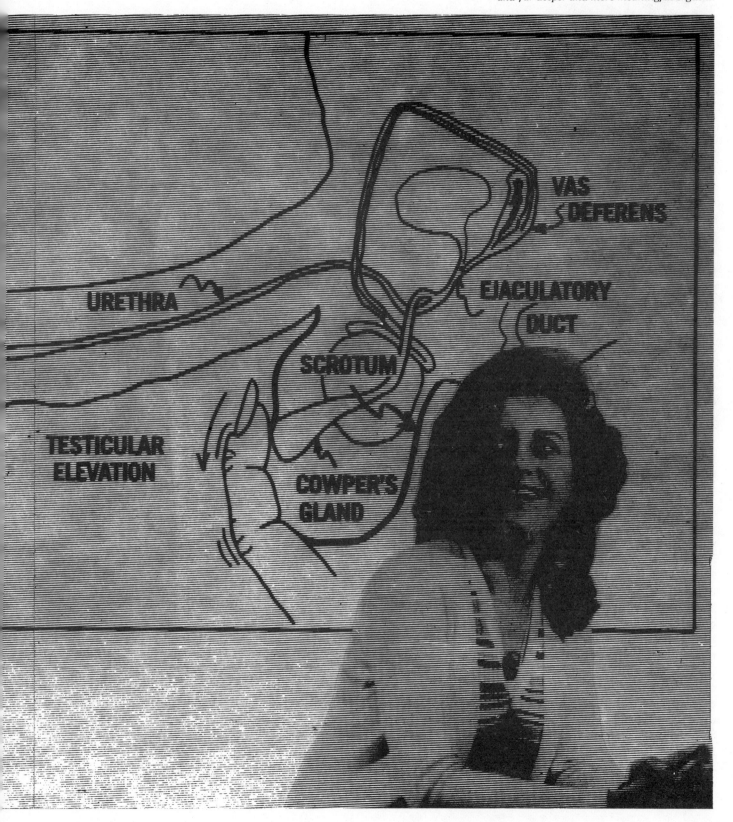

ORGASM— PRO AND CON

In the years following the International Year of the Simultaneous Orgasm, those who sought the simple physiological sensation of climax felt as if they had been tragically jerked asunder. Orgasms were prohibited outright in areas where authorities were especially sensitive to the connection between meat and physical pleasure; and in other jurisdictions that had been hard hit by the events of the IYSO, a strict limitation on orgasms—the so-called 'gasm rationing—was enforced.

But even among citizens in areas renowned for their toleration and liberal accommodation, the quest for orgasm could be a plangent journey. The memory of the terrible worldwide orgiastic moment was so traumatic for some that they remained forever among the ranks of the orgasm handicapped—repressing all memory of the pleasure principle, and of their own capacity for sexual relief.

Among the more fortunate, however—the majority who, though suffering from rampant societal dysfunction, could still remember having experienced the sexual act—many found themselves easy prey for those who proffered the quick fix.

The "Sex Aids" section of the average supermarket presented a sad assortment of Skin Brillo, Swiss Army dildos, and Aunt Millie's Hot Sauce. Mom-and-pop stores hawked a pathetic congeries of Mighty Wurlitzer Organs, anatomically correct inflatable Miss Piggy dolls, His and Hers Bullworkers, and Hammacher-Schlemmer Motorized Digits. In the bedrooms of suburbia, the Shtupperware party became commonplace. And perhaps the saddest symbol of the fate of the orgasm was highlighted in another way: many of those who could not achieve physical relief simulated the experience by buying the electronic video sex game, Poong.

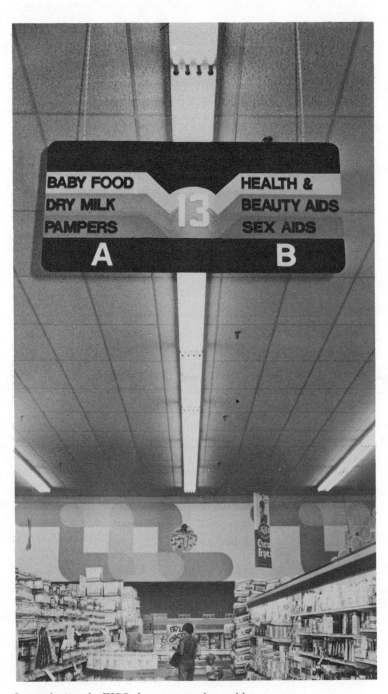

It was during the IYSO that supermarkets sold, for the first time, inorganic sex aids. This photo was taken in the El Paso, Texas, K & P-mart store.

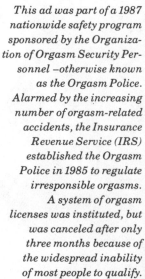

Humper the Rabbit says: Don't light fires you can't put out!

This ad was part of a 1987 nationwide safety program sponsored by the Organization of Orgasm Security Personnel –otherwise known as the Orgasm Police. Alarmed by the increasing number of orgasm-related accidents, the Insurance Revenue Service (IRS) established the Orgasm Police in 1985 to regulate irresponsible orgasms. A system of orgasm licenses was instituted, but was canceled after only three months because of the widespread inability of most people to qualify.

A secretive organization by nature, the Orgasm Police soon gained a reputation, however undeserved, for Gestapo techniques. It was rumored that a cigarette smoked in bed, or even a faraway smile, could result in a raid.

In order to counter this image, the Orgasm Police came up with Humper the Rabbit to carry their message to the public. Through posters, television, and radio spots, Humper spread the gospel of responsibility and restraint.

And in the process, little Humper became a celebrity, cherished and imitated all over America.

Orgasms are funny things.

In seconds, an orgasm can go from pleasurable spasm to nightmare terror. Especially when two or more go off at one time.

One young couple, overeager, were responsible for an apartment house collapse that killed 37 people.

A Des Moines, Iowa, woman and two houseguests were severely injured when a mirror fell on them during an afternoon frolic.

Their mistakes? They all came simultaneously. And they came too hard. Even one teenager, acting alone, can cause masonry to topple, endangering others.

Humper the Rabbit suggests a simple, three-point system for protection.
1. Don't come together. Check with your neighbors, too — stagger your schedules.
2. Take it easy. Restraint is its own reward.
3. Men, wear prophylactics to control sensitivity.

Remember—as Humper always says—

If you can't come nice–don't come at all.

THE ARMY

A two-man press gang of Ret. (retarded) Army Sergeants tries to shanghai an unsuspecting "recruit" on Chicago's Rush Street. The victim was later able to buy his freedom with a six-pack of Schlitz.

THE ARMY

It is winter, 1989, and a cold wind blows harsh across the Hudson River into Harlem. Corporal Kunta Kinte Jackson is glad he is inside. For the ninth time that morning he places his black hands on a sponge mop, hefting it and feeling its length. He wishes it were his M-16 rifle, but that was sold, long ago. So Kunta does with the mop what he used to do so expertly with the weapon: methodically, he takes it apart, cleans each piece, then reassembles it. He wants to "be ready" and, until he once again has the rifle in his well-practiced hands, the sponge mop will have to do.

A nation's history cannot merely be "made." It must be captured and forced to submit. Like no other nation on earth, our America has met—and conquered—its history with a strength and tenacity few other civilizations would care to think about. But it is no accident, for we have created the most technically advanced and morally sophisticated armed forces in history for precisely this purpose. In the '80s, these forces met unprecedented challenges—and, for the most part, they prevailed.

Much of the controversy surrounding the armed forces in the '80s concerned the Army. As more and more black, Colored, and Hispanic volunteers flocked to recruiting offices, eager to receive their free uniforms and one square meal a day, there were many observers who wondered: what had become of the army of Irving Berlin, and Sad Sack, and Sergeant Bilko? Some thought the trend a perfectly appropriate means by which these once-less-fortunate peoples could repay the debt owed by their ancestors, whose freedom had been so successfully defended by European immigrants in the two World Wars. But many—like cartoonist Alex Farmingham, whose antimilitary strip "Spickson Jiggs, PFC" was loved by millions until the demise of print—were disturbed by the phenomenon. When retired heavyweight boxing champion Muhammad Ali joined up in 1984, their disquiet concerning "an unrepresentative military" grew. "JOIN THE MAN WHAT JOINING THE ARMY," said the recruiting poster; after Ali's arrival, it seldom had to say it twice. But as enrollment rose, confidence in the Army dwindled.

WE HAVE CREATED THE MOST TECHNICALLY ADVANCED AND MORALLY SOPHISTICATED ARMED FORCES IN HISTORY.

These feelings of uneasiness spread. Perhaps it had something to do with Joint Chiefs Chairman Ali's refusal to have his men fight in Africa, Asia, or South America unless it be for the opposing side. Perhaps it was the result of a change in tradition: the once-universal army salute (right hand open, fingers extended, index tip touched to right temple) was officially replaced by the crude, controversial "Black Power" salute (right hand clenched in fist, fist held up in air at arm's length). Whatever the cause, white voters stripped Congress of its powers to allocate funds for the military.

To be sure, there were those who opposed these measures. Hastily organized blocs of liberals, in sympathy with underpaid Army personnel, staged an historic march on the Pentagon in 1987, calling for an increased defense budget and, if need be, outright war. Wrote journalist Norman Mailer of the demonstration:

> Yes, here at last was Ali (the Champ!) made Marx to Faust's Hegel, America herself going rope-a-dope in the ring of History, as the world's greatest Negro sought everything (at who knew what dread price to psyche, rhythm, soul, and fine cool hipster pride) and promised nothing to white liberal Mephistos.

Few understood it, or the march which occasioned it. But if the ground troops foundered in economic chaos—Ali ordered most of their weapons and heavy machinery sold to foreign powers to meet basic payroll expenses—there were still some forces capable of guarding the nation. It fell to the United Multinationals to shoulder the burden of protecting the United States of America. And shoulder it they did: their acquisition of the ships, planes, bombs, and other tactical weapons of the Navy and Air Force enabled them to direct these service branches with increasing vigilance and skill.

And what of Corporal Jackson? Ordered to return to his home during its occupation and "defeat" by the Army in 1989, he joins the growing number of trained (and possibly desperate) soldiers who form a sort of network of readiness (and potential terror) in the inner-city national parks and game preserves of the nation. Jackson plies his sponge mop and waits. But whether it is with the patriotic fervor of an Army man eager to serve his country well, or with some more sinister motive, only time will tell.

BLACK AND COLORED VOLUNTEERS FLOCKED TO RECRUITING OFFICES, EAGER TO RECEIVE THEIR FREE UNIFORMS AND ONE SQUARE MEAL A DAY.

THE PASSING OF THE WHITE ARMY

The debate about the effectiveness and the morality of the all-volunteer Army that had begun in the '70s continued unabated into the early '80s, but by the middle of 1983, there were at least two facets of the future Army that everyone was prepared to acknowledge: it was going to be black and it was going to be broke.

In the summer of 1983, as the result of a letter to his congressman by a disgruntled specialist 4, a presidential panel investigated the racial makeup of the Army and discovered that, far from being predominantly white, it was in fact 94 percent black. It was soon apparent that for eight years army recruiters across the country, never noted for their strict adherence to the truth, had been falsifying enlistment data on a national scale. Quietly informed that their promotions depended on signing up at least two white youths for every black enlistee, they simply listed two out of every three of the black Americans they attracted as suffering from "a mild skin condition causing whole body discoloration," "gross freckling," or "extensive birthmarks of a dark hue."

In retrospect, it was a tribute to the Army's legendary ability to maintain an official position in the face of overwhelming evidence to the contrary that the subterfuge had been so successful.

It was later discovered that some special units, made up of the few remaining white servicemen and the correct proportion of blacks, and highly trained in maneuvering into sight of the press and official visitors, had been in nearly constant motion throughout the decade. And the situation was not without its humorous aspects. Recruits recalled formations where the drill sergeant would call out, "What color are you?" and the trainees, black to a man, would shout back, "We're white, sergeant!" "And where are you men from?" "We're from Connecticut, sergeant!" "And what are you men going to do when you leave the Army?" "We're going to enter the insurance field, sergeant!" A black lieutenant told how he and his men donned specially developed whiteface camouflage for NATO maneuvers in Norway. And a career sergeant described how in "Operation Snow White" a special white public relations battalion, earmarked for duty in Europe, boarded a giant jet transport at an airbase ceremony, then slipped out the side of the aircraft and sped to another part of the field where they were welcomed as another battalion returning from Europe.

Taking the attitude, "If you can't drive 'em out, exploit 'em," the last white recruiting officers launched an aggressive promotional campaign to glorify the low-paying peacetime Army. With slogans such as, "He ain't a drill sergeant, he's my brother," and, "Uncle Sam want some soul," the canny recruiters saw enlistments soar.

For a few, however, the recruiting posters were alarming. When it was seriously suggested that Army flags, at least, should be recolored with black stars and stripes, the "veins of patriotism stood out to be counted," as the late Nat Hentoff put it. The pressure to recruit whites of any age, size, or shape into the Army became intense. Aided covertly by the Department of Defense, right-wing civilian groups organized press gangs of U.S. Army Sergeants (Ret.), empowering them to abduct and induct any likely looking whites, preferably when drunk. These Exceptional Forces (Ret. stood for retarded) made valiant attempts to shanghai recruits in bars and restaurants across the nation, but their beery emotionalism in one another's company tended to spoil their timing, and they ran up expense accounts beyond even the John Birch Society's willingness to pay. The program was abandoned when it was discovered that the only people the Retarded Army Sergeants had managed to recruit were other retarded Army sergeants.

I W
FOR
NEARE

MARY ANNE SHEA

ANT YOU
U.S. ARMY

RECRUITING STATION

Bowing to the inevitable, the U.S. Army —already almost entirely black — revised its recruiting campaign in 1982 with a new variation on an old theme. For obscure reasons, however, the unofficial name of the central character was changed to "Uncle Chicken George."

I am the Black infantry, pawn of battle. Follow me!

I have been in every war, but peace is worse.

I cooked the meals that fed the man who fired the shot heard round the world, and then I cleaned the rifle.

I was the first person shot in the Boston Massacre. I turned the tide at Bunker Hill. I and 5,000 of my brothers were in every major battle from Valley Forge to Yorktown, but at the beginning of the war, they almost didn't let me join, and at the end, they tried to find a way to send me back to Africa.

I built the barricades at New Orleans that broke the British lines. I cleaned the halls of Montezuma and picked up rubbish on the shores of Tripoli.

I was in the Civil War, 175,000 strong. I shined shoes at Shiloh and waited on tables at Antietam. The night before Appomattox, I polished Lee's sword and brought Grant his whiskey. And when it was over, Lincoln tried to find a way to send me back to Africa.

In World War I, the soil of France echoed to the ring of my shovel and the thud of my pick. I attacked the dirty pots at Château-Thierry, I fought stubborn stains in the Ardennes. And even after the Kaiser's goose was cooked, I was still the chef.

In World War II, I had my own units, but somehow I was always assigned to mop up the enemy.

In Korea, I fought side by side with white soldiers for the first time in a century. I never turned my back on enemy fire, and I tried to keep it out of the way of friendly fire, too.

But in Vietnam, I came of age. They said it was a dirty war, so I wasn't surprised that they left it pretty much to me. But I was just doing my part, and probably yours, too.

I was always there, and now I'm all that's there. Why do I volunteer? Well, having enemies everywhere, or being shot at, is nothing new to me.

I am the Black infantry, pawn of battle. Follow me!

CHIEF OF THE JOINT

"**W**ith so many brothers in the service, being in mufti makes me nervous," quoth Muhammad Ali on September 8, 1984. The balding, slightly paunchy heavyweight champion showed up at Fort Sheridan in Chicago with an entourage of 27 people, including his adviser, Drew "Bundini" Brown, and demanded induction. Cynics saw Ali's move as an attempt to build a domestic power base after he failed to win international recognition by punching out heads of state (*see SPORTS*). But certainly no one could fault his ability to "cut the mustard" in basic training. He negotiated the obstacle course in record time, and then flattened the base commander for suggesting that the spitshine on his boots was more spit than shine.

With basic training completed, he was quickly promoted to lieutenant, and then appointed (two weeks later) to brigadier general in charge of, as he put it, troop deployment, troop reployment, troop employment, and troop unemployment. "That rhymes, four times," he added.

Ali's tenure as a brigadier general was the shortest on record. President Carter evidently felt that some gesture to black Americans, who had gotten stuck yet again with one more of the nation's dirtier jobs, was in order. Accordingly, in a simple ceremony in the Rose Garden, Brigadier General Muhammad Ali was sworn in as the chairman of the Joint Chiefs of Staff. He promptly renamed himself "Chief of the Joint."

It was the chance the Joint Chiefs had been waiting for. Within days, all the other Army generals—who were among the few whites left in that branch of the services—announced their retirement. The Navy and the Air Force, going one better, proclaimed that they would no longer cooperate with the Army—nor did they wish to participate in the deliberations of the Joint Chiefs. Henceforth, they said, they were to be considered "neutral."

Across the nation, the secession of the Air Force and the Navy was widely praised. And Ali himself, in a speech to more than 200,000 cheering troops at the renamed Fort Mahalia Jackson in South Carolina, proclaimed, "Free at last! Good God Almighty, the Army's free at last!"

At a time when the disbursement of public funds was increasingly in the hands of television viewers through instant propositions, such a pronouncement was, of course, financial suicide. What happened was that a none-too-subtle shift of appropriations took place away from the Army and toward the Navy and Air Force. The Army was free—and broke.

The former heavyweight champion proved as agile in the Pentagon, however, as he had been in the ring. To keep his promise of "one square meal a day" to all enlisted men, Ali ordered the sale of the choicest pieces of abandoned Army real estate to private developers, including the Presidio in San Francisco and the barracks in Honolulu. Army property, from tactical nuclear weapons to dog tags, was available to the highest bidder. He also obtained (on an informal basis) some very substantial aid from the West German government for his troops in Europe by first scheduling a series of "mock amphibious landings" at popular German beaches and then canceling them.

But it was an uphill battle. In maneuvers of the First Armored Division on the outskirts of Newark late in '85, only 17 tanks were operational, and most of those had to be jump started. The only new weapon displayed was the Crispus Attucks rocket, which was in reality an old Nike painted green with a warhead full of hand grenades, and the air cover was provided by the Bronx Bomber, an aircraft knowledgeable aviation buffs could easily spot as a German PBY with the pontoons rigged up to look like missiles.

A rare photo shows General Muhammad Ali convening the Joint Chiefs of Staff before the other members retired. Two weeks after this picture was taken, the massive oak table was sold to the Greenwich, Connecticut, Board of Education, and the missile silo location map (Eastern Mediterranean sector) in the background went to an unnamed Libyan collector of Americana.

THIS IS THE ARMY, MR. JONES

To watch the U.S. Army on parade (left right jeté, left right jeté), with its precision, its expanse of bronze, bared chests, its often red sequinned pants, was to be overwhelmed by a perfect balance of power and grace. And if there were difficulties —the usual complaints about food and living quarters —they were minuscule in comparison with the discipline, the loyalty toward superiors, the ingenuity of the weaponry. Penniless, even occasionally bulletless, the U.S. Army might be, but its morale was higher than at any time since Valley Forge.

```
                                        March 23, 1986

Dear Mama, Pop, Charlene, Gregory, and Muhammed,

     I am sorry that you have not heard from me, but things
have been going crazy round here, and I mean CRA-ZEE.  I
mean dig it, I am lying under my blanket on my bed on account
that I have not got no uniform to put on.  Chief Ali has put
out the WORD that the honky voters won't give us no more money--
he ain't never lied, I mean when did the honky ever GIVE
money to a black man?  And so we're gonna have to sell all our
uniforms.  I hear tell a lotta white boys like to wear them
to go dancing.  Now YOU tell ME white folks aint drazy.  But
the WORD came down from Main Man Holder that he was gonna fix
us up some uniforms from the shit he's got left over from some
shows he's done in New York City.  HEA-VEE.  Some of the
brothers, the fat ones, they reFUSED.  One dude said he didn't
join no army to look stupid.  Main Man Montgomery sent him
to the brig and made him listen to Mantovani for ten hours a
day for a WEEK.  The dude is STILL sick.  Say Gregory, when
you gonna join up, bro?  The drills are something ELSE.
Every day they give us some new steps thats been worked out
by Main Man Ailey.  And we have got them DOWN..
     Oh yeah.  I have been PROMOTED from TOGETHA to SOUL
BROTHA.  Now I'm working on AMMUNISHUN.  One of the BLOODS
that went to College be giving us ideas.  Check it out.  He
made this bomb that looks like a basketball and he said that
we would pass it back and forth thru the enemy lines and
SLAM DUNK it on someone's face.  I said, what happens if I
drop the ball man, I mean you know I have been known to DROP
THE BALL.  And the BLOOD said, did I like Mantovani.  Then
he said that what we gotta do is get all the used car washes,
shine them up good, make them portable, camoflage them and
then when someone steps inside turn them on by remote control
and they be hot-waxed to death.  I said fine with me, so long as
I can be in REMOTE CONTROL.
     I gotta go now and catch me some sleep.  Don't have no
revellee no more.  Cut that shit out comPLETEly.  Start the
day out with a little Marvin, and you know CP time, nothing
gets moving till the sun is high.
                              Love,
                              Hassan Ahmed Saleen
```

The Army's most formidable weapon was the Giant Flying Radio, which could kill the enemy in one of two ways. Either the intense volume destroyed his brain, or the thought of meeting the owner induced a heart attack.

2/5/85—GENERAL MUHAMMAD ALI ANNOUNCED THAT HENCEFORTH THE ARMY WOULD BE GOVERNED BY THE ISLAMIC CODE OF MILITARY JUSTICE.

THE LONG MARCH

The new black Army was proud, but pride, as the saying goes, does not put meat on the table. Despite pleas from the Chief of the Joint, General Ali, that servicemen embrace the simple and inexpensive life of the Muslim, there were repeated incidents of soldiers looting small towns and hustling civilians at three-card monte. Tensions mounted as black soldiers awoke to the fact that they had been ghettoized once more, and as civilians, freshly equipped with weapons purchased from the Army itself, talked of mounting their own provisional force to quell possible uprisings. In the end, it was the ragtag legions of the old New Left that came to the aid of their black "brothers."

Donning fatigues to show their support, discoing to "la sousa"—a curious white misinterpretation of the new black Army's obsession with complex drill routines (*see MUSIC 'N DRUGS*)—but above all wanting, wishing, willing the Army to triumph, they came to the Pentagon. Five hundred thousand strong, comprising all the forces of antivegetarian, antientertainment, and anti-UM feelings, they marched to Washington. They sported hats reading, "Make War, F––k Love," "Give Them a Piece Now!" "Off the Web!" and, "Meat, Meat Is the Answer," and they came to make a point.

Cheering girls reverently placed bullets in the bulletless guns of black soldiers. Singers Baez and Seeger, ever on the side of the underdog, carried rifles where once they had carried guitars. Donna Summer, grand queen of everything, sang the anthem of the march, "We Shall Overrun (Some Day)." And the Pentagon, decrepit for lack of upkeep, the underground bunkers and war rooms robbing the complex of its foundations, did in fact sink into the ground.

The unfortunate collapse of the black Army's headquarters, widely misinterpreted by the white left wing, simply served to deprive the military of one more place to

Anti-war veteran turned pro-war activist Joan Baez holds aloft a "nonviolent" rifle during the 1987 March for the Pentagon. Sang Baez: "I am the princess of protest, I am the duchess of dissent."

find shelter. No more enduring symbol of the failure of the march and of the movement that generated it was to be found.

The most tangible result of the pro-war effort was a massive fund-raising drive for the impoverished Army. Within 12 months, citizens had chipped in to the tune of one billion dollars and it seemed that it was war as usual. But General Ali then stunned the nation by proclaiming that no whites would be inducted into the Army, because only Muslims were allowed to enlist. Legions of outraged contributors demanded their donations back, but the canny Ali pointed out that new weapons and uniforms had already been purchased on credit. Outfoxed citizens were forced to concede that the wily old puncher had scored yet another TKO.

Ms. *Abbie Hoffman, having undergone a sex-change, came out of hiding in 1982. In a triumphant gesture she sent her penis to the FBI, prompting the famous response from a bureau spokesman: "We'll need a much bigger file on him than we thought." Ms. Hoffman attended the Pentagon March in 1987, resulting in the book from which these passages are excerpted,* Blippie Nation.

I still don't believe it went down the way it did. I mean—far-out! The Pentagon really did sink!

What can I say? The Long March was a long time coming. The bullshit can back up only so far before the Potomac starts to stink. Know what I mean? Hey, if it hadn't been for Gloria Steinem-Mailer we'd still be up the Potomac without a paddle. Her book *Army Now*, resulting from an afternoon's maneuvers with the 23rd Infantry, did the trick. Even so, it took two years of street trashing before those knee-jerking liberals even knew what we were complaining about. I mean, no bullets? You can only shoot a flower so far. No wonder Billy Graham Cracker's pushing unilateral disarmament....

Wasn't till we got to Atlantic City that we knew we really had the issue by the gonads. Sure we lost Rubin. I told him to start small. Blow up a salt-water taffy stand or something, I said. That wouldn't be an event, he answered. Go argue with Rubin! So he blew up Penthouse International Casino. At least he took Mike Wallace with him....

Once we got to Washington, we circled the joint, shoutin' and singin' and clownin' and clappin'. Then for no reason people started beating each other into bloody stumps. I think it was Ginsberg who triggered it with a reading of "African Violets." A lousy sound system made it sound like "African Violence." Hotdogs and meatballs were flying, someone pulled down the flag and replaced it with a cheeseburger. Wild! You just knew it was going to happen. Then whooooosh! The grounds opened and the Granite Hulk sank faster than Babcock and Wilcox stock on a radioactive afternoon. The headlines bannered "PENTAGON'S UNDER-WAR ROOMS CAVE IN," but I'm telling you for a fact—it was Blippie magic!...

WE SHALL OVERRUN

Early in 1983 a group of executives, lawyers, actors, and doctors organized themselves into an exclusive society. The group was dubbed the Roots Club and its charter members were what was then known as black. Insisting with extraordinary courage (given the temper of the times) that they were not black but merely "colored," Roots Club members fought to give their class the status that indiscriminate bureaucratic definition had hitherto denied them. The society's very existence implied that its members had, through hard work or even inherited merit, achieved a predominance over their so-called brothers. Nothing typified this as well as the jovial form of hazing to which hopeful applicants were subjected. In effect a new version of the old practice of "paperbagging," used by black societies in the early part of the century to exclude those whose skins were darker than a paper bag, the Roots Club practice of "moneybagging" similarly excluded those who could not produce $100,000 in a paper bag at one hour's notice.

This is *the next time, sucker.*

BLACK SOLDIER TO OUTRAGED CIVILIAN DURING THE 1989 OCCUPATION OF CINCINNATI.

The split between middle-class and blue-collar black Americans, symbolized by the establishment of the Roots Club, grew throughout the decade into a chasm. "Silk-lining," the process by which cooperative banks and realtors gave preferential treatment to neighborhoods with large numbers of colored residents, became common. Black intruders in such neighborhoods were routinely "escorted" out of them by volunteer patrols. Fire hoses were turned onto a group of black demonstrators who attempted to "deintegrate" an Episcopalian church in the exclusive colored suburb of Ann Arbor. Busing into col-

ored schools was unsuccessfully proposed by militant black groups. Rebellious children of colored parents doffed their weekend dashikis for coveralls and grew bushy Afros in order to identify with their less fortunate compatriots.

It was no surprise that the proud but impoverished U.S. Army saw the Roots Club (three-quarters of a million strong by 1988) as a prime target for harassment. When General Ali announced in March 1989 that his troops were moving to reoccupy their "turf," which observers correctly interpreted as meaning the cities, few were more alarmed than Roots Club members. Their clubhouses, usually situated on prime pieces of real estate in impeccable urban and suburban areas, were highly visible manifestations of the racial tension between black and colored, and they properly feared for their safety. Accordingly, they requested protection from, and if necessary retaliation by, the forces of the United Multinationals.

The UM Security Council was reluctant to move against the U.S. Army. Certainly—thanks to the judicious acquisition of the U.S. Air Force by its subsidiaries, McDonnell Douglas and Lockheed—it had the means to do so. And the "reoccupation," although it appeared so far to have involved little more than incredibly elaborate parades in the main thoroughfares of major cities, was an ominous development. Nevertheless, the UM's reaction was that inner turmoil was something the U.S. economy—still in the recovery room—could do without.

The declaration by General Ali that Chicago was applying for membership in the United Islamic Republic took the confrontation to another stage. On September 1, the UMAF began overflights of all urban centers with a view to monitoring "possible hostile action and/or insurgent activity against the American people by the U.S. Army."

Arms "sales" were commonly held by a U.S. defense industry deprived of its domestic market and saddled with enormous inventories of death-dealing weapons. Other promotion techniques included the offer of toasters to purchasers of neutron bombs and death rays, and late-night television spots featuring "Greatest Hits" packages. This ad appeared on February 22, 1988, in the classified section of the Johannesburg Daily Thug.

George Washington's Birthday

Arms Sale!!

What could be a better day to provide for the safety of you and your country than the birthday of the father of the world's leading arms-producing nation? At **Crazy George Vootze's Arms-Mania Center,** you'll get unheard-of power at fabulous savings! All you need is your Department of Defense charge card, and you can roll home the most staggering instruments of death you've ever seen! When's the last time you could get . . .

- **Flame-throwing armored tanks for an insane $400,000??!!**
- **XK-4 Missile-Launchers for a ridiculous $50,000??!!**
- **Floor-sample almost-new neutron bombs for $400,000—yes, only $400,000??!!**

Now's the time to stock your arsenal!

Holiday Bonus! Free with every anti-aircraft gun: 5 sets of snappy factory-second riot-control gear!

IF PERFECT, THESE MEGADESTRUCTION UTENSILS WOULD GO FOR 2 . . .3 . . . .4 TIMES WHAT WE'RE CHARGING! BUT GEORGE VOOTZE WILL NOT BE UNDERSOLD! RUSH ON DOWN BEFORE THE RUSSIANS DO!

The United Multinationals reluctantly began over-flights of the U.S. Army after its occupation in 1989 of several once key cities. Here, a fighter of the AT&T First Airborne ("Ma Bell's Mothers") prepares to land after a routine strafing of Toledo.

FOOD

"Just browsing" ... this man of the food-short mid-'80s is pricing the Vegetable Market—"looking at the long green"—with an eye to a bank loan for a pound of potatoes on margin.

FOOD

It is a sunny Tuesday afternoon in the year 1987, and Mrs. Phyllis Lomax has a problem. It concerns her youngest—and, now, only. It seems that Timmy, age three, is "tired" of potatoes. But potatoes are her local supermarket's specialty—it stocks two name brands of the hardy, hearty vegetable. With a rueful sigh, Mrs. Lomax wheels her cart down the aisles, and ponders.

If an army travels on its stomach, then a nation lives on its mouth. And few nations have a bigger collective mouth to feed, or life to lead, than America. Ours is food that is like the people who buy it: simple, wholesome, but withal substantial, and possessing a certain irreverent "kick" that suits our ethos. During the '80s, this was truer than ever.

From Daniel Boone munching a hickory branch in the wilds to Neil Armstrong pausing on the lunar surface for his Tang, American food has always been fast. In the '80s, retail chains such as Eat It 'n Beat It and Feast 'n Flee became an integral part of the American foodscape. Some purists thought that the proliferation of fast food would mean an end to such traditional American delicacies as the backyard cookout hot dog and the bologna sandwich eaten over the kitchen sink. They needn't have worried. Late in 1982, McDonald's pioneered the first at-home "family franchise" operation, bringing burgers, buns, and special sauce into Everyman's dwelling.

FEW NATIONS HAVE A BIGGER COLLECTIVE MOUTH TO FEED, OR LIFE TO LEAD, THAN AMERICA.

But as chef Harlan Sanders of New York's Le Cygne remarked, "Politics don't have table manners," and with the prohibition of meat in 1983 came a new and challenging sequence in the feature-length adaptation of the cookbook that is America's gustatorial saga. Quick to respond, our nation's agribusiness set about the task of coaxing (or forcing) more and more from the soil and, by and large, it succeeded. Experiments with strip-farming yielded impressive results: after careful crossbreeding with the oft-ignored coconut, they created a species of tomato protected by a natural shell capable of withstanding pressures of up to 9.7 tons per square inch. This was Yankee ingenuity with a vengeance, and there was more. Thalassa Cruso's *Houseplant Cook "Book"* became a perennial bestselling disc. "To perk up an ordinary potato salad," she advised, "boil spider plant leaves for three hours in a solution of brine and vinegar. Mash well, salt heavily, and let sit overnight." Millions did, and gratefully.

Of course, the prohibition of meat meant a scarcity of cattle and, therefore, of dairy products. But solutions to such problems were often as nearby as one's trusty old dog. Appropriately, the Pet Milk Company was the first to market what many found to be a quite delicious line of dog milk and cat cheese products.

"BOIL SPIDER PLANT LEAVES FOR THREE HOURS IN A SOLUTION OF BRINE AND VINEGAR."

Professional dog dairies perfected the use of piped-in music to stimulate canine lactation—and discovered that an all-disco format both encouraged paw-tapping conviviality among the bitches and resulted in the direct manufacture of dog butter without need for mechanical churning.

The process of creating these foods from house pets was not simple, but those do-it-yourselfers who botched the job could take ample solace in such hearty—if technically illegal—dishes as "beagle bourguignon" and "chihuahua cacciatore." So widespread did pet-eating become, in fact, that it drew public protest from the renamed American Society for the Prevention of Cooking Animals.

With the latter part of the decade came oil, and with oil came many experiments—some surprisingly successful—with petroleum-based edibles. To be sure, there was much we had to learn about the delicate art of cooking polymers. (Water could not be used, and fireman/trouble-shooter Red Adair had to be summoned in May of 1989 to "cap" Manhattan's posh Lutèce.) But as the oil and agriculture industries worked more and more closely—sometimes going so far as to merge entirely—many held hope for the future that the problems would be solved.

As for Phyllis Lomax: with so few distracting alternatives to slow her down, she is able to choose her potatoes, apples, and tomatoes in 10 minutes, race home, and have them on the cutting board and ready to go when James Beard's "The Potatoes, Apples, and Tomatoes Show" airs. And even if Beard's latest recipe fails to please the finicky Timmy, Mrs. Lomax can take some consolation in the fact that her efficient trip through the market enabled her to miss—by a scant 8 minutes—the explosion of a bomb planted in the tomatoes section by the FLANC (Fuerza de Liberazion de Alimentos Naturales con Carne), a Puerto Rican pro-meat terrorist group. Such extremist acts are not uncommon in the tumultuous decade.

THE FOOD CHAIN

At noon on Saturday, July 12, 1981, a great grumbling noise as of a hundred million stomachs gurgling echoed across the cities and hamlets of America. (It was a hundred million stomachs gurgling.) Ed Hanley, of 10 Sycamore Street in Fargo, North Dakota, was one who heard it. He felt uneasy: his stomach rumbled too, a cold sweat broke out on his brow, his hands began to tremble, and a sudden overpowering urge to unwrap something, anything edible, seized him. He looked around the room — his wife, Beulah, and little Tod and Marisa were also trembling. Why?

The surgeon general's 1981 report "No-Fry-Day and After" yielded an explanation. On Friday, July 11, for the first time ever, there was no gasoline at all at America's pumps. At lunch hour on Saturday, a hundred million immobilized American families experienced the same symptoms: cold sweat, mass stomach growling, muscle cramps, hallucinations involving fried foods and parallel parking, and a sudden overpowering urge to find a clean rest room. Homebound America was suffering from fast-food withdrawal; the nation, to use a now familiar phrase, had gone "cold burger."

As America rounded into the '80s, the fast-food industry — like a cheap hamburger — was already overextended. One could not drive an appreciable distance along the nation's vast network of superhighways without passing clustered vermilion turrets, golden cupolas, and puce pavilions with mock-Spanish interiors of exquisitely veneered plasterboard. These

"You do it all for you." McDonald's, reacting to multiplying competition and the gas shortage, made its uniforms, patties, condiments, buns, and rest room signs available to the American family. The "McDonald's-at-home" became a popular eating-out place.

palaces offered whatever could be fried, broiled, barbecued, and packaged for instant oral gratification. And there was the rub: without gas no one could drive an appreciable distance.

No all-beef patties, no pickle, no sauce in a great big sesame seed bun. . . .

Hold the pickle, hold the lettuce, we ain't got 'em, don't upset us. . . .
FAST-FOOD TELEVISION COMMERCIALS, 1987

From No-Fry-Day, the industry got the message. America was seriously hooked on fast food. If the nation couldn't come to it, it would come to the nation. Chains pulled in their outposts: within six months the famous "onion rings"—dense bands of fast-food restaurants—encircled every city and town at an average driving distance of three miles (one-quarter gallon).

Most popular was the ingenious Pit Stop chain that took over disused gas stations and pumped a slurry of meat and potatoes through a gas nozzle directly into customers' mouths. "It's just like the old days," said one delighted American. "I can drive right in, point to my wife, and say, 'Fill 'er up!'" The overwhelming popularity of Pit Stop was attributed by a prominent behaviorist to "breast-feeding anxiety and the frustration of the gas-tank surrogate."

Business boomed; new franchises burgeoned. Americans like the Hanleys had a dazzling choice of rapid-dining spots at which to perform the drive-and-eat ritual. Speed-eaters enjoyed new chains called Nip 'n Zip, Eat It 'n Beat It, and Peck 'n Check; health food freaks went to Sprout 'n Out and Vim 'n Skim; the ethnic food market had Pasta fa-Zoom! (Italian), Chop 'n Hop (Chinese), and Feta Compli (Greek).

Today, if you are what you eat, you're pretty dull.
CRAIG CLAIBORNE, 1987

The gas glut of the mid-'80s and the growing food shortage completely reversed the trend. Nineteen eighty-seven saw the Hanleys driving hundreds of miles on Saturday in search of an open fast-food place for a meatless "Small Mac" or a dab of the Colonel's "Kentucky Fried batter." And when they found an eatery they also found a line of cars, often a mile long. By decade's end, it was not unusual to wait up to three hours for fast food. Between 1988 and 1989, Americans were stabbed, tire-ironed, or shot to death for cutting into fast-food lines. But America's hunger for a quick feed continues unabated; like our leather-stockinged ancestors, we are on the trail again, stalking the vast wilderness in search of sustenance, food hunters once more, westering, always westering. . . .

Food was in short supply, but there was no lack of food chains thanks to the shrewd marketing strategy of organizations like Grubs 'n Roots (menu, right), which sold its first franchise in 1988 and soon earned the title: "The World's Number One 'Fast' Restaurant."

Welcome to
"A Whole Third World of Food"

Grubs'n Roots Specialties

ALASKA KING CRABGRASS Liberally laced with Crabgrass Helper and prepared with our own over-baked smoked hickory. $31.25

SIZZLING CHARCOAL BROILED SIRLOIN STICK

Served with crispy French flies and a pickleweed wedge

$37.85

NEWT ROCKNE Chilled garden fresh green salamanders topped with a crown of thorns $28.50

DEEP FRIED GULF BUTTERFLY Drowned in our own savory dog-butter $29.95

LEAF STROGANOFF

Choice oak leaf clusters in a sow-thistle sauce

$33.25

Above served with celery-flavored sticks

FREE

From Our Sand Bar:

All the Sand You Can Shovel
WITH EVERY ENTREE

And, for Dessert:

Famous Lice Cream Cake

Our own homemade lice cream on a fluffy square of golden sponge, topped with luscious raspberry fruitworms $11.95

Before Dinner May We Suggest a Cat-tail?

$6.75

Locust of the Day

ROAST SUCKLING PYGMY GRASSHOPPER

Served with aphid stuffing and purée of squashed acorn

$23.75

Especially
for the Kids:
TUBBY THE TUBER
Jumbo Char-Broiled Burdock Root,
served up with
a lode of coal slaw
$23.50

Beverages

Milkweed Shakes	$4.95
Creme de Cicada	$7.95
Grub Soda	$3.25
Lint Julep	$8.25
Grubs 'n' Roots' Famous Root Beer	$3.50

HAUTE CUISINE WITH NO INGREDIENTS

Of the appetizers the best was the fake ham (shambon de Bayonne), which had the smoky vigor of the real thing, though made of pressed farina. The imitation Tripes à la mode de Caen were stringier than most (Lutèce uses less string). The dessert, a simulated orange mousse, tasted disappointingly of simulated apricot. A pleasant surprise was a single stalk of that rarity, real broccoli, on a huge platter. Another was the splendid soup, Campbell's '81 (a good year), made from real tomatoes . . . remember?

Thus wrote food critic Fifi Chippendale in the *New York Variety Times* on May 4, 1986, reviewing a new gourmet restaurant, Le Souvenir de Cuisine. She gave it three stars. Clearly, with the food shortage, *haute cuisine* had fallen on low days.

The reason was simple: among the first things to disappear from the world's table were calves' brains, veal kidneys, pheasant, partridge, lobster, artichokes, asparagus, shallots, baby lettuce, and fresh cream. In a world short of food, growing tiny carrots and *petits pois* was economic suicide. Even caviar had dwindled: sturgeon, sharing the loss of sex drive in the early '80s, had laid fewer eggs. Truffles

---

In the nineteen hundred and eighties, hunger is the only sauce.

CHEF PAUL DE ROQUEFORT, WINNER
1985 PRIX D'ESCOFFIER

---

had waned: the pigs that had rooted for them were now too valuable as food.

Deprived of all these ingredients, the great cooks of the world faced a new challenge—how to preserve the grand tradition of gourmet cooking.

Their answer was *cuisine farceur* (loosely translated as "funny" or "mock" cuisine). This was made with substitutes to *resemble* the great classic dishes and was embodied in such books as Julia Child's *The*

Pseudo-French Chef, Craig Claiborne's *Favorite Fakes*, and *The Ploy of Cooking*.

One school of *cuisine farceur* preferred in the United States was the *cuisine semblable* ("lookalike cuisine"), using everyday ingredients, sculpture, and coloring to make things that looked like the great traditional dishes. Its glories included rack of yam, beets *à la bourguignonne*, fillet of half-sole *à la dauphine*, and rock *au vin*.

The French preferred *cuisine odeur*, dishes that *smelled* like the real thing. The secret of *cuisine odeur* lay in using essences of the great ingredients, such as pheasant concentrate, *eau de veau* (veal), *jus reviens* (beef), *mon poulet* (chicken). These added to plaster forms regaled the gourmet nose with such treats as *haleine de faisan sous cloche* (breath of pheasant under glass), *bouffée de fromage* (whiff of cheese), and lobster thermid-air.

Perhaps nothing reveals the combined desperation and resourcefulness of the great chefs more than this typical recipe from a famous cookbook of the era.

MOCK MOCK TURTLE SOUP

1 quart water
1 tea bag
1 turtle (*rented*)
2 ounces sherry
1 jar mock turtle soup (*borrowed, optional*)

Bring the water in a saucepan to a rolling boil. Soak the tea bag in the water until it is the color of mock turtle soup (if unsure, use the borrowed jar of mock turtle soup as a standard). Let cool. Feed one ounce of sherry to the turtle (to raise its threshold of pain). Reserve the other ounce. Holding the turtle firmly, dip its feet into the soup water and bring the heat up *very slowly*. When the turtle shows sings of discomfort, remove feet. Add the other ounce of sherry to the soup, and simmer. When the turtle quiets down, the soup is ready to serve. Garnish with mock mock turtle meat (*page 125*) and simulated croutons (*page 690*).

With pigs in short supply, truffle lovers like Russ Whitely of Seattle, Washington, were forced to root for the exotic food themselves. "After a hard week on my ass, I like to use my face on the weekend," said Russ.

RICH FOOD: CUISINE GROSSEUR

It was a hot afternoon in August 1987 when reporter/food critic Pierre Marcuse, on vacation, drove the unavoidable miles through the scorched wasteland of southern France.

Hungry, thirsty, Marcuse was astonished suddenly to spy a small wayside inn only yards ahead. With a reporter's determination and a food critic's need-to-know, he pulled his car into the parking lot to discover how the restaurant had endured. By evening, having sampled its fare, he knew. It seemed to Marcuse that he had witnessed a French revolution.

The reporter's plate was heaped in a rococo splendor of gorgeous *pain en croûte* that was further glazed with a slather of ruddy peanut butter. There were delicately molded shells of lard swimming among islands of cannelloni peaked by mounds of bulgar wheat and angelica. Pots of scrapple were constantly replenished as waiters scurried to assist the diners. Acorns, turnips, parsnips were caramelized into the medley of always-available candy placed in shimmering glass bowls on every table in the small dining room.

Elaborately constructed roasts of aged oatmeal and porridge arrived hot and tempting from the oven. And, for dessert, Marcuse was plied with enormous servings of rice pudding with nutmeg, double egg custard, apple brown betty, and—the *pièce d'occasion*—towering carrot cake. Curiously, Marcuse's appetite seemed boundless, even piggish, and he could resist nothing. As he sank back, sated for the first time in years, a phrase floated into his mind—*cuisine grosseur*.

As the news of the breakthrough cooking spread, the wealthy everywhere scurried to learn the unknown chef's professional techniques.

While most of the world's population subsisted on grubs and twigs, those who could afford it ate everything in sight. Capturing the spirit of the movement, fashionable

women checked into "fat farms," spas that offered rigid behavior control and the sometimes delicious—but always plentiful—*cuisine grosseur*.

PAIN EN CROUTE

This dish, one of the centerpieces of cuisine grosseur, is properly made with only the most authentic bread, flour, butter, lard, and eggs. The legendary French willingness to spend a small fortune on palate and figure need not be emulated by Americans: a mouthwatering version can be concocted with modern industrial foods. You will need:

> 5 cups real-grain flour (or 2 cups real-grain flour, 2 cups Flour Helper, 1 cup hydrogenized lint)
> 1 cup Seven Sisters Butterette–109
> ½ cup Lard Twin
> 1 pinch Sugar Cousin
> 2 secondhand eggs (or Egg Friends)
> 1 pinch salt (sea or desert)
> ½ cup cold water
> 1 loaf French bread (where available—French-style bread substitute will do)

Preheat oven to 350°.

Place real-grain flour, half of the Butterette–109, Lard Twin, Sugar Cousin, eggs, salt, and water in pastry blender. Blend pastry at ultrasonic setting until dough light flashes *Knead*. Remove and place in kneader. Allow one full cycle or until screen reads *Rich and Starchy*. Hoist or fork-lift dough into roller-compressor and process at ⅛-inch thickness. You should now have a uniform 18-inch square sheet of dough.

Next, trim the loaf of French bread into brick 12 inches by 4 inches by 4 inches, using McCulloch bread saw. Place scraps in julienner and julienne. (These will be pressurized and served as a garnish.) Spray loaf with remaining Butterette–109, and dust lightly with flour-duster (you may use a flour-tunnel if you have one).

Place dough sheet in wrapper-folder with automatic plate transfer and fork-lift the French bread to position 3 inches from one side of dough sheet and 7 inches from the other. Activate wrap-fold and staple edges of dough sheet together. Hoist into shallow pan and bake until screen reads *Ready*. Remove and serve hot in thick slabs drizzled with Cream Acquaintance, using Servomatic in drizzled-slab mode or by hand.

NEW FOODS

The search for new comestibles in the '80s went through two phases: the first, finding something better, tastier, and more convenient to eat; the second, finding something to eat.

Before the food shortage, America experienced a revolution in convenience foods. By mid-1980 we already had the pay-cable TV dinner (no advertising on the carton), the frozen Betamax dinner (reheatable, erasable, and reusable), and the closed-circuit TV dinner (for doormen in posh apartment houses). Other intriguing developments included the frozen "mood meal" (for instance, the Swanson "Angry Man" dinner) and the self-basting cryogenic frozen turkey, which came to life when thawed and rolled in butter. It had to be caught, killed, plucked, and cleaned, but it was guaranteed fresh.

With the prohibition of meat by the Congress of Nuts, the food industry faced the new challenge of supplying us with protein and amino acids in a viandless society. Strict regulation of cows (under the Controlled Species Act) led the dairy industry to experiment with other kinds of milk.

For sale: Florida Grapefruit, pink, 8" diameter, one owner, 2 mos. old, never used. $100 or best offer.

FROM THE *NEW YORK VARIETY TIMES* MERCHANDISE OFFERINGS, 1987

Dog butter and dog yogurt (Land O' Lassie) and a cheese called Le Chat Qui Rit had a brief vogue, but as America's pet population dwindled suspiciously, production was banned. In 1984, a forest ranger died trying to milk a cougar. A plan to milk whales foundered because the protected animals herded so thickly it was impossible to get under them to determine their sex (even when milked they would not hold still, tending to broach and upset the bucket).

The introduction of petrofoods in 1989 brought a false dawn of hope. Petroingredients, such as ashpharagus, cantelube, and chickenol, tasted strikingly like the real thing. But it was soon discovered that the new miracle comestibles had one drawback: they exploded when cooked. Subdued by this information, the great chefs kept for a while to cold buffet. But in France the temptation was too great. Working at heats just below flash point and in small amounts to limit the explosions, they had some success; but triumphs such as Duval's *croustades de fruits de mer sur le plafond* (sea food in patty shells on the ceiling) and Chevallier's *rognons par la fenêtre* (kidneys out the window) were deemed too dangerous to reproduce.

Still, smelling the old smells and mistaking them for victory, the chefs of France grew bolder. In the summer of 1989, the cooking capitals of France were rocked by a fusillade of major explosions. It is estimated that in just 60 days France lost more chefs than in the entire period of the Napoleonic Wars. But France honors her dead; today in Lyon's city square the Eternal Gas Flame flickers in their memory beside a monument with this simple inscription:

ALLONS, ENFANTS DE LA PETROCHIMIQUE

A smorgasbord of the decade's food breakthroughs. (Clockwise from left) Milk Helper, typical of substances that provided much-needed assistance to basic foodstuffs; the cocomato, a sturdy agribiz hybrid with an estimated shelf life of 15 years; dog butter (and cheddar), dairy firsts that converted Man's Best Friend into Man's Best Sandwich; Hamburger Helper Helper, which refined food assistance still further; Ms. Paul's New Fishstix (discontinued when they were found to be made from whale phalli); Nogurt, the decade's slimmingest substance; Aide Beaujolais (Wine Helper), a fitting accompaniment to any bottle of Burgundy; and last, but not least, the Two-Time Turkey,℠ which graced so many Thanksgiving tables so often that for many it came to be regarded as a member of the family.

THE PIGALO AND THE POTATOLO

In late 1986, with the meat ban honored more in the breach than in the observance, scientists at Texas A & M University, encouraged by the success some years earlier of the beefalo, a cross between bull and bison that yielded choice steaks on grass forage, began new breeding experiments. Less than a year later, they announced the development of the pigalo, a shaggy beast with a curly tail and pink snout, equally at home in a sty or on the range. It lived on slops or grass and, being half-kosher, was a favorite with Jewish agnostics. (The project floundered somewhat when it was discovered that, perhaps due to difficulties at the breeding stage, the pigalo was irretrievably gay.) Despite a two-million-dollar United Multinationals' grant, however, the Cornell University Agricultural Extension Service failed miserably to breed a potatolo (a cross between a bison and a potato), conceived as an animal that would grow rooted in one place, have 50 eyes (2 functional), and when cooked, taste vaguely like beef stew. The breeding experiments were said to be messy and embarrassing, and of them the less said the better.

(Right) The widespread practice of strip-farming —harvesting crop, roots, and the first six inches of topsoil —led agribusiness to concentrate on solid, hardy produce with thick shells. Delicate crops like lettuce, spinach, and endive, however, which tended to be pureed by the vast strip-farming machines into a greenish mud, became rarer and rarer. On February 29, 1988, broccoli was declared an endangered vegetable.

KIDS

By 1987, youngsters hung out in "single-kids bars" such as
Maxwell's Plum Pudding (above), nursing Shirley
Temples and waiting to "score" with new parents.
"One-night stands" and "cribbing around" were common,
as was shoptalk. ("Their Christmas tree was really hung.")

KIDS

It is 10:00 A.M. on a pleasant April day, and a court in Richmond, Virginia, is convening. As the judge enters the courtroom, five-year-old Stevie Klopman Franklin DeWitt rises and, obedient to his counsel's advice, takes his thumb out of his mouth. Several feet away, Joan and Robert DeWitt also rise. In a moment the judge will announce his decision—a ruling that could take Stevie out of the DeWitt's lives forever. As all are seated, Stevie asks the bailiff for a cookie. The request is granted.

When the gods convene after the end of the world, surely one of them will ask: why was the United States of America the most famous nation on earth? There can be but one response: freedom. And if that curious god should inquire, why freedom?—then the answer must be: for the children. For they are the commodity futures with which any society invests in its destiny. If, during the 1980s, America's children seemed somehow older, stronger, more independent, and in shorter supply than the children of other nations, it was precisely because America's destiny is to be older, stronger, more independent, and in shorter supply than any other people.

In 1980, Dr. Lawrence A. Child of Harvard University was the first to realize that a baby, far from being the passive recipient of the actions and attitudes of its parents, is in fact the active determiner of those actions and attitudes. The child cries; the mother responds.

WITH THE 1987 SUPREME COURT DECISION IN *CHIP JR. V. CHIP SR.*, CHILDREN WERE GRANTED THE LEGAL RIGHT TO DIVORCE THEIR PARENTS.

The child laughs; the mother smiles. With the discovery of this phenomenon, known as "childing," America's youngsters became a self-aware, politically powerful sector of society. Tots stood up on their own hands and knees and announced themselves to the world.

But "What children?" asked many, for during the '80s children themselves seemed as rare as broccoli. Experts pointed fingers everywhere: at the "Baby Bust" of the childless 1970s generation of self-absorbed narcissists; at the alarming shortage of orgasm, which afflicted everyone from ditchdigger to professional historian; at the off-putting necessity for test-tube conceptions and artificial insemination procedures. Demand was up and supply was down; it was a seller's market. With the 1987 Supreme Court decision in *Chip*

Jr. v. *Chip Sr.*, children were granted the legal right to divorce their parents and seek, in a process not unlike that employed by "free agents" in professional sports, new ones. It was a momentous decision and, as "Divorce Court" became a popular Saturday-morning children's show, the nation agreed with the wisdom of it.

The economy agreed, too. With the parental bond now legally breakable, children became as marketable as beets, and took their place alongside the other great prod-

> **"WHAT CHILDREN?" ASKED MANY, FOR DURING THE '80s CHILDREN THEMSELVES SEEMED AS RARE AS BROCCOLI.**

ucts of American merchandising. Baby trading flourished, bringing satisfaction to parent, child, and customer alike. "W.M., 2 yrs. old, dstnt. Kennedy cuz., 1 prev. owner, a steal," read one ad. As prospective purchasers took the tykes out for a test stroll, all knew a reawakened pride in that marketplace that is America. For it was this process that would enable a great many children to grow to happy adulthood, secure in the knowledge that they were the best children their parents' money could buy.

To be sure, this scarcity of offspring created some troubling social problems. Patty Hearst's daring daylight robbery of the Beverly Hills First Spendings and Clone Association served to dramatize the plight of the wed un-mother. Children for whom no parents seemed acceptable lived alone, giving rise to the so-called single-kid phenomenon. Such a child's entire day often centered around his or her quest for still another set of parents. Living on a child support "allowance" paid directly into his or her Pigibank account, the youngster would "cruise" the "single-kids bars" in an often frantic attempt to "get folked."

And so eager were some parents for offspring—either natural or replacements—that some couples took turns "raising" each other on a weekly basis. Gay couples hired themselves out as substitute children. "It was an example of *ad hocism* at its best," wrote cultural critic Joyce Maynard. "For the gays, the 'new' mother and father became the warm, understanding parents they had never had. For the parents, the gays became the sweet, agreeable children fate had denied them."

"Fate?" Or rather, "progress?" Stevie Klopman Franklin DeWitt claps his hands gaily at the judge's decision. He has been granted his divorce—his third—and will toddle out of the courtroom a free man. And although he may be unaware that his emancipation echoes that "divorce" by which his nation attained its own independence from an equally unsuitable "mother," it does not matter. For the moment he is free of everyone—as indeed all Americans should be.

BABY'S FIRST RIGHTS

What many called "the trial of the decade" was occasioned by a casually smoked cigarette in a San Fernando Valley cockfighting disco. Enterprising attorney Marvin Mitchelson saw well-known superstar of the day, Cher Bono-Allman-Orlando, light up a low-tar cigarette at the snack bar. She happened to be pregnant.

Within hours, Mitchelson had filed a massive civil suit under a little-known clause of the National Environmental Protection Act authorizing third-party actions. The suit, filed on behalf of the singer's fetus, charged the mother-to-be with endangering the infant-to-be by exposing it to a known carcinogen.

Mitchelson's claim was deceptively simple: if a mother's cigarette caused an increased risk of cancer in the future neonate, that creature should have equal rights to sue for damages. Likening fetuses to persons in a coma ("Would Cher offer a cigarette to Karen Ann Quinlan?" he asked rhetorically), Mitchelson maintained that any interested attorney should be able to enforce those rights through an *amicus feti* ("friend of the fetus") lawsuit. Judge Herbert Kalmbach, presiding in a courtroom cleared of all spectators to make more room for reporters, ruled that the implied intent of the 29th (anti-abortion) Amendment was to "protect the rights believed to belong to the unborn fellow or gal in the tummy." Thus, with superlawyer F. Lee Bailey defending the pregnant actress-singer, the landmark trial began.

After a two-week continuance granted to allow designer Bob Mackie lead-time on a wardrobe for the defendant, the sessions at courtroom 41 commenced. By the end of the case, publicity surrounding the trial fashions had snowballed into a craze for maternity wear, even among women who were expecting nothing more than their next period. Oscar de la Renta designed one of the biggest sellers—a red tent with sequined script lettering over the stomach that said *Occupado*.

Jury selection consumed the first two months of the trial. Mitchelson candidly admitted that his goal was to pack the panel with cancer victims and young children as the only logical way for the case of an endangered fetus to be heard by a jury of its peers.

From Bailey's opening defense onward, it was clear that Cher had a two-pronged defense strategy: (1) she denied smoking while pregnant, and (2) she pleaded temporary insanity. Bailey refused to let the singer herself take the stand, fearing it would lead to the use of fetal monitoring devices to extract evidence from the client's womb. "A woman's uterus," Bailey thundered at one point, "is her castle."

The case took a bizarre turn when Kalmbach reluctantly allowed Mitchelson to be sworn in to testify on behalf of the fetus. Mitchelson's performance, complete with a convincing hacking cough, was the hit of the proceedings. Later he won two gold statuettes of President Lincoln at the American Bar Association's first annual Abie Awards—one for Best Lawyer and the other for Best Witness in his role as the fetus.

The verdict awarded Cher's unborn relative a judgment of seven million dollars: a million in medical expenses for the possible future lung cancer, and the rest in punitive damages. Mrs. Bono-Allman-Orlando's various husbands were apparently not in a generous mood, however. Hours after the baby's birth, it was placed on auction at the prestigious Sotheby Parke Bernet gallery in an attempt to raise enough funds to satisfy the judgment. ("Selling Peter to pay Peter," one columnist called it.) When the auctioneer's gavel fell for the third time, Chastity's half brother (named Poverty by the distraught mother) had fetched a whopping two million seven hundred thousand dollars, at that time a world-record price for a newborn child.

SUBSTITUTE KIDS

It's an ill wind, the saying goes, that does no one some good, and that was certainly true of the great birth dearth of the '80s. Of course, the Baby Bust decade was a tragic time of heartbreak and thwarted nurturance for some; but for other energetic and industrious Americans, it was a time of fulfillment and downright plenty. Commented Roger A., one half of an enterprising gay couple that hired themselves out as substitute children for needy moms and dads, "It's meant more to our lives than Stonewall."

Not only homosexuals profited from capitalism's reassuring response to the Baby Bust. Eager heterosexuals also found employment as surrogate children, and, by the end of the decade, the "home temporary" market was a booming business. Computer-parenting services sprang up across the land, along with a host of new "surrogate bars," where role-playing "children" could size up prospective "parents." For greeting card manufacturers, there were new birthday cards to be designed for "Our Surrogate Son" and "Our Substitute Daughter"; for day-care centers, there were unforeseen new profits to be made from the sudden influx of the "older children" who were farmed out by working moms and dads. For Mattel, Incorporated, there was spiraling demand for its full-size, inflatable "Son" and "Daughter" dolls ("They talk, they walk, and they're anatomically correct"), and an enterprising chicken mogul named Frank Perdue, wiped out by the 1983 Meat Prohibition Act, launched his line of brand-name babies in 1985. Thousands of lonely parents were made happy by Mr. Perdue, even though the children did bear—especially in their hindquarters—an inexplicable resemblance to his former product.

I've got twelve mothers
and I ain't ashamed,
I've got twelve mothers,
I love each one the same—
Let me tell you 'bout my first
mo-ther,
She's sweet an' kind . . .

POPULAR SONG, LATER ADOPTED AS
RECRUITING LYRIC IN ADVERTISING
CAMPAIGN FOR LITTLE DAUGHTERS OF
AMERICA, INC.

daddy

daddy

daddy

daddy

daddy

missed my hit.

How to keep 20 lecturing, pompous, overbearing Dads happy and involved? It's all in an afternoon's work for this Little Son! "I usually take 'em to the park," says Skippy, who at age nine has been a Little Son for two grueling but deeply rewarding years. He hikes every Saturday afternoon to the local sandlot with 20 gawky, sonless Dads. Displaying awesome patience and never-failing affection, he takes turns with each one, pretending to let them teach him how to play ball. "I guess the toughest thing is remembering to pretend to flinch when they hit grounders at me. Some of the Dads get real mean and give me a punch for every flinch," says Skippy. "But I know how much they really need me—to bully, to shout at, to be distant and insensitive to. I always try my best to be awkward, even with the last Dad on a long afternoon." Skippy, whose real, away-from-the-Dads name is Herbert, is one of the more than 400,000 members of Little Sons of America who selflessly sacrifice their evenings and weekends to make sad Dads glad.

SINGLE KIDS

We present it here in all its stark brutality. The shocking dialogue from the moment of cinematic madness that has become the anthem for a whole generation. Few could have dreamed it possible, that these words—from an unheralded 1986 low-budget remake called *Looking for Mr. and Mrs. Goodbar* —would be picked up and repeated by an entire cohort of '80s children.

Everywhere, long lines of children would wait hours outside big-city art theaters to see midnight showings of the cult film. Inside, they would mouth every word of dialogue and mime every filmic moment. The words from the brutal spanking scene became a rote-learned ritual, a *lingua franca* in the sordid single-kids bars that blighted the cities of America. "There is nothing you can do to me that will make me betray my dignity as a child," these youngsters would say to one another, in their "spank talk" jargon. But all too often the dignity was tinged with despair. This was the dark side of the '80s dream: the wanton, degrading world of the tot rooms and crib clubs. They gathered there after play, or during "happy hours," or even way after bedtime. In the darkness, illuminated by the flickering light of juketubes playing old "Brady Bunch" and "Make Room for Daddy" reruns, they would seek out one another and the lonely parents who were drawn to the "scene." Solitary and rootless, many of them recently divorced from their mothers and fathers, single children would promiscuously pick up parent after parent in an attempt to recapture some of the warmth that lingered after—as the nay-sayers would call it — the fission of the nuclear family. But as literary philosopher David Wallechinsky would later write in his autobiography, "The transition of the American family under the tutelage of the single kid was a thoroughly natural state of growth. The single kid delivered the family from its adolescence."

FADE IN

EXT. KID KAT LOUNGE -- NIGHT

LONG SHOT of the Kid Kat Lounge, a notorious single=kids bar in a strip of crib clubs on a seamy street in Manhattan's Soho district.

MED. SHOT of TERRY walking up to the entrance, and pausing under the sputtering neon sign over the door.

CLOSE=UP of Terry's face, bizarrely lit by the harsh neon. She pauses uncertainly, furtively glances about the street, and then, impulsively, pushes through the door.

INT. KID KAT LOUNGE -- NIGHT

MED. SHOT of Terry as she threads her way through the sordid single kids, cruise tots, and lone parents in the dark and noisy bar.

CLOSE=UP of Terry, talking to a predatory=looking Mom. Terry's words are drowned out in the roar of singles bar sounds.

CUT TO MED. AND CLOSE=UP SHOTS of Terry talking to other single kids and a series of Moms and Dads. CROSSCUT to shots of strung=out single kids and impatient parents arranging assignations as Terry continues to seek companionship amid the roar of noise and the swirl of movement.

MED. SHOT of Terry talking animatedly to a silver=haired, jovial Dad, who smiles at her warmly and pats her gently on the head.

CLOSE=UP of Terry, who places her hand tentatively in his.

EXT. KID KAT LOUNGE -- NIGHT

MED. SHOT of Terry and her new=found Dad, MR. GOODBAR, leaving Kid Kat Lounge and walking over to a dark pink Buick parked nearby. At the wheel is a kindly, silver=haired Mom, MRS. GOODBAR, who smiles happily at Terry and embraces her when she gets in the car.

EXT. GOODBAR RESIDENCE -- NIGHT

LONG SHOT of car pulling into the driveway of a landscaped suburban ranch house. Terry and Mr. and Mrs. Goodbar leave the car, and, arm in arm, walk to the door and enter the house.

INT. GOODBAR RESIDENCE -- NIGHT

MED. SHOT of Terry, smiling, turning to talk to Mr. Goodbar. He and Mrs. Goodbar have ceased smiling, and Mrs. Goodbar is hurriedly chain=locking the front door.

                    MR. GOODBAR
                    (menacingly)

          Now we have you here, Terry.

Mrs. Goodbar finishes locking the door and turns to Terry.

                    MRS. GOODBAR
                    (threateningly)

          Yes. Now that we've got you here, and you can't
          escape -- we want you to <u>clean up your room</u>.

Terry cringes away from them, moving into the den.

                    TERRY
                    (fearfully)

          I --what? You want me to what?

                    MR. GOODBAR

          You hear us! We want you to CLEAN UP YOUR ROOM!
          NOW!

                    TERRY

          Oh, my God.

Mr. and Mrs. Goodbar advance toward Terry.

                    MRS. GOODBAR

          Do it. Now.

Terry edges away from them, backing through the den and ending
in a child's room. It is strewn with toys and its only furniture
is an unmade child=sized bed.

                    TERRY

          Please, I --

                    MR. GOODBAR

          If you won't do it, well, we can make you. We
          just might not be telling you a bedtime story
          tonight. Lit=tle Terry.

                    TERRY

          You just cannot be serious. I --

                    MRS. GOODBAR

          Do it! This minute! You little brat ...

Terry stops backing away and stands to face Mr. and Mrs. Goodbar.

                    TERRY

          I -- wait a minute. I -- I'm not afraid of you.
          Do you hear? I am not afraid! I am a responsible,
          independent, full=grown child. I have rights.
          Don't you ever forget it. There is nothing you
          can do to me that will make me betray my dignity
          as a child. Next you creeps will threaten to
          feed me spinach!

Mr. Goodbar glances at Mrs. Goodbar.

                    MR. GOODBAR

          I think this little pick=up kid needs a lesson,
          Mrs. G.

                    MRS. GOODBAR

          I'll say. And we're the ones to teach it.

                    MR. GOODBAR

          Grab her! Now! Down with her pants! Hold her
          now -- WHILE I SPANK HER!

Mr. and Mrs. Goodbar throw Terry on the filthy bed.

CLOSE=UP of Terry's face, her expression a mix of anger and agony.

                    TERRY

          No. No. No. No. No --

FADE OUT

Note: *The parent deduction may be filed by qualified children only for expenses incurred in parent care while the child is pursuing an employment opportunity or educational study that leads to a vocation.*

J. K. LASSER
YOUR INCOME TAX, 1986

334.2. STRICTNESS OR PERMISSIVENESS? I may as well let the cat out of the bag right away as far as my opinion goes and say that strictness or permissiveness is not the real issue. Good-hearted children who are not afraid to be firm with their parents can get good results with either moderate strictness or moderate permissiveness.

DR. BENJAMIN SPOCK
BABY AND CHILD CARING, 1987

Ah, the age-old problem. What to do with a houseful of fractious, squabbling parents on a rainy day in the country?

Try this. Tell them you MUST have their help in building a tin-can telephone! Pretend that you don't know how to tie together two tin cans with a piece of string. There's every chance that you can keep them busy for as much as an hour while they empty the cans, find the string, and tell you to keep your thumb away from sharp edges. And, after the project is finished, tell them to go and talk to one another from adjacent rooms! Maybe then you can get some hard-earned rest.

STEVEN CANEY
THE RAINY-DAY WHAT-TO-DO BOOK, 1988

THE FACE OF AMERICA

SFX (stomach rumbles)
JOHN HUNGRY: It's a good thing I'm not hungry, because if I was I could eat a horse.
BLUE: Or an ox!

1.

SFX (loud stomach rumbles)
JOHN HUNGRY: Say, what's that over there?
BLUE: Nothing worth . . . wait . . .

2.

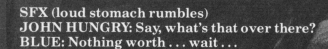

THE FACE OF AMERICA

It is near midnight, December 31, 1989, and Alex Parsons has just been told by his wife Louise that the bottle of champagne she has stored in their refrigerator since December 31, 1979, has been stolen. She hands him the only beverage left with which they might toast the new decade: a small can of Milk Helper, its label bearing the familiar repetitive pattern of cow, and can, and label, and cow, and so on. Alex sighs—it has been that kind of year—and reaches for the can opener. It, too, has been stolen.

A nation that fails to read the fine print of the social contract is a nation destined to be clubbed senseless by the blunt instrument of history. No society can—or, indeed, should—endure, when it confuses change *qua* change with promiscuous, arbitrary upheaval. We have always known this—yet, particularly during the 1980s, it sometimes seemed that, in the words of social critic Gene Shalit, "So much history happened in such large quantities that everyone wanted to run away." Some called it "the decade of irritation"—but many knew that, behind every irritation, there waited a challenge, if only it could be found.

Just as the lion tamer's skill is tempered by the snapping of his animals, so is our American character strengthened by the occasional rebelliousness of Nature. With the desertification of our great Midwest, and with the slippage of the San Andreas Fault in 1986,

SOME CALLED IT "THE DECADE OF IRRITATION."

America learned the true meaning of inconvenience. The effects of the epochal Simultaneous Orgasm of 1983 were even more severe. For that brief moment of ecstasy—experienced only by some, and missed by more than is commonly supposed—mankind the world over suffered greatly. But, many reflected, what is the history of man if not that chronicle in which the worthy, disciplined few pay dearly for the wanton excesses of the common herd?

Yet sometimes human history is the sum total, not of major cataclyms, but of small events at the interstices of life. Irritation increased as Unidentified Flying Objects, appearing with greater and greater frequency, mocked us with their unfulfilled promise of advancements in civilization. We looked skyward and saw, over several major metropolitan areas, terrifying drag-races of extraterrestrial vehicles—and not once did any occupant of such a spacecraft deign to stretch forth a hand, tentacle, or pseudopod in a gesture of interplanetary friendship. Rejected, we went about our human

IT WAS A WORRISOME DECADE, AN AGGRAVATING DECADE ... AN ANNOYING DECADE.

business: of having to dress to use the videophone; of signing endless petitions to save the endangered mass transit systems; of joining still another Inhuman Potential movement, in which a Provocateur would hurl insult and abuse at us, and to whom we were encouraged to respond with merely a glassy smile and a murmured, "Oh, really? That's nice."

It was a worrisome decade, an aggravating decade, and, for all its noble challenges, an annoying decade. During the guerilla land war between the Northern California Vietnamese and the Southern California Vietnamese, a self-immolating Buddhist monk ignited a brush fire in Bakersfield that claimed 12,000 acres and took six days to extinguish. Maps became obsolete overnight, as states—as if to cause personal aggravation to journalists and popular historians—seceded from each other in hideous mitosis. Such monstrosities as New Old New York and North-East South Dakota cluttered the nation's roadmaps, and brought migraines to the nation's psyche.

Even American technology—invulnerable god of an earlier era—faltered. The Year of the Total Recall, in 1984, saw the complete crippling of our economy as every single item produced during 1983 was ordered returned to its producer for inspection. Woe to the journalist and popular historian who purchased a new typewriter during that unlucky year—his refusal to allow its recall brought rude and thuggish company "representatives" pounding on his door at 10:30 in the evening, and threats of physical violence unless he comply. It was all he could do—it was all anyone could do—to remember that in such adversity is to be found the means by which we become stronger, that America is that land of lands in which pain, misfortune, difficulty, incompetence, and threats of physical violence lead to a better way of living for all mankind.

Having punctured the can with a screwdriver, Alex Parsons holds his cup of Milk Helper aloft and touches it to that of his wife. Behind their mutual wishes for a "Happy New Year" lies the tacit understanding that to live is to endure challenges. Many lie behind them—and their country. Many more lie ahead.

LAS VEGAS: RIEN NE VA PLUS

"The jewel of the desert," they used to call it. In 1980, more than eight million cash-crazy thrill-seekers from Boston to Baja passed through Las Vegas, Nevada, a glittering neon mirage whose streets seemed paved with saw-bucks. Today it lies dying in the desert, just another sagebrush-scattered ghost town, a panned-out buccaneer gasping for air in the scorching sun.

For years, the Rio of the Rockies had been America's favorite playground; the entertainment capital of the only state in the Union to legalize casino gambling. The most explosive stars in the show-biz firmament sang and joked their hearts out in lavish showrooms at luxurious resorts while wide-eyed vacationeers staked their paychecks on the roll of a wheel. But when New Jersey opened the doors of Atlantic City to gambling fiends in 1978 and six other Northeastern states quickly followed suit, the race for the American gaming dollar was on.

As the casino craze spread nationwide in the following years, Las Vegas tourism dropped sharply and its glow began to dim. Top-flight performers began passing up Vegas in favor of New Jersey's Resorts International, Detroit's Black Jack's Palace, and Miami's Moneyworld. As casinos sprouted in small towns across the country, Vegas could no longer offer the exotic vacation. A sign of the times in Canton, Ohio, in 1983 read, "Why pack for Vegas when you can lose your shirt right here at Joey's Kit-Kat Casino?"

A series of ill-fated schemes to head off impending city bankruptcy followed. The introduction of contact greyhound racing and cock fights only cut the shrinking pie into minuscule slices; the desperate L.A.– Vegas monorail drained precious tax dollars only to open three days before the California legislature approved casinos in that state.

An 11th-hour push to preserve the city as a landmark of Americana fell short. Old-time singer Joan Baez was coaxed from retirement to lead a musical benefit to "Save Old Sin City," but few turned out and fewer contributed. Finally, Mayor Joey Adams declared a fiscal emergency, banning the casino chip as a form of negotiable currency and designating the once-majestic Caesar's Palace a welfare hotel as out-of-work croupiers and comedians swelled the relief rolls. Those few performers who had remained loyal to Vegas fell on hard times; one guided tour of "Ol' Las Vegas" included the sobering sight of Sammy Davis, Jr., playing solitaire in the lobby of the Sands Hotel and Shecky Greene and Lainie Kazan pitching pennies on the Strip. A last-ditch national fund-raising effort was a lottery with the Silver Dollar Casino as the grand prize, but only 180 tickets were bought—and the pleasure palace was leveled and sold for scrap.

And so Las Vegas stands today, a garish pinball game with its glass smashed, its plug pulled, its neon colors run together in a muddy mosaic of desolation. It is a monument to the times, a discarded toy, a hot-winning streak that turned deadly cold.

"Las Vegas is so broke . . ."
"How broke is it, Johnny?"
"Las Vegas is so broke that these days when Ed passes out he has to carry himself to the car."

Now this song, well, it's not really a song, it's more of a holler. . . and it's very simple, wait, let me get my banjo fixed here . . . O.K., I want you all to join in and sing the chorus with me . . . and it goes like this . . . "Place your bets red or black, place your bets red or black. . . ."

PETE SEEGER PERFORMING
IN LAS VEGAS AT A 1987 BENEFIT
FOR THE SANDS HOTEL

NEO-IRVINGTON

"Perhaps it was a dream that could not survive reality; or perhaps it was a reality that could not survive the dream."

This perceptive observation by one onlooker sums up possibly the most exciting, and ultimately the most dramatic, social experiment of the entire decade: the community of Neo-Irvington.

Named for neo-conservative guru Irving Kristol, plans for the totally unplanned community drew on the principles of thinkers as diverse as Daniel Patrick Moynihan, Seymour Martin Lipset, Norman Podhoretz, and Jack Kemp. Its premise was that "the vibrant spirit of free men—and an occasional woman—can govern itself free of the dead, stifling hand of bureaucrats who went to fancy colleges and got big fat foundation grants and smoked marijuana and hated Catholics and had no respect for traditional values and laughed at the National Anthem and wanted to tell everybody else what to do including be sexually perverted."

From this thoughtful critique, however, it was a long way to the practical operation of a community. The intention was clear: to demonstrate that a town could function "with the market as a guide." Zoning requirements were limited to severe restrictions on the sale of pornography and the operation of clubs "featuring heavy, insistently rhythmic music." Automobiles were freed of all safety requirements. The whole panoply of "restrictive regulations" were lifted from plants, factories, restaurants, and utilities. Stop signs and traffic lights were banned.

The first months went smoothly. Homebuilders, freed from building codes, began work on 25,000 new houses; the unemployed, promised jobs "for all who seek them at wages the market can bear," flocked to Neo-Irvington, living in tents in a community that came to be known as "Resubmission City." Prominent conservative figures were attracted as well. Five members of the United States Supreme

Court moved to Neo-Irvington, as did a third of the members of the United States Senate. And what problems did exist were minor. There were the long lines at movie theaters, for example, since each patron was free to negotiate a separate admission charge at the ticket booth.

Then, as City Administrator Midge Decter recalls, "We had a series of bad breaks." All five Supreme Court justices were killed in a car crash. (Car crashes were common since motorists refused to slow down at intersections, arguing that this was "a bow to the power of the state.") The Adam Smith nuclear power plant released what was called a "spontaneous nocturnal emission." Three months later, 8 percent of Neo-Irvington's newborns turned a shade of pale green and developed nostrils in the middle of their foreheads. And locusts suddenly began spurting from water faucets after the utility company proudly announced the suspension of an elaborate inspection system. Its cost would have to have been passed along to consumers.

The end came for Neo-Irvington, however, when the black population organized a demonstration to protest the average wage of 75 cents an hour paid to unskilled workers. They booed Milton Friedman, who explained to them that the alternative was joblessness; and when Irving Kristol began to lecture the crowd on the dynamics of postindustrial capitalism, the crowd tore him limb from limb. A rampage ensued. By morning, nothing was left of the town.

Some of Neo-Irvington's strongest supporters took the destruction hard. Norman Podhoretz, for example, was last seen wandering the ruined streets in a robe, his mind gone, urging the workers to "arise." But press spokesman George Will was philosophical, commenting: "Perhaps it was destiny—almost as if an invisible hand had dealt a losing card." For the few who survived, Neo-Irvington would remain the memory of what had been; and the hope of what might be again.

Conservatives were indeed a dying breed at Neo-Irvington, as was proven by this sign on its main street, Laissez Thoroughfare.

BACK TO TECHNOLOGY

■t started as a trickle early in the decade; in a few years, it was a flood. After nearly twenty years of rejecting the fruits of 20th-century technology for the simpler life, Americans were by 1986 going "back to junk" in droves. They were tired of living in yurts, domes, sod hogans, and tepees; tired of everything rough-hewn, homespun, and handmade (usually badly); tired of squatting on their hams listening to Hindus rant; tired of the monotony of the mass counterculture, the millions of one-of-a-kind belt buckles, the lumpy ceramics, the ten-pound necklaces, the strange teas. They wanted to watch game shows, not babies being born. They wanted to root for the Yankees, not for odd nuts and lumps of fungus. They had learned that there was a reason why, a century earlier, their ancestors had deserted the simple life by the millions: it was so damn hard. Further, in a world in which wasting oil was a moral obligation, "back-to-technology" made sense. The bible of the movement was *Mother Lode News*, a monthly periodical of chatty articles, practical advice, and ads. Crammed with literally thousands of helpful how-to hints, *Mother Lode* ran such articles as "101 Simple Plastix You Can Make in Your Basement," "The Fun—and Profit—in Drop Forging," "Lead—the Gray Wonder-Worker," "The 'Lost' Art of Food Coloring," "A Simple Backyard Catalytic Cracking Tower You Can Build Yourself," and "How to Build a Rubber Tire Bonfire That'll Burn for a Week."

The movement had a profound impact on the public as well as the private sector. New uses for the abandoned products of bygone technology became imperative, if only to recoup the vast investment they represented. Among the more dramatic signs on the American landscape of a society that no longer needed alternative energy sources were the almost 3,000 nuclear plant coolant towers.

Surrounded by countryside, close to running water, within striking distance of large population centers, yet undisturbed by birds, field animals, insects, and most other rural irritations, these majestic structures would clearly be of benefit to society.

It took the Urban Deployment Task Force of the UM to put two and two together. In August 1987, work began to convert the towers into low-income housing.

After some token resistance (it was pointed out to protesters that the habitual consumption of lead-based paint would make them immune to radiation), the first of more than 50,000 families took up residence in time for Christmas, 1987. Since then, despite unsubstantiated rumors of mutations, the vast majority have lived happy, useful lives. The Towers, as they are affectionately known, stand as a silent tribute to a society that will not allow its homeless to go without shelter, nor its children without heat and light.

The Towers under construction near Concord, Massachusetts. Set in rolling countryside, this former "nuke" would provide ample, spacious housing for disadvantaged members of society, with guaranteed solitude and tranquillity, plus built-in heating and lighting.

From Mother Lode News, *April 1987: "Back to the Land—in a Limousine!" by Myra Kennerly.*

A few years ago, after my husband and I sold our temple bell business, we started looking for a place in the country like our folks used to have. After a long search, we found what we wanted last year in northern Connecticut. It wasn't much to look at, but the price was right. We knew it would take a heck of a lot of work. The house itself was a solid 1953 colonial split ranch, but it had been badly altered. The roof was covered with bubble skylites, solar panels, and a Fuller dome; mandala windows had been cut in the north side; and—can you believe it—there was a working woodburning stove in the living room!

To round off the picture, the grounds had gone to seed; there was some kind of smelly bean all over the place, a compost heap the size of a mountain smack dab in the middle of the yard, and a windmill right where it was sure to cause year-long blizzards on any TV screen for miles around.

Well, we got right to work. John has a friend, Fred, who got fed up with yoga and yogurt a couple of years ago and set about restoring an old junkyard in Springfield. Well, Fred showed up one day with a D-9 on a flatbed! That dozer sure did the job. We had ourselves a nice yard and the foundations for a pair of 5,000-gallon corrosives tanx in two days flat. The windmill went in ten minutes!

We got 3,000 square feet of green asphalt shingles—the real stuff—from another friend of John's, and a real beauty of a heat pump—a late '70s Carrier. John also turned up a mint KitchenAid dishwasher and a one hp In-Sink-Erator.

As I'm writing this, the sweet smell of diesel exhaust is wafting across the yard where John is using a forklift to stack some drums of oxalic acid we got for a song down in Hartford. There's no place like home!

CALIFORNIA NUEVA

On May 11, 1984, California became the first state to rescind voting rights for women. It was one of many signs that, several years ahead of the predicted date, El Estado del Oro had become more than 50 percent Mexican-American.

For non-Hispanic Californians it was a volatile period. Many eagerly adopted the customs and fashions of the new majority. "Passing" for Chicano was less a fad than an economic necessity. For others there were problems. When La Siesta took on the force of law that winter, for example, it caught many blacks and Anglos by surprise. Try as they might, these minorities could simply not get to sleep in the afternoon. The crime rate rose dramatically between 11 A.M. and 2 P.M. Community Clinics were organized to teach workoholics and other culturally deprived Protestants how to cope with rest. Siesta Crisis Centers and Free Time Hotlines were staffed by sympathetic Chicanos experienced in "talking down" daytime insomniacs. In time, the three-margarita lunch became a fixture on the California scene and disappointment gave way to a general midday euphoria. So successful, in fact, were these social programs that in April 1986 the civil service, the Teamsters, and the American Medical Association agreed to extend siesta from 11 A.M. to 6 P.M.

In this historic raising of Anglophonic consciousness, non-Hispanics soon found that speaking Spanish entailed more than merely adding the letter *o* to every English word. Hard-working English speakers were quick to realize that while *banco*, *telefono*, and *matrimonio* indeed mean "bank," "telephone," and "matrimony," words like "horso" (as in "el cowboyo rides el horso") mean nothing at all and may be vaguely obscene.

Many young Anglo and black Californians enhanced their future job opportunities by spending a few months in Sonora working as maids or busboys. There they developed, if not actual Spanish, at least the ability to speak English with an accent.

Nor was language the only hurdle these enterprising minorities overcame. At community colleges across the state, crash courses in tortilla-making, mural-painting, car-upholstering, decorating graves, and safe driving at slow speeds were filled to capacity.

Schools, faced with the legal requirement of teaching all courses in Spanish, had

Suddenly Spanish . . . this amazing Santa Monica couple broke the Barrio barrier in just 90 days, turning from laid-back Anglos (left) to hot-blooded Chicanos (right)

two major obstacles. First, not enough Chicanos could be found who actually spoke Spanish. Second, Jewish families, faced with California's mandatory First Communion for second graders in addition to the Spanish language laws, threatened a mass exodus from the state—a move which would have crippled the en-

ough diet, salsa, and intensive body work (see Schlitz Book of World Records, *issing: non athletic").*

tertainment industry. Faced with this dilemma, state legislators in 1986 created exemptions from the Spanish Language Act and First Communion Law for children of comedy writers.

There was great civic support for public artwork. La Ciudad de (formerly the City of) Los Angeles commissioned powerful anti-imperialist murals to be painted on all city walls. A landmark feature of this renascent art form is the masterpiece executed in 1985 by Andres Warhol, Incorporated, on the side of Wilson's House of Suede. In classic social-realism style, it features savage tableaux of Sam Houston reintroducing slavery into Texas, James K. Polk annexing the Southwest, and internationalist Woodrow Wilson persecuting Pancho Villa.

And these were not the only visible signs of the new majority. City buses throughout California took on the look of "low riders" and sported pink shag carpet along the window sills, black and red velvet seat cushions, and pompom fringes across the windows. Each bus was named after a saint and some had an appropriate statue or small shrine near the driver. The buses traveled slower than walking speed and were canted to lean *way* back and ride only two inches off the ground.

In what was perhaps the most significant religious development of the decade, the Catholic church canonized César Chavez (San César) in 1987. Thus, the former farmworker became the first person in the history of Holy Mother Church to be declared a saint while still alive. In honor of the occasion, California agronomists developed a special strain of lettuce, which grew with the union label right in the leaf.

In 1988, the resilient Californian peoples embraced legislation reinstituting the firing squad, so that condemned Anglos might have the opportunity to "die with honor." The doomed but honorable prisoners were allowed to smoke one last "pitillo de marijuana" before the shots rang out.

For many, it was perhaps the most telling evidence that La Transición was complete.

THE BIG SLIDE

San Francisco, here I am!" This was the theme song for sun-tanned, laid-back Southern Californians during one hectic week in the summer of '86, when nature, helped along by the U.S. Army Corps of Engineers, "redrew" the map of the nation's westernmost state.

For millennia, the strip of California west of La Falla Sismica de San Andreas (the San Andreas Fault) had been slowly bumping and grinding northward at a rate of approximately 2.5 inches a year. The biggest bumps were felt as "earthquakes." By the middle of the decade, earthquake anxiety was epidemic in El Estado del Oro (the Golden State). When the Chinese reported that the aggressive behavior of vibration-sensitive snakes warned peasants of any impending tremors, there was a boom in the Californian snake market. Top seller by far was the pit viper, which was heavily promoted as a combination "earthquake-sensor and watchdog" by an ex-used-car salesman named Friendly Fernando.

Unfortunately, the vipers turned out to be so sensitive that they were driven into a killing frenzy by the tread of golf shoes on soft greens or by any tone of voice louder than a hoarse, terrified whisper. In wealthier communities, where "Beware of Viper" signs proliferated, few people ventured from their homes except for absolute necessities such as heart attacks and real estate closings.

When the state government tried to ban the vipers (or at least require owners to buy licenses, collars, and pooper-scoopers for them), the Naranja (Orange) County Chapter of the National Reptile Association argued that the people's right to bear venomous snakes should not be infringed.

To avoid a confrontation between pro- and anti-viper forces, the Army Corps of Engineers took steps to eliminate the need for snakes—by harmlessly releasing the geological tensions that had built up over the years in La Falla (the fault). On the night of July 4, 1986, a team of specially trained lubricationists squeezed 47,000 quarts of surplus 3-in-1 oil—from an estimated 752,000 little red-and-white cans—into La Falla outside Las Fuentes de la Palma (Palm Springs). The results of "Operation Quaalube" exceeded all expectations. The natural process of continental drift, which would have brought Los Angeles del Oeste (West L.A.) into alignment with San Francisco over a million-year period, was simply speeded up—and completed in five days.

Since the Army Corps' action was a tightly kept secret, there were a few moments of panic when the northward slide of the coastline suddenly accelerated from 2.5 inches a year to four miles an hour. Wild speculations about causes ran the gamut from "Commie sabotage" to "the gods are angry." Calm returned, however, when Engineer General Rastafar Omani went on television to explain what had been done.

Some grumbling continued. But attempts by owners of earthquake insurance to collect on their policies were thwarted when a state court handed down a "no fault" decision, which found that most Californians were better off than they had been before. The commute from Los Angeles to San Francisco was reduced to a bicycle ride across La Puente de la Entrada del Oro (Golden Gate Bridge). The state university system now had a single contiguous campus the size of Vermont. The economy of the Watts area received a shot in the arm when Fisherman's Wharf, complete with three picturesque crab boats, ended up on Imperial Highway. The San Joaquin Valley's climate, however, was altered to such an extent that henceforth its only practical crop was potatoes.

The dust had pretty much settled by the end of 1987, when a U C L A S F geologist announced that the effects of "Operation Quaalube" might be temporary—and that the entire coastline could be expected "to snap back like a rubber band" any day, restoring all previous jurisdictions, mineral rights, and sports franchises.

The Big Slide of '86, in which Los Angeles merged with San Francisco, allowed Californians to enjoy cold smog, left-wing surfing, and militant gay gas stations.

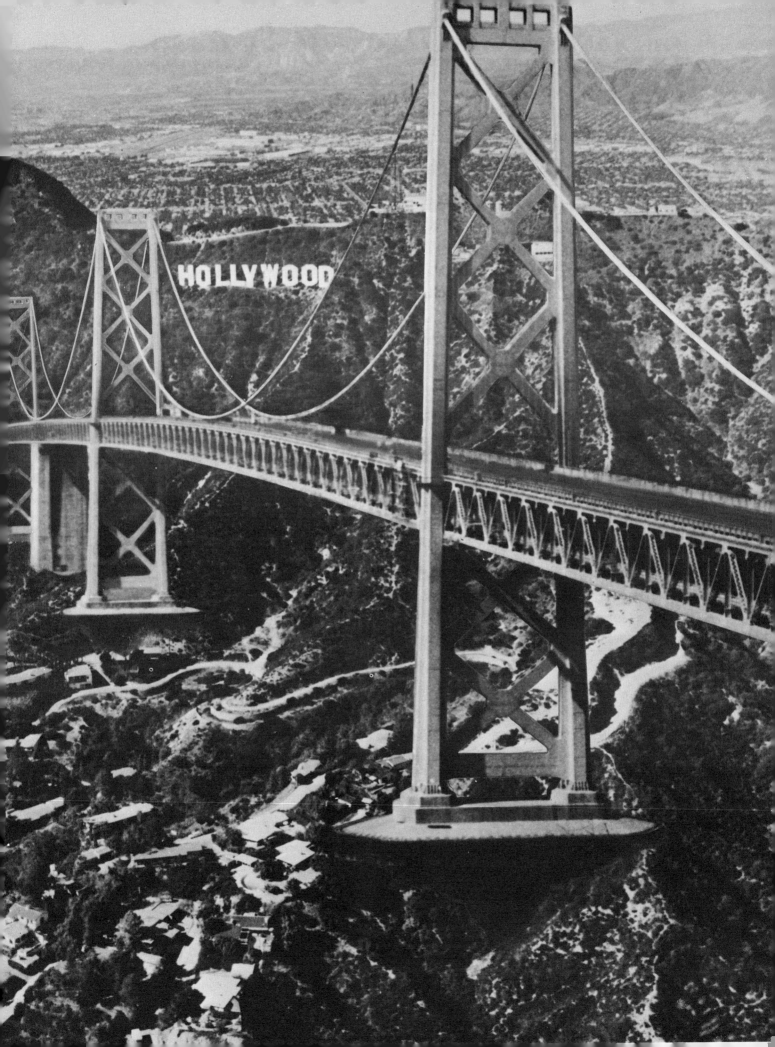

THEM

Just who were they? Or as many put it, just who did they think they were?

In 1983, UFOs became IFOs.

On the evening of March 10, approximately 200 UFOs descended on the newly constructed Silver Creek Motel some miles outside Boulder, Colorado, and parked their vehicles in its lot. The occupants then attempted to check in.

"They spoke perfect English," recalls manager Fred Gruening, "but frankly, I would've washed their mouths out with soap. If they'd had any mouths. I told them we were booked but they just swore at me and told me to check the computer. I did. It had been cleared—don't ask me how they did it. So I gave them the rooms. But I didn't like their attitude."

Gruening was right. By morning the Silver Creek Motel was a shambles. Thirty-three of its rooms were burnt to a crisp—the result of the occupants' indiscriminately lasering the walls. Its bar had been ransacked, and every bottle emptied. The "parsnips on pogo sticks," as historian Hunter Thompson later described them, apparently ingested alcohol by pouring it over their heads. Fifteen teenage girls had been raped in some manner that was not clear—their bodily orifices subject to various kinds of intrusion by prods that may or may not have been attached to the aliens' bodies. Whatever had happened, the girls left with their molesters in the morning.

It was the start of a rampage that continued for almost a year. The aliens drank, destroyed, and debauched their way first across the Southwest, then through Mexico and South America as far as Rio. They showed a predilection for fashionable beaches, nightclubs, and expensive hotels. Police and even military forces were never able to apprehend them because of the advanced technology of their transports, and despite their loathsome appearance they left a trail of broken hearts behind. This may have been due in part to their apparently inexhaustible supply of money, which made them welcome in chic water-

The widespread designation of UFOs as "undesirable" led to municipalities from Hawaii to Monte Carlo prohibiting their use of public facilities. The UFOs' speed and maneuverability, however, made such bans hard to enforce.

ing places and even private homes. Their short, translucent, vegetable-shaped bodies, visorlike brows, and hairy monopods soon became familiar items on gossip pages from Paris to Southampton. Clients of Regine's from Buenos Aires to New York politely looked the other way when they indulged in their idiosyncratic method of vomiting. The aliens discovered cocaine—which they took by rolling in it—and the havoc that followed was the talk of two continents. Their indiscriminate sexual exploits were marked more by stamina than any observable enjoyment—since sex alien-style usually involved the insertion of large, random portions of their highly flexible bodies into a human orifice. The total impression was less that they were sexually aroused than that they were curious about their partners' internal organs, but this very fact made them much sought after by the more sophisticated. As one veteran of several alien orgies giggled, "They really want to get inside you."

Their relationship to one another was close and exclusionary. Quite intelligent when sober, they would mercilessly humiliate any human foolish enough to try to become part of their circle. And, when drunk or drugged, they verbally or physically abused anyone who came within range, which often involved them in fistfights especially with ordinary hardworking citizens. This was a problem, firstly because they had no fists and secondly because they had no compunction about lasering their opponents.

Something had to give. And on February 23, 1984, it did. After a weeklong Mardi Gras celebration in which the aliens emptied more than 21,000 bottles of assorted liquor over themselves and rolled in an estimated 700 pounds of cocaine, a UFO drag race was organized from New Orleans to Nice. Halfway across the Atlantic, the leading two UFOs struck a westbound Boeing 767 carrying 814 people. All died. The occupants of the UFOs, as usual, were unhurt. And unrepentant. Refusing to pay any compensation to the families of the deceased, they insisted that they had had the "right of way" and referred to their victims in an interview with one distinguished gossip correspondent as "disposable peasants."

The public outcry was unprecedented. Interpol was instructed to apprehend the aliens at any cost and bring them to justice, summarily if necessary. The police surprised and surrounded their prey at London's Claridge's Hotel, where they were engaged in a "767 wake" with much of the better element of British society. The aliens refused to give themselves up and a shootout seemed imminent.

As both sides prepared for a pitched battle, an unforeseen development occurred. Three large UFOs appeared from nowhere and hovered over the hotel. They appeared to be armed craft and each one carried three flashing lights on its upper surface. A team of aliens, similar to those in the hotel but much bulkier and more wrinkled and wearing an assortment of gadgets on glowing belts of light around their bodies, descended to ground level in transports and made contact with the law-enforcement officers. They formally expressed regret for the accident, claimed custody of the "perpetrators," and proffered a cash settlement amounting to exactly a million dollars apiece for each of the bereaved families. There was a period of intense conference between police brass, but as the Scotland Yard superintendent of operations said, "We knew these chaps could handle the situation. They were real pros."

Granted safe conduct, the team entered the hotel. No one is sure what happened inside, but eyewitness accounts mention considerable crashing and shouting, the flash of several lasers being fired, and a series of "loud 'squishy' sounds like two-by-fours hitting oatmeal." Moments later, the team emerged from the hotel leading the recalcitrant aliens who had been bound with a glowing ropelike substance and looked very much the worse for wear. They were shepherded roughly onto the ground transports, while the leader recorded the proceedings on what appeared to be a pocket calculator.

The giant UFOs took off and disappeared within seconds into the upper atmosphere. No sign of them, or any other UFOs, was ever reported again. The only reminder of the 300 days that shocked the world is a badly dented and still faintly glowing UFO in the Smithsonian in Washington, D.C.

MEET ME IN ST. LOUIS

Some have called it one of the Seven Wonders of the Modern World. It stretches from Gateway Arch in what was formerly St. Louis to the foothills of the Rocky Mountains—the parched wasteland of the "new" American desert.

When the earth's axis shifted during the International Year of the Simultaneous Orgasm, climatic changes brought a virtual end to rainfall in the American Midwest. The process was gradual but inexorable. As the decade wore on, even the great historic rivers of the region began to dry up. On the Mississippi, where paddle-wheelers once churned their way down to New Orleans, enormous mudboats—poled by swarthy teams of "gondoliers"—carried a dwindling commerce.

While sand drifted through the ruins of Lincoln, Nebraska, and Sioux City, Iowa, desperate displaced farmers, the Okies of the '80s, descended on Utah's Great Salt Lake, which offered the most fertile land within a thousand miles. (Their principal crop was a thin but very clean potato aggressively marketed as "Mormon Chips.")

In explaining what had turned the former "breadbasket of the world" into a second Dust Bowl, experts were divided. One school, headed by Pakistani geologist Ali ul-Hag, felt that the condition was temporary: "We are predicting that rainfall in the affected area will be back to normal by the end of the Holocene period, in roughly 20 million years."

Others held a darker view. Meteorologist Herbert Call of the New York Central Park Observatory said, "I think we've seen the last of Kansas City beef—not to mention Kansas City."

Saarinen's majestic arch still soars beside the remote Missouri-Kansahara Highway, a buoyant reminder of the indomitable spirit of St. Louis, and gateway, if not to the Midwest, then certainly to America's future.

INDEX OF AUTHORS

BEARD, HENRY:
Congressional Squares, 78-79
The Congress of Nuts, 80
The Halfway House, 82-83
The Horrible Hundredth, 84-85
A Man for Four Seasons, 86
The Second U.S. Constitutional
 Convention, 88-89
The New Bill of Rights, 90-91
Half-Life, 121-123
Dealing with the Black Hand,
 186
"I Am the Black Infantry," 213
Back to Technology, 254
Mother Lode News, 255

CERF, CHRISTOPHER:
"Five Steps to a New OLD You,"
 19
Universal Literacy Optical
 Code, 25
South Vietnam! Playbill, 71
The Halfway House, 82-83
Contract, 102-103
Half-Life, 121-123
"How KGB Fly Pens, Jam TV,
 DC Quiz Rx," 124
The Best and the Last, 137
Grubs 'n Roots, 229

COLLINS, GLENN:
One Healthy Nation, 196-197
The Legions of the TV Blind, 198
The Death of Cancer, 200
"The Lives of a Cancer Cell," 201
The International Year of the
 Simultaneous Orgasm,
 202-203
"The Little Man in the Scrote,"
 204
Orgasm—Pro and Con, 206
Kids, 238
Substitute Kids, 241
Little Sons of America, 242
Single Kids, 244
"Looking for Mr. and Mrs.
 Goodbar," 244-245

CORCORAN, JOHN:
This Is the Army, Mr. Jones,
 216-217

CRIST, STEVEN:
Olympics, 96-97
Contact, 98-99
Los Juegos, 100
The Champs: Ali's
 Parliament-Storming Tour,
 106
Prime Times, 126
Meatleggers, 144-147
Meatheads, 148-150
La Sousa, 152
"Neurosurgery City Bargain
 Basement Sale," 197
The Long March, 218
Washington's Birthday Arms
 Sale, 221
Las Vegas: Rien Ne Va Plus, 250

CURTIN, VALERIE:
Hollywood, 66-69
Where Are They Now?, 132

DICKINSON, TIMOTHY:
New Gods: Mergers, 117

DRYSDALE, PHILIP:
The Dealth Penalty—A New
 Lease on Life, 188

EGAN, JACK:
¡Viva Mexico!, 159
Futures, 160
Shortage, 162
Glut, 164-167

ELBLING, PETER:
An Interview with a Dolphin, 51
Hollywood, 66-69
Camelot II, 76
Congressional Squares, 78
Where Are They Now?, 132
This Is the Army, Mr. Jones, 216
John Hungry and His Big Rat
 "Blue," 246-247
Back to Technology, 254

GEISS, TONY:
Jihad! Revenge of the Prophet,
 30-33
Russia—The Iron Curtain Call,
 42
Inside Russia, 44-45
The Death of the
 Three-Network System, 56
Waltergate: The Eye Closes, 59
The Last Ratings War: The Big
 Tune-In, 60-61
The People Maybe:
 Programming from the
 Masses, 62-63
The New York Variety Times,
 125
The Food Chain, 226-228
Haute Cuisine with No
 Ingredients, 230
New Foods, 232
The Pigalo and the Potatolo, 234

GENG, VERONICA:
The Past Masters: Catch-88, 133
Prime Time Terms, 178-179

GERSHEN, HOWARD:
Where Are They Now?, 132

GILMAN, RICHARD:
The Best and the Last, 137

GOODROW, GARRY:
Religion, 110-111

GOTTLIEB, CARL:
Italy—La Soluzione Finale, 40

GREEN, JOEY:
Olympics, 96-97
Fred, 127-129

GREENFIELD, JEFF:
The Death of the
 Three-Network System, 56
Waltergate: The Eye Closes, 59
The People Maybe:
 Programming from the
 Masses, 62-63
Hollywood Cleans House:
 HUAC's Hawkhunt, 64-65
Julia's Bi-Weekly cartoon strip
 text, 64-65
Camelot II, 76
The Congress of Nuts, 80
The Halfway House, 82-83
A Man for Four Seasons, 86
The Inside-Out Look, 175
A Court for Our Time, 190-191
Neo-Irvington, 252

HENDRA, TONY:
"Le Shoe," 21
United Magic Kingdom, 34-35
Plastic China, 36-37
"Glorious Detergent of the 23rd
 of September," 39
Russia—The Iron Curtain Call,
 42

This Is Not a Perfume Ad, 49
Hollywood, 66-69
Broadway—Bust and Boom,
 70-71
Congressional Squares, 78-79
Andre el Giant Rooster, 101
The Champs: The Great Wide
 Hope, 107
The Church Modernizes, 112-113
New Gods, 114-117
The Final Edition, 124
Columbia Gossip Review,
 131-132
The Past Masters: El Castillo de
 Tremarric, 136
Music 'n Drugs, 140-141
A Beatle-Maniac, 142-143
Meatleggers, 144-147
La Sousa, 152-153
The Movie of the Decade, 172
The Sheetrock Suit, 177
Citizens for Murder, 189
The International Year of the
 Simultaneous Orgasm,
 202-203
The Long March, 218
We Shall Overrun, 220
"Pain En Croute," 231
Save the Broccoli, 235
John Hungry and His Big Rat
 "Blue," 246-247
Them, 260-261

HIRSCH, JANIS:
Broadway—Bust and Boom,
 70-71

HOFFMAN, ABBIE:
Prime Times, 126
The Run Run Rickshaw Corp.,
 162-163
Blippie Nation, 219

JONAS, GERALD:
Humpback and Sperm Galore,
 48
Chief of the Joint, 214-215
The Big Slide, 258
Meet Me in St. Louis, 263

KANFER, STEFAN:
Contract, 103

KELLY, SEAN:
The White League: Red Herron's
 column, 104

KLIBAN, B.:
Rats, 181

LEE, STAN:
Ratman and the Hulk, 180

MACK, STAN:
Real Life Funnies: "Meatheads,"
 151

MAEGHT-MUSEUM, DINAH:
"The Ten Days," 77

MARTIN, BERNARD:
California Nueva, 256-257

McCALL, BRUCE:
United Magic Kingdom,
 34-35
Mad. Ave. Comes to the United
 States of China, 38
Zufti Nog Hummo: 1988 Tirana
 World's Fair, 46
Where Are They Now?, 132
This Is the Army, Mr. Jones, 216

McQUADE, LARRY:
Viva Mexico!, 158

MEYEROWITZ, RICK:
John Hungry and His Big Rat
 "Blue," 246-247

MILLER, ED:
The Best and the Last, 137

OBST, DAVID:
Olympics, 96-97

PETERSON, MAURICE:
Where Are They Now?, 132
We Shall Overrun, 220

PLAYTEN, ALICE:
"Le Shoe," 21

PLIMPTON, GEORGE:
The Yacht People, 50
The White League: "Ol' Valise,"
 105
Where Are They Now?, 132
The Past Masters: A Fragment
 by Truman Capote, 134-135
"Vaunted Vole Top Rodent at
 Westminster," 180

ROBERTS, JONATHAN:
"Hippie Days," 57
New Gods: Cults, 114-117
Where Are They Now?, 132
WWWD: "Today," 130
Downwardly Mobile Fashion,
 174
"Don't Light Fires You Can't Put
 Out," 207

ROGERS, JENNIFER:
Wide Women's Wear Daily, 130
Rich Food: Cuisine Grosseur,
 231

ROMITA, JOHN:
Ratman and the Hulk, 180

SHEARER, HARRY:
Where Are They Now?, 132
Baby's First Rights, 240

SOKOLOV, RAYMOND:
Rich Food: Cuisine Grosseur,
 231

WEINER, ELLIS:
Introduction, 8
Section Openers:
The World, 28-29
Showbiz, 54-55
DC, 74-75
Sports, 94-95
Religion, 110-111
Adieu, Print, 120
Music 'n Drugs, 140-141
Oil, 156-157
Fads 'n Fashions 170-171
The Law, 184-185
Sex 'n Health, 194-195
The Army, 210-211
Food, 224-225
Kids, 238-239
The Face of America, 248-249

WHITE, TIMOTHY:
Meatheads, 148-150

WOLFF, JEREMY:
Olympics, 96-97
Fred, 127-129

YOUNG, CHUCK:
Meatheads, 148-150

Captions, news heads, and visuals were conceived and/or written by the editors and many others, most notably Tony Geiss, Jonathan Roberts, Ellis Weiner, Jeff Greenfield, Carl Gottlieb, and Harry Shearer.